"Why did... what the conditions for getting the job were?"

"Because," Wade grated softly, "I wanted to teach you a lesson."

"A lesson in how to choose the right man?" Elissa rasped furiously.

"If you're going to use such techniques to rise to the top, I'm in a position to assist your career efforts."

Elissa stalled. "You may think I was dumb enough to sleep with the wrong man once for business purposes, but don't make the mistake of thinking I'll make the same error again!"

"I want you. I don't know how long I'll want you, but while I do, you might be able to benefit considerably. Perhaps if you play your cards right and keep me interested, you'll move up right along with me."

Elissa whitened. "I see your career path is on course, Mr. Taggert. There's no doubt in your own mind that you'll be the next CEO?"

"If I want it badly enough, I'll get it...."

* * *

Dangerous Magic

"I told you on the dance floor that the choice would be yours tonight."

Dark velvet was in his words. "Just remember that I will hold you to your decision, even if you choose to take the risk."

"What risk?"

"The risk of inviting me into your bed."

Hearing it spelled out so bluntly sent a tremor through her, but she managed not to lower her lashes in spite of the confusion she was experiencing. "What is the risk, Ryder? That you won't stay long in my bed?" she provoked deliberately, ignoring the pain of that possibility.

His mouth crooked and he lifted his fingers to spear them through the sleek knot of her hair, dislodging the clip. "No, you little idiot, the risk you're taking is that I will stay there. Don't you understand, Brenna? I won't let you go after I've made you mine!"

* * *

Affair of Honor

JAYNE ANN KRENTZ

writing as Stephanie James

Dangerous Affair

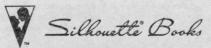

Silhouette® Books

Published by Silhouette Books

America's Publisher of Contemporary Romance

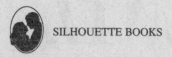 SILHOUETTE BOOKS

DANGEROUS AFFAIR

Copyright © 2004 by Harlequin Books S.A.

ISBN 0-373-21877-X

The publisher acknowledges the copyright holders
of the individual works as follows:

DANGEROUS MAGIC
Copyright © 1982 by Jayne Ann Krentz

AFFAIR OF HONOR
Copyright © 1983 by Jayne Ann Krentz

CONTENTS

DANGEROUS MAGIC

Chapter 1

Elissa Sheldon sat stunned, letting the full force of the insult wash over her in an icy wave. The only thing which kept her from drowning under the impact, she realized dimly, was the internal rage which rose to meet it. But that, too, was a problem because it took all her not inconsiderable will to master the fury before it mastered her.

"Would you," she said quite clearly, her low, slightly husky voice sounding incredibly restrained to her own ears, "mind repeating that?"

Her blue-green eyes, normally so alive with humor and a contagious enthusiasm for life, darkened rapidly to green flames, but the effect was lost on the tall, hard man standing at the window behind his desk. He had his back to her, apparently absorbed in watching the Seattle business-day traffic fifteen floors below.

"You heard me, Miss Sheldon," Wade Taggert

growled softly. "I merely pointed out that you picked the wrong man to sleep with in your efforts to secure the promotion to head the editing and graphics department." He paused significantly. "You should have tried your wiles on me. Not Martin Randolph."

For an instant longer Elissa simply stared, appalled, at the lean, powerful masculine back across from her. Wade Taggert was dressed all wrong, she thought as a finger of near hysteria touched her mind. He ought to have been wearing skins and carrying a spear instead of being attired in a conservative dark suit, white shirt, and tie. But perhaps such clothing was *de rigueur* for the modern-day predator.

"Mr. Taggert," Elissa began a little desperately, all thought of the promotion disappearing in the face of the potential ramifications of his outrageous insult, "there is some mistake! I don't know where you got the idea that I would...would lower myself to that sort of behaviour, but you're wrong! I suppose you're one of those men who assume any woman anxious to get ahead in the business world will do anything to climb her way up the ladder, but I can assure you that you owe me an apology in this case!"

But even if he got down on his knees and apologized, Elissa realized as she tried to contain her anger, there was no way in the world she could continue to work for this man. His accusation would always be the dominant factor between them, making any sort of business relationship impossible.

"I saw the necklace, Elissa." The deep, heavy-timbred voice was curiously devoid of intonation, almost weary-sounding, as Wade Taggert turned around at last.

Elissa met the shock of his icy gray eyes and

wanted to turn and flee. Only her fierce pride and grim determination to set him straight kept her in the chair. Facing Taggert was a formidable task at any time, but when he was in this remote and glacial mood, all normally intimidating features were magnified.

He was thirty-five years old, and none of those thirty-five years looked to have been easy. He had recently been appointed manager of the Seattle office of the computer-design firm for which Elissa worked, and the office grapevine rumored him to be in line for the chief executive officer position of the company. Elissa didn't doubt it. Wade Taggert had made his way rapidly and ruthlessly up through the ranks in a relatively short time, and there was no reason to think he wouldn't keep going. He had done a lot for CompuDesign, and the company would undoubtedly keep rewarding him.

The image of a predator hardened in Elissa's mind as she absorbed the sight of him outlined against the city skyline. Taggert's near-black hair was cut in an unfashionably severe line, revealing wings of gray at each temple. Heavy brows framed deep-set eyes which ranged from the present wintry gray to a strange silvery color, depending, Elissa supposed, on the light. The planes of his face had been chiseled with an iron hand, leaving the tanned skin stretched tautly over the commanding cheekbones and a square, aggressive chin. Fine lines fanned out from the corners of his eyes, making it appear as if he had spent a fair amount of time outdoors. There were harsh grooves etched at the sides of his stern mouth. And, as was the case with most efficient predators, there wasn't an ounce of extra weight on the man. Broad shoulders and chest tapered to lean waist and hips which were emphasized by the close, conservative cut of his clothes.

Elissa felt his gaze raking her as she sat tensely in the chair, and she realized he was taking in the neat tailored green suit along with the short, sassy style of her dark auburn hair, which was cut into the nape and made a perfect frame for the slightly slanting sea-colored eyes. There was no great beauty to be discovered in the face, she knew, although her small, firm chin, faintly tip-tilted nose, and well-drawn cheekbones went together in a reasonably attractive fashion. It was the expressiveness of those features and the overall impression of laughter and challenge which drew the occasional second glance. Her five feet four inches of slender height put her at a disadvantage, she felt, compared to her accuser's six feet of coordinated strength. But her clothes were expensive and fit the small, gentle curves of her breast and hip well without being overpowering.

Very coolly, Elissa crossed her legs in a small gesture of feminine challenge. She was twenty-seven years old, and she hadn't gotten this far without having learned something about staying calm under fire. She would not let this man see how badly affected she was by the unexpected and shattering scene.

"What necklace, Mr. Taggert?" she demanded, lifting her chin and narrowing the blue-green eyes a bit further to let him know she didn't appreciate his use of her first name.

"The one Randolph gave you the other night, presumably for services rendered. Too bad he didn't have the power to repay you in full, but you should have verified that before getting involved with that sort of bargain. If it makes you feel any better, he did put your name in for consideration," Taggert drawled bitingly.

"But you, in your infinite wisdom, disregarded the recommendation?" Elissa concluded evenly, unaware that the knuckles of the hand clenched in her lap had gone quite white under the force she was exerting.

"You were very well qualified, being the supervisor of the technical writing department," he admitted.

"But I, er, bestowed my favors on the wrong man?" she gritted.

"I'm surprised at you, Elissa," he told her bleakly. "You should have done your homework better."

"Could we get back to the little matter of the necklace? It appears to be the chief item of evidence."

"What about it?" He shrugged, turning slightly away and prowling across the room to sample the view from the side window. The advantages of a corner office, Elissa thought with a sigh. She knew what he was seeing from that vantage point; the busy harbor and Elliott Bay with its myriad white ferries gliding to and from the various islands. The Seattle winter day was as cold and gray as the atmosphere in the office.

"I only want to know where and when you saw me receiving the thing."

"After work the other night, down in the garage. You were standing with Randolph beside his car. I saw him take it out of the box and hand it to you."

"And on that basis you denied me a promotion and accused me of sleeping my way up the corporate ladder?" Elissa blazed.

He swung around and trapped her flaming gaze. "It's not the first time I've seen you under less than innocent circumstances with Martin Randolph. You were out with him the other night in the cocktail lounge in the lobby of the hotel down the street. He's a married man, Elissa, and you know it.''

''If you know that, then you should know the necklace was a present he'd bought for his wife. I was merely admiring it,'' she shot back, still trying desperately to keep her temper from exploding completely.

''You put it into your purse,'' he retorted grimly. ''Don't lie to me, Elissa. It won't work.''

''I'm keeping it for June Randolph's surprise birthday party, which happens to be tomorrow night. At my apartment, I might add! June and I are good friends.''

''Then you shouldn't be having after-work drinks with her husband, should you?'' Taggert snapped.

''Just how many such occasions have you witnessed, Mr. Taggert?'' Elissa got out between painfully dry lips.

''Enough,'' he muttered laconically, walking back to his desk and dropping into the chair behind it. ''Two or three, at least.''

''And you're not in the least prepared to believe they might have been totally innocent events, are you?''

''It's a bit too convenient, Elissa. You didn't start meeting Randolph after hours until the time for this promotion drew close—''

''As close as June's surprise party! That's all that was being planned during those incriminating little meetings!''

''Don't try to play me for a fool,'' he ordered, leaning back in the large chair and eyeing her harshly.

"On at least one occasion I saw you take the elevator upstairs. Randolph followed a few minutes later."

"I hope you enjoyed yourself playing I Spy," Elissa hissed, unable to believe what was happening. "If you knew that hotel well, you'd know the rest rooms are on the second level where the convention facilities are located. Good grief! What did you do? Hide behind the potted palms and conduct surveillance operations on your employees? Perhaps you should try working for the government!"

"I had to be sure," he stated flatly, ignoring her sarcasm. There was something very heavy and final in his dark voice. Elissa shivered involuntarily.

"And now you are sure?" she demanded, startled at the degree of her own anger. Never had she been so infuriated. She glared at her tormentor, her mind whirling with alternative courses of action.

"I think the evidence of my own eyes is fairly conclusive, Elissa," Wade Taggert said coldly. "There's really not much point in going through it again, is there? Why don't you just accept the fact that I found out what was going on and that your methods worked against you?"

"And Evelyn Keenan got the job, even though she's had less experience and has been with the company for a shorter time," Elissa stated.

"Are you going to accuse her of having slept with the right man?" he asked, one heavy brow lifting quizzically.

"Don't be ridiculous," she snapped back in utter scorn. "Evelyn would never do such a thing!" Which was nothing less than the truth, Elissa thought moodily. Pretty, blond, hazel-eyed, and quite competent,

Evelyn was also very much in love with her new husband.

"I must admit you're being fair about the matter, at any rate," Wade retorted. "You're right. Evelyn got the job because she was the second-most-qualified person around."

"The *most* qualified person having foolishly put herself out of the running by choosing the wrong man to seduce?" Elissa could almost feel the blood simmering in her veins now. Somehow she would find a way to take this man down a peg or two if it was the last thing she did on earth! "Tell me something, Mr. Taggert, did you put pressure on Evelyn to sleep with you and then have to give her the job anyway when she wouldn't?"

"No!" he flung back, sounding genuinely outraged himself. "Unlike you, I choose my bedmates from the unmarried crowd!"

Elissa felt the wave of red storming into her cheeks, and it became all she could do to maintain eye contact with that bitter gray gaze. In spite of the knowledge of her own innocence of the charges the man had leveled against her, it was difficult to meet the power in him on an even footing. My God! she thought wonderingly. If I had been guilty, I would have been crawling out the door on my hands and knees by now!

"I see," she managed gamely. "Then why didn't you simply come to me and tell me what the conditions for getting the job were?"

"Because," he grated softly, significantly, "I wanted to teach you a lesson."

"A lesson in how to choose the right man next time?" she rasped furiously.

"Something like that," he acknowledged sardonically. In an absent gesture, Wade reached out and picked up a yellow pencil lying near his hand. He tapped it gently on the blotter while he assessed her bitter gaze. "If you're going to use such techniques to rise to the top of the heap, Elissa, you might as well practice them on me. I'm in a much better position to assist your career efforts than Randolph, and I hope this little matter of the promotion proves it."

"You," she gritted between fiercely clenched teeth, her slender body almost shaking now with the force of her emotions, "are the most unprincipled, egotistical, ruthless man I have ever had the misfortune to meet!"

"I think we understand each other perfectly," he shot back dryly.

How could he sit there as if he were lord of all he surveyed? Elissa asked herself almost frantically. There was such absolute masculine certainty on that hard face, such undisguised, aggression in those gray eyes. Wade Taggert was, indeed, a predator, and she had been elected the prey!

"There's not much point in carrying this conversation any further, is there?" she finally asked bleakly, shaking her head once in a gesture of disbelief. This couldn't be happening! "I'll let you have my resignation as soon as I can get back to my desk." She moved her trembling fingers to the arms of her chair in preparation for rising, but his next words brought her head up with a snap, the short auburn hair dancing gracefully about her small ears.

"I'm not asking for your resignation, Elissa. I'm merely pointing out the facts of life to you. Your work for CompuDesign has been excellent in the month and a half that I've headed this office. The records show it's been excellent for the four years you've worked for the firm. You had no need to resort to the methods you used in trying to land this latest promotion, but if you are going to use such methods..." The pencil in his fingers snapped as the sentence was allowed to trail off meaningfully.

"If I am going to use such methods I might as well learn to use them where they'll do the most good, is that it?" she heard herself say.

"As I said," he repeated in a voice of sandpaper on silk, "I think we understand each other very well."

"There's a term for what you're doing to me," she breathed tightly, still keeping her seat in the chair but feeling as if she would leap to her feet and run like any other small creature if the hunter made a sudden move toward her. "It's called sexual harassment, and it's illegal!"

"There's a term for women who use their bodies to get what they want on the job," he snarled, spreading his palms flat on the top of the hardwood desk and holding her pinned beneath his contemptuous gaze. "Several terms, in fact. None of them particularly flattering!"

"If you think so little of me, I'm surprised you're even bothering to issue a proposition," Elissa bit out. The first faint glimmerings of an idea were beginning to shape themselves in her much-pressed brain. This man was so certain he had everything figured out. What would it do to his ego to discover he was wrong?

"Men, to their eternal bewilderment, cannot always account for their own tastes, Elissa," Wade Taggert told her with something approaching wry humor in his words. "I want you. It's as simple as that, and I'm using the main lure I have to get you."

Elissa stared at him, uncomprehendingly. "Want me," she repeated dully, her blue-green eyes blinking once as if to clear away a figment of her imagination. But he was still there, sitting behind the wide desk with all the cool, waiting patience of a large cat. The gray eyes were enigmatic pools of cold, icy rain, and the grim line of his mouth was made no less harsh by the curious little upward quirk at one corner. One hand continued to play with the broken piece of pencil in an idle fashion.

"You find that so difficult to understand?" he asked almost mildly. "In the short time I've been here I haven't noticed you suffering from a shortage of admirers."

"They're called friends, Mr. Taggert," Elissa snapped, goaded. And it was true, she thought somewhat vaguely. She did have a lot of friends, and certainly some of them were male; but the one man who fit the description of admirer didn't even work for CompuDesign! Wade Taggert couldn't have been further off base then to think of her as a *femme fatale!*

"And what do you call Martin Randolph?" he prodded bluntly.

"I call him a friend who happens to be fifteen years older than I am *and* happily married as I told you before!"

"Which puts him out of the risk category, doesn't it? You can use him on the assumption that he isn't in a position to demand anything more than you feel like giving. But what happens if he goes crazy, as other men have been known to do, and leaves his wife for you? What will you do if he comes knocking at your door some night expecting to be taken in by the woman who's been showing him so much attention? Will you feel even a little guilty, Elissa?'' Taggert was suddenly surging to his feet, but he made no move toward her. Instead he turned back to the window behind his desk, and she was once again left with his broad back as a target.

''That's hardly likely to happen!''

''I agree,'' he said surprisingly, glancing back at her over his shoulder. ''Because I've put a stop to your little game with him by removing the prize and giving it to someone else. Randolph's no fool. He'll soon realize you're pursuing more promising avenues of advancement, and if he's smart he'll thank his lucky stars he got out of the situation before he did something really stupid like leaving his wife!'' He shifted completely back around to face her, planting his large hands flat on his desk and leaning forward with cool challenge in every line of his body. ''Well, Elissa?'' He waited.

Elissa pulled her scrambling thoughts into some order, trying to come up with a way to handle the incredible situation. Only one thing seemed very clear in the chaos, and that was that if there was any way of achieving even a token revenge against this man, she was going to take it.

''Well, what?'' she taunted bravely. ''You can't expect me to leap at your offer when I still don't know why you've made it.'' She was stalling for time now as her earlier idea took firmer shape. ''You might think I was dumb enough to sleep with the wrong man once for business purposes, but don't make the mistake of thinking I'll make the same error again!'' There was no point arguing her own case any longer.

Elissa accepted that with bitter resolve. She would devote all her energy now to finding another tactic to use against Wade Taggert. A tactic that would show him once and for all he had no right to play havoc with the careers of the women who worked for him. A tactic that would demonstrate his own fallibility...

"I've told you why I'm inviting you to investigate other possibilities for career advancement," he drawled. "I want you. I don't know how long I'll want you," he added ruthlessly, "but while I do, you might be able to benefit considerably. I'm sure your imagination can supply you with all the potential inherent in the situation. You couldn't aim any higher than the division office manager, could you, Elissa? Unless, of course, you tried for the CEO! But perhaps, if you play your cards right and keep me interested long enough, you'll find yourself moving up right along with me."

Elissa whitened. Never in her life had she been subjected to such unsubtle propositioning! "I see your own career path is on course, Mr. Taggert. There's no doubt in your own mind that you'll be the next CEO? The next chief executive officer of CompuDesign?" she demanded gratingly, trying to achieve a semblance of cool contempt.

"If I want it badly enough," he told her starkly, "I'll get it." Quite suddenly Elissa believed him. If this man really went after a goal, he fully expected to get it.

"It doesn't make any sense," she murmured after a second's tense silence. "Why me? There are far more beautiful women working for you, Mr. Taggert, and you're not blind. Several of them are even unmarried!" she concluded mockingly.

"I agree you're not the most beautiful or sophisticated woman I've ever met, Elissa Sheldon," he told her, his mouth twisting slightly. "But there is something about you which attracts me. For the time being, at any rate," he added with casual menace.

He circled the desk then, moving so quickly that Elissa was only half out of her chair and nowhere near en route for the door by the time he reached her. In two long pantherlike strides he was in front of her, reaching down to pull her up out of her seat. His hands clamped around her arms, and she was held immobile as he brought her very close to him.

"For a while," he went on in a voice of distant, grating thunder, "I want to know what it's like to be included in the warmth of your smile. I want to answer the challenge in your eyes, and I want to join with you in the laughter. I want to argue about the stock market and about politics, and I want to enjoy your enthusiasm, for life. In short, Elissa, I want to be part of your charmed circle. But there's one stipulation: While I'm circling in your obit, I will be the *only* one there. Is that understood?"

"Let me go!" Elissa cried in astonishment and a hint of genuine fear. "Take your hands off me this instant!" Her fingers splayed against the dark material of his jacket as she faced him, wide-eyed and wary. Desperately she pushed, trying to put distance between them, but he didn't appear to notice.

"I asked if you understood my basic requirement for this affair of ours," he countered roughly, giving her a small shake.

"I heard what you said, damn it!" she flung back, stung. The look on his face and the unshakable strength in him warned her to tread carefully until she was once again free of his grasp. "But we have no affair, so your 'requirements' don't matter a whole lot, do they?" That had been unwise, but Elissa was too angry to still her tongue.

"We will be having one," he swore softly, "when you've had a chance to simmer down and think about what I can do for you. And I'll throw in something else for your consideration," he went on, tightening his grasp until she was pressed unwillingly against the length of his tough, hard frame.

"What's that?" she taunted bitterly. "A diamond necklace? It *was* diamond, you know, the one Martin gave me the other evening—"

"This is what I had in mind," he interrupted harshly and lowered his head in a swift, unexpected move that caught her vulnerable mouth unprepared.

Elissa's small sound of outrage was totally muffled by the impact of Wade's kiss. It was a marauding, claiming, branding thing that promised fire and male dominance in no uncertain terms. Without any subtlety he forced apart her lips, his tongue sweeping boldly into the dark warmth of her mouth. It was a short, punishing foray designed only to demonstrate her inferior strength, and it succeeded in leaving her trembling with dismay and fury.

Hating her own helplessness in his arms, Elissa tried the only defense left to her and deliberately went passive in his ironclad embrace.

"That's better," he approved huskily as he sensed her lack of struggle. "Things will go much more smoothly if you don't fight me." His mouth continued to move over hers, seeking out the corners. When she would have turned her head aside, his teeth somehow caught her tender lower lip and closed on it with insolent, gentle promise.

She stood very still, letting the force of his chastising passion spend itself, her eyes shut against the reality of what was happening. Later, she vowed silently, later she would teach this arrogant man a lesson he would never forget!

She felt his hands move at last, releasing their grip on her arms and sliding around her waist. Elissa waited tensely, hoping for an opportunity to free herself, but even as she weighed the odds, she was being arched into the hard line of his thighs and her throat was becoming the focus of his determined mouth. She was aware of the intent in him in the most elemental way a woman can become aware of a man, and the knowledge was an added danger Elissa recognized only belatedly. It was only when the fundamental electricity in him began transferring itself to her through the contact points of hands and thigh and lips that she faced a new kind of fear.

"No!" she breathed grimly, refusing to allow her new inner despair to show in her voice. "I won't allow you to do this to me!" Could he know, she wondered desperately, just *what* he was beginning to do to her? How could her body react so traitorously to a man who promised nothing but insults and punishment! But it was beginning to react, and she had to stop the assault before her knees gave way completely.

"Why don't you allow me to kiss you, Elissa?" he mocked, dropping tiny, stinging caresses along her jaw and at the edge of her mouth. "Think of all I can do for you in exchange. And there's no wife waiting in the background to make matters difficult this time," he went on coaxingly. "You'll have entire nights to practice your magic on me. Who knows how far you can go in this company?"

With all her self-control, Elissa stifled the temptation to hurl all the verbal abuse she could think of back at him. At this dangerous juncture she must keep her priorities straight, and the most important thing was to get free of him. The second most vital matter was to set the stage for revenge, no matter how puny it might turn out to be. She would not let Wade Taggert treat her like this and get off scot-free!

"I'm listening to you," she muttered bitterly. "There's not much else I can do until you stop playing out your little scene. But you have to admit I've got some readjusting to do. I hardly expected this when you summoned me to the office this afternoon."

He lifted his head at that remark, leaving one last rather fierce kiss on her mouth before he did so. The gray eyes gazed broodingly down at her upturned face, and she could see the deliberation in them. He was wondering if she'd begun to see matters his way.

"You expected to be told you'd gotten the promotion, didn't you?" he demanded musingly.

"It was a logical assumption on my part," she retorted, aware of the bruised feeling of her mouth. His embrace had been more in the nature of an attack, she thought fleetingly. As if Wade Taggert wanted it clear from the outset that he would be calling the shots between them.

"There will be other promotions, other possibilities," he told her with cool promise. His hands were still around her waist, and she could feel the strength in his fingers as they almost absently kneaded the lower curve of her back. It was a startlingly erotic sensation, she discovered to her horror, and one he wasn't even going out of his way to perform.

"Will there?" she questioned carefully, moving slightly and finding herself able to put a couple of inches between their bodies. She waited breathlessly for the next opportunity to push for her freedom. Deliberately she kept her wide, sea-colored eyes on his face, trying to project the uncertainty of a woman seriously considering exchanging lovers. She would allow him to think he was winning the cruel game. It was the surest way to free herself for the moment. The future could take care of itself.

"Give me what I want, little witch," he whispered hoarsely, searching her face intently, "and you have my word I'll take care of you. Your time spent amusing me will pay dividends."

"And what you want is me?" she verified one last time, a small part of her still not entirely able to believe the shock which had occurred in his office this afternoon. "For some unspecified length of time?"

"Yes!" he grated thickly, and the fingers along her back dug into her flesh with controlled violence, as if he would take her then and there had he seen any way to manage it.

Elissa winced at his touch and what it implied. "Have you always satisfied your male urges in this manner? Using your position to tempt the woman you want?" It was difficult to keep the scorn out of her voice, but she strove for neutrality. He mustn't suspect she was forming plans of her own.

"Different women are tempted by different things," he retorted unhelpfully. "I've never tried quite this approach before, however." He smiled with a touch of cruelty. "But, then, I've never encountered one quite so determined to advance her career. Would you believe it? Most of them start thinking in terms of marriage rather than promotion.''

Elissa flushed under his mockery. ''You, of course, would never go that far to satisfy a temporary craving.''

''Of course not,'' he agreed at once.

Elissa stepped back experimentally, and his hands dropped to his sides as he watched her move a few paces away and put the barrier of the chair between them. Clutching the edge of it with hands that might have shook otherwise, she faced him again, her head high.

''What guarantee do I have that you would keep your end of the bargain?'' she challenged, working through the final steps of her poorly formed plan.

''Not much,'' he admitted freely, sweeping aside the edges of his jacket to plant his fists on his hips. He propped himself casually on the corner of the desk, legs stretched out straight in front of him, and watched her with lazy interest. She knew he sensed victory. Let him enjoy it, she told herself furiously. My time will come. ''You really have only my word to rely on at this point,'' he concluded.

''And that's supposed to be enough?'' she retorted.

''What more do you want?'' he asked in some amusement.

''Perhaps a necklace…'' she suggested baitingly.

''Necklaces, especially diamond necklaces, come after you've shown you can be trusted to keep your end of the deal,'' he murmured softly, the gray rain in his eyes washing over her face.

''You're asking me to trust you?''

"I'm less of a risk than Martin Randolph, and I have more to offer," he pointed out laconically.

She lifted one delicate brow but did not contradict him. "Aren't you afraid others will talk?" she asked instead.

"It's a big town," he growled. "We can get sufficiently lost in it after hours. There would, naturally, be no open signs of a—shall we call it an association?—between us at work. You wouldn't want people to say you were rising in the company because of me, would you? I think we can do a little better in the discretion department than you were doing with Randolph. We certainly won't see each other in the local lounges where the crowd hangs out after work." His sarcastic tone implied she wasn't well versed in the fine art of romantic intrigue.

Unconsciously Elissa tipped her pert head to one side and drummed the fingers of one hand against the back of the chair. "How soon," she murmured deliberately, "do you want an answer?"

"Is there any need for a delay?" he pounced immediately, his gray gaze slitting as he watched her.

"I, uh, think I deserve some time to consider the matter in more depth," she grated dryly. "A woman doesn't just plunge into these things without some thought."

"What more is there to consider? It all seems pretty obvious to me."

Elissa drew a deep breath and then jumped in with both feet. "Would you," she asked quietly, "wait until tomorrow night for your answer?"

There was a tense pause, and she was left with the conviction he had fully intended to seal the bargain that very night. Arrogant, pompous, egotistical male!

"Saturday night?" he repeated slowly, thoughtfully.

"Yes. Could you come by my place around seven? I'll have an answer ready by then," she promised, excitement threatening to swamp her at the boldness of her own plans. "Please, Wade?" she tacked on in as artfully pleading a style as she could manage under the circumstances.

It did the trick, however. With a curt nod of his head, Wade Taggert straightened, coming to his full six feet beside the desk. "Seven o'clock tomorrow evening, then. I'll be there," he vowed coolly, the male anticipation in him very evident. He was granting her the time, she realized abruptly, because he had no doubt about the outcome.

Biting her tongue to keep from screaming at him like a fishwife, Elissa grabbed her purse and fled with as much dignity as possible from the panther's cage.

Chapter 2

Of all the humiliating factors involved in the disastrous meeting on Friday afternoon, the one which kept returning to haunt Elissa all day Saturday was the look of triumph which had been in Wade Taggert's eyes when she'd left his office. Never had she seen that expression in the eyes of a male looking at her. The cold gray gaze had held an elemental masculine promise which appeared totally unhampered by the layers of civilization and sophistication that should have intervened.

It was only later in the day as she finished preparations for June Randolph's surprise party that Elissa realized her astonishment at her boss's behavior toward her had prompted her to overlook another, equally astounding matter: the way she had reacted to him and to his accusations.

Elissa paused halfway through icing the cake and

stared unseeingly at the painting of a bizarre, other-worldly landscape hanging on the opposite kitchen wall. The painting didn't quite fit into the extraordinarily comfortable apartment furnishings, nor did it seem to go with the functional, neat kitchen. But, then, the five other strange, alien landscapes hanging throughout the one-bedroom high-rise apartment didn't seem to complement the overall decor, either. When visitors pointed that fact out, Elissa laughed, declared she was entitled to one idiosyncrasy, and motioned them to one of the very comfortable over-stuffed chairs. Said visitors generally proceeded to prop their feet on the convenient hassock, settle back with the cup of tea or glass of wine which was always offered, and pour out their hearts on whatever subject happened to be uppermost in their minds at the time. And Elissa, in her instinctively enthusiastic, sympathetic fashion, gave her visitors, in addition to tea or wine, what it was they seemed to want most from a friend. Sometimes that involved an understanding ear, a gentle lecture, a crafty suggestion, or a good laugh.

Elissa gave such things automatically and easily, fully aware of what she was doing but not begrudging the gift. The rewards for such charm had come frequently and easily to her. They included good friends, good grades through college, relatives who had thought her enormously mature even as a young girl, and a good job.

Or at least, Elissa sighed grimly, returning her attention to the cake in front of her, a good job with steady advancement *had* been a part of the taken-for-granted things in her comfortable life-style until yesterday afternoon!

Her fingers wielded the icing knife with absent skill

and she frowned down on her work as she considered
the shock she had been put through on Friday. The
greatest shock of all, naturally, was that anyone could
have even conceived of her being guilty of the sort
of behavior Wade Taggert had suggested. And if
someone had been so crazy as to believe her capable
of stooping to such unscrupulous actions, the incredible mistake should have been recognized as soon as
Elissa declared her innocence. No one in his right
mind could have believed Elissa Sheldon guilty of
anything underhanded or degrading!

But how much did she really know about Wade
Taggert? Elissa asked herself seriously as she stood
back to admire her handiwork on the cake with a
practiced eye. He'd only taken over the reins of
CompuDesign a month and a half earlier. Perhaps he
wasn't in his right mind, she told herself with a rueful
attempt at humor. There had to be something a little
crazy about a man who trailed his female employees
to local cocktail lounges after work!

She set the cake aside and began getting out the
plates and napkins. Elissa entertained so frequently
and so successfully that the work involved in a major
production such as Jane's surprise party was almost
second nature. The food would be elaborate and very
good; the wine and other alcoholic beverages would
be excellent. She would see to it that no one became
embarrassingly or dangerously drunk, and everyone
would have a great time. They always did.

But tonight, Elissa thought with a strange satisfaction as she artfully arranged the buffet table in front
of the huge living-room window, there would be one
exception to the rule. Wade Taggert was not going to
enjoy himself in the least. And for very nearly the

first time in her life since she was a small girl, Elissa found herself looking forward to another person's discomfort with a degree of enthusiasm that amazed her.

She wondered idly if having invited the boss would bother her friends, most of whom worked for CompuDesign. They would all be aware by now of the surprising fact that she hadn't gotten the promotion, although they couldn't know the humiliating reason why it had been denied. Elissa winced once again at the recollection of the Friday interview.

It wasn't just the fact that Taggert had denied her the advancement which would make people wonder why he was invited. It was also the fact that he was new and a complete change from the branch's former manager, a paternal gentleman who had retired. During his short time at the helm Wade Taggert had made it clear that he did not follow in the kindly footsteps of his predecessor. Nor did he go out of his way to fraternize with his employees as the older man had done.

Taggert was, Elissa decided as she showered an hour before the party, the perfect example of the lone wolf who had risen through the ranks on the basis of ability and ruthlessness. And wolf, she told herself as she toweled dry with one of the huge oversized bath sheets, was the operative word!

No, she would never have deliberately set out to make a friend of Wade Taggert, and he, in the normal course of events, would never have drifted into what he himself had termed Elissa's charmed circle. He was one of the rare individuals who would not have been welcomed there, nor could Elissa envision him as wanting to be a part of it.

But for tonight, she decided with grim anticipation,

he would be invited into the comfortable, cheerful warmth which surrounded her. Because that was the most efficient technique she could use to prove to him how completely wrong he had been about her.

As she stood in front of the bedroom mirror, which was flanked by two of the strange landscapes featuring crumbling castles and grotesque creatures, Elissa wondered what sort of apology she would receive from the arrogant, so-certain-of-himself Wade Taggert. A curiously expectant little smile touched the corners of her generous, expressive mouth, and the blue-green eyes looked back at her from under long auburn lashes with an unfamiliar gleam. Taggert would find his disgusting challenge met with the full force of the truth, and she hoped his masculine pride would prod him into a suitably abject act of contrition.

Elissa spent the last few minutes before the party began thinking of various ways in which she could receive her boss's apology. She glanced at the hall clock as the doorbell rang. It was just six. With any luck, by the time Wade Taggert arrived at seven the party would be in full swing. She would time the cake so that he would be there when June discovered the lovely diamond necklace inside. And that, she decided vengefully, would be the *pièce de résistance!*

A last negligent glance in the hall mirror satisfied Elissa that she looked the proper hostess. Her long plaid wool skirt and lacy, old-fashioned blouse provided a warm, homey look that was at the same time fashionable. The sleek, sassy cap of dark red hair was brushed to a natural shine, and when she opened the door to her first guest, she knew her appearance was more than acceptable.

"Dean!" she exclaimed happily, flinging open the door to see the polished, handsome man standing outside in the hall. "You're the first to arrive! Come in, come in," she urged happily, putting a hand on Dean Norwood's expensively attired arm and standing on tiptoe for his light kiss. She smiled up at him as she led him inside, thinking, not for the first time, that this man, who was steadily becoming more and more important in her life, was a most attractive specimen. His light brown hair was cut and styled in a fashionable but not the least radical manner. The perfectly trimmed mustache added a touch of sophistication which was well carried out in the expensive tailoring of his designer suit, and Elissa knew the leather in his shoes was Italian. Dean's cheerful blue eyes smiled down at her as he followed her into the living room.

"And how was Wall Street this week?" she demanded, escorting him to a chair and moving over to the small bar to pour him his favorite drink. "I didn't catch the news last night, I'm afraid." Primarily, she added wryly to herself, because she'd been so upset after the meeting with Wade Taggert.

"The market closed down a bit, but not bad. The latest government figures on consumer spending affected it, of course, but things should be bouncing back on Monday," Dean told her pleasantly, reaching happily for the martini she was holding out to him. Elissa always mixed perfect martinis, just the way he liked them.

"The eternal optimism of the professional stockbroker," she teased, perching lightly on the wide arm of the overstuffed chair and tilting her head to smile down at him. "But I suppose when you're handling other people's money you have to keep them thinking there's hope around the corner.''

''Can't have the clients panicking on me.'' Dean grinned, lounging back comfortably and reaching out to pat Elissa's knee with casual affection. ''You're supposed to be the one with the big news tonight, though, love. Let's have it. I assume I am now drinking a salute to the new head of editing and graphics at CompuDesign?'' He cocked a confident, querying eyebrow up at her.

Elissa grimaced and then attempted a rather rueful smile. ''You are saluting the old and familiar supervisor of technical writing, Dean. My friend Evelyn Keenan got the promotion.'' Two seconds of inner debate was sufficient to convince Elissa not to go into details. She could think of no suitable way of telling her friend that she had been accused of trying to sleep her way to the top.

''Evelyn? The little blonde who got married a couple months ago?'' Dean frowned in surprise. ''But she's rather new, isn't she? She couldn't possibly have your experience.''

''Taggert thought her perfectly qualified,'' Elissa said quietly. ''And she is, Dean. I'm sure she'll do a fine job.''

''But I was sure from what you'd told me that you had it in the bag.''

''A good lesson in counting one's chickens before they're hatched,'' Elissa muttered, getting to her feet to answer the door as the bell sounded again.

''Elissa, you should have had that job! What went wrong?'' Dean's offended tones were balm to her spirit as she glanced at him over her shoulder.

''I'll tell you all about it later. Promise me you

won't say anything to make Evelyn or her husband uncomfortable?''

"Of course not," he denied instantly. "But…"

"Later, Dean," she promised, her hand on the doorknob. "Although there's really nothing much to say about it."

The doorbell began to ring more and more frequently after that as the guests hurried to make the six-thirty deadline. Everyone wanted to be present when Martin Randolph escorted his wife into the room.

Over and over again Elissa listened to the same dismayed greeting as people bustled in from the wintry Seattle night. "Elissa! I heard about the promotion going to Evelyn. Thought sure you had it!"

And over and over again, Elissa summoned her most self-mocking smile, made jokes about counting chickens, and urged everyone to forget the matter with a shrug and the assuring words, "Evelyn will do a terrific job."

When Evelyn and her new husband arrived, there was something besides dismay in the younger woman's pretty hazel eyes. There was a kind of nervous wariness which Elissa saw at once and set out to remove with automatic, efficient ease.

"Evelyn! Congratulations!" she beamed, holding open the door and urging the couple inside. "I know you're going to do a heck of a job. Taggert knew enough to recognize the quality work you did on that quarterly report last month, and I'm very glad for you." With a casual, congratulatory hug that set everyone who witnessed it at ease, the small tension passed as if it had never existed. No one ever stayed tense long at Elissa's parties.

The exception tonight, Elissa reminded herself with satisfaction, would be Wade Taggert, who, if he had an ounce of integrity in his large, hard frame, would be properly tense with the knowledge of his error. Or were wolves ever repentant? That thought occurred to her as she stood temporarily to one side, watching her guests relax and begin to enjoy themselves. She sipped idly at a glass of wine and considered the matter. Well, time would tell. It was six-thirty, time for June to walk in and be properly surprised. After that the real countdown would begin for Elissa. The turning point of her evening would be the instant she opened the door at seven o'clock and Wade Taggert absorbed the fact that her excuse about the surprise party had been valid.

The first highlight of the evening went off in a perfectly orchestrated fashion. Dark-haired and attractive, June Randolph entered the room on her equally dark-haired and attractive husband's arm. Both were in their forties, well-dressed, and clearly in love. The marriage was a second time around for each, and Elissa knew they were committed to making it a success.

The shouts of surprise and congratulations stormed over the apartment as June stood flushed with pleasure and excitement. Martin Randolph caught Elissa's eye over his wife's head and grinned conspiratorially.

"I told her we were just going to stop by for a drink." He chuckled, slipping off June's coat.

"Good heavens!" June gasped, laughing. "How long have you been planning this?"

"Almost a month." Martin smiled, vastly pleased with the success of what he had come to think of as his own idea. Somewhere in the excitement of planning the party the fact that Elissa had given him the notion had slipped his mind. She didn't mind. There was nothing as nice as watching a man enjoying himself by making his wife happy.

After that Elissa moved with easy charm through the lively crowd, one eye on the clock as it slowly crawled toward seven. Her sense of anticipation grew in vast leaps as the magic hour approached, and it lent an added fillip of excitement to the evening that was new to her. Soon, she told herself every two minutes or so, soon...

"Elissa!"

She turned to smile at Martin approaching with a drink in his hand, his jacket unbuttoned over the slight paunch at his waistline. His dark looks were little marred by the signs of good living, however, and the thinning hair at the crown of his head was barely noticeable.

"I can't thank you enough for all this," he announced gratefully, waving a hand to encompass the successful party. "June was thrilled. She's never had a surprise party before. She's like a little girl with a new toy tonight," he went on delightedly.

"Don't thank me." Elissa grinned. "It was a brilliant idea on your part, and you know I love to entertain."

He nodded, not disputing the statement that the idea had been his. A lot of people came up with brilliant ideas around Elissa Sheldon. "Listen," he said, his features sobering as he talked. "I got the word about Evelyn late yesterday afternoon. I wanted you to know I'm sorry you didn't get the job. You deserved it and you would have been perfect for it." The brown eyes watched her glinting blue-green gaze for a moment. ''Are you upset about it? I mean, Taggert hasn't been here very long and he likes to do things his own way. He probably made his choice without sufficient input…''

''I'm sure he had excellent reasons for his decision, and you're not to worry about me, Martin,'' Elissa admonished firmly. ''No career ever advances straight up without one or two setbacks, and it's a good experience for me, I'm sure.'' She laughed with an ease she really didn't feel. Five more minutes, assuming Taggert would be on time. Somehow she was certain he would be. The wolf in him would be wanting to collect his prey.

''I'm glad you're taking it so well,'' Martin said, looking relieved. ''I don't mind telling you Evelyn's going to need some help from you for the first couple of months. She's got ability, but she lacks your experience.''

''Don't worry, she'll be welcome to all the assistance I can provide,'' Elissa promised, meaning it. Across the room, Dean looked up from his conversation with a woman who worked in Elissa's editing group and smiled. She returned the small intimacy and was about to excuse herself from the little conference with Martin when the doorbell rang.

For an instant Elissa froze. In spite of all the anticipation and the planning, she abruptly realized she wasn't totally prepared for the next few minutes. Quite belatedly she acknowledged to herself that Wade Taggert was a very unknown factor. Unlike the others in the room, who responded so readily to her charm, Taggert had already proved his resistance to it. He might want her, but he wasn't exactly *charmed* by her, she thought wryly, shaking off the momentary paralysis and going toward the door.

She hesitated once more before opening it, taking a deep breath and letting the anticipation flow through her. Few others in the crowd had paid any attention to the bell summons, and when Elissa mastered her suddenly trembling fingers sufficiently to unlock the door, most didn't even glance toward the newcomer. Whoever it was would be drawn into the cheerful group soon enough under Elissa's expert guidance.

Wade Taggert, as expected, dominated the hall outside the door. Dressed in a dark green pullover sweater and close-fitting slacks, he looked no less formidable than he did in the more formal suit and tie Elissa had always seen him in at the office. What Elissa hadn't expected, for some strange reason, was the flash of hungry, glittering intent in the silvery gaze. She had known deep down that it would be there, just as she had known enough to expect the stern, harsh set of his mouth and the aura of unruffled power around him because she had seen them yesterday in his office. What she hadn't fully expected was to find them more intimidating than ever when the man stood at her threshold, waiting to step into her life.

To her own private disgust, Elissa felt her breath catch in her throat as his eyes clashed with hers. He didn't look beyond her into the room full of people. It was as if he had no curiosity whatsoever about the change in his plans for the evening. His whole attention was focused on Elissa's challenging, upturned face as she stood poised with one hand on the doorknob and one braced against the jamb.

"A party, Elissa?" he drawled with a deceptive

mildness which didn't fool her at all. "You amaze me. I had assumed you'd want discretion to be the keyword for our little arrangement. I had no idea you intended to celebrate." The darkness of his hair gleamed in the hall light as he waited for her response with a taunting nonchalance which rasped along her nerve endings.

"Not a celebration, Wade," she murmured coolly, facing him with the sum total of her self-possession. "More of an object lesson for you on the perils of leaping to conclusions!"

"Are you sure it's a lesson you're trying to teach me, or did you organize all this with the idea of providing yourself with an illusion of safety while you negotiate? I thought I made it clear yesterday there's no point in bargaining with me. I hold the high cards in this little game." There was no threat in his words, only a calm statement of fact. Wade Taggert was very, very sure of himself.

"And in a few minutes when you realize you were completely wrong about me there will be no need to negotiate at all," she assured him, lifting her chin in a small, regal gesture. "Except, perhaps, when we discuss the nature of your apology. I'm assuming you will have enough integrity to want to do that, but I could be wrong. You may simply slink off into the night, unable to face me after you're forced to admit the truth."

"You're going to play this scene right out to the end, aren't you?" he noted with mocking admiration as he stepped forward, forcing her back into the room. For the first time he glanced around at the other guests, a few of whom were beginning to notice his presence.

Elissa was acutely aware of the astonished silence that descended briefly on the room as word went through the group that Wade Taggert had arrived. The others must be flabbergasted that she had invited the man who had denied her the well-earned promotion.

And for the first time in years there was an awkward stretch of silence at an Elissa Sheldon party. A silence she moved instinctively to deal with before it ruined June's celebration. Whatever her private battle with the tall, cold man at her side, her guests would not be involved.

"Look who managed to drop by, after all, everyone," she announced brightly, her fingers hovering lightly on the sleeve of Wade's sweater as she forced herself to lead him forward in a welcoming fashion. When his other hand came up to cover hers, clamping it to his forearm in a possession which to others might have appeared to be only a casually polite move, she realized she was trapped. The single option available to her now was to continue with her plan.

"Where's our guest of honor?" Elissa demanded cheerfully, searching the crowd for June's neat, dark head. "Ah, there you are. Come and meet your husband's boss. Martin, I didn't want to tell you Mr. Taggert might drop by in case he couldn't make it. "

"Oh, there was never any doubt that I'd get here," Wade demurred, bending his head politely to a smiling June Randolph and releasing his grip on Elissa's hand to take the other woman's fingers in his. Elissa wisely used the momentary freedom to jerk her own hand off his sleeve and safely out of reach.

"I'm so happy to meet you," June chattered, unaware of the constraint in the room. "You're just in time to have a piece of birthday cake. I'm going to cut it in a moment.''

"Thank you," Wade said softly, glancing at Martin Randolph, who stood behind his wife. "I believe this was to have been a surprise party for your wife?'' he commented in an even tone which alerted Elissa at once.

"June's first one." Martin chuckled, putting an affectionate arm around her shoulders.

"And a complete success! I had no idea Elissa and Martin had been plotting," June grinned, slanting a happy look at her husband.

"I'm sure they worked very hard on it. It appears to have gone off quite well," Wade said dryly, his gray eyes gliding over Elissa's carefully composed smile like a shark considering its next meal.

In spite of herself, she shivered, keeping the charming smile in place at a considerable cost. Bravely she challenged him with a mockingly raised eyebrow. Surely he must be getting the picture. June and Martin were clearly very much in love, and the excuse of planning a surprise party had been shown to be completely truthful. How long before he backed down? Elissa wondered, running an unconscious tongue tip over her lower lip in expectation. And how gracious would she allow herself to be when the time came to accept his apology? She was certain now she wouldn't allow him to escape without one.

"I was just going to bring out the cake," she declared, slipping lightly through the crowd toward the kitchen. The brief conversation with the Randolphs seemed to be breaking the brittle moment nicely. Others in the group who knew Wade and worked for him closed around him with polite, mildly curious greetings. He was still something of a stranger in the midst, she realized, stepping into the kitchen and picking up the beautifully constructed cake. Most of his employees had seen Wade only in brief, formal sessions at work. Finding him a part of their social world was bound to stimulate curiosity.

"Need any help, love?" Dean stuck his head around the corner and smiled.

"I think I can manage. Would you mind bringing that knife along, though?"

He picked it up obligingly. "So that's Taggert, hmm? The one who didn't give you the job?"

"That's the one, I'm afraid." She chuckled wryly.

"He's a little different from what I expected," Dean began slowly.

The voice which responded to the comment wasn't Elissa's. It was Wade's dark, heavy tones, and she whirled in surprise to see him lounging in the kitchen doorway, arms folded across his chest as he watched the other two.

"What, exactly, did you expect?" he asked the younger man a bit too gently.

"Never mind," Elissa commanded immediately, stepping between the two men, cake in hand. "We've got more important things to do right now. Bring that knife, Dean, and you, Wade, bring those extra napkins over there."

She moved forward with the attitude of a queen leading a procession and hoped she was leaving the men nothing else to do but follow obediently behind.

A chorus of oohs and aahs greeted the arrival of the cake, and June was pushed cheerfully forward to cut it. Dean graciously handed over the knife, and out of the corner of her eye Elissa could see Wade standing aloofly to one side, a handful of napkins clasped rather incongruously in his fingers.

"Now, this," Elissa began dramatically, "is a very special cake, June. Might I suggest you make the first cut about here?" She guided the woman's poised hand to a point over a pink rose. "Yes, I think that's about right. I would also suggest you cut very carefully."

There was a burst of laughter over the elaborate cake-cutting directions, and Martin shushed everyone with a wave of his hand. "This is very serious, folks," he joked and eyed his wife with mock warning. "Make that cut exactly as Elissa suggests, June!"

"You've both got me terrified of a simple cake," June complained laughingly, nevertheless sinking the knife into the icing with proper care. "I don't see what could be so difficult..." She paused a second later as the knife refused to continue its downward progress. "What in the world...?" She bent over slightly to peer at whatever was impeding the knife's efforts. "Good heavens! There's something in here!"

Excited chattering and laughter urged her to finish the task, and poor June was nearly pushed into the icing as the other guests crowded in to see the grand surprise of the evening. A moment later June extracted a small plastic bag, the cake crumbs which clung to the outside failing to obliterate the glitter from within.

"Oh, my God!" June breathed as she held the plastic package in both hands and simply stared at it. Then her delighted, unbelieving eyes went to her proud husband. "Martin, you didn't! I can't believe it!"

Elissa stepped back out of the way as Martin

moved close to his wife to accept her grateful kiss. The diamond necklace inside the plastic wrapper was released and passed around the room as tiny tears of pleasure trickled down the guest of honor's cheeks.

"A nice touch," Wade murmured, coming up behind Elissa's shoulder and keeping his voice so low that only she could hear it. "You were quite determined to prove me wrong tonight, weren't you, witch?"

She shrugged, not without a sense of satisfaction. "You wouldn't listen to me yesterday. But I figured even you couldn't ignore the evidence of your own eyes. And this sort of visual proof is the only thing you trust, isn't it?"

"You look extraordinarily pleased with yourself, Elissa Sheldon," he growled softly. She didn't turn around to look at him, keeping her attention on the furor the necklace was causing as it moved through various hands. But she could feel his massive presence behind her, and the image of a stalking wolf again came to mind. "I suppose," he went on coolly, "that you're expecting an apology? Or did you think I'd tell Evelyn she couldn't have the job, after all?"

Elissa did turn around at that, shocked. "Don't be ridiculous!" she charged, her eyes flashing at the suggestion. "You can't possibly take that job away from her. No, an apology is the only thing I expect to get out of this mess, Mr. Taggert. But by rights it ought to be a good one!"

"You expect me to get down on my knees?" he drawled interestedly, watching her with a deliberately provocative twist to his lips.

"That wouldn't be overdoing it one bit!" she

vowed, aware of the excitement sparking through her as they neared the final confrontation.

"You'd be satisfied with that?" he mocked.

"Since I can hardly call you out for pistols at dawn, I shall have to be satisfied."

"In the old days defending a woman's honor was the responsibility of the man who protected her," Wade commented silkily, his eyes flicking briefly across the room to where Dean was busy admiring the necklace together with someone else. "I take it you're not going to sic your friend Dean on me?"

"I wouldn't think of involving him in this disgusting matter. Besides, I can take care of myself, Mr. Taggert," Elissa told him coldly.

"Tell me something," he invited almost casually, his eyes once again on her challenging gaze. "Have you been looking forward to the grand denouement all day long?"

"I've been looking forward to it since it first occurred to me to invite you over here so that you could see how wrong you'd been," she assured him tauntingly.

"In that case, I wouldn't want to spoil matters by acting precipitately," he retorted calmly. "I'll wait until after the party to let you know what I think of your efforts. In the meantime you can pour me a drink. I'm really not much of a birthday-cake eater." He pushed the napkins he'd been holding into one of her hands and then took her wrist firmly between steel fingers and forced her along to the bar she had arranged at the far end of the room.

There was nothing to do but allow herself to be dragged in his wake, Elissa realized with an inner sigh. She had no intention of creating a scene at her own party, and she would, after all, be getting her payment shortly.

That thought was enough to keep her going for the rest of the evening as the party sailed into high gear and eventually began to wind down. The leavetaking was reluctant on almost everyone's part, but eventually people did glance at their watches in resignation and began moving slowly out the door. Elissa saw each off on a rising tide of excitement, which dimmed only momentarily when she realized it was going to be awkward saying good-night to Dean Norwood, who was one of the last to leave.

"I'm not sure I like leaving you alone with that guy," Dean whispered at the door. He nodded his head surreptitiously toward a large chair where Wade sprawled, whiskey in hand, and appeared to study one of Elissa's strange paintings on the wall across from him.

"It'll be all right," she whispered back. "He just wants to discuss a business matter with me. He'll be leaving almost immediately."

"Are you sure?"

"Very," she breathed confidently.

"Do you think he's changed his mind about giving the job to that other woman?" Dean wondered vaguely, a small frown still drawing his brows together.

"I'm not certain, but it probably has something to do with my future at the company." She put a hand on his shoulder and lifted her lips for his kiss.

"Good night, love," Dean said, edging politely out the door. "It was a great party, as usual. I'll give you a call in a couple of days, okay?" He glanced uncertainly once more in Wade's direction. The other man ignored him completely. Rudeness came easily to Wade Taggert, Elissa decided.

"That will be fine, Dean."

With a last reassuring smile she closed the door on the remainder of her guests. Then, drawing a deep, anticipatory breath, Elissa turned and leaned back against the wood, her hands behind her on the knob, and waited for the satisfying conclusion to the evening.

Wade stirred in his chair, but he made no move to look at her. Instead he raised the glass of whiskey to his mouth, took a long swallow, and set it down on the table beside him.

"Well, Elissa," he said after a moment, and she straightened away from the door, prepared, she suddenly realized, to take an attitude of gracious hauteur.

"Yes, Wade?" she prompted cooly, coming forward slowly to receive the apology she had waited for so long. Her blue-green eyes gleamed with an unaccustomed brightness as she paused in front of him.

But his next words took her breath away with their sheer audacity, leaving her speechless as she met the dry ice of his eyes.

"You've put it off for an entire evening, but the time has come to give me my answer. I'm waiting, little witch. No more games."

"You're answer!" she finally managed, stunned. She stared at him, in bewilderment and rising anger. "What answer? I'm waiting for the apology you owe me, damn it! Why else would I have invited an overbearing, egotistical, rude male such as you to my party in the first place?"

"Because you thought you could fool me into thinking you'd been telling the truth about your relationship with Martin Randolph. Oh, it was all nicely staged, Elissa, but I'm not a complete idiot, you know. I realize the party has been a convenient cover for you and Martin, but don't expect me to buy the whole illusion!''

He moved, surging out of his chair and reaching out to snag her wrists in one hand. The cold flames of his eyes lashed her as he pulled her incredulous face close to his. ''So let's have it, Elissa, my sweet witch. Have you made up your mind to accept a new lover in your life, or do you still need convincing?''

Chapter 3

"**You**," Elissa stated with great certainty, "must be out of your mind! Crazy! How did a crazy man ever get to be the manager of CompuDesign, for God's sake?"

"By a lot of hard work," Wade retorted, and for the first time since she'd met him, Elissa could have sworn an ingredient very close to humor stirred for an instant in the gray eyes. It was gone almost at once, but not before it had managed to catch her attention. She didn't tell herself she'd been mistaken. Elissa Sheldon knew people too well to think herself mistaken in a matter like that.

"You're hurting my wrists," she pointed out grittingly. "Would you mind letting me go? I'm not going to run anywhere. In case you weren't aware of the fact, this is my apartment!" She tossed her head in a small gesture of infuriated disdain. The dark red-highlighted hair moved gracefully, like the rippling coat of an animal.

"You're not accustomed to being hurt, are you?" Wade observed laconically, glancing down at the slender wrists he was holding prisoner.

"I most certainly am not!" she agreed fervently, wriggling her fingers suggestively. But he didn't release them. Instead he seemed to lose interest in the cause of her protest, continuing to chain her in front of him with idle ease as his gleaming eyes moved back to her taut face.

"Think of it as a new and educational experience," he advised dryly. "Or perhaps as an object lesson, such as the one you tried to give me tonight!"

"You don't seem to have learned much from what I was trying to teach you!" she snapped, beginning to plot various ways of scratching out his eyes as soon as she had the use of her hands.

"I wouldn't say that," he disagreed mildly. "I learned, for example, just how incredibly charming you really can be. How many women, I wonder, go out of their way to give parties for their lover's wife?"

"Martin Randolph is not my lover! How many times do I have to tell you?"

"He won't be any longer, I'll grant you that." Wade smiled with dangerous promise. "As I told you yesterday, while I'm in your inner circle I won't tolerate any other man sharing it with me. But even if I hadn't decided to find out for myself what's behind the bewitching facade you present to the world, I still think poor Randolph would have been shown the door. He had, after all, outlived his usefulness, hadn't he? He failed to get you that promotion."

"What a ghastly thing to say!" Elissa hissed. "Martin is a friend of mine, and he will continue to stay a friend!"

"That's the amazing thing, isn't it?" Wade nodded thoughtfully. "He probably will continue to be your friend. In fact, he'll probably come up with the notion that it was all his idea to break off the more intimate relationship and go back to being just friends. I could see from the way he acted with his wife tonight that already he's thinking about his marriage again. You're a very clever woman, my dear."

"He never stopped thinking about it!" Elissa shut her eyes in brief despair and disgust: "What's the point of arguing? You've made up your mind, and all the proof in the world won't change it, will it?"

"Who was going to be next on your list?" Wade persisted, and Elissa felt his fingers tighten further around her bruised wrists. "The stockbroker you had a little trouble getting rid of tonight? Norwood?"

And then a very strange thing happened in Elissa's mind. She allowed the raw frustration and rage seething inside to take control for a few short seconds, long enough to grate a scathing response to his demand.

"Yes," she heard herself say. "As a matter of fact, Dean is next on the list. Very good-looking, don't you think? Also quite successful. I might do more than charm him into bed—I might charm him into marriage!"

"I don't doubt for one minute that, left to your own devices, you could do exactly that," Wade growled. "But, as of tonight, you are no longer your own boss, free to glide through the world like some sort of sorceress, causing any man to whom you take a fancy to roll over and play dead or leap to do your bidding.

You have power, Elissa Sheldon, but, unlike everyone else, I'm fully aware of it, and I'm going to see to it that you exercise some control in its use.''

"You mean that I'm going to use it the way you want it used!" she said heatedly, wondering how she had ever gotten into such a devastating conversation.

"Now you're getting the idea," he approved, separating her wrists and enclosing one in each of his hands. Very deliberately, as if defying her to break free, he twisted her hands behind her back, arching her resisting softness against him. "Don't worry," he went on softly. "I wouldn't dream of trying to crush your enchantments. I only intend to see to it that you practice them on me for a while."

Elissa turned her head frantically to avoid the plundering of his mouth, but it was impossible. He held her too firmly, too closely, and there were no avenues of escape. His lips moved hungrily on hers, bruising her when she tried to fight him, softening seductively when she ceased struggling. The cycle of his attack was at once unswerving and inevitable. Elissa felt her senses begin to swim with the hopelessness of trying to break out of the circle. Each attempt at freeing herself brought only a punishing intensity in his kiss. Passiveness brought forth a gentler, intriguing exploration of her mouth.

"It's called conditioned response," Wade told her on a note of victorious masculine humor. "Soon you'll realize it's much more pleasant to stop fighting altogether."

"I want you to leave, Wade," Elissa tried ordering in desperation. She had to get rid of the man, and soon. There was a compelling danger in his embrace, and she was woman enough to recognize it. It weakened her with its sense of inevitability, but sought the embrace in the first place. And that was a very novel situation for Elissa Sheldon. Past romances had always been of a very *comfortable* nature, deftly managed by her with unerring instinct for what she liked to think was the benefit of both parties. She was not at all accustomed to being taken by storm, and she had no intention of growing used to the idea.

"But I'm not ready to leave," he whispered. "We have a great deal to discuss, you and I. Come over to the couch and I'll show you." With that he stepped back, retaining only a casual hold on her arm, and began to lead her toward the fat, pillowy sofa.

Elissa knew she wasn't going to get a better opportunity. She was dealing with a desperate situation, and it called for desperate remedies. Heart pounding, she allowed herself to be reluctantly dragged past the bar she had arranged earlier, now cluttered with used glasses and bottles. Appalled at her own daring, she reached out and snagged the nearest bottle.

You couldn't attempt this sort of thing with a faint heart, she challenged herself bracingly, and you had to do it quickly while there was still an element of surprise. Already Wade had turned to glance back in annoyance to see what was happening. She wouldn't aim for his head, she reassured her queasy stomach. Only his shoulder. The cloth of his sweater would protect him from being cut, but the impact should startle him enough to loosen his hold on her for a vital second or two....

Her hand clutching the bottle was moving in an arc as the gray eyes collided with hers over his shoulder. In that instant she knew he realized what she was about to do and that she hadn't gotten enough of a head start. He would put out his free hand and catch her arm before the bottle found its target!

But he didn't. With sudden horror Elissa became aware that Wade was simply going to stand there and let her crack a half-full bottle of bourbon across his shoulder. The ice in his gaze dared her to go through with it, but she knew she couldn't. Not possibly!

It didn't take much to halt the blow before it landed. Elissa recognized that the effort had been rather half-hearted from the beginning, and the knowledge increased her fury severalfold. What was the matter with her? Had she no spirit whatsoever?

Still clutching the bottle by its neck, Elissa lowered her hand to her side and stood her ground grimly as Wade dropped her wrist and turned fully around to face her. There was a baiting attitude in him which was reflected in the wicked curve of his mouth and the narrowed gray eyes.

"Don't look so disgusted with yourself, little witch," he murmured, surveying her defiant glare and the unused weapon at her side. "I could have told you violence isn't your style. You're more at home with magic than you are with physical methods of attack."

"Unlike you!" she shot back daringly, regaining a measure of confidence as she realized he was no longer holding her.

The curve of his mouth widened, and he nodded agreeably. "Unlike me. If that bottle of bourbon had landed, there would have been hell to pay, Elissa Sheldon. You were very wise to think twice before you went through with the plan."

She eyed him scornfully. "Why? What would you have done? Beaten me?"

"With the greatest enthusiasm," he affirmed laconically. "You wouldn't have been able to sit down for a week."

Elissa eyed him with a new thoughtfulness as she hoisted the bourbon and set it on the bar. "Why didn't you try to stop me? So much simpler than messing about with a lot of broken glass!"

He shrugged. "A calculated risk. I didn't expect you to go through with it, and you didn't. The advantage of letting you find out for yourself that you couldn't do it was worth the risk."

"What an insufferable creature you are," Elissa breathed wonderingly. "I can't imagine how you've survived this long. You must have a great many enemies, Wade Taggert."

"Possibly, but I don't intend to count you among them," he informed her quite gently. "Besides, you never make enemies. You make it a point to charm everyone you meet, don't you? Has it always been easy for you? I'll bet you were born with the ability."

"Too bad the same can't be said of you! I've never met a less charming man in my life!" she glazed, flushing under his accusation that she somehow used her many friends.

"No, I haven't gotten where I am by enchanting everyone around me," he allowed easily. "I've fought for everything I've ever wanted. It's a different way of getting what one wants out of life than the method you've employed, but effective, nevertheless."

Elissa saw the mockery in him as he watched her, and she found herself wanting to flatten him. "It might be effective but I'd rather have people like me than think of me as a wolf!"

"Is that how you see me?" he demanded with great interest.

"Yes," she confirmed with relish. "A lone wolf, taking what you want out of life with no regard for anyone else. A predator! That's what you reminded me of tonight, trying to socialize a little, put people at ease as if they were sheep you wanted to calm. But it never quite works, does it? People may relax a bit, even try some casual conversation with you, but a part of them is always slightly wary. Their instincts tell them the wolf is still there under the surface."

"But even big bad wolves want some kindness in their lives, Elissa," he muttered in a new, lower, almost purring tone as he lifted a hand to touch a finger to the line of her jaw. "Just because I see your sorcery for what it is doesn't mean I'm immune to it, you know. For over a month, since the first day I saw you, in fact, I've been giving you opportunities to draw me into your web and try your charms on me, but you've always ignored me. Is it any wonder I finally decided to take matters into my own hands?"

"What in the world are you talking about?" she yelped, astounded. "You and I have rarely crossed paths since the day you arrived!"

"Only because you kept avoiding me. Every time I tried to create an opportunity for you to get to know me, you acted oblivious to my bait."

"If you're talking about the afternoon you called me into your office to discuss the career paths for the various members of my writing group..." she began heatedly, thinking of that short, businesslike meeting.

"I am." He smiled quirkingly. "You came totally prepared with case histories on everyone who reports to you, spent half an hour extolling their virtues, and left without even giving me a chance to get a word in edgewise.''

''You'd made it clear you wanted a concise report, and that's what I gave you!'' she snapped, incensed.

''I had intended,'' he informed her dryly, ''to extend the discussion through cocktails at my place, but you raced in and out of my office like a whirlwind. Then there was the morning I stopped you in the hall and suggested I get to know more about the writing group over lunch. I thought I was making progress until you showed up at the appointed time and place with the five writers you supervise.''

Elissa reddened, remembering the occasion. ''They were all thrilled by your interest,'' she mumbled, her eyes lowering self-consciously to the knot of his tie.

''Tell me something,'' he urged, lifting her chin between thumb and forefinger. ''You didn't really misunderstand my invitation that morning, did you? You deliberately chose to interpret it as meaning I wanted to take the whole group out to lunch. Why, Elissa? I've seen you turn a corner at the end of a hall just to avoid having to walk past me!''

''That's not true,'' she defended, thoroughly irritated at his perception and at herself for having allowed her instinctive avoidance response to show. She had found herself going out of her way to forestall small encounters, and she had purposely misinterpreted his invitation to lunch. Exactly why she had done so wasn't entirely clear to her on the various occasions involved, but now she knew. Her feminine instincts had been working overtime, warning her of a new kind of danger in her life—warning her of a man who couldn't be handled the way she automatically handled other men.

"It is true!" he countered. "But why me, Elissa? Why haven't I qualified for your magic circle? You didn't even invite me to your last party even though most of the rest of the staff went, and I understand my predecessor always had a standing invitation to your parties."

"Don't act as if you're some poor waif from the storm to whom I've refused shelter and comfort," she snarled, jerking herself away from his touch on her face and stepping a pace out of reach.

"You've known from the beginning that even if you could succeed in charming me, you'd never be able to make the thorough job of it that you do on others, isn't that right?" he pressed, closing the space between them but not touching her again. The gray flames of his eyes swept her outraged face. "You'd never be able to dazzle me to such an extent that I wouldn't be aware of how little of you I was really getting. I'll always know if I'm being short-changed, witch, and I won't tolerate it. Wolves aren't noted for taking less than their full share. And I do want my share, honey," he added in suddenly cajoling tones. "I want to have your softness and your wide-eyed, fascinated interest and have you remember the way I like my drinks and all the rest. Surely you can understand that? I'm only a man, Elissa, and I want to be charmed like the others...."

"Don't give me that line," Elissa grated furiously. "I've read Little Red Riding Hood!"

"Then you know the wolf got everything he wanted in the end."

"This time the story is going to have a different conclusion, Wade Taggert!" she vowed, trying to stifle the leap of her pulses as she confronted this new

and dangerous element in her life. It would be the
height of folly to allow the intrigue of the situation
to pull her under. She knew, deep inside, she might
never resurface.

"No," he denied in deep, blighting tones. "It's
not. I'm going to get what I want, too. Even though
I'm going to have to reach out and take it for myself
instead of having you give it to me. But that's all
right. I'm used to doing things that way. And before
you and I are through, Elissa Sheldon, I'm going to
have everything. Not just the bits and pieces you be-
stow so sweetly on others, but the part that no one
ever even gets close to...."

"What are you talking about?" she blazed, a
strange and curious fear licking down her spine.

"I'm talking about the part of you that goes into
your paintings," he tossed back with casual ruthlessness.

Elissa swallowed tightly. "My paintings?" she repeated distantly. No one had ever guessed she was
the creator of the unearthly landscapes. No one had
even asked if she had painted them. Everyone just
assumed she had the idiosyncrasy she claimed to have
where art was concerned, and people promptly forgot
about the subject as soon as Elissa had gently turned
them aside from it. Yet this man who hardly knew
her and who had never been in her apartment before
tonight had instantly recognized them as her work.

"Did you think I didn't know you'd done them?"
he asked in some surprise, seeing the bafflement and
wariness in her face. "But of course I knew." He
frowned, shaking his head at her obtuseness. A flicker
of understanding flashed across the hard planes of his
face, and then he smiled very slightly. "But others

don't know, do they? And if they did, they wouldn't understand. Just as they don't understand why you have such things hanging in your apartment in the first place. Most people would be floored to know you'd painted them yourself. After all, they're so *unlike* you, honey,'' he drawled mockingly.

"What's that supposed to mean? There's nothing wrong with those paintings!''

"Except that they reveal a side of you no one has ever had the sense to see was there,'' he whispered huskily. "The side of you I'm going to take, along with all the rest of you!''

Once more Elissa stepped back, but this time she was too slow and he caught her before she could get out of reach.

"No!'' she snapped, slapping at his hand as he used it to pull her close. His arm moved, but only to form a cradle with his other one as he swooped and lifted her off her feet with soft violence. "Wade!'' she protested, genuinely alarmed now. "Put me down this instant! I won't have you treating me as if...as if...''

"As if I own you?'' He grinned daringly, stalking across to the overstuffed sofa and tossing her lightly down into it. Before she could scramble aside, he was sprawling on top of her, anchoring her beneath him. "But that's the way it's going to be, little witch,'' he went on beguilingly, his rough palms framing her infuriated features. "You wouldn't take me into your world willingly, so I'm going to make a place for myself there.''

"Not a chance!'' she got out between gritted teeth. "I've got news for you: my job doesn't mean that much to me! Certainly not enough to convince me to be your mistress!'' She could feel the weight of him along the length of her and was vaguely amazed at the latent demand she sensed in that heaviness.

''You're not such a coward as to quit merely because you've learned the price you'll pay for holding on to your position,'' he taunted, the thumbs of his hands probing the corners of her mouth intimately.

''It's not a question of cowardice, damn you!''

''Are you admitting you don't have sufficient power to charm me into giving you what you want?'' he retorted gently, challengingly. ''Come, no, Elissa, just because everything's been so easy for you up until I appeared on the scene, that's no reason to quit at the fist sign of trouble.''

''Don't you dare make fun of me,'' she breathed tightly, aware of her helplessness and painfully aware of the sensual tension enveloping them both. ''Your behavior is utterly despicable! Any man who would use his position to try and force one of his female employees to sleep with him is beneath contempt!''

''No more so than a woman who uses her body to get what she wants!''

''Wade, I swear I never did such a thing!'' she tried frantically. ''I invited you here tonight to try and prove it to you. Since you refuse to believe the only evidence I have, you leave me no choice but to quit my job!''

''Suit yourself,'' he rasped. ''There are some pretty obvious benefits in the deal for you if you stay on at CompuDesign, but leaving the company's not going to get rid of me. I know what I want, and every day that passes makes me more certain.'' He relaxed slightly. ''But you want your job. Admit it.''

She heard the absolute promise in his voice and

sucked in her breath. "You can't *hound* me, Wade! I won't have it!" she wailed.

"I'm not going to hound you, sweet witch," he vowed, bending his head to find the hollow of her throat under the lacy collar of her blouse. "I'm going to make love to you. Every chance I get!"

Once more Elissa drew in her breath sharply, but this time for a different reason. Try as she would, and as dangerous as she knew it to be, she could not build up sufficient resistance to the overwhelming demand emanating from him. There was a fire on her skin everywhere his mouth descended, and he used his weight to force an intimate, electric contact against her hips.

Elissa had one brief moment of hope when he abruptly elevated himself for a few seconds, but the respite lasted only long enough for him to angle her more directly beneath him, and then she found herself crushed again into the cushions of the sofa.

"Wade! Please!" she begged as one of his hands began to explore her body with arousing hunger.

He silenced her protest with his mouth, fastening it on hers in carefully controlled ferocity that demanded entrance for the invasion of his tongue. She lost the battle to keep him out when he used his teeth with delicate savagery on her vulnerable lip. She gasped at the implied pain which was not yet pain, and he used the short weakness in her defenses to taste the warm honey behind her lips.

Simultaneously with the unlocking of her mouth Wade's hand closed possessively over her small breast, and she felt the tremor that went through both of them at the contact. Elissa sensed the rising tide of the assault and began to panic at her own inability to stem it.

There was need and demand and desire and promise in the way Wade's fingers left her breast momentarily to seek the buttons of her blouse. His mouth slid moistly across hers, withdrawing from one conquered territory to search out another. He found it in the sensitive tip of her earlobe just as his probing fingers found the entrance to her blouse.

"Sweet witch," he husked as he toyed luxuriously with the earlobe he had captured. "You're so good at knowing what others need. You wouldn't turn me away at the gate, would you? Not when I need you more than the others do."

"You want too much," she cried softly, despairingly as her buttons gave beneath his efforts. The front clasp of her bra was soon dealt with, and then her flesh tingled unmercifully as he palmed the nipple he had been stalking.

"How could I want any less than all of you?" he demanded hoarsely. She shivered involuntarily and knew at once that he sensed it. Instantly, his fingertips tightened tantalizingly around the tip of her breast, coaxing forth the nipple as if luring a small creature from its burrow.

Elissa shut her eyes against the force of her own response, dazed at the impact he was having on her senses. Against her volition her hands freed themselves from where they had been wedged against his shoulders and went to the thick darkness of his hair. Cautiously at first and then with increasing urgency she slid her fingertips through the gray at his temples and on into the blackness beyond. She heard him groan in unrestrained hunger as her fists eventually settled at the nape of his neck, clenching and un-clenching the muscles there.

He *did* want her, she thought in wonder. With a power she'd never sensed in other men. It was nearly impossible to imagine Dean Norwood, for example, demanding and forcing this level of response. But Dean Norwood was a civilized, polite human being who would be a gentleman even when he made love. Wade Taggert's needs and masculine desire went beyond the level of a gentleman's. And he had no inhibitions about letting her know the intensity of his demands, Elissa thought dimly, her mind whirling.

"Randolph and that damn stockbroker might be satisfied with what you choose to give them, and in the end, when you tire of them, they'll leave still thinking of themselves as your friends," Wade muttered fiercely as his lips began tracking down her throat to the curve of her breast. "But if and when our affair comes to an end, there will be no friendship between us, my witch! I can't look at you without wanting to posses you—and whatever happens, that element will never change!"

"Wade! You don't know what you're saying!" And then Elissa's words were broken off in a gasp as his tongue found the tip of her gentle curve to replace the hand which had been at work there and had now moved on.

"Yes, I do." He grated against her breast as he traced a feathery pattern on the warm skin of her stomach. "I want to know the part of you living in that crumbling castle in your painting. The part that's protected by the dragons you've got hanging all around this apartment. You look out at the world from some inner sanctum and find the rest of us amusing little pets, don't you? But not me, Elissa,'' he vowed, lifting his head for a moment to rake her startled, tense face.

"I'm not a pet for you to gently, kindly, control and manipulate or please because it amuses you or because it keeps everything in your world flowing comfortably along. I'm the wolf you called me a few minutes ago, and I'm going to sit beside you in your castle, not beg outside the door! You'll pet me, Elissa, but no more often than I'll pet you. And in the end you'll be as chained in my power as I will be in yours.''

"That's utterly absurd!'' she managed, knowing the feel of hot honey flowing through her veins and appalled at it. "We're two very ordinary human beings, Wade! Not enchanters from another world who can cast spells over each other and see which of us is the stronger!'' Her blue-green eyes had deepened in shading until they reflected the depths of a remote sea as she looked up into his uncompromising features.

"Shall I tell you your own great secret?'' he asked musingly. "Will that prove my power is at least a match for your own?''

"What nonsense is this?'' she hissed uncertainly, searching the gray gaze for some hint of his meaning.

"Your best-kept secret, little witch, and the source of your magic is that, in spite of all the friends and admirers you so easily cultivate, you could close the door on all of them tomorrow, retreat into your painting or read books of fantasy, and not miss any of them. You're completely self-contained inside the walls of your castle, aren't you? And no one even has a clue. Except for me, naturally,'' he added calmly, matter-of-factly.

Elissa was dumbfounded. The one remark which finally penetrated her reeling brain was the comment he'd made on the science fiction. ''What do you know of my fantasy collection?'' she charged, a new wave of fury roaring through her senses. She thought of the books on her shelf and winced.

He moved his hands back up to cup her face and smiled with patent triumph. ''I wandered into your bedroom during the party. I wanted to see more after I saw the paintings.''

''My bedroom!'' For some unknown reason Elissa felt as if some part of her had been violated, invaded. ''You took it upon yourself to do a thing like that? Haven't you ever heard of private property? What kind of person are you?''

''You've already decided I'm a predator. We wolves set out own boundaries.'' He grinned, clearly enjoying her shock and anger.

''I'm glad you're so damned pleased with yourself,'' she ripped at him violently.

''Calm down, Elissa,'' he ordered, the grin fading as he felt her tremble with the force of her anger. ''I already knew there were mysteries about you. It was natural for me to go looking for them.''

''And what are your secrets, Wade Taggert?'' she asked fiercely, sea eyes narrowing with menace even though it would have been clear to any observer that she was in no position to threaten Wade. All the menace was plainly on his side.

''Secrets?'' he repeated softly. ''I don't have any secrets. Not from you. Only a need to be charmed. A need for you to want me, really want me, not just find me comfortable for a while. Is that so much to ask?''

Elissa couldn't believe the near wistfulness of his tone. His most dangerous tactic yet, she told herself grimly. She must not allow herself to be seduced by the depth of his desire and need. Who would have realized that she, of all people, would be in such danger from this aspect of the man? It didn't bear contemplation! Her head moved restlessly, negatingly, on the cushion as she continued to focus on the soundless gray pools of his eyes. He must have known of her chaotic thoughts, because his smile suddenly gentled in a way which was altogether new. And every bit as dangerous as his strength.

"Elissa, Elissa," he whispered, "I tried to work my way into your spells through normal routes; I tried to bribe my way in with promises of advancing your career, the one thing I thought might be important to you; I've demanded admission on my own terms. And now I'm asking very politely. I want to know your magic, little witch. Come be my woman and find out what it's like to put yourself in someone else's power for once. I promise you won't regret it, my sweet. I'll take good care of you…"

"The way you already took good care of my promotion?" she snapped, trying to fight the weakness in herself and fearing failure.

"I had to do something to show you that you couldn't use Randolph to get what you want," he explained, as if to a small child to whom he had denied candy. "I'm the one who can make life difficult or pleasant for you, Elissa. And I might prove more complicated to manage than men like Randolph or

Norwood. But think of the challenge!'' he urged goadingly.

''You still think I tried to sleep my way into that position, don't you?'' she muttered forlornly, not understanding how anyone could think that of her. No one ever thought the worst of Elissa Sheldon. Everyone who knew her would realize she wouldn't have dreamed of using sex to get that job.

''It doesn't matter now,'' he soothed, stroking her cheekbones with his fingers. ''That lesson is over, and I won't allow you to stray again…'' The cold rain in his eyes turned a deeper shade for an instant. ''Except with me!''

''You want me in spite of what you think is my history of sneaky, underhanded, conniving behaviour, is that it?'' she murmured disbelievingly. No one had ever thought the worst of her, but if someone had she certainly wouldn't expect him to pursue her so intently after learning the awful truth. What manner of man was Wade Taggert?

''I think you're salvageable,'' he informed her bluntly. ''You've always worked your charms so easily that you've grown accustomed to using them to smooth your path through life. But I don't believe you're really bad. You require a firm hand and some guidance from a man who sees through your magic even while he's availing himself of it. And you need to find out what it's like to want a man so much that you couldn't just walk away and close the door on him!''

Chapter 4

Elissa closed her eyes against the astounding presumption of the man who still held her pinned against the couch and then she let her lashes flutter open very wide. "You think you're the man to keep me under control?" she drawled very coolly.

"I want you, Elissa," he stated categorically. "And that means I've got to control you, make you want me, or I'll find my fingers very badly burned, won't I?"

"The experience of getting yourself singed might be quite salutary," she offered bitterly.

She saw the reluctant smile touch his eyes and the edges of his mouth.

"I think I can take care of myself," he promised meaningfully. She could feel the certainty in him. It had a palpable presence. He was so sure he'd win....

"And what's in all this for me?" she demanded a

little too gently, feeling the rage mingle with the other new emotion she was experiencing tonight. Together they made a potent combination in her bloodstream.

"Your career back on track," he said immediately, not appearing the least reluctant to enumerate the material advantages of an association with him. "The challenge of finding out if you've met a man you can't ultimately control. I'm counting on that as a lure as great as advancing in your job, by the way." He smiled bleakly. "The temptation of discovering what passion can be with a man who doesn't think of himself as merely a good friend, and..." He hesitated and then said with shattering callousness, "Perhaps a necklace or two thrown in on the side. Something to make up for the one you had to give up to June tonight."

It was too much. Elissa knew she could no longer resist the risk of trying to bring the pompous, overbearing Wade Taggert down into the dust at her feet. Never had she experienced such violent feelings toward another human being, but, then, never had she been treated like this, either! If there was any justice in the universe she was going to bring it crashing around his ears!

But such a goal meant playing his repellent game very, very carefully, Elissa realized with surprisingly cold logic. She must lead him delicately, cleverly, to the point of final victory. And then hurl everything back in his face!

The punishment of Wade Taggert would be a new adventure for her, Elissa thought as her pulses pounded in anger and excitement. It would take her far out of the normal, comfortable routine of her life. The man would be as dangerous as any of the strange beasts in her paintings, and she would have only herself to blame if she got in over her head.

But the apology she had been seeking from him earlier in the evening had become a goal she couldn't ignore. In fact, she decided boldly, an apology alone would not be enough to satisfy her newly awakened craving for revenge. Not nearly enough!

"My career back on track..." she repeated thoughtfully, as if turning the idea over in her mind. "You give me your word to restore my promotion— or one equivalent to it, since you can't very well take the job away from Evelyn at this point?" She moistened her slightly parted lips in a faintly provocative gesture, her eyes wide and interested. Elissa had never set out to play a *femme fatale,* but every woman had a few instincts to fall back on in a crisis.

"Behave yourself and give me what I want, and I'll take care of everything," Wade promised with a pouncing effect in his voice. She could almost see his thoughts spinning out plans. He was so sure he had her, so sure that he'd found the key to her when he'd taken control of her future at CompuDesign.

"I'm...I'm not quite certain if I can trust you," Elissa hedged, allowing feminine caution to flicker in her searching gaze.

"You have my word," he told her arrogantly, as if that should be sufficient.

"But I hardly know you," she pointed out gently. "Perhaps your word is worthless..."

"You can trust me, Elissa," he told her with a sudden frown. She realized he wasn't used to having his word of honor questioned, and that gave her a great deal of encouragement.

"Perhaps," she mused baitingly. "Perhaps not.

You're asking me to risk a lot, aren't you? A woman wants to have some faith in a man's intentions before she agrees to a situation like this. You've already told me I won't be able to count on charming you into completing your end of the bargain..." She let the words trail off suggestively, and his frown intensified. He hadn't expected this particular hitch, she thought gleefully.

"What are you recommending?" he demanded forcefully. "That I give you a promotion first? Before I collect what's owed me? I'm not that foolish, little witch!"

"I didn't expect you would be." She smiled placatingly. "I'm only going to suggest that we give ourselves some time to get to know each other before embarking on a full-scale affair. In spite of what you may think of me, I don't wander through life hopping from one bed to another!"

"Yesterday I gave you a day's grace to think the matter over, and I arrived for my answer tonight only to find you'd spent the time planning to prove me wrong. You didn't have any doubt you'd be successful, did you? Now you're asking for more time. Will I come back in a few days only to find you've erected other fortifications and defenses? I don't feel like wasting any more nights, Elissa," he concluded warningly. His hand moved to settle once more over her breast in flagrant possession.

She shivered involuntarily at the touch and took a firm grip on her nerves. "I'm not suggesting I spend the time in solitary thought about the matter, Wade. I'm offering to spend the time getting to know you. Is that so much to ask?" She knew she'd hit a vulnerable point when she'd expressed doubt in his word, and she homed in on it with intuitive accuracy. Elissa was good at diagnosing the weak points in others, but her automatic reaction when she located one was to treat it gently, kindly. To build and strengthen, not use the advantage. Tonight constituted one of the rare moments in her life when she deliberately hammered at a sensitive area in a man's ego. The last time she could clearly recall doing so was the time she had found a young boy mistreating a small dog. Her anger had caused her to rip the boy to shreds, reducing him to tears in a matter of minutes. Later she had been sorry, wishing she'd used positive instead of negative tactics to show him the error of his ways, and she'd made an effort to do so in other encounters.

But tonight she would think only of herself, she vowed silently, and that meant using every advantage she could garner.

"You'll spend the time only with me? No one else?" he verified as if going over the terms of a bargain. His palm scraped a little roughly on her delicate nipple, and Elissa realized he wasn't even aware of the tiny roughness.

"Yes, Wade." She nodded quickly, appealingly. "We'll…we'll treat it like the start of any normal romance, discovering each other, getting to know one another. A dating relationship."

"I hope you don't expect me to keep my hands completely off you during the course of this game," he mocked. But she could see the triumph still swirling in his eyes. He was sure he could handle everything.

"I expect you'll try to seduce me, but don't expect me to be easily persuaded into your bed." She couldn't keep the tartness out of her voice, but he didn't seem to mind.

"You won't allow that to happen until you're sure I can be relied upon to complete my end of the bargain, is that it?" he bit out. "In the end you'll come to me on faith alone, witch, because I'm not going to let you talk me into giving you the things you want until I've got what I want!"

"We shall see, won't we?" she murmured provokingly, lowering her dark auburn lashes so that he wouldn't see the look in her eyes.

"So it's a game you're playing!" Wade eyed her consideringly for an instant and then slowly, resolutely, lowered his head and kissed the small bones of her exposed shoulder with cool aggression. "Very well, witch," he grated against her skin, letting his mouth taste her. She could feel his tongue curl raspingly on her and had all she could do not to flinch from the barbaric caress. "I'll play your games with you," he told her challengingly, confidently. "You'll find I'm an opponent worthy of your best magic!"

"Then," she essayed boldly, "if we're agreed on the terms and conditions, it's time you left."

"Kicking me out already?" he mocked, making no effort to move his weight off her. The black brows climbed upward with quelling intimidation. "I've hardly begun to explore some of your most interesting secrets." His eyes holding hers, Wade slid his hand down the length of her rib cage to the waistband of her skirt.

"I want you to leave," Elissa demanded as her breath seemed to catch at the back of her throat. "You've got what you came for tonight..."

"Not quite," he contradicted, letting his fingers stray inside the waistband.

"Let me phrase that a little differently," she snapped. "You've got all you're going to get tonight!"

"I can see that even though you've lost this evening, your spirit isn't anywhere near crushed." He suddenly chuckled, a rich sound from deep in his chest. The gray eyes glinted with the awakened humor in him.

"Is that what you want? My spirit in tatters?"

"Oh, no," he denied at once. "Never that. I only want it controlled. Properly chained and controlled by me!"

"I learned a lesson about not counting chickens before they're hatched yesterday," Elissa said sweetly. "Perhaps you're due to learn the same thing."

He grinned savagely. "I knew you wouldn't be able to resist a challenge of suitable proportions."

"Your proportions are large, all right," she retorted. "You're crushing me!"

"Too bad." He sighed humorously, moving at last to sit up beside her on the couch. "I find you extremely comfortable." he watched as she hastily struggled to a sitting position and tried buttoning her blouse with shaking fingers. She wasn't certain if it was rage or sheer reaction which caused her to tremble, but it made the small task difficult.

"Here," he told her quite gently, "I'll do that."

"No!" she said waspishly, pushing his hands aside. "I want you to go, Wade. I've had enough of our little 'game' this evening!" She stopped trying to fasten the blouse and held the edges clutched tightly in her fingers, lifting resentful, defiant eyes to meet his.

"Yes," he agreed surprisingly, the hand he had been intending to use to help her with the blouse going to her hair and ruffling the now-tousled stuff with a tenderness which astonished Elissa. "I think you have had enough for tonight. It can't be a familiar experience for you to find yourself facing such complications in life. I suppose I should show some understanding, especially since I've won so heavily this evening. I'll go, Elissa, and leave you to retreat temporarily to your tower and consider the situation. But only for a short while. I shall be back tomorrow to shake the bars on your door again."

"What are you talking about?" she grumbled, pleased that he was going to leave without much more fuss but wary of his willingness to do so.

"Tomorrow is Sunday, and I'm going to spend it with you. Just as you suggested when you bargained for time a few minutes ago," he said, acting surprised that she hadn't expected him to be back in the morning.

Elissa's eyes slitted ever so slightly. Well, the game had to commence sometime. It might as well be tomorrow. How long, she wondered, would it take to bring this man to his knees? And what would constitute a proper penance? Not just an apology, not anymore. He'd had his chance to get away with that alone!

"What did you want to do tomorrow?" she asked loftily, trying to appear unconcerned.

He smiled. "I think I'll take you on a picnic."

"A picnic! That's impossible! You can't have a picnic in Seattle in the winter. It will be raining!"

"It won't be raining in my apartment," he tossed back, getting easily, lithely, to his feet.

She frowned, ignoring the hand he had stretched down to help her up beside him. "I'm not going to your apartment."

"Yes, you are," he told her significantly. "You're committed to the game, witch. There's no way out. If you want me to play within your rules for a while, you'll have to obey them yourself. And that means spending time with me. A great deal of time! We're supposed to be getting to know each other, remember?" he finished mockingly.

"I remember!" she flashed, incensed that he would imply she wasn't going to play fair. "What time will you pick me up?" she demanded rashly.

"A little before noon. Good night, Elissa, my sweet witch," he added, his voice darkening several shades as he tipped up her chin and feathered her lips with a kiss of offhand power. "Go off to your solitary bed and dream about the night when you'll have a wolf in your bedroom!"

Before Elissa could come up with a properly crushing retort, Wade was gone, smiling boldly as he strode toward the door and let himself out into the hall.

For a long moment she stood very still amid the aftermath of the party and stared at the door which had been closed so quietly behind her last, marauding guest. What had she let herself in for in her determination to punish Wade?

It was only as she was dumping soiled napkins into the garbage and thinking about the picnic to which she had been forcibly invited that a tiny, worrisome thought made its way to the forefront of Elissa's mind.

When all was said and done, Wade had left with rather more willingness than she would have expected in the situation. He had, after all, not believed her innocent of his accusations. In a sense, for him nothing had changed. Yet he had agreed quickly to her demand for time to get to know each other. Elissa paused in her work, frowning with an unpleasant suspicion.

What if, she asked herself grimly, Wade hadn't really expected her to leap straight into an affair even with the lures he thought he held, such as helping her career? What if his goal tonight had been only to assure a place in her life and make it impossible for her to ignore him as she had been doing for the past month? Had he demanded much, hoping for the compromise she had come up with herself?

Elissa slammed a stack of plates heavily on the counter, wincing as she thought she heard a crack from the one on the bottom. Surely she hadn't been so stupid as to allow herself to be manipulated!

No, she assured herself an instant later. Her own motives were clear. She was going into this strange and reckless game for one reason only: to make Wade eat his words. He would grovel at her feet before she was through with him! He wanted an affair with her, did he? One he controlled? Well, by the time she'd finished with him he would be humbling himself and begging for marriage!

That, she knew with a flash of sheer inspiration, was the proper punishment for Wade Taggert's crime. He would find himself begging to marry the woman he was convinced he could manipulate into an affair.

Begging to marry the woman he thought was so unscrupulous she would sleep with a man in order to
advance herself. How much pride would he have to
swallow before he reached such a stage? Elissa wondered with mounting excitement. A great deal, no
doubt!

And when that lovely moment arrived when Wade
Taggert was pleading for her hand in marriage, she
would coolly, mockingly, hurl his offer back in his
teeth, together with the damn job he thought meant
so much to her. She would crush that rampaging ego
of his if it was the last thing she did!

A little shaken at the unfamiliar intensity of her
emotions, Elissa went to bed.

Sunday dawned, as Elissa had predicted, cold and
wet. But that was only to be expected of Seattle in
the winter, and she went about her normal weekend
routine without giving the matter much thought. It
was difficult, she acknowledged honestly, to think of
anything else except Wade Taggert, anyway.

What would have happened, she asked herself more
than once as she sprawled on the couch with the Sunday paper and a cup of coffee, if she had invited
Wade into her life in the beginning? If she had picked
up one of the more conventional lures he had claimed
he'd tried? Would they still have arrived at this juncture? The question was fairly academic, she decided
wryly, turning to the comics first. Try as she would,
she simply couldn't see herself as ever willingly inviting the man into her circle of friends. He just didn't
fit the way others did. How could a wolf fit comfortably into her life?

Besides, she declared with silent conviction, there

was something distinctly uncomfortable about being
wanted as intently as Wade Taggert seemed to want
her. She had never encountered anyone like him, and
she was glad of that. But she couldn't keep her pulse
running at a normal speed as noon approached.

Once again she was watching a clock and waiting
for Wade, Elissa realized with dark humor as she
checked her casually elegant designer jeans and silky
sapphire-blue shirt in the hall mirror. The jeans fit like
a glove, emphasizing the feminine curve of her hip
and the sweep of her leg. The shirt had a dashing air
in its style which left her throat bare to reveal the tiny
gold chain she wore. The outfit suited her mood, she
decided, a little bold and reckless. For a moment she
envisioned herself on a pirate ship, cutlass in hand, a
scarf rakishly tied around the flame of her hair. Yes,
the clothes suited her mood.

The nervous tension raced into high throttle as the
doorbell sounded a moment later, and Elissa braced
herself mentally and physically as she opened the
door.

Wade stood in the hall as he had done last night
with the same hungry wolf gleam in his eyes. He was
dressed as she was in jeans, but not the designer variety. His were the rugged, faded, lean sort which
would have looked at home on the range and had
plainly seen some action outside the city. There was
a plaid flannel shirt to go with the jeans, and Wade
had a weathered-looking suede jacket with fleece lining slung over his shoulder. He smiled broadly as he
eyed the length of her.

"Is this the latest thing in Red Riding Hood out-
fits?" he drawled, the gleam in his gaze approving.
Elissa could have sworn there was a lightness about

his mood which she hadn't seen before, and she wondered if it was because he thought he held the winning hand.

"I would have thought a professional wolf would keep in touch with the latest fashions for visiting grandmother's house."

"In touch is exactly what I want to be when you're looking that tasty," he drawled outrageously, stepping forward and catching her close with a firm hand planted on the neatly outlined curve of her rear.

"Wade!" she gasped, a bit shocked by his audacity. "Behave yourself!" She frowned at him in ferocious warning which he appeared not to notice. Gingerly she stepped back out of reach.

"We wolves have our own code of behavior," he murmured, watching as she collected a leather jacket from the hall closet.

"A fascinating sociological study, no doubt," she gibed, telling herself there was nothing wrong in going along with his mood. She wanted him off guard, didn't she?

"I'll tell you all about it over lunch," he promised, stepping aside so that she could precede him through the door.

"Shall I take notes on the tablecloth in case there's a quiz later?" she inquired dryly as they waited for the elevator.

"That won't be necessary. I'll be happy to keep going over the fine points with you until you've learned the subject thoroughly."

In the lobby of the apartment building Elissa allowed him to help her on with her jacket, shrugging lightly into it and tying the belt. "Where's your car?" she asked, glancing out into the wet street.

"Over there. Only a short dash!" He chuckled.

"You're illegally parked!" she scolded as he pushed her out the door with an encouraging hand.

"I was counting on your being ready on time," he admitted, turning up the collar of his own jacket as they hurried through the mist. "And the fact that it's Sunday."

"Living dangerously, I see," she remarked, slipping into the passenger side of a sleek silver Jaguar which undoubtedly raised appreciative eyebrows on all those like herself fortunate enough to ride in it.

He slid into the seat beside her, filling the cockpit area with his massive presence, and turned to smile at her before starting the engine.

"You're the dangerous element in my life at the moment, witch. All other risks pale in comparison."

Suspense flashed along her nerves at the intimate, warning timbre of his voice, and it was all Elissa could do to keep her response pert.

"You're not trying to tell me you've reconsidered during the night and decided the whole game is too much for you! If you're so afraid of me we can call a halt right now."

"I'm not about to lose by default," he growled, putting the car in gear. "In fact, I'm not about to lose at all. I merely remarked that there is an element of risk involved."

"But you're convinced you'll get what you want in the end?" she murmured with mocking curiosity, slanting a sideways glance at his rugged profile as he negotiated the city streets.

"I'll have you eating out of the palm of my hand in a week," he returned silkily.

"And if it doesn't quite turn out like that?" she prodded dryly.

"Then I'll have you eating out of my hand in two weeks!" he flung back with a slashing grin.

"The bigger they are..." Elissa began warningly.

"The harder they fall?" he finished helpfully, cocking a heavy brow.

"Precisely. And your ego is definitely of the large-scale variety!"

"Well, I'm getting a good start on my goal today, you have to admit. At least you'll be eating my food in my lair. It's only a short step from there to my palm, I'm sure," he purred teasingly.

"Don't count on it," she advised coolly, convinced that if she had anything to say about the matter he would be the one eating out of *her* hand.

"How can I help but be optimistic? See how far our relationship has come since Friday!"

She groaned almost good-naturedly. "You're impossible. You know that, don't you?" It was going to be a little too easy to get into the spirit of his banter, she thought reluctantly.

"Not impossible, honey, just a bit different from what you're used to dealing with in men. That's my big advantage in this game, you see. I don't mind admitting it."

She shot him a quick, speculative glance. "You call it a game, but you don't really see it that way, do you?" she hazarded with a flash of intuition.

"How do you think I see it?" he asked mildly, slowing for a stoplight and using the small break to trap her glance across the short distance between them.

"More in the nature of open war, I think," she proffered dryly.

"A battle is a battle. Only the stakes involved and the ruthlessness of the day determine whether it slides over the boundary between game and war," he said with sudden soft intensity.

She stared at him in an appalled little silence. "And you're very familiar with war games, aren't you?"

"I've told you, I'm used to fighting for what I want." He shrugged as the light changed and he put the powerful car back in motion with easy expertise.

Elissa swallowed to soothe a dry mouth. She was accustomed to getting what she wanted, too, but not by fighting. Things just happened easily in the normal course of events....

Wade's apartment turned out to be an attractive town house overlooking Lake Washington. Elissa could see the modern West Coast influence in the angled lines of the roof and the wide expanse of glass.

"You were lucky to find this place," she remarked, following him up the path to the front door and glancing back over her shoulder at the vast gray lake.

"I put the whole business in the hands of a real-estate agent. I didn't have any time to scout the market on my own. When the agent suggested this place I took it sight unseen." He pushed open the door, and Elissa stepped into the almost severe interior.

And the first thing which caught her eye was the painting on the far wall. She paused, staring at it in mingled wonder and cold unease. It was a seascape, and in a way it was more alien than the pictures she herself had painted, although the subject was ostensibly a real-world shore-line scene. But it was a seascape of devastating loneliness and power. There was

in the bleak fierceness of it something more dangerous and awesome than any element of fantasy Elissa
had ever inserted into one of her own works. Yet her
first reaction was to cry, of all things! She fought that
back with determination, thrusting her hands into the
pocket of her jacket and stepping closer to the
strangely affecting painting. She was about to say
something purposely noncommittal when she realized
there was another on the wall to her right. A desert
scene this time, but conveying the same raw isolation
and grimness as the first.

Abruptly Elissa realized how Wade had known
she'd done the unearthly scenes hanging in her own
apartment. The part of him which was attracted to
these forbidding paintings was able to recognize the
part of her she put into her paintings. Wade might not
be an artist himself, but she knew at once he had an
artist's intuition.

"Unusual," she stated flatly. "They look as if they
were painted for you alone." She didn't look at him,
concentrating on the seascape. She could feel him
standing very still behind her and wondered what he
was expecting.

"They were," he agreed neutrally.

"They're good," she said simply, honestly. "Much
better than my own work." It was the truth. She knew
her own work wouldn't have this impact on a casual
observer.

"But you don't like them?" he prompted. His tone
remained curiously neutral and he still didn't move.

"Liking doesn't come into it," she said before
stopping to think. She bit her lip, hoping he wouldn't
pick up on the hasty phrase. But of course that was
a futile wish.

"I couldn't agree more," he commented wryly. "Just as liking doesn't come into our own relationship. What do you think of the paintings, Elissa?"

"I find them…" She hesitated. "Disturbing."

"Not charming?" There was a hint of humor back in his voice, and she turned to look at him.

"No, not charming." She half smiled, untying her jacket belt.

"Good," he rasped gently, coming forward to take the garment from her hand. "My friend who did them would have been thoroughly insulted if you had reacted to them too comfortably. You knew at once they had been done for me, didn't you?" he went on with a perceptive glance.

"Oh, yes. I knew at once. Did you have them commissioned, Wade?" she asked, looking for a way to steer the conversation aside from the path in which he was trying to take it. When he had removed the jacket from her shoulders she wandered deliberately across the room, noting the masculine restraint in the furnishings of leather and wood.

"Yes," he told her, his eyes following her meandering progress around the living room. "I asked Hal to do the first one on a whim. I'd seen his work from time to time in local galleries and gotten to know him. He told me he'd paint a picture for me but that I might not like it."

"Do you?" Elissa queried.

"The first one suited me." He shrugged. "A few months ago I commissioned him to do another one, the desert scene."

"Which suits you just as well?"

"I think so," he said with a slow, quirking smile. "For some reason, something in me identifies with what's in those paintings. They…'' He hesitated, looking for the right word. "They satisfy me," he concluded.

Elissa nodded, understanding the statement if not her own reaction to it. She was wondering a little desperately how to get the subject off the lonely, desolate, stark canvases when Wade went on lightly.

"Are you hungry?" he asked, shaking off the mood and heading toward the kitchen with an unspoken invitation to follow.

"Don't worry, I'll do justice to your food. Nothing like a picnic to bring out one's best appetite. Can I help?" she offered politely, watching with a degree of curiosity which surprised her as he began hauling various items out of the refrigerator. It took Elissa a moment or two to realize she was genuinely looking forward to the small adventure. Telling herself it was only the prospect of ultimate revenge which was attracting her, she moved toward the counter to examine the food being stacked there.

"You can spread the blanket out in front of the hearth," Wade instructed, closing the refrigerator door and reaching for a bottle of wine standing nearby.

"A blanket! On top of the carpet?" Elissa asked in amused surprise.

"What's a picnic without a blanket to eat it on?" He grinned engagingly. "Go ahead, I've got one waiting on the back of that leather recliner. I'll take care of this end of things."

"Are you going to supply ants, too?" Elissa demanded as she obediently headed toward the living room to find the blanket.

"No," he retorted very smoothly, very intently.

"My affair with you is a personal and private matter. No one else allowed, not even ants!"

Elissa was glad she was out of sight at that particular moment. Not for anything in the world would she have wanted him to see the red color which she knew was rushing full tilt into her cheeks. To hear him blatantly talk of an affair still bothered her. She was going to have to strive harder to retain a cool composure in this dangerous game.

"But, then," she managed distinctly, although it took considerable effort to achieve the cold warning in her voice, "we don't really have an affair going between us, do we? Only a small case of blackmail!"

She sensed his presence behind her as she studiously bent to spread the colorfully striped Hudson's Bay Company wool blanket in front of the hearth. For the life of her, Elissa couldn't bring herself to turn and face him.

"The blackmail," he drawled very silkily, stalking forward to stand immediately behind her as she slowly, reluctantly, straightened from the small task he had assigned, "is the initial hook I'm using to snag you, little witch."

Elissa stood perfectly still, unable to move as she felt his arms circle around her. She realized he was holding a bottle of wine in one hand and a stemmed glass in the other. The glass was pushed into the fingers of her right hand and, his lips hovering in the vicinity of her ear, he calmly poured the wine.

It was a very neat trap, Elissa thought on a tiny wave of panic. She couldn't move away from the cage of his arms at first because of the sheer tension of the moment. Now she couldn't move or the red wine would be splashed across the chocolate-brown carpet.

She stood watching in a kind of blank astonishment as the liquid slowly, inevitably, flowed into the glass.

"But once snagged on the hook, I will immediately begin steps to transfer you to the net. A clever little fish can wriggle off a hook, but a net is a much different proposition, isn't it? A net is impossible to fight. It encloses and binds and traps and allows no freedom at all."

Elissa trembled as he ceased pouring the wine and, with a subtle pressure on her shoulder that she didn't dare resist for fear of sloshing the liquid out of the glass, turned her around to face him.

She met the glinting, purposeful silver in his eyes and forced herself to counter it with deliberate, taunting arrogance, a most unusual attitude for her.

"What will this net of yours be made of," she whispered haughtily, "that I will find it so irresistible?"

"Tempting things, dangerous things. Toys for a witch who is more accustomed to orchestrating games than she is to being a participant. I may have to catch you with blackmail, Elissa, but I'll hold you with other kinds of bonds," he promised in a voice of velvet-covered steel.

Chapter 5

A hundred times during the course of the afternoon Elissa told herself she should walk away from the decidedly unreal situation in which she had found herself. But each time some undeniably intrigued and dangerously curious portion of her pushed the common sense aside, assuring her that she could handle the man and the net he was weaving. And always she reminded herself that walking away at this stage would ruin any chance she had for revenge. And besides, she decided with an inner flash of humor, his food was very good.

"I think," she announced languidly at one point, watching the soaring flames of the fire Wade had built, "that this will definitely rank as one of the more exotic picnics in my life." She absently swirled wine in her glass and reached for another cracker spread with paté. Her feet were tucked neatly under her as she sat curled on the blanket, and she felt an almost sensual pleasure in the way the fire drove away the gray gloom of a rainy Sunday afternoon.

"Even though I didn't provide any ants?" Wade quipped, watching with satisfaction as she consumed his food with delicate greed. He was stretched out on his side, propped on his elbow, and he put Elissa very much in mind of a relaxing panther. No, wolf, she told herself, munching the elegant paté. Wade was definitely a wolf.

"I wouldn't want to share these goodies with anyone or anything," she murmured luxuriously. "You keep a much more interesting pantry than I do."

"That's because you do your own cooking." He chuckled, helping himself to the last of the small mound of dark caviar. "Me, I've got to rely on imported tins of fancy stuff to impress my guests."

"Do a lot of this sort of entertaining, do you?" she noted with a mocking, slanting glance.

"Not a very subtly loaded question," he accused easily. "You might as well come straight out and ask about the women in my life as make a comment that pointed."

"I wouldn't think of prying into your personal life," she informed him aloofly, wishing it were the truth. She found herself very badly wanting to know about the other women in his world. The knowledge of her own inquisitiveness was thoroughly annoying and she would not give in to the temptation to press him on the issue.

"I don't see why not," he observed carelessly, although she could hear the laughter in him. "I certainly have no compunction about prying into your privacy."

"Don't tell me you're one of those men who want a detailed description of a woman's past romances!" she tossed back disparagingly.

"No," he assured her, sounding completely honest. "I care nothing about the past. I know you're not carrying the torch for anyone, and that's the only important thing. But I do intend to concern myself very deeply with your present."

"Are you attempting to give me a word of caution?" she teased with a cool little smile. She felt the sudden urge of inner defiance and was bemused by its intensity.

"That's a nice, polite way of saying it, I suppose. A word of caution." He repeated the phrase as if mulling it over for appropriateness. "But I think that comes off as too weak. A clear warning would be a better approximation of what I'm getting at."

"You expect me to steer clear of other men while you're interested in me?" she clarified with great civility even as her blood pounded in response to the challenge. She watched him through her lashes as he examined her in return. There was a tightening of the electrical charge between them.

"Most definitely," he confirmed, taking a thoughtful sip of his wine, his eyes never leaving hers. "I told you on Friday that while I'm circling in your orbit I will be the only one in your inner circle." His mouth twitched, as if a sudden thought had just struck him. "This is probably a new experience for you, isn't it? Having a man tell you that you're no longer free to exercise your spells on other males?"

"I thought you weren't interested in my previous relationships," she countered.

"I'm not, but it might have made things easier for

me if you'd learned a healthy respect for the male of
the species at some point in your life. Still, if some
man had succeeded in teaching the lesson you probably wouldn't be available now for me to instruct. He
would have caught you in his own net and I would
never have encountered you myself.'' He smiled, appearing enormously pleased with the workings of fate.

"Perhaps," Elissa suggested with cool daring, "the
reason no man has attempted to lay down the law to
me before is that he knew he couldn't enforce it."

"Are you now trying to warn me?" he asked
gently.

"I would hate to see that lovely ego of yours become unduly bruised," she said just as gently.

"You've already bruised it, honey," he allowed
wryly. "Each time during the past month when you
ducked out of sight to avoid meeting me or refused
one of my carefully held out lures, you inflicted un-
told damage on it. Damages for which I mean to collect, by the way!"

Elissa said nothing, merely smiling her taunting response. He reached out and removed the glass from
her hand, and then, maintaining a grasp on her wrist,
he pulled her toward him with just enough unexpected
force that she tumbled against his chest, her fingers
splaying out to brace her fall.

Before she could do more than summon a frown,
he had wrapped his hands in the pelt of her hair and
pulled her mouth down to his.

"Umm, you taste good," he growled, his lips moving warmly, tantalizingly, on hers.

"I should," she breathed between his sampling, devouring kisses. "You buy only the best wine."

"One doesn't set about seducing a witch with inferior weapons," he explained, nibbling his way to a point just behind her ear and back to the corner of her mouth. Tiny shocks followed in the wake of the questing kisses.

Elissa felt the tremor which rippled through her body and wasn't certain if it emanated from him or from her own roughened, heightened senses. She told herself first that she ought to put a stop to the slow, compelling embrace, and then came the consoling, rationalizing thought that the lovemaking was an important part of her plan. How could she hope to charm Wade into asking for marriage if she didn't give him the satisfaction of responding to his kisses?

"Aren't you afraid," she demanded a little breathlessly, "of being caught in your own net?"

His hands tightened, and she felt the smooth, coordinated muscles of his body tense as he moved, pinning her carefully on her back and rolling over so that his chest covered hers.

"Afraid of it!" he mocked, his gray eyes leaping alive with a lambent fire. "I'm looking forward to it with the greatest of pleasure!"

The tasting exploration of her lips made way for a more demanding hunger which seemed to grow eagerly in him. His kisses ravaged the inside of her mouth, his tongue dueling for excruciating moments with hers, forcing a response her body did not seem loath to give.

As the sensuous intensity of the assault continued Elissa felt herself give ground before it. The man was as overwhelming in his lovemaking as he was in his choice of paintings. In both he expressed himself with bold, masculine power. The impact of her senses was impossible to ignore, and somehow it grew difficult to distinguish between the two vastly different forms of attack.

In the paintings which had been done for him she had been exposed to the bleak isolation of a man who has always fought the world on his own terms. The artist had caught that quality with indisputable sureness. In Wade's arms she experienced the relentless demand for her to meet him on the shores of the wild sea or in the middle of that searing dessert and temper the isolation for a time.

And by answering his fierce demands could she succeed in charming him? In weaving the spells he accused her of being able to cast could she exert some measure of power? The heady thought somehow mingled with the exciting sensation of his hands on her body as Wade began searching out the warmth of her skin.

"No," she whispered achingly as he made short, efficient work of the buttons on her sapphire-blue shirt.

"Yes," he muttered huskily, his mouth on the pulse in her throat. And Elissa knew she didn't have the will yet to stop him. Soon…soon…

Fumblingly she tried to catch his hand and push it gently back from its goal, but he trapped her restless fingers in his and transferred them to the buttons of his own flannel shirt.

"Touch me, little witch," he grated as he left her fingers clinging precariously to the edge of his shirt. "Let me feel your hands on me. Pet your wolf and see what happens!"

The demand was irresistible. Even as she felt her breast swell beneath his cold caress she was obeying his orders and undoing the fastenings on the plaid flannel. She heard her own breath catch in her throat as her shaking fingers found the crisp, curling hairs of his chest and began to thrust through them.

His groan of response was utterly entrancing, Elissa discovered. It made a woman yearn to elicit more evidence of his rising passion. It made her feel reckless and daring. She traced soft circles around the male nipples and sensed his spine arch rigidly in reaction.

"Ah, my sweet Elissa," he breathed as he finished his work on her shirt and eagerly pushed back the material. She closed her eyes as she felt him drinking in the sight of her soft curves. She felt first his hands and then his lips on the hardening tips of her breasts as he disposed impatiently of her lacy bra.

"One way or another I'm going to join you in your fortress, even if I have to make the foundations shake! And you'll welcome me when the time comes, I swear it!"

Elissa was aware of him sliding lower, his hands shaping the curve of her hip as he sowed strings of kisses down to her navel. The almost unbearable excitement arced through her limbs and one knee lifted in reaction.

At once Wade's hand moved to the jean-covered inner part of her thigh, stroking her through the material until both of her legs shifted languidly. He leaned farther over and dropped a heated kiss on the contoured line of her waist precisely where it disappeared into the protection of the denim.

Elissa's fingers groped blindly across the strong expanse of his chest, probing at the lean, tight skin along his rib cage and seeking the flat stomach beyond.

When he began working his way caressingly back

up to her mouth she involuntarily clung more closely, her body demanding more of his warmth and fire. The level of passion was new to her, and the temptation to reach out and leave her mark on his splendid isolation was enthralling in itself.

A self-sufficient male was probably a challenge for any woman, but one who taunted you with that challenge, invited you to change him, was like a drug in one's bloodstream, Elissa decided. And the fact that he was so intent on raiding her own cool, remote tower made her long to try her power on him in a way she had never been tempted to do with other men.

"Tell me," she whispered in a throaty, husky voice as she placed a soft palm on either side of his face and raised his head to look at him, "is it ever lonely being a wolf?"

"Is it ever lonely being a witch?" he returned, not answering her question.

"It hasn't been," she said honestly, watching his flickering eyes for some sign. She wasn't altogether certain what sort of sign she expected to find.

"Perhaps you just haven't been aware of it," he suggested deeply, holding himself very still above her.

"And you?"

"Perhaps I haven't been aware of it, either."

"It's there in those paintings, I think," she told him and saw the passion in the gray gaze thicken.

"Is it?"

"I think so. It's difficult to be sure, because so much else is there, too," she breathed gently.

"What else?" he invited.

"Remoteness, isolation, aloofness. All those things

certainly," she began honestly, working through the puzzle of him in her own mind as she spoke.

"Do you want to find loneliness in me, little witch?" he smiled.

"It might give me some sort of power over you," she admitted, searching his face.

"You already have that," he mocked feelingly. "I would never have set out to force my way into your life if you didn't."

"But it's no good as long as you can see it and control it," she protested wistfully.

"I won't let you use your power to play with me," he agreed steadily. "But that doesn't mean I'm not under its influence."

Elissa smiled with charming menace. "And I'm not willing to risk myself completely in a relationship I'm not sure I can control, so we are left at an impasse, aren't we?" She waited, sea eyes full of the baiting, goading, daring feelings filling her body.

"I wouldn't say that," he murmured with unruffled assurance, eyes gleaming. "We've already made great strides. Yesterday you wouldn't even admit you wanted to control the men in your life. Here you are today, lying in my arms and telling me you're afraid to risk losing that control."

Elissa took a savage grip on her emotions, which seemed to be in chaos, and smiled brilliantly up at him. She would not let her ultimate goal of revenge slip out of sight, not when he held her like this and told her he could dominate her.

"Thank you," she told him with utmost demureness, her auburn lashes concealing the mix of emotions in her eyes, "for a wonderful picnic. It's time you took me home now."

She felt him stiffen and knew he had counted on much more than a few kisses and tantalizing caresses in front of the fire. The knowledge that she had managed to surprise him with her cool ending to the day gave her added strength.

"The meal is over," he conceded, his words laced with soft resolution, "but the evening hasn't even begun. Stay with me tonight, Elissa, and together we'll find out whose power is the stronger."

"I'm not ready for a contest of that magnitude," she hedged gracefully. "I need the time we agreed to last night. The time to get to know each other. Surely you didn't expect to win this war so easily?"

"A man can hope." He sighed, reading her firm intention in her eyes and giving way to it.

"Come, now," she charged on a thread of soft laughter. "What wolf wants an easy victory?" The knowledge that she would be the one controlling the ending to the intimate picnic filled Elissa with a sense of power that made her almost lightheaded.

"You don't have an understanding of the species," he retorted, his fingertips playing with the vulnerable line of her throat. "A wolf is interested only in the spoils of victory, not in how the game is played."

Elissa heard and decided to disregard the clear warning. She could handle this man. All she had to do was keep her wits about her. "You must think my job means a great deal to me."

The look of surprise which appeared in his eyes at the mention of what he had called his hook came and went in an instant. It was almost, Elissa thought wonderingly, as if he had temporarily forgotten how she had come to be here in his home, caged in his arms. Had he fooled himself into thinking the afternoon's interlude had removed the memory of the blackmail from her mind? What arrogance!

"Your job," he promised on a determined threat, "isn't going to be the main factor in this skirmish. The challenge between us goes far beyond that level. It was only a useful tool."

"Would you have thought so lightly of it if I were the one threatening your job?"

The gray eyes narrowed. "You wouldn't have done it. Those aren't your kind of tactics. Stick to the weapons you know best, honey. Your witchcraft will be sufficient for your purposes."

"I'm ready to go home," she murmured imperiously. Damn the man for being so sure of himself! There would come a day...

"And if I'm not ready to let you?" One near-black brow arched quizzically.

"Then I'll know your word is completely unreliable, won't I?" she tossed back with forced lightness. "You did promise me time...."

"I never said exactly how much time." There was wary hunger in his eyes, as if he were calculating how far he could push his prey this day.

"Certainly long enough for me to forget the real reason I've even agreed to see you, surely?" Elissa made no effort to keep the taunt out of her cool tone. "Long enough for me to forget a matter of blackmail!"

"You'll forget it by morning if you stay with me tonight," he insisted, the roughly cut lines of his face hardening with conviction.

"I'm not yet ready to take that chance. This is, after all, our first date," she flung back quickly, not caring for the way his hands had tightened on her throat. She mustn't lose her nerve at this point. Feminine instincts and her inborn ability to sense another's needs were functioning well at the moment, and they assured her she was on the right track. If she wanted a proposal of marriage from him, she must play her cards very carefully.

There was a suspenseful hesitation in him, and then Elissa saw the lines at the corners of his hard mouth relax slightly and knew she had won. He was not going to push too hard. Not yet.

Slowly he sat up beside her, the gray eyes never leaving her face as she took advantage of the opportunity to do the same. When she broke the nonverbal contact and lowered her eyes to struggle with the sapphire shirt, he reached over and stilled her hands.

"This time I'll do it."

Patiently, with great precision, he redid the buttons and ran his fingers through her hair, bringing back a semblance of order. Elissa sat unmoving through the small attentions, not understanding the almost erotic pleasure she was deriving from them.

Wade stood at her door half an hour later and waited as she turned around to say goodbye. The drive from his town house had been made largely in silence.

"Thank you for a most interesting picnic, Wade." Her voice prim and her manner too reserved, Elissa faced him from the safety of her own apartment.

He ignored her politeness. "Elissa, I have business at the home office in San Jose at the end of the week. I want you to come down to California with me."

Startled first at the suggestion and then at the ragged note hidden behind the steel in his tone, she stared at him, her astonishment clear.

"That's impossible, Wade! You must know that!"

"Why?" He stood, feet braced a little apart, the suede jacket slung over his shoulder, and defied her to come up with a reasonable excuse. The silvery-gray eyes were fixed on her face with unrelenting demand.

"I should think that's obvious," Elissa snapped, growing rapidly annoyed with his merciless approach. He had promised her time, damn it! Time she meant to use for her own purposes! "For one thing, everyone at work would be bound to find out about it and talk. For another, I'm not about to travel anywhere with you. You'd be certain to construe the action as an invitation. As a sign you'd won!"

"Is that how I'll know, Elissa?" Wade watched her, his gaze softening ever so slightly, as if the thought appealed to him. "Will I know for sure you've surrendered on the day you agree to go away with me?"

"Stop putting words in my mouth!" she grumbled furiously.

"Yes," he agreed with a bleak smile. "I'd rather fill your mouth with kisses, anyway!"

Before she could step back out of the way, he had curled a hand around her neck and pulled her face close for his short, hard kiss.

"Goodbye, Elissa," he told her tersely, surveying her wide-eyed, irate expression. "I'll pick you up for dinner tomorrow night about seven. We can talk about the California trip then."

"What makes you think I'll be meekly waiting for

you here tomorrow evening?'' she blazed, incensed at his easy assumption.

"Just a hunch.'' The slow, mocking grin spread across his grim face. "And the promise that if you aren't, I'll make life very miserable for you at work on Tuesday morning.''

"You wouldn't dare!''

"Wouldn't I? The only reason I'm going to make an effort to keep our affair a secret for a while is that I thought you'd appreciate the privacy. Personally, I don't care if the whole world knows!''

"You'd embarrass me like that at work?'' Elissa choked, knowing that if their private quarrel spilled out into the open she would have no choice but to quit and surrender her hope of revenge. She couldn't bear to have the entire staff thinking the worst of her.

He must have seen the incipient panic in her eyes and guessed that he was pushing too hard, because all at once Wade's voice softened.

"There's no need for me to threaten, is there, Elissa? You'll be here Monday evening, waiting for me. After all, I'm not suggesting anything more than another date, am I? A chance for you to get to know me better?''

Elissa slanted a suspicious glance at him, a small frown creasing her brow. "You won't push too hard about the California trip?''

He lifted one shoulder negligently, eyes lighting with amusement. "Surely it's a man's privilege to try and convince a woman to come away with him. I keep telling you I'm no different from other men, honey.''

"Don't take that coaxing, wheedling tone with me,'' she ordered briskly. "And if you think I'm going to spend tomorrow night listening to you threaten me about what you'll do if I don't go to California with you, you've got another think coming!''

"I swear I won't threaten," he soothed, stroking her cheekbone with the slightly rough edge of his finger. Sensitive fingers, she thought inconsequentially, even if they did seem hard and strong. "I promise to limit my discussion of the subject to rational appeals and the usual male pleading.''

"All of which will get you nowhere," she promised with fine hauteur.

"Perhaps. We'll find out tomorrow night, won't we?''

Not waiting for her response, Wade reached for the doorknob and pulled it shut behind him, leaving Elissa to gape angrily at the closed door. For a moment she simply stood there, trying to assimilate the events of the day into some meaningful pattern. A pattern in which she could see whether she was winning or losing.

But it wasn't that simple, she realized, turning away and trailing through the living room, an intense, thoughtful expression on her intelligent features. Try as she might, it was impossible to tell who had won the first skirmish that afternoon. Had she made any progress, or had everything gone in Wade's favor?

Shaking her head fretfully, Elissa came to a halt in front of the crammed bookcase in her bedroom, her eyes automatically searching for the new fantasy novel she had bought during the week, the novel she had originally intended to spend the day reading.

She needed it now, more than ever, she told herself, plucking the exotically illustrated paperback from the stack. Her eyes canned the cover painting, which depicted another artist's concept of an alien world, and then she kicked off her shoes and settled herself in the middle of the bed with a grateful sigh.

What she needed now was to lose herself in a tale of real magic and sorcery, she realized. For her that reality had always been found between the covers of a book, or else it had flowed from her paintbrush. She was thoroughly at home with the business of retreating into a world of imagination.

But she had never had to retreat from the real world because it bordered on the dangerous, she thought, opening the book to the first chapter. The real world had never been anything other than completely comfortable and totally manageable. It was in such fantasy tales as the one in her hands that her mind found the adventure and magic it craved.

But even as her eyes absorbed the first sentence, Elissa recognized that something was different this time. The book promised to be a good one, full of excitement and the wizardry of a far-off world. So why wasn't she plunging into it with her usual enthusiasm?

Deliberately she forced herself to finish the first page, and then, with a groan of self-disgust, she let the cover close.

Morosely she stared down at the colorful scene of a warrior mounted on a creature that was half dragon, half horse. In the background an evil-eyed sorcerer lifted his hands, frozen by the artist in the act of casting a spell. A good book. She knew it was going to be a good book. And it had started off well, lots of excitement right there on the first page. And she had meant to read it today, anyway.

Damn that man! With a muttered oath, Elissa grimaced down into the unresponsive face of the hero on the book's cover. She knew why she couldn't throw herself into this book tonight. She might as well acknowledge the reason and be done with it.

It was simple enough. The book offered her nothing more exciting than her own real-life adventure. For the first time since she could remember, Elissa had found an adventure that tugged at her emotions and excited her mind as thoroughly as any novel of the far future or the mythical past. Whatever Wade Taggert had intended to achieve today, he had certainly spun his web skillfully.

Elissa lifted her eyes to stare blankly at the painting across the room, her fingernail tapping gently on the slick cover of the paperback book. But instead of her own fantastical work, she saw again the stark isolation in the paintings Wade had commissioned from his friend. A friend who had seen the truth in his patron.

But that isolation was there because Wade wanted it, she told herself forcefully. She had no business feeling a tug of sympathy for a man who certainly wouldn't welcome it. He was a wolf, and wolves were, by nature, lonely creatures. How could creatures who viewed the rest of the world as a battleground ever develop close, meaningful relationships? Wade wanted a woman, and he had singled her out as the chosen victim. He would try to take what he wanted. It was his nature.

And if he could achieve his goal by seduction, that's the weapon he would use, Elissa realized. If he thought threats were the means to his end, he would try them. And if he thought he could use his self-imposed isolation and loneliness to appeal to her gentler nature, he wouldn't hesitate to do so.

She would be a fool to soften toward Wade Taggert in any way. She must remember she was only seeing him so that she could pursue her own goal, that of revenge.

"You think it's going to be easy, don't you, wolf?" Elissa whispered through gritted teeth. "You think you can just make up your mind to have me and that's all there is to it! But I'm on to you. I know what you are. You're a predator, and predators deserve no sympathy whatsoever. And they don't deserve the least amount of kindness!"

No, she was involved in this adventure strictly for her own reasons, not because she was actually attracted to Wade Taggert. such a thing couldn't possibly be! It would be impossible to love a man...

Elissa's thought broke off in sheer panic. Love! Where in the universe had that idea originated? Of course she wasn't in any danger of falling in love with a wolf! Her imagination really was running away with her tonight!

Grimly she forced herself to reopen the fantasy novel in her lap. She had always been able to control the real world, and Wade Taggert's advent into her life could be controlled as well. It was only in tales like the one in her hands that life genuinely became an adventure.

Chapter 6

"Wise girl" was Wade's dry observation when Elissa opened her door to him Monday evening.

"I assume that remark is in reference to the fact that I decided to go out with you tonight," she muttered coolly. "Let me tell you, Wade, such comments are not calculated to put me in the best of moods for an evening. But you must know that already. Are you deliberately trying to antagonize me?"

"If you must know," he told her, detaching himself from the doorframe and sauntering into her living room, "I half expected you to stand me up tonight." He tossed her a casual, satisfied smile that said volumes.

"That would have been a pity when you took so much effort to dress for the occasion." She raked his expensive charcoal-gray suit and the white shirt with its subtly woven pattern, her eyes derisive. He did look good tonight. Polished, sophisticated, and sure of himself. You almost had to look twice to see the wolf under the surface. But it was there, hidden behind the fine leather shoes and the silk tie. And the wolf in him had fully expected her to be ready and waiting tonight.

"No more effort than you so obviously took," he murmured appreciatively, returning her perusing glance with interest. "You look very lovely, little witch. Turquoise is a perfect color for you."

"Would you like a drink?" Elissa could think of nothing else to say as she endured his open regard. His eyes traveled with possessive approval over the unusual blue, long-sleeved sheath, lingering on the silver at her neck and wrists.

"Have I moved into the ranks of the privileged?" he inquired as she turned her back on him and disappeared into the kitchen.

"What privileged?"

"The men whose drinks you remember."

"Whiskey isn't hard to remember," she tossed back, reaching for the bottle in the cupboard.

"It may be a little thing," he pointed out industriously as she reappeared holding a glass of amber liquid, "but I like to think it's a sign of progress." He took the drink from her hand, glancing at the glass of sherry she was holding for herself.

"If I were you, I wouldn't put too much stock in the fact that I remembered your drink." Elissa smiled with an air of cool mockery, choosing to ignore the sudden pounding in her veins as the gray eyes met hers.

"You mean because such little courtesies come second-naturedly to you? That may be true for your associations with most people, but not with me. I think you remembered my favorite drink because you thought about me last night and today. To us!'' he added, clinking his glass lightly against hers and taking a good-sized swallow.

She ignored the toast, frowning slightly. ''What makes you think I'd spend so much valuable time thinking about you?'' She took a sip of her sherry, striving for a mocking attitude.

''Because I spent the same amount of valuable time thinking of you.'' He grinned unabashedly. ''It wasn't easy, you know, concentrating on my meeting with a new client while wondering if you were going to make me chase you all over town this evening.''

So that's why she hadn't seen him at work during the day, Elissa thought. He had been tied up with a new client. She had been lucky. Although Wade had virtually promised not to reveal their relationship at work, she was dreading that first time when she had to react naturally to his presence in front of co-workers. Of course, when had she ever reacted naturally to him?

''Chase me all over town!'' Elissa scoffed. ''Is that what you would have done?''

''Most assuredly. And the longer I was forced to chase, the more upset I would have been. Which is why I congratulated you on being wise enough to be ready this evening.'' The look in his eyes was pure satisfied hunter.

''It doesn't bother you that I'm going out with you under duress?''

He looked surprised. ''Should it?''

''Some men might be a little bothered by the fact

that they had to ensure a date with threats," she growled.

"Some men," he repeated, nodding his dark head thoughtfully. "But not me."

"You don't care how you achieve your goals as long as you get what you want, is that it?" Elissa demanded, setting down her glass of sherry and walking over to the closet for her coat.

She heard him start to say something and then change his mind.

"I really didn't intend to spend the evening bickering with you," he offered ingratiatingly, finishing his whiskey and crossing the room to help her on with the belted white coat.

She flicked a startled glance up at his intent face. "Then we'd better find another topic of conversation, hadn't we?" she managed flippantly.

"How about California?" he asked, sliding his large hands under the wide collar of her coat and holding her still for his brief, hard kiss.

"Another bad choice, I'm afraid," Elissa muttered, acutely aware of the feeling of having just been branded by his lips. She ducked her head and pulled free of his hands. "Where are we going tonight?"

"The Space Needle," he replied readily enough, making no attempt to force the discussion of California on her. He took her arm and opened the door. "Any objections?"

She raised an eyebrow. "Would it matter if I did object?"

"Oh, yes," he assured her deeply. "It would matter. But I don't expect you to do so."

"Why not?" she asked, intrigued in spite of herself.

"It's your kind of building. A revolving restaurant perched on top of the more than five-hundred-foot spire. It looks like something off the cover of one of your fantasy novels." He chuckled as they made their way toward the elevators.

Elissa grimaced, acknowledging the appropriateness of his choice. It occurred to her that, while she had eaten at the Needle on occasion, no one had ever taken her there specifically because it was her kind of building.

City lights gleamed wetly in the Seattle night as Wade drove through the downtown district, underneath the monorail which carried visitors back and forth to Seattle Center, and finally parked near the Needle. They walked through the grounds of the center en route to the glass elevator which would take them over five hundred feet into the air to the restaurant. Wade glanced around with interest, and Elissa smiled.

"The grounds are all left over from the World's Fair held here in the early sixties," she explained. "Seattle has turned the whole thing into a very useful city park and recreation area. There's a science center and rides for the kids and restaurants. Something special going on almost every weekend."

"What else can you do with leftovers from a World's Fair?" he joked as they joined the crowd getting into the elevator.

Elissa was about to respond when, in the crush of nicely dressed people, she found herself pushed inevitably closer to Wade. Without a word he put out his arm, pulling her against his side with a casual possession. There wasn't much she could say or do in the tightly pressed crowd, and Elissa realized Wade was as fully aware of that as she was.

"Don't worry, honey," he murmured directly into her ear. "I won't let you get trampled."

"I wasn't aware I was in danger," she retorted tersely.

"Um, but you are. A great deal of danger," he countered in a low, seductive tone that brought the red into her cheeks. "But I'll take care of you, never fear."

"I'll bet!"

"I've told you before you're going to have to come to me on faith, little witch," he reminded her.

Before Elissa could think of a suitable rejoinder, the elevator doors slid open, spilling the crowd into the elegant lobby of the restaurant. Wade took over with easy assurance, and without any delay they were guided to a window booth.

"For a stranger in town, you did all right in securing the best view in Seattle," Elissa had to say as she slipped happily into her seat and instantly turned to study the spectacular revolving scene of the city below.

"The maître d' is a businessman, like maître d's everywhere," he noted laconically, his gray eyes on Elissa's profile as she stared, fascinated, at the view.

"Meaning you tipped him well?" She smiled, glancing around and colliding with his gaze across the candlelit table. It was a small, intimate shock.

"Meaning we came to an amicable arrangement."

"I tried tipping a maître d' once," Elissa confided, her eyes full of laughter at the memory.

"And?" Wade prompted expectantly.

"And he gave me the seat I wanted and then

handed me back the money. It was very embarrassing!''

"The poor man probably took one look into those sea-colored eyes of yours and knew he was dealing with a witch. You charmed him into giving you back the tip, didn't you?'' Wade chuckled knowingly.

"I most certainly did not! I was trying to practice the proper way of taking a gentleman out to dinner, and having my tip thrust back at me ruined everything,'' she snapped indignantly, remembering the incident with chagrin.

"Taking a gentleman out to dinner?'' he echoed, sounding surprised. "Trying to put the 'new equality' into practice?''

"What's the matter? Don't you approve?'' she taunted, pleased at the faintly disgusted expression on his rugged face.

"No!'' he stated unequivocally.

"Good!'' she said with relish, thinking his words confirmed his basic hunting instinct. A wolf wouldn't like his victim even nominally in charge of the evening, and paying the bill went a long way toward giving one the upper hand. "Just for that, I hope that someday you get a woman boss!''

He gave a crack of laughter—a rich, deep sound that turned an amused head or two at a nearby table. The gray eyes flared more brilliantly than ever. "I've got news for you. I've had one! It was several years ago, and it worked out fine.'' He looked mildly proud of himself. "And not the reason you're thinking, either,'' he added smugly when she eyed him skeptically. "I didn't seduce her.''

"I wasn't inferring that.''

"Yes, you were, and it's totally untrue. We got

along fine because she was competent. In the business world that's all I demand of anyone, male or female.''

"You're forgetting something," Elissa purred gently. "You also demand that they live up to certain moral standards. I was quite competent."

For the first time since she had known him, Wade looked momentarily uncomfortable, but he recovered immediately. "I do demand a bit more of someone when he or she is being considered for promotion," he clarified smoothly.

"I see," Elissa said stiffly and turned her attention back to the jeweled night outside the window. "Fantastic view, isn't it?" she went on with determined chattiness. "From this perspective you can really see how much Seattle loves the water. The stuff is everywhere! That dark blob over there is Lake Union, and then there's Puget Sound and Elliott Bay and Lake Washington…"

"San Francisco has a lovely bay," Wade interposed coolly. "Come down to California with me and we'll spend the weekend there."

Elissa met the waiting gleam in the gray eyes and smiled sweetly. "Not a chance. And you're going to ruin this evening if you continue to bring up the subject."

"It's an important one to me," he protested, contriving to look hurt.

"I'm sure you'll have plenty of company when you get to California. Lots and lots of old friends to look up," she told him nastily.

"I thought you decided I was a *lone* wolf."

"Not that *lone!*"

Somewhat to her surprise, Wade allowed Elissa to get away with the light banter, not pushing the California trip again during dinner. They dined leisurely and elegantly, with good wine, good food, and Elissa had to admit, good conversation. It was, she reflected at one point, a new experience to be so personally involved in a conversation. Her normal role, the one she chose deliberately, was that of listener or confidante. She couldn't remember ever having had a man ask so many personal questions of her before in her life. The only explanation was that she wasn't really guiding the conversation as she normally did. This one just seemed to flow. She glanced apprehensively at the low level of the wine bottle and wondered if that was a factor.

"When did you start reading those fantasy novels of yours?" Wade demanded as he refilled her glass.

"I don't remember," Elissa replied honestly. "Somewhere in grade school I got involved in science fiction, and when fantasy became such a big part of it I guess I naturally gravitated in that direction."

"Naturally," he mocked gently. "It suits you."

Elissa cocked her head speculatively. "What suits you, Wade?"

"You," he answered unhesitatingly. He smiled his wolf's smile.

"I mean," she retorted firmly, "what sort of hobbies suit you?"

"I don't have any except you."

"I find that hard to believe."

He shrugged uncaringly. "It's the truth. The rest of my life is filled with work."

Elissa frowned. "Work? That's the most important thing in your life?"

"It has been until recently."

"Well, to each his own, I suppose," she remarked

slowly, wondering how he classified the women in his life but not quite daring to ask. Perhaps, like herself, they constituted temporary hobbies. She thought again of the paintings in his home and realized that whatever status women held in Wade's world, they didn't manage to penetrate the essential loneliness of it. Because he didn't want them to do so?

"No lectures on the evils of devoting one's whole life to work?" He grinned challengingly, watching the flicker of expression in her eyes.

"Obviously you have a lot of energy to channel," she replied carefully, perceptively. "It's probably safest to channel it into work. At least, if you bite an employee once too often he or she can quit."

"Is that what you're going to do?" he inquired deliberately, watching her through narrowed eyes, as if assessing how many bites he could take out of her before she fled.

Elissa only smiled, letting him read anything he wanted into the nonverbal reply. She wanted a lot more than the satisfaction of quitting her job.

"I thought," he went on after a moment, "that we would go down to the wharf when we've finished dinner. You can show me around the waterfront."

"If you like," she agreed politely, for the first time beginning to wonder if matters were going to get awkward when it came time to go home. She must make very certain he understood she wanted to be taken back to her own apartment, *not* his place!

But Elissa put the nagging problem out of her mind as she toured the lively Seattle waterfront with him after dinner. It was a bustling, touristy place filled with fascinating import shops, colorful bars, and sea

gulls who appeared more interested in eating than
sleeping.

She was aware of the contact Wade retained
throughout the meandering tour, his large hand folded
firmly around her own, and wished the clasp didn't
convey overtones of masculine protectiveness. She
didn't want to feel protected by this man. For one
thing, it would be a false sensation. His protection
would last only as long as he was interested in her,
and there would be an extremely high price tag attached. She knew that in her bones.

As usual, the import shops proved most attractive
to Elissa, and she drew Wade to a halt beside a huge
wicker chair.

"I've been thinking of buying that chair for six
months," she confided.

He glanced curiously at the fan-shaped back and
exotic styling. "Why haven't you?"

"Because, although it looks beautiful, it isn't very
comfortable." She sighed morosely.

"And you always put comfortable things in your
apartment, do you?" He grinned suddenly.

"Always!" she snapped, goaded by his teasing.

An hour later, chilled from the brisk breeze off the
water, Elissa found herself expertly stuffed into the
Jaguar and headed for home. Her own home, she realized, relieved that there wasn't going to be an argument over the matter. Perhaps Wade was intuitive
enough to know she wouldn't have reacted well to
the notion of being taken back to his place. Of course,
now she had the decision to make about inviting him
in for a nightcap. Why was this revenge business so
full of dangerous little pitfalls?

At the door of her apartment she tried turning to

make a formal, emphatic good-night, but somehow he was moving into the living room with her and closing the door behind him with a definite finality. Elissa frowned. She might have been of two minds about inviting him in for a drink, but she did not appreciate having the decision made for her.

"Thank you for a lovely evening, Wade," she began carefully as he calmly slipped off his jacket and loosened his tie. "Since we both have to be at work early in the morning, I think we had better—"

"I'm not going to be at work in the morning," he interrupted easily, casting her a mocking glance as he slung his jacket over a chair and stepped close to her. "I'm going to be on my way to California."

"I thought you were going down at the end of the week," she said in surprise, uncertain of his mood.

"I've changed my mind. The only reason for making the trip at the end of the week was so that I could have the weekend there with you. But if you're not going to come with me…" He let the sentence trail off invitingly as he lifted a hand and wrapped it gently around her neck.

"I'm not!"

"You're sure, Elissa?" he whispered throatily, bending his dark head to tease her lips with his own.

"I'm sure," she mumbled against his mouth, conscious of the electricity in the air. What would it be like if she were to fling caution to the winds and run off for a weekend with this man? Instantly she squashed the idea. He had insulted her, mocked her, and now he wanted to use her. How could she even think of running off with him? Revenge was what she was after, and she must not let herself be seduced by the charm he could wield. She had to keep her goal firmly in mind, or she would be swept up into the vortex of the passion he could create between them.

"If I asked you very nicely?" he coaxed softly, his mouth tasting hers and then beginning to nibble appreciatively. With his other hand he toyed with the thick pelt of her hair.

"I don't think you know how to ask anything very nicely," Elissa managed to contradict, standing very still beneath his light, intriguing caresses. A dangerous man. Already she could feel the flicker of excitement and warmth beginning to build toward a flame. Her body remembered the way it had luxuriated in his arms on Sunday afternoon and instinctively sought to move closer to him. Desperately she strove to control her reactions.

"You do like to push a man, don't you?" he grated, and then, instead of the delicate little nibbles he had been taking, Wade began to devour her mouth fully. With the eager, hungry forcefulness of the predator, he parted her lips and explored the warm, honeyed place beyond.

"Oh!" Elissa moaned the small sound from deep in her throat, trembling beneath the onslaught and searching wildly for a way of handling herself. Why did it have to be this man who had such an effect on her? If only it were Dean or any of a number of others she knew! It didn't seem fair.

"Come with me, Elissa!" he growled, raising his mouth an inch from her own and meeting her wide, uneasy gaze. "Let's make a weekend of it, honey. It will be perfect."

Elissa felt herself drowning in the silver quicksand of his eyes and struggled desperately to pull back.

"Everyone would know. The people at work would

find out about a thing like that, Wade,'' she protested, clutching at the only straw available.

"I've had second thoughts on the practicality of trying to keep our affair a secret," he admitted, a thread of humor running through the passion in his voice. "I don't think it's going to be possible."

"You wouldn't tell anyone!" she gasped, shocked back to reality at the thought of her co-workers learning of Wade's interest in her.

He hesitated, as if seriously thinking about it.

"Wade!"

"Listen to me, Elissa," he said softly, sounding as if he were trying to reason with her. "Even if neither of us says a word, people are going to realize something's going on. Why shouldn't we be honest about it?"

"Because so far there is no affair, damn it!" she hissed. "So far I am merely studying the possibility, remember? I may decide my career at CompuDesign isn't worth putting up with your attentions." Elissa was angry now—angry at his presumption, angry at how difficult it was going to be to achieve any measure of revenge, and angry at herself for wanting to go to California.

"All right, sweetheart," he soothed. "Take it easy. We'll do it your way."

"You give me your word not to say anything to anyone?" she charged.

"I promise not to make a general announcement," he agreed lightly. "But it's not going to be my fault if someone happens to see us together or notices the way I look at you."

"Oh, yes, it will be your fault. I'll hold you personally accountable if you give anyone the idea that you're interested in me.''

''That's a little extreme,'' he pointed out dryly.

''I happen to feel extreme about it! This whole damn situation is extreme!'' she gritted, thinking helplessly that the evening had been quite pleasant up until now. ''Blackmail generally is considered *very* extreme, you know! Wade…!''

Elissa's railing words were abruptly cut off as he jerked her toward him, pinning her in his arms. She gazed up at him furiously, her sea eyes stormy with the force of her emotions.

''Stop using that word, damn it!'' he almost snarled, and then he was crushing her mouth, not seeking her cooperation this time but taking his fill of her. She struggled for a moment and then went rigid as his hand lazily prowled up from the curve of her hip to find her breast. It settled there, branding his possession through the material of her dress and into her skin.

''The next time you're tempted to lose your temper with me, little witch,'' he cautioned thickly, ''remember that not all of us fight magic with magic. Some of us have other techniques.'' He emphasized the threat by dragging his thumb heavily across the outline of her nipple, sending sparks along Elissa's nerve endings.

''You mean men like you resort to brute force when you can't hold up your end of an argument?'' she managed to hiss.

He loosened his grip, retaining only the mildly punishing grasp on her neck, and smiled wickedly.

''Wolves use the most efficient means to end a hunt, darling, didn't you know that? I keep telling you they're interested in the final results, not the game playing that goes before the victory.''

Elissa glared at him seethingly, knowing that the excitement racing through her veins was every bit as dangerous as his threats. She would bring this man to his knees for the rude, uncivilized way he was pushing past the dragons and into the privacy of her castle, she promised herself violently. Wade Taggert would pay for his presumption.

"You see me as a victim?" she muttered.

"I see you as a prize," he corrected softly.

"Strangely enough, that doesn't relieve my mind one bit!"

"It isn't supposed to relieve your mind. I'm not out to make life comfortable for you, honey." His momentary anger over her use of the term *blackmail* seemed to have disappeared. Wade was back to the bantering, mocking; seductive man she had known all evening, and Elissa stared at him mistrustfully.

"But you expect me to make life comfortable for you?" she countered vengefully.

"Oh, yes. Eventually. Or, at least, as comfortable as one can be around a witch."

The fingers on the back of her neck moved, giving her the smallest of shakes, as if trying to secure her entire attention for his next words.

"You will behave yourself while I'm gone, won't you?"

"I always behave myself," Elissa announced haughtily, hoping he would take his hand away from her neck before he inflicted damage.

"I'm very glad to hear that." He nodded. "I would hate to come back to find out you hadn't taken our relationship seriously."

"More warnings, Wade?" She lifted one eyebrow interrogatingly.

"If you need to ask, I'm being too subtle," he muttered gruffly. "Just remember that you're wriggling on my hook and you're headed for my net. I wouldn't take it kindly if you were to allow yourself to be stolen in the middle of the process."

"What? You have so little faith in your own abilities?" Elissa tossed her head, freeing herself from his grasp as she mocked him, daring to laugh at him with her eyes.

"Do us both a favor, honey, and don't push too hard," he advised almost cordially. "Wolves can get awfully short-tempered if sufficiently provoked. I'll see you as soon as I get back from California." He turned and strode away down the hall toward the elevator, not looking back.

Elissa slammed her door as loudly as she dared, instinctively not wanting to disturb the other tenants, and collapsed back against it, reviewing the evening morosely.

Had she accomplished anything at all? There was no doubting Wade's genuine, if temporary, interest in her. The offer of the trip to California had not been made lightly. He had wanted her with him.

But that was a long way from offering marriage, she thought gloomily, straightening slowly and heading dejectedly toward the bedroom. How did one go about maneuvering a wolf into marriage? The problem would have been ludicrously simple with a man like Dean, but with Wade it became far more difficult.

The problem in dealing with Wade, Elissa decided as she slid down the zipper of her dress and slipped the garment over her hips, was that a woman couldn't always be certain who was doing the maneuvering. She might be operating from the relative safety of a castle wall, but Wade had the undeniable advantage of the lone hunter's mentality: a relentless drive that didn't acknowledge defeat easily.

She stopped for a moment and glanced at one of the paintings on the bedroom wall. An alien world full of challenge and mystery. She felt as if she had just finished an evening in such a place.

Chapter 7

It was a relief to be able to go into work the next morning and know she wouldn't run into Wade, Elissa thought. The past few days had been more than a little traumatic, she acknowledged ruefully, and the idea of pretending nothing had happened between them was more than she wished to deal with at that point. Knowing she had two days of grace at the office was enough to enable her to deal with friends and co-workers on an ordinary basis.

It was early afternoon when the phone rang, and she set aside her work on the final draft of a software manual to answer it.

"Dean!" she exclaimed mildly, pleased with his call. "I had no idea it had gotten so late. Where has the day gone?"

"What do you mean, late?" he demanded cheerfully. "It's only a little after one o'clock."

"I know. That's what I mean." She chuckled. "I never get calls from you until after the stock market's closed back east. I worked through lunch and hadn't realized the time. How are things going?"

"Not a bad day," he admitted, sounding pleased with himself.

"Sounds like you pulled off a coup among the bulls and the bears."

"Umm. Why don't I tell you some of the choicer details over dinner tonight?" She could hear the smile in his voice and knew he really was pleased with his accomplishments for the day.

"I'd love it," Elissa heard herself say even as the tiny warning jolt of memory flashed alive in her head. She could see Wade standing in her doorway the previous evening telling her to behave. Coolly, firmly, she pushed the image aside. Whatever Wade Taggert might think, he did not have any genuine control over her life. She was only stringing him along until the moment of revenge, and she would not disrupt her ongoing relationships with others just because of that. "What time?" she demanded, reinforcing her decision.

"I'll pick you up around six. I thought we'd try that new French restaurant downtown."

"A successful day, indeed!" she teased. "That place is expensive."

He laughed. "This is a feast-or-famine business, and today we're feasting."

"Give me the steady salary any day. I like to know where my next meal's coming from, even if I can't always afford to have it at French restaurants," Elissa told him roundly.

"No sense of adventure," he complained good-naturedly.

It was only later, after she'd hung up the phone, that Elissa thought about his words. No sense of adventure. A slow smile tugged at her lips as she went back to the draft of the computer manual. If only people knew how much adventure had recently been injected into her life!

By her normal standards, dinner was a success, Elissa told herself resolutely several hours later as she said her good-night to a smiling and contented Dean Norwood. Smiling and contented even though he was being shown her door after only one short brandy in her living room.

"It was a lovely evening." She smiled dazzlingly. "And congratulations again on the huge block trade today."

"Too bad the market opens so early." He sighed, somehow having come up with the notion that the evening had to be ended prematurely because of his work. He was usually in the office before seven o'clock.

"Stockbrokers should save their socializing for weekends, I guess." Elissa grinned, contriving to look properly reluctant to see him go. It was amazing, she thought, that he was so very easy to manage. Skills she had taken quite for granted before she had met Wade were beginning to appear in a new light. She realized how easily she had kept the evening flowing without allowing the conversation to become too personal. Such a trick wouldn't have been possible with Wade.

"You're probably right." Dean smiled, leaning

over to kiss her lightly on the mouth. There was no overwhelming male passion in the caress. It was exactly the sort of good-night kiss Elissa had wanted from him. "I'll call you sometime next week and we can talk about weekend socializing in more detail, okay?" he asked pleasantly.

"I'll look forward to it," Elissa promised. Very gently she shut the door behind him as he walked down the hall. For a moment she closed her eyes in bemusement, wondering at herself, and then she slowly trailed through the comfortably furnished living room, turning out lights as she went.

Last week she had seriously contemplated engineering a different ending to her next date with Dean Norwood. Yet tonight when the opportunity had arisen she had carefully maintained a distance between them. A distance Dean hadn't even been aware of. It would have been very simple to steer the conversation toward the two of them, Elissa thought with a sigh. It would have been very simple to encourage a far more impassioned good-night embrace from him. But she hadn't done it. And she was honest enough with herself to admit that the reason she hadn't was Wade Taggert.

Not that his warnings alarmed her unduly, she decided, removing the soft green jersey dress. There was no reason to fear the man, and besides, she reminded herself bracingly, there was almost no chance he would ever find out she'd spent the evening with Dean.

But in the course of her recent turbulent association with him Wade had made her aware of something she hadn't worried much about in the past. It wasn't that she had never realized how easily she handled people, she mused, slipping into her nightgown and pulling back the soft satin comforter. It was that she hadn't realized that anything had been missing in the curiously one-sided relationships which tended to develop—relationships she controlled easily.

Elissa lay in the middle of her wide, comfortable bed and gazed around at the brightly patterned green-and-white bedroom. A soft, comfortable bedroom. Exactly like her life. Soft and comfortable. Until Wade Taggert had charged into it. That thought brought her eyes to the paintings hanging beside the mirror. The only things in her bedroom which were not soft and comfortable. Her mouth quirking downward at the corner as she gazed at them, Elissa reached out to turn off the bedside light.

Her hand was on the switch when the phone on the nightstand blared shrilly. Elissa frowned and picked it up, aware that it was almost midnight and that calls this late at night could mean unpleasant news.

"Where the hell have you been?"

Elissa drew in her breath sharply at the shock of Wade's silky aggression. He wasn't in a towering rage, she decided at once. He was cool and controlled and dangerous. But he was nearly a thousand miles away, she reminded herself firmly, and he had no real power over her.

"Out," she retorted bluntly, not bothering with preamble any more than he had.

"I've been calling since seven."

"Why?" she asked with deliberate innocence.

"To see how reckless you really are, of course," he shot back smoothly. "You managed to live up to my worst expectations."

"I assume that's a compliment?"

"Not to your intelligence. Who were you with? Norwood? Is he still there?" The questions came rapid-fire, as if he didn't want to give her time to think up an excuse.

Elissa drew on her reserve of inner control and said quite softly and encouragingly into the phone, "Would you like to speak to him?"

There was a heartbeat of frozen silence, and then Wade was the one taking a deep breath. She could hear the forced sound of it even through the phone lines.

"You don't even know enough to be scared, do you?" he observed with unnatural dryness.

"Well," she hedged, "it's been a good job and I would like to hang on to it—"

"I'm not threatening you with your job, little one," he broke in on a drawl. "Whatever you may think, that's not the only weapon I'm holding over your pretty red head. Now tell me the truth, is Norwood there?"

Elissa heard the command in his voice and decided to give in to it. She was already being bold enough on several fronts, and she didn't want to completely infuriate Wade, she realized. That wouldn't help her plans along. No, she needed to walk a very cautious middle ground here....

"No, he's not here."

"But you did go out with him, didn't you?" he demanded roughly.

"Yes, as a matter of fact, I did. He's a friend of mine, Wade, and I don't intend to give up my friends for you."

"You didn't waste any time asking for the lesson I promised you." He swore softly.

"What lesson?" Elissa's brows drew together in a fierce frown as she eyed the telephone receiver suspiciously.

"I seem to recall telling you I wouldn't tolerate other men in your life while I was in it, and then I went on to say you needed a lesson in developing some respect for the male of the species. You may recall the incident. It only took place Sunday," he chided grimly.

"You *are* threatening me!"

"But not with your job," he told her evenly.

"What, then?" she snapped, irritated, but curious in spite of herself.

"You'll have tonight to worry about it," he said with great gentleness. "And tomorrow, too. I'll be home sometime tomorrow evening. I hope you'll have the courage to be in your apartment when I get there. If you're tempted to spend the evening elsewhere in order to avoid me, you might take into consideration the fact that I'll be twice as annoyed with you if I have to track you down."

"If you think I'm going to sit around and wait for you to arrive just so that you can yell at me, you're out of your mind!" Elissa accused furiously.

"Why don't you spend the time thinking of ways to charm me into a better mood when I get there?" he remarked.

"Would it do any good?" she flung back through clenched teeth.

"It might," he allowed thoughtfully. "Tell you what. Why don't you fix dinner for me and see if that does the trick? I'll be there around seven."

Confused and intrigued by his sudden switch to an

almost bantering tone, Elissa hesitated. "Are you telling me I can avoid the lecture if I feed the beast?"

"And pour him his drink the way he likes it, let him put his feet up on your furniture, and ask him all about his hard business trip. It might just work, little witch."

"And if it doesn't?" she couldn't help inquiring.

"As they say," he quoted philosophically, "'Into each life a little rain must fall.' The only reason it will seem more like a storm breaking over your head than a light shower is that you're so used to good weather."

Elissa hung up the phone with a small crash.

By six-thirty the following evening she had fully rationalized the work she had put into the meal which simmered temptingly on the stove. She was not in the least afraid of Wade Taggert. Indeed, the whole thing was becoming something of a game, she decided. He had dared her to try to charm him out of his anger, and she had taken up the challenge.

It wasn't that she feared his anger, she thought with an inner smile as she checked the coq au vin. Only that it amused her and fit into her plans to see if he was as vulnerable as other men. This evening would be something in the nature of a test.

She felt a twinge of unsettling anticipation when the bell sounded at seven, but she went toward the door with determination, a glass of whisky in her hand. She had deliberately sought for a homey, soothing image this evening and took a quick glance in the mirror to make certain it had come off properly.

The skirt was a soft border print in tones of gold and brown which swirled lightly around her ankles.

She had selected a blouse of liquid gold to go with it, one cut with a deceptively demure neckline. Her hair was brushed to a bouncing shine, and there was a sparkle in the blue-green eyes which owed nothing to makeup. A frilly apron tied around her waist added the final homemaker touch, she thought. How could any man bring himself to yell at a woman dressed like this when she answered the door with his drink ready and his food elegantly prepared? There was a welcoming smile curving her lips when she turned the doorknob.

"Hello, Wade. You're right on time," she murmured sweetly, stepping aside for him to enter. "Do come in, won't you?"

He was still dressed in the business suit he'd undoubtedly worn back from San Jose. The near-black hair was neatly combed, the touches of gray very properly complementing the crisp, conservative whiteness of his shirt. He looked tired, she thought with unexpected surprise, but the gray eyes were as hungry and watchful as ever.

"Good evening, Elissa," he returned politely, raking her slender figure with an intent, interested glance. "Do I take it you're going to try and ease my weary body and uncertain temper, after all?"

"You do look tired," she informed him with a sympathy she couldn't have said was real or false. But it sounded real, she consoled herself, and that was what counted for the moment. "Here, take off your coat and I'll hang it in the closet."

He did as he was bid, shrugging out of the garment and casually loosening his tie with what sounded like a small sigh of relief.

"Was the trip unsuccessful or just tiring?" she

asked gently, leading him over to the largest of the comfortable overstuffed chairs and handing him his drink as he settled into it.

There was a fractional pause behind her as Elissa picked up her own drink and returned to take the seat across from him. It occurred to her that Wade was thinking seriously about his response. Had he really come prepared to read her the riot act?

"It was successful, I think," he owned at last, putting his feet on the hassock between them and watching her through mildly narrowed eyes. "At least, Roberts is willing to listen to reason."

Elissa handed him a plate of cheese and crackers, which attracted his attention immediately. "What was it you were trying to reason with him about?" John R. Roberts, she knew, was the head of CompuDesign. The man whose position was said to be going to Wade when the older man retired.

"He'll grant the Seattle office more autonomy in contractual matters as long as I will guarantee the results with my neck." Wade smiled wryly.

"Which you're willing to do?" Elissa sipped her drink idly, her eyes on his tired face.

"Of course," he said flatly, leaning back in the chair and exhaling heavily.

"Somehow that doesn't strike me as terribly reasonable on the esteemed Mr. Roberts's part!" she noted. "Why should you be held personally accountable for the results of what is clearly an experiment!"

"Why shouldn't I be?" He half smiled. "In his shoes, I'd demand the same accountability."

"Yes," Elissa agreed after a moment, thinking of Wade's first month at the Seattle office, "I expect you would. Perhaps that's why the old wolf is grooming you for his job when he retires. He recognizes a fellow traveler!'' She grinned teasingly and received a speculative smile in response.

"For a Little Red Riding Hood who's on rather shaky ground at the moment, you seem in excellent spirits this evening.''

"What?'' Elissa exclaimed in mock distress. "Is that all the thanks I get for setting the stage exactly as you wished? Stop trying to bare your teeth at me, and tell me more about the trip.''

He obliged, relaxing visibly as the whiskey and quiet conversation took effect. For her part, Elissa was privately interested to discover that her responses weren't the casual, automatic ones which came easily to her in similar situations. She succeeded in creating the pleasant atmosphere she wanted, but there was a different element in it than there usually was. With an inner start she finally realized she wasn't playing her role because it was easy or because it was second-nature after so many years. She was enjoying herself on a different basis altogether. There was an underlying warmth and excitement in the give-and-take of the conversation which was vaguely satisfying and stimulating.

"Ready to eat?'' she asked half an hour later, rising smoothly to head for the kitchen.

"I'm starving,'' he confirmed. "But I don't know if I have the energy to get out of this chair!''

"Not necessary,'' she assured him airily. "I'll serve the meal in here on the coffee table.''

With a few deft arrangements, Elissa transformed the small table into an intimate, beautifully set service for two. Candles flickered, and the china and silver gleamed in their light.

"A man could get used to this," Wade observed some time later, helping himself to more of everything.

Elissa blinked but said nothing. The comment had been a throwaway one, not to be taken too seriously. She was fairly certain Wade hadn't taken it into his head to seek a long-term commitment from her. He was still angling for an affair. Well, she would find a way to push him deeper than that before this business ended.

"You're an excellent cook, Elissa," he continued blithely. "Part of being charming, I imagine."

"Goes with the territory," she affirmed pertly. She poured a little more wine into his glass and splashed the last few drops into her own. "Any complaints?"

"About the food? Absolutely not. Nor about the conversation. I got precisely what I ordered. Do you know how badly I've wanted this invitation?" He fixed her with an inquisitive gray stare.

"Was it an invitation?" She mimicked surprise. "I had the impression it was more in the nature of a command."

"Let's compromise and call it a strong suggestion, shall we?" he offered politely.

She heard the hint of gravel in his voice and smiled very sweetly. "You're the boss."

"So I keep telling myself when I'm around you. But it's been difficult making you understand."

"Has it ever occurred to you," she retorted very carefully, wanting to test the ground before she trod on it, "that I might have been a bit afraid of you?"

"No," he declared without hesitation. "It hasn't." He buttered the last portion if his crusty French roll and slanted a glance across the small table. "Why should you have been afraid of me? At least up until the time I caught on to what was going on between you and Randolph?''

''That was unnecessary,'' she reproved sadly. ''Must you bring that incident into the conversation? I'm trying to forget the whole matter.''

''Sorry,'' he apologized without any sign of repentance. ''Go ahead and tell me why you were afraid of me for the past month.'' He popped the roll into his mouth and chewed reflectively, eyeing her.

''To begin with, you're considerably different from the man whose place you took. You must know that by now,'' Elissa said calmly, sitting back in the large wing chair and crossing her legs languidly.

''Granted. But every new boss seems a great deal different from the one who went before. Hardly a reason for going out of your way to avoid me.''

''You've agreed you're not exactly a household pet,'' she murmured wryly, her sandaled foot swinging gently as she locked gazes with him.

''And my predecessor was?''

''Definitely. A kind, grandfatherly sort of man. He hired me originally, you know. That was a few years ago, before the Seattle office was large enough to have a separate personnel department. I've always had a soft spot in my heart for Mr. Jensen.''

''And he always had a place on your invitation list?''

''Certainly. He *and* his wife,'' she added a trifle grimly.

''I wasn't about to suggest you had seduced him,'' Wade told her quietly.

''Thank you.'' Elissa's voice was cool now. ''One never knows with you.''

"I sense the sweetness and light going out of this evening," he stated with mild regret.

"Forgive me," she purred instantly, soothingly. "I expect I overreacted. As I was saying, I was accustomed to working for Mr. Jensen—"

"More likely you were accustomed to wrapping him around your little finger." Wade swallowed the last of his wine.

"And then you came on the scene," she persisted, choosing to ignore the interruption. "Stepping on people's toes, reorganizing, issuing directives right and left…"

"It's called assuming the reins."

"It's called shaking up the staff," she corrected firmly, lowering her lashes. "With considerable roughness, I might add."

"The bottom line to this endearing little confession being that you thought it was safer to stay out of my way?"

"Something like that," she agreed softly, injecting a certain amount of appeal into her words. She waited expectantly for his understanding.

"Is there any dessert?"

"What?" She frowned in astonishment, lifting her lashes to meet the gleaming gray pools across from her.

"I asked if there was any dessert," he repeated obligingly, an expression of total innocence struggling to look at home on his hard features.

"Yes," she bit out impatiently. "There is a dessert. Cheesecake."

"That sounds delightful," he murmured enthusiastically. "I'll help you clear the table."

"Don't bother," she grumbled, rising to her feet

and sweeping up a stack of dishes. With an air of grand disdain she headed for the kitchen. Annoying, irritating, overbearing man!

She had regained control of her temper by the time she returned to the living room with brandy and cheesecake, and she made a point of smiling very pleasantly.

"So you don't believe you might have made me a trifle, umm, nervous?" she pressed gently, watching him polish off the cheesecake in a few short, efficient moves and hand back the plate for more.

"I'm fully prepared to accept that you found me" —he paused as if searching for the right word— "different. That something about me made you wary." He watched her cut the second slice of cheesecake and hand it back to him. "That much is obvious. But I don't think you were afraid of me. I doubt if you've ever had anything as uncomfortable as real fear in your life." He sat back in the chair again, taking his time with the second slice of cake.

"I think you're jealous," Elissa said suddenly, reclining across from him, the brandy glass cradled in one hand. She smiled with a kindly, patronizing expression as he looked up. "Not of a man in my life," she hastened to add, seeing the narrowing of the gray eyes, "But of what you perceive as my ability to charm other people. You've said yourself that you've fought for everything you've ever wanted. My way must seem much easier and far less wearing to you. Are you hoping that if I let you hang around me for a time some of the ability will rub off on you?"

"I take it you don't think that's likely." He smiled, showing a hint of white teeth.

"Not the way you're going about it," she returned

promptly. Deliberately she sipped from her brandy snifter.

"What would be the correct method of obtaining that goal, supposing I wanted it?"

"You should try imitation, not force. You should practice charming me, not laying down the law." Elissa waited while he appeared to be turning the notion over in his mind.

"There's one problem with that," he decided thoughtfully, setting aside his empty plate.

"What?"

"I think your definition of charm in me would be my letting you do exactly as you pleased. Which, in turn, would hardly be very pleasant for me. No, you can forget that idea. Jealousy I might feel, but not of your techniques. I'm satisfied with my own way of doing things."

Elissa pounced, catching him up on the small admission he'd dropped. "What would you find yourself jealous about, then?"

"The usual thing," he told her blandly, heating the brandy by cupping the snifter in his palms. "Other men. If you really want to charm me, you'll have to convince me you're capable of being faithful."

"A high price to pay merely to keep one's job." Elissa sighed regretfully, aware of the exhilaration she was experiencing in bantering with him.

"Have you got a better offer at the moment?" he growled, not moving but appearing ready to spring even though he was, to all appearances, fully relaxed in the chair.

"Let's just say I'm working on it," she demurred.

"And so," he declared, "the discussion finally gets around to the main topic of the evening." He settled more deeply into his chair, looking prepared to spend the next several hours there.

Elissa tilted her head appraisingly and lifted an inquiring eyebrow. ''What,'' she asked clearly, calmly, ''is that supposed to mean?''

''We are about to go into detail on the subject of you and Norwood and last night, aren't we? Since you brought it up yourself, I figured you were ready to discuss it. Of course, if you'd rather wait a while longer…'' He let the sentence trail off helpfully, as if trying to be gracious. He waited politely for her to express her wishes. But the gleam in the gray eyes was anything but polite, Elissa decided.

''I have no intention of discussing Dean with you. Or last night, for that matter. We've already discussed it. Besides,'' she went on, smiling most appealingly, ''I've spent the evening following your instructions for charming you. You did imply on the phone that you would refrain from the lecture if I served up the proper amount of hospitality tonight, you know.''

''Did I?'' He appeared to be recalling his own words, examining them. Then he shook his head decisively. ''No, I don't believe I said it would work. I merely said you could *try*.''

''I did try,'' she defended drawlingly. ''You have to give me credit for that.''

''Yes. An excellent attempt,'' he agreed approvingly.

''But it's not going to work?'' Elissa felt the tiny thrills down her spine as she prepared for the battle to come.

''No,'' he said smoothly, ''it's not going to work. You didn't really think I'd let the whole incident pass,

did you? That I'd let you get away with seeing another man the first night I'm out of town?''

"I don't really *think*," she returned evenly, "that
there's much you can do about it. You were enormously lucky, in fact, to get dinner!" She couldn't
resist taunting him, Elissa realized abruptly. He had
claimed to be able to master her, and she now knew
a part of her could never have let that claim go un-
challenged. No one had ever made such claims before. In the end she was going to have this man on
his knees in punishment for his unjustified accusations about her relationship to Martin Randolph. It
was only fitting she let him find his own way to failure by giving him enough rope to hang himself.

For a highly charged instant their glances clashed
across the short distance between them, and then
Wade smiled. A very dangerous sort of smile. But
there was nothing overly alarming in his next words.

"Actually, I am a little tired at the moment. And
there are other things I'd rather do than yell at
you...."

"Such as?" Elissa was ready for a verbal skirmish.
Every sense was alert and eager. She could win this
argument, she knew. He hadn't a leg to stand on.
What right did he have to tell her she couldn't see
other men?

"Such as kiss you," he whispered, his deep voice
husky as his gaze dropped to her mouth.

Was he going to back down without a fight? she
wondered, a little disappointed. On the other hand,
Elissa told herself, she wanted to reach her own goal
as quickly as possible, didn't she? If Wade was more
interested in kissing her than he was in scolding her,
she was making great progress.

"You can't," she said very softly, "do both."

"I can't yell at you one moment and kiss you the next? Then guess which activity I'm going to choose." Slowly, deliberately, he set his snifter down on the table beside the chair and uncoiled to his feet.

Elissa watched, her mouth going dry in anticipation, as he paced the single step to her chair and put out a hand to remove the glass from her fingers. Like taking candy from a baby, she decided gleefully. She could make this man want her even more than he wanted to berate her for defying him.

She let him pull her up to stand in front of him, and then he wrapped her arms around his waist and held them there.

"You do deserve something for all your charming efforts tonight," he said very softly, promisingly.

"Something besides being yelled at?" she hazarded provocatively, aware of the feel of his hardness as she was forced gently against him. Head tipped back, lips slightly parted, she watched the very male, very hungry flames melt the gray ice in his eyes.

"Yes," he agreed, his words barley above a whisper and thickening rapidly with desire. "Something besides being yelled at..."

His hands still pinning her arms around his waist, Wade took advantage of her tilted chin to feather the side of her throat with his lips. The lightest of touches, it sent a tiny shiver through Elissa. A small voice warned her that she was beginning to respond more and more quickly to Wade's kisses, but she pushed the thought aside. Hadn't she won tonight? Why shouldn't she sample some of the fascinating sensations she was coming to expect in his arms? She could handle the man....

A curious, sensual recklessness urged her to kiss the exposed column of Wade's neck where it disappeared into his loosened collar. She pressed her mouth to the tanned skin and felt his instant response. Her arms around his waist were freed as he shifted to hold her more firmly against him.

"You are a very slender thing for such a formidable witch," he groaned in her ear as his hands slid down the length of her spine to the curve of her hip. "How can you be so little and so dangerous?"

"Am I dangerous?" Elissa murmured, tensing for an instant and then relaxing as he used his strength to arch her closer to his warmth. She began exploring the muscles of his back through the fabric of his white shirt and shivered yet again as first his lips and then his tongue teased her ear.

"Very," he affirmed readily enough. "I doubt if you even know the full extent of your power. You've never had anyone to experiment on with the full range of it."

"Until I met you?" she finished dreamily as his fingers edged lower to cup her hips.

"Until you met me!" He crushed her completely against him, leaving her in no doubt of the rising demands of his body. Elissa felt her knees weaken as the knowledge of the strength of his hunger was forced upon her. The fingers she had been using to stroke his back sought for support instead as she clung to him.

His mouth began moving slowly, teasingly, temptingly along the line of her cheekbone, pausing to drop a kiss at the corner of her eye. She squeezed her lashes more tightly closed in response. When his lips neared hers she moaned unconsciously with a hunger which was rising to match his.

"That's it, little one," he encouraged, letting one hand glide up from her hip to her waist and higher to circle her ribs just below the soft weight of her breast. "Cast your spells, and see if you don't get caught up in them yourself!"

Elissa leaned heavily against him, using him unabashedly for the support she craved as she lifted her arms around his neck. His mouth slid along the remainder of its path and closed firmly, commandingly, over hers with an impact that was like the closing of a door.

"Oh, Wade!" His name was a summons, an order, an imperative that he seemed to understand at once. And just as quickly he responded to it, scooping her into his arms with a small rush of power that left Elissa's head swirling. To still it, she rested her cheek against his shoulder and clung tightly to his neck, aware that he was carrying her through the room and down the short hall to her bedroom.

The light from the hall shafted across the expanse of her bed, and Wade settled her gently in the middle of it. An instant later he was beside her, dropping urgent, biting kisses along every inch of her skin as he exposed it.

Elissa felt the coolness on her flesh as her blouse was pushed aside, and she heard his sigh of satisfaction as she searched for the fastenings of his own garments. Her legs shifted restlessly, and he slid a knee over them, anchoring her in place until he undid her skirt.

She made a small, futile attempt to stop him before he had removed all her clothes, some warning bell

sounding belatedly in her passion-fogged mind. But
he gently caught her wrists, imprisoning them while
he completed the task.

"Are you cold?" he whispered as she shivered beneath his touch. By now she was wearing only the
lacy scrap of her bikini underpants, and in the slanting
hall light she was almost totally exposed to his sweeping gaze.

"Yes," she breathed, not knowing if it was the
coolness of the bedroom or the clamoring of her
body's demands which made her seek his warmth. It
was all bound up together, she realized vaguely. Only
Wade could warm her tonight. Only Wade.

He pulled away for an instant, removing his shirt
and tie completely, and then returned to tug her close
to his chest. He was still wearing his slacks, she knew,
and her fingers went to the buckle of his belt.

"You'll soon be warm enough, little witch," he
promised, leaning forward to crush her breasts softly
against his chest. The crisp hairs teased at her nipples,
exciting the stimulating. "We'll both warm ourselves
at the fire we've built between us!"

She had his belt undone now, but when she would
have tried to strip the remainder of his clothes from
him he caught her hand and brought the trembling
fingers to his lips, kissing them lingeringly. Then he
placed the hand around his neck, his own fingers
searching for her small breasts.

Elissa strained against his touch, clutching fiercely
at him as he lowered his head to kiss the valley between her breasts and then sought the tips with his
mouth. His hand trailed lower, prowling toward her
stomach and then moving on to the promise of her
thighs.

With teasing, provoking little forays he inserted his fingers just inside the waistband of her lacy underwear, and Elissa cried out.

"Wade!"

"Tell me, sweetheart," he ordered gently. "Tell me how much you want me!"

"I want you," she gasped, her breath coming quickly between parted lips. "You must know I want you!" She could no longer think properly.

His mouth burned on her skin. "You aren't going to turn away from me tonight the way you did on Sunday?" he prodded.

Elissa tried very hard to remember Sunday and why she had refused him then. Surely the same reasons applied tonight, a thread of common sense tried to say. But she had won tonight! He was here on her terms. He was at her mercy! Wasn't he?

There was something else, she realized dimly. Something more she wanted from Wade Taggert. But she could sense the need in him, was aware of the depths of his desire in every fiber of her being. It was becoming very important to satisfy that desire. More important than anything else she had ever done...

"No, Wade," she breathed, her heart pounding as he placed the palm of his hand against the sensitive area of her inner thigh. "Not if you want me, too...." She longed to hear him tell her of his need, his desire, and—her pounding heart nearly skipped a beat—of his love. Yes, that's what she wanted to hear him say! And he would say it, she was certain of it. No man could do this to a woman unless he loved her, could he?

"I want you, sweet witch," he vowed heavily, using his nails lightly, flickeringly, on that vulnerable inner thigh in an enticing touch which made Elissa moan. "I want you, and I'm going to take you. Make you mine so completely, so thoroughly, that you'll never look at another man!"

Elissa heard the rough, sensual threat in his voice. It cut through some of the passionate mist he had evoked, reaching the nearly silent part of her brain which had tried to urge common sense on her earlier.

"Wade?" she pleaded questioningly, uncertainly, crowding closer to him in an effort to convince herself that she was wrong, that her tremor of fear was a false alarm.

"After tonight," he vowed, his hands tightening possessively as his mouth nipped her shoulder and then soothed it with his tongue, "after tonight there will be no more games with Norwood or anyone else. No other men, Elissa, my lady witch. Only me!"

She heard the ring of grim male resolve in his voice. Heard it and reacted to it the way she wouldn't have reacted to anything else in that emotional, highly charged moment.

"No!" she managed to get out from a tension-clogged throat. "No!" she said again, louder, more forcefully, as she used every ounce of her nearly banished willpower to call forth resistance from her reluctant body.

"Elissa…!" She heard the velvet tearing away from the steel.

"How dare you!" she gritted, finally locating the energy to struggle in earnest, her blue-green eyes on fire with a heat that had nothing to do with fading passion. "How did you dare to think you could come here tonight and…and *seduce* me into agreeing to stay away from other men?"

Wade's eyes hardened as he took in the sight of her gathering rage, and he reached for her pushing, punishing little fists before she could find a more vulnerable spot than his chest.

"Calm down, Elissa, before you get hurt!" he ordered harshly.

"Now you're threatening to hurt me!" she flung back, outraged. She would have used her bare feet to kick at him, but he perceived the danger and pinned her ankles with the weight of his leg. Unable to move now, she glared up at him, her anger and scorn flashing from the aroused sea of her eyes.

"You have no scruples at all, do you?" she charged bitterly, her breasts heaving with the force of her fury. "When you can't get what you want by tricking me—"

"I never tricked you. What the hell are you talking about, woman?" he blazed tightly, the cold rain of his eyes drenching her taut features.

"I'm talking about coming here tonight, eating my food, pretending to be...to be *charmed*..." She was beginning to hate the word but couldn't think of a better one. "And then pretending to...to want me..."

"That's not exactly a pretense!" he rasped, giving her a small shake.

"The way you did, it is!" she retorted with a snarl.

"I thought I was very honest about that particular aspect of the situation," he grated, and she thought for an agonized instant there was a spark of humor in the gray eyes. "What's so unscrupulous about the way I set about showing you that I want you?"

"You made me think you were...you were..." Elissa gulped, realizing the direction her words were

taking her and trying vainly to find an alternative way
to end the sentence.

"That I was what, Elissa?" he demanded sharply,
his fingers bruising her wrists as he waited for her
answer. When she could only lick her lower lip in
nervous agitation, he finished the sentence for her.

"You thought I was falling completely under your
spell, didn't you? That you could control me the way
you control the others! But that's not quite the case,
little witch. I was charmed enough this evening, but
did you really think I'd forget all about last night just
because you fed me well and soothed my weary
brow?"

"Yes!" she swore, stung. "Yes, I thought that because you made me think that! You tricked me! You
were going to…to make love to me in the hopes that
I'd be so weakened I'd agree to anything you demanded, including giving up my freedom. But it
wouldn't have worked, Wade Taggert," she hissed.
"Never in a million years!"

"You think not?" he growled, his gray eyes mocking her. "You think that if we'd finished what we
started here tonight you wouldn't be eating out of my
hand by morning?"

Elissa flushed furiously, acutely alerted to the reality of what he was saying. She wasn't at all certain
she could have gone on fighting him if he'd succeeded in making love to her tonight. How could any
woman fight a man like this after he'd made her his
completely? For the first time she saw the real danger
in allowing herself to be seduced by Wade. It would
brand her forever his. The realization sent a cold chill
down her back.

"We'll never know, will we?" she bit out nastily,

"Because you aren't going to finish what was started here!"

"What's the matter, witch? Afraid to find out how powerless you'd be if you surrendered to me?" he taunted dangerously.

"No!" she cried proudly, lying through her teeth. "There's no danger in such a thing because there's no love between us!" And then, with more boldness and sheer courage than she had ever exercised in her life, Elissa added, "I could spend the night with you without risk, Wade—that is, if my pride would allow it! But I can't say the same for Dean Norwood. If he were the one here with me tonight, things might be very different!"

The sudden still silence was colder, more threatening, than an iceberg floating toward her, only the tip of it showing above the surface of the water.

"Don't," he finally grated, the menace in him plain, "try telling me you're in love with Norwood!"

"Why not? He has far more to offer than you do!" Elissa could hardly believe what she was saying. This wasn't the way she had meant to seek her victory. She shouldn't be precipitating matters like this! It was far too risky, too dangerous. But she couldn't seem to stop herself. It was as if the unreasoning elements of a genuine witch had taken control of her body, pushing her into what she was going to say next.

"What can he possibly offer you that I can't?" Wade demanded with royal disdain for his rival. The gray gaze ravaged her scornfully, daring her to compare him to Dean Norwood. She could feel the outraged wolf in him and wanted to laugh hysterically. Was Wade truly so arrogant, so utterly sure of himself, that he couldn't even conceive of her preferring

Dean to him? She would show him, Elissa vowed silently. There were other things a man could offer her besides challenge and a continual assault on her senses.

"I'll tell you what he can offer," she smiled, baiting him. "He can offer marriage!"

Once again the iceberg floated, pressing increasingly cold water ahead of it to announce its arrival. But it was too late, far too late to return to the safety of the shore....

"Marriage." Wade repeated the word as if tasting it, examining it the way he would a business deal. The enigmatic gray gaze trapped her, wide-eyed and breathless, beneath him. "Is that what you want, lady witch?" he asked slowly, meditatively.

"Yes!" It was too late to back down now, even though she knew she had rushed her fences, that she was probably going to lose any chance at revenge.

He shrugged with massive indifference. "All right. If it will put an end to this game you're playing, I'll marry you. It wasn't exactly the method I had planned on using to keep other men away from you, but I suppose it will be effective enough."

Chapter 8

Elissa was never sure how she managed to drag herself into work on Thursday morning. She cringed at every mirror she happened to pass, keenly aware of the dark circles under her eyes she had tried to cover unobtrusively with makeup. She shuddered as she sat crouched over a cup of tea at her desk, grateful for the privacy of her small supervisor's office. She could not remember ever having had a sleepless night before in her life. Wednesday night would have to go down somewhere in a book of world records.

The dreadfully long hours had not passed in wakefulness because of Wade's presence. Elissa shut her eyes and grimaced wryly as she remembered the calm, utterly cool and collected way he had taken his leave after telling her so casually he would marry her. Her lashes fluttered open again as she instinctively searched for something breakable on her desk. Anything would do, she decided grimly, reaching for a pencil. Even as it snapped obediently in her fingers the memory of how Wade had snapped the yellow pencil during his interview with her on Friday sprang to mind.

Elissa hastily tossed the remains of her victim into the trash can.

"Elissa? Got a minute?" Marie, one of the writers under Elissa's supervision, stuck her pert, closely cropped head around the corner of the office door. She was smiling as she did so, confident of her welcome. Elissa was always welcoming. "I wanted to ask you about this chapter on data entry I'm working on for the manual on the Z100 series machine."

Elissa, with incredible effort, summoned a smile. The very fact that it took an effort was a distinct shock. She was in for another jolt when she realized she didn't want to welcome Marie at that particular moment and assist her with her problem. She wanted to scream for some help with her own problems! But, she admitted honestly to herself, how could anyone help her out of this mess?

"Come on in, Marie," she forced herself to say with a fair imitation of her normal pleasant attitude. "What's the matter?"

"I think we'd better get the programming group to explain in more detail how they've structured the entry screens. It looks like they've put in some protection to prevent obviously numerical fields like dates from accepting alpha characters, but I can't be sure. I don't want to put the instructions in the client's manual unless it's certain."

"Okay, I'll get hold of Rob and Mandy. They're handling the programming for this client, aren't they?'' Elissa remarked, trying to get back into a businesslike frame of mind as she glanced through Marie's notes.

''That's right,'' Marie nodded helpfully.

''We've got to get better coordination between the writers and the programmers,'' Elissa added with a frown. ''These notes they make are so much garbage half the time. We need to be working much closer with that group.''

''Perhaps you could talk to Mr. Taggert about it,'' Marie suggested brightly and then bit her lip. ''I guess you'll have to go through Evelyn now, won't you? She's our new department head....''

''Yes,'' Elissa agreed fervently, exceedingly grateful that she wouldn't have to go directly to Wade over the matter. ''I'll mention it immediately to Evelyn.'' She shook her head absently. The interdepartmental lack of communication was one of the things she had planned to devote a great deal of time to improving once she'd been given the new, higher-level position. She would have to work through Evelyn now. Elissa stifled a sigh.

After a bit more professional discussion of the task at hand, Marie left, leaving her supervisor to her private thoughts. And said thoughts returned at once to Wade's incomprehensible leavetaking the night before. Elissa still couldn't understand it, although she had gone over the scene a thousand times during the night, searching for a clue. She had been prepared to tell him flatly what he could do with his proposal the moment she had gotten it.

But she hadn't expected to get it so soon and not under such conditions. The small revenge to be derived from the scene in her bedroom hadn't been what

she was after at all. She wasn't even sure Wade would
care one way or the other if she threw the offer of
marriage back in his face. He was simply extending
the proposal because she'd more or less implied his
competition was prepared to do so. She'd pushed him
into it. He hadn't come crawling on his hands and
knees begging her to marry him! Some revenge!

Elissa got to her feet and paced the limited area in
front of her desk, her forehead tense with her whirling
thoughts. There was one interesting option open to
her, she decided after a moment. She could continue
with the farce of an engagement, hoping to wring
more satisfaction from the situation. Wade did want
her, she told herself, even though he'd made no effort
to consolidate his position last night. Not that she
would have allowed him to do so, Elissa added re-
gally. But he hadn't even given her the chance to
refuse him. He'd simply rolled off the bed, tossed on
his shirt, told her he'd see her at work, and left.

She gritted her teeth in a grin that would have appeared astoundingly savage if she'd seen her face in
a mirror.

Fortunately, running into Wade at work was not
that common for someone on her level. She might
conceivably have to pass him in a hall, but she would
do her best to stay clear of the executive suite of
offices where that sort of encounter was most likely.
She needed time to think. She *must* think!

But fate was definitely against her, Elissa decided
at lunchtime as she made her way quickly down the
hall toward the exit. She was rounding the corner,
preparing to grab the slowly closing doors of one of
the elevators, when she saw Wade at the other end of
the hall. He glanced up from scanning the front page

of the business journal he had in his hand and saw
her at the same time. He was already walking in her
direction, and on seeing her he increased his pace.

Elissa thought of how he had accused her of ducking around corners in order to avoid running into him
in the past. She took a deep breath. He was just going
to have to add another instance to his list of times she
had deliberately avoided him, she thought forcefully,
stepping into the elevator and letting it close. There
was a certain satisfaction to be had from the annoyance in the gray gaze which watched in grim frustration as she made good her escape.

Confident she'd gained sufficient time to allow her
to disappear into the noonday crowd on the Seattle
street, Elissa stepped out of the elevator a few minutes
later and into the building lobby. The guard at the
reception desk was in the act of replacing his telephone receiver when he glanced up and saw her.

"Oh, Miss Sheldon," he called cheerfully.

"What is it, Russ?" Elissa said politely, wanting
to be on her way out but not wanting to offend this
friendly older man who greeted her so cheerfully each
morning.

"Wanted to show you those pictures of the grand-
kids I told you about last week. Finally got them back
from the developer this morning."

"Could I see them after lunch, Russ?" Elissa
pleaded desperately, conscious of being vulnerable as
long as she stood in the lobby. "I've got to dash.
Some errands to run on my lunch hour. You know
how it is…" She was already halfway toward the
revolving doors when Wade's voice called her name
and she knew she'd lost the small race.

"Elissa!"

She turned in resignation, hearing the iron command vibrating under the assumed friendliness of his call. He was stepping out of the other elevator, moving toward her.

"Thanks, Russ," he threw over his shoulder as he walked past the smiling guard.

"No problem, Mr. Taggert," Russ beamed, his bushy white brows lifting as he regarded the other two. "Always glad to help."

"On your way to lunch, Elissa?" Wade inquired blandly, slipping his hand firmly under her arm. His eyes glittered down at the coolly composed face.

"Yes, as a matter of fact, I was." There was little else she could do except submit to his unrelenting lead as he started her out the door.

"How convenient. So am I. I was on my way down to your office to invite you along when I saw you stepping into the elevator. Too bad you weren't able to hold the doors open for me, but these modern elevators do shut quickly, don't they? Lucky I was able to use the phone in the other one to call Russ and tell him to detain you."

"The elevator phones are only for emergencies," she snapped, irked at her failure.

"This was an emergency, I think," he drawled. "As I said, lucky I was able to get hold of Russ."

Elissa shot a suspicious sideways glance up at his too-bland face. He returned it with gleaming malice in his eyes. "I'm assuming, of course, that the elevator's shutting and not reopening was an accident. I wouldn't want to think you'd gone back to your old trick of ducking out of sight whenever you happened to come across me in the hall."

"Wouldn't think of it," she told him airily, refusing to be intimidated.

"Good." He nodded. "Now, then, about lunch…"

"I was only going to grab a quick bite at the deli down the street," she said bluntly.

"I'll join you." He smiled. "As soon as we pick out the ring."

Elissa froze, coming to a full stop in the middle of the sidewalk and swinging around to glare up at him. "What ring?" she asked very distinctly.

"Your engagement ring. What ring did you think I meant?" he retorted mildly. "There's a good jeweler in the next block. He's expecting us."

"But how could he? I mean, we only decided last night! That is…" Elissa broke off in a morass of confusion as she contemplated the new development.

"I called him an hour ago. That's why I was on my way down the hall to fetch you," he explained kindly. "I was under the impression I had plenty of time." He glanced pointedly at the thin gold watch on his wrist. "Most of the staff go to lunch from twelve to one."

Elissa flushed, aware that it was not yet twelve. "I, er, had some chores and thought I'd take a couple of extra minutes…"

"So you ducked out fifteen minutes early?" He made a small clucking sound of disapproval. "Not a good example to set for the rest of the staff, is it? You do still have people reporting to you, even if you aren't the new head of editing and graphics!"

"It won't happen again!" Elissa lifted her chin haughtily. "I was feeling somewhat pressured this morning."

"Were you? I wonder why.…"

"Stop teasing me, Wade!" she snapped, goaded. Whirling, she started up the sidewalk again, jamming her hands into the front pockets of her belted wool coat. Instantly he fell into step beside her, pacing along like the wolf he was.

"What gave you the idea I was teasing, Elissa? I'm going to put a stop to this furtiveness of yours if it's the last thing I do! Hard on my ego, you see," he explained laconically.

"I doubt if anything could demolish your ego!" Except when I tell you I wouldn't marry you if you were the last wolf on earth, she added silently.

"If you keep talking like that I might get the idea you're a tad reluctant to marry me," he observed coolly. A little too coldly.

Elissa went on the alert. She didn't want to ruin matters at this delicate stage. Not when the situation had begun to promise some interesting possibilities in the way of revenge.

"It was a bit sudden," she murmured wryly, not certain how to pursue her new course of action but committed to it. It seemed easiest to follow Wade's lead for the moment. After all, she would always be able to bring everything to a screeching halt when she was ready to make her grand refusal. That thought gave her a small lift.

"I was only meeting your terms, honey," he purred. "You made it clear the competition was offering marriage: That's a tough offer to beat with only the promise of an affair and a little assistance in your career. I upped the ante in order to stay in the game. I think I mentioned in the beginning—was it only last Friday?—that I'd use whatever lures would work. The way I figure it, I'm holding all the aces again. With marriage thrown into the pot along with good career potential, how can you resist?''

Elissa flicked a half curious, half enraged glance at him out of the corner of her eye and surprised a strangely watchful expression on his features. Something tight in the lines of his mouth…

''You really believe I'm quite mercenary at heart, don't you?'' she muttered, unwilling to admit to herself that the evidence of tension in him had disturbed her. ''Have you given any thought to what's going to happen when you lose interest in me and my career? You did say originally you didn't know how long you'd want me!''

''We'll burn that bridge when we come to it,'' he promised, pulling her to a stop in front of a jeweler's door. ''First things first, however.…''

The selection of the ring didn't turn into a major event for the simple reason that Elissa refused to become overly involved. She scanned the first tray of rings presented her and randomly picked the least gaudy one, declaring herself satisfied.

''We'll take that one,'' Wade instructed the helpful, hovering jeweler, and Elissa ground her teeth in disgust as her new fiancé indicated a different ring from the one she had selected. It was easier not to argue. Besides, she would only be giving it back shortly, anyway. Throwing it back, perhaps, if she managed things with a proper amount of drama.

''About announcing our engagement to the rest of the staff,'' Wade began some time later as he pulled off the small coup of finding a table at the overcrowded little deli much favored by office workers in the vicinity.

Elissa glanced up, startled. ''I…I hadn't thought

about that,'' she admitted slowly, turning this new wrinkle over in her mind as she took her seat.

''Well, you'd better. A well-handled, discreet little affair might have been something we could have kept out of the limelight, but an engagement is more complex, I'm afraid.''

''You sound very knowledgeable on the subject,'' she retorted, gradually regaining some of her normal poise. She'd allowed herself to become dizzy with the rush of events, but she could deal with them, she reminded herself.

''Common sense,'' he returned smoothly. ''I didn't get where I am by not being able to do good contingency planning.''

''Too bad I wasn't more versed in contingency planning myself,'' she grumbled with great depth of feeling as she glanced through the menu.

There was a split second's hesitation before Wade's reply. ''You mean if you had been you might have approached the right man at the start of your campaign for the promotion? Well, live and learn. You're headed in the right direction now. What are you going to have for lunch?''

She told him, and he gave the orders to the waitress, who bustled off in the direction of the kitchen. Wade turned his attention immediately back to Elissa, who waited warily.

''Returning to the matter of our announcement to the staff,'' he began again firmly. ''I think the most appropriate way would be a casual cocktail party at my place. I haven't done any entertaining to speak of since I took over CompuDesign, and this should provide a good excuse.'' He nodded, apparently pleased with his plans. ''We'll make a little announcement

sometime during the middle of things when everyone
is on his or her second drink, and I'll present you
with the ring. It should go over very nicely.''

Elissa thought briefly of her engagement ring,
which had been left at the jeweler's for sizing. Then
she thought of receiving it in front of the entire staff
of CompuDesign. Her mouth went quite dry.

"Perhaps we should be quieter about the whole
matter," she tried tentatively. That was instinct speaking, though, she told herself bracingly. *Practically*
speaking, this might be just the event she was looking
for....

"Nonsense," Wade said dismissingly, smiling with
an intimidating show of his good white teeth. "The
staff will love it. Possibly enough to make them forgive me for choosing Evelyn over you for that promotion!" He tacked on the last statement with a wry-
ness that caused Elissa to lift an interrogating
eyebrow.

"Has anyone said anything along those lines?" she
demanded in surprise.

"Not directly." He grimaced ruefully. "But I've
gotten the message."

Elissa frowned, "I hope it's not going to make life
difficult for Evelyn."

"Our announcement should go a long way toward
taking everyone's mind off the subject," he pointed
out.

Elissa nodded, thinking about the positive effects
the action would have for Evelyn, and then her mouth
tightened as she reminded herself that Evelyn was not
her primary consideration at the moment. The party
was going to be used for the benefit of one Elissa
Sheldon, damn it!

"I think I'll schedule the cocktail party for Sunday afternoon, say between five and seven. Most people are free Sunday afternoons, and as this is such short notice, that's an important factor...."

"*This* Sunday afternoon?" Elissa blinked her astonishment.

"Why not?" he said carelessly as their sandwiches were presented by the waitress. He thanked the woman with a smile which she didn't seem to find wolflike at all.

"But...so soon?" Elissa wasn't sure why the short time frame was upsetting her. Didn't she want to get the whole thing over with?

"What's the point of waiting? Can't you get things organized by then? You always seem quite efficient."

"Me! I'm supposed to organize the engagement party?" Elissa squeaked. Things were getting rushed again, and she wasn't sure she liked it.

"I'll handle the food," he assured her quickly. "Don't look so annoyed; you'll have the easy part. My God! You're glaring at me as if I'd just told you or organize your own execution!"

Elissa drew in her breath at the analogy. An execution, she thought harshly, was exactly what the party would be. An execution of the overinflated, overbearing, and vastly annoying ego of a wolf!

"I'll see what I can do," she promised sweetly, unaware of the gemlike glitter in her eyes.

Wade nodded, looking much too satisfied. "Yes, I thought you'd agree," he murmured softly. He took a huge bite of his sandwich. "When you've finished your lunch we'll take care of another detail."

"Which is?" she demanded tartly.

"The license."

That afternoon Elissa pulled out the old résumé every serious career person is supposed to keep tucked away and began the task of updating it. Whatever happened Sunday afternoon, she would be job hunting Monday morning.

It was strange, she thought gloomily, scanning the one-page summary of her entire working experience, how attached she'd gotten to CompuDesign. She would be sorry to leave. Not *overly* sorry, she realized truthfully, but mildly sorry. Elissa bit her lip and considered that for a while. When was the last occasion when she had been *very* sorry about anything? She shook her head. The only event she could work up strong emotions over lately was the explosion of Wade Taggert into her life. She began to look forward to Sunday afternoon.

She wasn't quite sure what gave her the notion of dragging out her acrylic paints and brushes that evening. The urge to paint had popped into her head after she'd eaten a quiet, solitary dinner in front of the evening news, and she didn't fight it. When she felt like painting, there was nothing else to do but obey the summons. Nothing else would be satisfactory at that particular moment, as she knew from experience.

Carefully she spread a sheet to protect the rug, set out the paints on the palette, and erected a small canvas. Before beginning she went over to the stereo and, after a moment's close thought, put on Bach's Brandenburg Concertos. A little lilting pizzazz was called for, she decided, turning the volume up higher than usual. She bit her lip as the rich strains filled the apartment. Neighbors, she reminded herself guiltily, and reached for the earphones.

Much better, she told herself, the long cord to the

earphones dragging behind her as she headed back toward her canvas. The music now filled her head, not the apartment, and picking up a brush, Elissa began creating another world.

It was like a drug, this business of projecting herself into the landscape of a planet circling under a different star. The music swirled in her mind, somehow getting mixed up with the paint on her brush, and except for having to change the record occasionally, Elissa lost all track of time. She forgot about everything except the adventure taking place under her fingertips, an adventure in which magic too, the place of science and strange beings conversed on subjects which had nothing to do with computers or cocktail parties.

She wasn't sure how long the doorbell had been sounding before it finally penetrated the earphones. For a moment longer she hesitated, hoping against hope that whoever was outside her door would give up and go away, leaving her to the painting and music. But it was not to be. The bell chimed again, imperiously, and with a sigh Elissa went to answer it.

The shock of finding Wade on the other side of the door caused her to freeze, brush in hand, as she opened it. A strange disorientation persisted which she couldn't quite comprehend. Her mind was still partially in her landscape, she thought vaguely. She stood staring up at him, saw his lips move, and realized she couldn't understand what he was saying.

The brush waved distractedly through the air as she shook her head, scowling, and then he smiled, put out both of his large hands, and removed the headphones.

"I said, good evening, Elissa." He grinned, holding the source of her music in his fingers. Instantly silence descended, and Elissa found herself emerging back into the real world.

"Hello, Wade," she managed, shifting with a twinge of uncertainty. "What are you doing here?"

"Why shouldn't I be at the home of my bride-to-be?" he quipped, leaning down to plant a rather husbandly kiss on her forehead. He stepped inside and closed the door firmly behind him. Elissa backed up, not having much option, and her eyes narrowed.

"Don't point that thing at me." He laughed, indicating the brush in her hand. "I come in peace!" He held out a palm in the traditional gesture, and Elissa smiled in spite of herself.

"I suppose you've come to plan your grand party." She grimaced, glancing down at her paint-stained jeans and blue cotton work shirt. "As you can see, I've had other things on my mind."

He was dressed casually himself, although his jeans weren't spattered with paint and the maroon sweater he had on under the fleece-lined jacket looked expensive.

"No problem." He chuckled, shrugging out of the jacket and tossing it unconcernedly over the back of a chair. Immediately he made for the canvas across the room, and Elissa grew unaccountably nervous. "I've always wondered what you'd be like caught up in the middle of one of your painting binges," he said reflectively, coming to a halt in front of the scene created out of paint.

"Wade, that's not finished yet, and I…" Elissa felt her unease increase and begin to crystallize until she was abruptly aware that she didn't want him looking at the painting. Normally it didn't matter if others saw her work. They never understood it, and it made no difference. But this man was too perceptive, and Elissa realized she was vulnerable in this, her most private area.

There was a tension-fraught silence as he studied the painting with an intentness that bothered her. She was standing on the other side of the canvas, unable to view it, so her mind recreated the scene for her. The memory of what she had done made her wet her lips in anxiety. Surely he would not, could not, see what she had quite unconsciously put into the landscape.

But when he looked up, the gray gaze meshing with hers over the top of the canvas, Elissa knew he had, indeed, seen far too much.

"Elissa, Elissa, my sweet witch," he growled with a beguiling roughness that did nothing to disguise the hint of wolfish triumph in him. "Are you trying to tell yourself something? Or are you trying to communicate with me?"

"I don't have the vaguest idea of what you're talking about," she hissed, moving forward to turn the easel with its too-revealing painting toward the wall. "Come and sit down. I'll get you a brandy. I assume you've had dinner?"

"Good old Elissa, using her charming-hostess qualities to try and take my mind off what I just saw." Wade obediently took the large chair she indicated and made no effort to prevent her from hiding the painting. "But I'm not as easily deflected as that, little one. I would have thought you'd realized that by now."

"Stop talking nonsense," she ordered, hurrying into the kitchen to find the bottle of brandy and a snifter. "It's merely another one of my weird paintings, and you're only fooling yourself if you try reading too much into it.''

''I want it for a wedding gift, Elissa,'' he told her bluntly as she reappeared, glass in hand.

She stopped for a second, appalled. ''What?''

''You heard me,'' he repeated gently, his eyes glowing with gray flames. ''I want that painting for my wedding gift. It's traditional, isn't it? For the bride and groom to exchange gifts?'' One black brow lifted quizzically.

''Why?'' Elissa forced herself to continue her forward progress, carrying the brandy carefully to his side and putting it on the small table near the chair. She didn't look at him as she busied herself with the task. She was able to avoid his eyes completely, in fact, until after she'd seated herself in the chair across from him. Then it became quite impossible.

''Because,'' he told her calmly, ''when it's done it's going to be my invitation into the witch's castle.''

''You think so?'' she couldn't resist taunting. ''What makes you believe you're the one being invited?''

''Don't play that particular game with me, Elissa,'' he grated, eyes narrowing with warning. ''It's the one tactic I won't let you use. I thought we had that understanding clear last night when I asked you to marry me!''

''That I'm not to imply the existence of other men?'' she confirmed, an unholy sense of mischief rising inside her as she sought for some defense against what he had seen in her painting. ''Very well, I suppose it's only civil if I keep my other interests out of your sight. After all, as my husband I accept

you're entitled to some small consideration...
Wade!''

His name came out on a tiny shriek as he pounced.
He was out of his chair and hauling her up beside
him before she even had time to comprehend what
was happening.

"What do you think you're doing?" she gasped
furiously, her shoulders bruising under the hard clasp
of his fingers. She gazed up at him in a strange fury.
Strange because it was tempered with sheer, unadul-
terated fear. Elissa discovered that she did not like
being afraid. It was a highly uncomfortable sensation,
one which sent tremors through her limbs to the tips
of her fingers and the ends of her toes. It made her
heart pound and her breath quicken painfully.

"I should think what I'm doing is obvious, even to
an independent, irritating, willful little witch who
hasn't got the sense to know when she's gone much
too far out of line," he rapped out in a voice that
seemed to roar at her even though he never raised it.
The gray eyes swirled with a freezing storm that
threatened to turn her into easily shattered ice.

"I am going to beat you, Elissa Sheldon. Another
new experience for you, I'll bet. I'd stake a lot of
money on the idea that no one's ever even thought of
doing such a thing to sweet, charming Elissa!"

"Wade!" Elissa's mouth fell open in utter shock.
"You wouldn't dare!"

"There you go again, mixing me up with the other
men in your life who fit so easily around your little
finger," he mocked, giving her a slight but violent
shake. "Perhaps when I've finished you'll be able to
remember which one I am!"

"Wade! Please don't!" Elissa resorted to primitive

feminine instinct. Enraged males were to be placated, appeased. It was the weaker female's only defense when matters had gone this far. "Please don't hurt me," she begged, disgusted with her pleading but not so disgusted as to continue the defiance. Discretion was called for here, she told herself grimly. "I was only baiting you because I was upset that you'd seen the painting. You can have it, Wade, I promise," she added quickly, not noticing any signs of the lightning in his eyes abating. She waited, the trembling in her slender figure not in the least faked for the sake of authenticity.

"When I arrived at your door this evening," he told her gruffly, eyes still very hard and metallic, "I was in a good mood. I want to be restored to that mood."

Elissa felt hope flare amid the nervous wreckage of her poor stomach.

"Isn't there..." She moistened her lips and tried again, eyes wide and pleading. "Isn't there anything besides beating me that will restore your better mood?" With all the female power inborn in a woman, she loaded the delicate question with soft promise and soothing appeal.

"One hell of an abject apology from you might do the trick," he growled unhelpfully. "The sight of Elissa Sheldon groveling is about the only thing that will have any impact on my recent decision!"

"I'm sorry, Wade," she murmured, lowering her head dejectedly and letting her lashes flutter gently on her cheeks. Pride didn't come into the matter just then, she told herself morosely. She would worry about that wounded pride after she'd gotten herself off the hook. "It was only that I was upset...."

There was a tense, dangerous pause, and Elissa waited in an agony of suspense to see which way his mood would swing. She clutched her hands, palms damp, in front of her, keeping her gaze on the rug at her feet. When this fiasco was over, she swore silently, she was going to look forward to Sunday evening with immeasurably increased enthusiasm. Wade Taggert had a great deal to pay for, and she was going to extract that payment. Every ounce of it!

"No more arguments about the painting?" he challenged with a certain ferocity. "You'll give it to me as a wedding gift?"

She nodded, head still bent. "Yes, Wade." She wanted to cross her fingers as she uttered the false promise but didn't quite dare.

"And there will be no more taunting me with hints of other men still flitting to and fro in your life?" he persisted vengefully.

"No, Wade."

Again a pause. Elissa swallowed with difficulty.

"Congratulations, Elissa," he suddenly drawled, the velvet in his voice not fooling her for a minute. "I do believe you've learned a new spell tonight. One you've probably never had occasion to use in the past, but you might find it quite useful in the future. The thing to keep in mind is that it might not always work on me. You got lucky this time, however. I accept your apology. Now sit down and we'll go over the details of the party. I'll want to order the food and drink as soon as possible."

Elissa stirred, stepping carefully back out of reach. He let her go. She met his eyes, and her own slitted in sudden suspicion.

"You're rather quick to change your moods," she

observed dryly, studying him with her head tipped to one side. The storm in the gray gaze was gone as if it had never been.

"Your apology was very nicely delivered," he said by way of explanation, settling back into his chair with a sigh of contentment. He closed his eyes.

"I tricked you," he agreed, not opening his eyes. He appeared the picture of contentment.

"You wouldn't have beaten me." It was a statement, uttered with a certain seething violence. She flung herself down into her own chair, propping her feet on the hassock and leaning back with a sensation of complete self-disgust.

"Not for a little wolf baiting."

"What were you doing? Practicing witch baiting?" she gritted, wishing he would open his eyes so he could get the full effect of the angry flags flying in her own.

"Perhaps," he said enigmatically. "It's a bit more complicated than that, though. I'll explain it to you on our wedding night." He lifted his lashes at last, and the grey eyes actually shimmered as they caressed her sprawled figure. "Now, about that party..."

"Speaking of our wedding," Elissa whispered glumly.

"Oh, yes I forgot to mention I'd set the date, didn't I? It's Monday."

Chapter 9

It was midway through Friday that Elissa finally remembered Dean Norwood. With a small start she glanced up from her work and frowned absently at the far wall of her office. What was she going to do about Dean?

Not that she had any desire to continue her association with him, regardless of her impending freedom from Wade. No, the lukewarm relationship was best ended, and the sooner the better. But there was no reason it couldn't be handled gently and comfortably for all concerned. Dean had been a most pleasant escort, and Elissa automatically searched for an appropriate way of slipping him out of her life.

When Marie knocked politely on the doorframe to announce her presence, Elissa smiled with more enthusiasm than usual. The answer to her small dilemma was suddenly obvious.

"Come in, Marie."

"Hi, Elissa, just wanted to check and see if you'd heard from Rob and Mandy about those entry screens."

"Yes, as a matter of fact, I did. They'll have the data for you this afternoon."

"Good. I'll be able to complete the manual on Monday, then." Marie nodded, pleased.

"That will be fine. Say, Marie!" —Elissa smiled dazzlingly—"would you like to have a drink with me tonight after work? There's someone I'd like you to meet...."

Marie's warm brown eyes brightened for a moment and then assumed a slightly cautious expression. Her attractive features shaped themselves into a tentative smile.

"You know I'm a bit rusty at social situations these days," she said diffidently.

"You're not going to get over John's defection until you start dating other people, Marie. You know that," Elissa advised gently. Elissa had been the one Marie had turned to for a confidante when her boyfriend had casually announced his engagement to another woman. But that had taken place two months ago, and it was time Marie improved her social life.

"I know," Marie admitted. "Guess I'm just feeling scared."

"You won't around my friend," Elissa promised cheerfully. "What about it? We can leave right after work and meet him in the lounge of that hotel up the street. He'll be delighted to make your acquaintance."

"Well..."

"Come on, Marie, I'll be there, too!" Elissa smiled winningly.

"If you think he won't feel like I'm being pushed at him…"

"Trust me."

Marie suddenly grinned. "Okay, Elissa. If I can't trust you in a situation like this, who can I trust?"

It would be easy, Elissa decided a few minutes later as she hung up the phone after speaking to Dean. She and Marie would make a quiet exit from the office promptly at five. Wade, who always worked an hour or so later than the rest of his staff, wouldn't even know. If he chose to stop by her apartment during the evening, she would be home. The business with Dean and Marie would only take a few minutes. Elissa was very efficient at handling easy situations like this.

The buzzing of her office intercom interrupted the smooth flow of her plans.

"Elissa?"

She swallowed, taken aback. "Yes, Wade?"

"I'm going to be able to get away for lunch, after all. I'll meet you at the elevators at twelve. You will hold the door for me this time, won't you, honey?" he added as if it were an afterthought.

She sighed. "Yes, Wade."

"I thought you would. We'll go down to Pioneer Square."

Many more calls like that one, Elissa thought disgustedly, and Wade wouldn't have to wait until Sunday to make the engagement announcement! The office rumor mill would do the job for him.

There were a few covert glances of surprise and interest at noon when Wade coolly guided Elissa into the elevator, but no one had the nerve to ask any questions. Elissa was grateful when the majority of the crowd spilled out at the lobby floor, on their way to nearby restaurants for lunch. She and Wade continued silently down to the parking garage where the sleek Jaguar waited for its master.

"You've certainly learned your way around Seattle in a hurry," she remarked politely as he nosed the car out onto the street and headed for the restored older part of the city. The historic section, once a bustling meeting place for men on their way to the Klondike gold rush or those involved in the lumber business, was now a popular complex of galleries, shops, and restaurants. The fine old architecture had been preserved, along with cobblestone parks now filled with a host of colorful street people who regarded the well-dressed business crowd tolerantly.

"Somebody in the office mentioned an interesting little restaurant down here." Wade smiled. "I believe he said it qualified as romantic."

Elissa flushed, glancing out the window at the brick and stone buildings dating from the nineteenth century. "Is that why you chose it?"

"Don't you think I'm romantic?" he demanded, offended.

She pretended to consider that, pursing her lips provocatively. "No," she finally announced. "I'd say you were pragmatic, not romantic!"

"Just goes to show how much you still have to learn about me!"

The restaurant was a delightful little spot tucked away in the corner of an elegant red-brick building, its decor done with an early Seattle theme.

"I'm surprised you're able to find time to get away today," Elissa murmured noncommittally as she perused the menu. "I thought you'd be busy with that crowd from Oregon."

"The lumber firm? They called and asked if they could meet to discuss computerizing their records after lunch instead of during lunch," Wade said. "It will probably tie me up a bit this afternoon, so I may be late getting away from work. Thought I'd better take advantage of the free lunch hour to see you."

"I'm flattered," she said dryly, her eyes laughing at him as he glanced up speculatively.

"No, you're not," he contradicted. "You're used to people rearranging their schedules for you."

"Not true! You have a very low opinion of me, don't you, Wade Taggert?" she grumbled.

"A realistic one. I think I'm going to have the veal. How about you?"

She sighed thoughtfully. "I'm not very hungry."

"Nervous about Sunday night?" he queried solicitously.

"Should I be?" she managed gamely.

"No," he said with sudden, unexpected gentleness, his gray eyes warming. "I'll take care of everything. There's nothing at all to worry about."

Elissa stared at him for a timeless, whirling moment and then took a grip on her senses. She would not allow this man to drag her under, damn it!

"I'm sure everything will go very smoothly," she agreed quietly and tried to still her pulses as they began to race under the heat of his gaze.

His words were still on her mind that afternoon as Elissa collected her belongings and her friend Marie.

"I'm still not sure about this, Elissa," Marie whispered nervously as they entered the dark lounge together. The expensive well-upholstered room was beginning to come alive with the normal Friday after-work crowd, and Elissa automatically searched the ranks of business suits, seeking Dean Norwood's cheerful face.

"Don't worry, Marie, I'll take care of everything," Elissa assured her friend, realizing with a flicker of humor that she was using the same words Wade had used to her earlier in the day.

"Elissa! Over here!" Dean's call came cheerfully through the murmur of voices, and she turned to see him guarding a small table. She lifted a hand in acknowledgment and started forward, Marie following hesitantly at her heels.

"Glad you could make it, Dean. I want you to meet a friend of mine. Would you believe it? She's into sailing!"

With easy grace and natural skill, Elissa made the introductions and then carefully began to guide the conversation. In a very few moments she was no longer even a part of the discussion as it flowed happily between the other two. Things were going very nicely, she decided with satisfaction. Of course, her task had been simplified by the knowledge that both her friends were interested in sailing, she admitted modestly. Still... The corner of her mouth lifted with self-mockery as she wondered whether or not there really was any magic involved. It was all so easy!

She stayed long enough to make sure Dean and Marie were safely headed in the right direction and then smoothly injected her apologies into the conversation.

"I've got to be on my way." She smiled fondly, getting easily to her feet and reaching out for her coat. "You two have a good time, and I'll see you both soon."

"Oh, Elissa, must you go?" Marie looked momentarily startled to find herself in such a comfortable, casual situation with an attractive male.

"I'm afraid so," Elissa said with light regret. "I've got a thousand and one things to do this evening, and I..."

"And she didn't want to have her fiancé catch her having a drink with another man," interposed a familiar gravelly voice that sent instant chills down Elissa's spine. She whirled to find Wade less than a foot away, directly behind her. He seemed very large and very dangerous in the dark room.

"Wade!" she gasped, striving to regain control of the situation. "I didn't see you..."

"I gathered that much," he noted wryly, taking the belt of her coat out of her nervous fingers and cinching it tightly at her waist. The intimate task brought him very close indeed, and she was violently aware of the leashed anger in him.

"Fiancé?" Dean's mildly confused question interrupted the tension for an instant.

"We're making it official Sunday evening," Wade declared quietly, his eyes flicking from Dean's surprised expression to Marie's curious one. "I trust you'll be coming, Marie? That's what the invitation to my house is all about. You did get it along with the rest of the staff this afternoon?" he added politely, ignoring Elissa.

"Yes, sir," Marie responded immediately, her gaze going at once to her supervisor's flushed face. "I'll definitely be there. We all wondered what it was about...."

"Actually," Wade purred deeply, his arm tightening around Elissa's waist, "it's supposed to be something of a surprise announcement. I'd appreciate it if you didn't give the game away until I put the ring on her finger Sunday night."

"Oh, no, sir." Marie smiled nervously. "I won't say a word!" And she wouldn't either, Elissa realized grimly. The staff was far too much in awe of their new boss to risk his displeasure.

"Elissa, I had no idea..." Dean said, frowning slightly as he looked up and met her eyes.

"It's been very...very sudden, Dean," she said hurriedly, aware of Wade's slanting, mocking glance. "I hope you'll congratulate me."

"Yes, I suppose so," he began uncertainly, his eyes shifting from her features to Wade's implacable face. "But why didn't you mention it earlier? I thought, I mean..."

Damn Wade! Elissa thought savagely. He had ruined everything!

"I'm afraid I'm guilty of rushing her off her feet," the subject of her heated thoughts murmured with patently false apology. "Aren't I, honey?"

"Yes," she bit out and then saw the confusion on Dean's face increase. First things first, she told herself resolutely, turning away from Wade's enigmatic gaze. "Dean, I'm sorry about this. I hope you'll understand..."

With every bit of skill she possessed, Elissa sought to project a wistful, hopeful plea for understanding and friendship as she smiled tremulously at her former boyfriend. "I wanted you to be the first to know, but you and Marie seemed to be so involved with your conversation I didn't quite get a chance to bring up my little surprise."

"Was that why you called me and asked me to

meet you here after work?'' Dean asked, frowning slightly as he considered developments.

''As I said, I was going to explain everything, but I didn't feel right interrupting...'' She looked sadly at him and felt Wade's hand clenched into her waist. He knew exactly what she was doing, and he was letting her know he was aware of it. Deliberately she forced a brighter smile.

''I brought Marie along because she's a friend of mine who needs to get out more,'' Elissa went on chattily. ''She's had some bad times lately, and I thought your company might cheer her up, Dean. You're so much fun.''

''I see,'' he said slowly, clearly confused, perhaps a bit upset, but more than willing to try the obvious escape route Elissa was extending. ''I'm sorry you didn't get a chance to tell me your news,'' he went on, nodding as if it really had been his fault. ''I certainly wish you the best. And don't worry about Marie, here; we seem to have a lot in common....'' He turned a broad smile on his companion, who smiled back at first self-consciously and then with genuine enthusiasm.

A perfect match, Elissa thought. If only Wade hadn't spoiled it! But it looked as if matters were going to sort themselves out after all.

''You two won't mind if I remove my fiancée from the discussion, will you?'' Wade was saying equably. ''She and I have a lot to discuss. You know how it is. So many last-minute details...'' He let the sentence trail off suggestively, easing Elissa away as the other two nodded politely.

Before she could say another word, Wade had somehow put a great deal of distance between Elissa and her two companions. And with every step, the sinewy muscles of his arm seemed to tighten more and more forcefully. By the time they reached the foggy street, Elissa could barely breathe.

"Of all the stupid, poorly timed, oafish things to do!" she hissed, struggling for breath. "What in the world did you think you were doing? I had everything so neatly set up! It was all going so perfectly…!"

"If I were you," he informed her bluntly, half guiding, half dragging her to where the Jaguar crouched at the curb, "I'd be very careful about throwing a tantrum just now. It wouldn't take much to convince me I ought to chew the hell out of you right here in front of the whole world!"

"You'd have absolutely no right!" Elissa began imperiously and then found herself stuffed ungently into the front seat and the door slammed on her angry words. She didn't let that stop her. As soon as he opened his own door and slid behind the wheel, she picked up where she had left off.

"I wasn't doing anything wrong, even by your exalted standards, Mr. Taggert," she gritted loftily.

"You call meeting another man for a drink doing nothing wrong?" he charged coolly, pulling out into traffic with a smooth caution that belied his obviously irate state of mind.

"I wasn't meeting another man for a drink, damn it! I was…I was trying to arrange something." She stumbled over the explanation, because what she had tried to arrange *had* involved meeting another man for a drink.

What was wrong with her? Why should she feel even faintly guilty? She owed no loyalty to this man—only the promise of revenge! Confused and appalled by the unnerving realization that Wade was making her feel guilty, Elissa sought refuge in a more heated tirade.

"I was trying to casually introduce Marie and Dean," she went on bitterly. "I thought the two of them would be perfect together. What's wrong with a little matchmaking?"

He threw her a derisive glance. "Nothing, as long as I'm going to supervise."

"Well, I could hardly have brought you along," she muttered. "Having the boss around doesn't make for the most relaxed of atmospheres. As it is, you came very close to ruining everything. I can only hope that, between the two of them, they'll be able to salvage the situation. I thought you were going to work late this evening, anyway," she added belatedly.

"Is that the reason you picked this evening to meet Norwood?" he retorted coolly, his eyes on the traffic. "Because you thought I was safely out of the way?"

"I was not meeting Dean!"

"Strange," he murmured laconically, "that's certainly what it looked like when I walked into that lounge. For one very dramatic moment, I thought you might be up to your old trick of meeting men on the sly in local bars." Some hint of warning in his voice shook her.

"What a horrible thing to say!" she gasped, outraged.

"It was a horrible thing to contemplate, I assure you," he returned a little too casually.

Elissa shot him a questioning glance. Something didn't quite fit here. Wade was clearly disapproving of the situation, but he wasn't in the rage she might have expected if he really had thought she was meeting Dean behind his back.

"And what about you?" she gibed deliberately. "Were you up to your old trick of tailing your employees to local lounges?"

"I came looking for you just after you'd left the building. One of the women in your group was still there, and she remembered Marie talking about having a drink with you after work. She also remembered the name of the place, and of course as soon as she mentioned it…"

"You remembered that was where I was in the habit of carrying on my illicit affair with Martin Randolph!"

"You can't blame me for being a little upset by the prospect of you heading off to the nearest swinging lounge after work," he pointed out calmly.

"And when you saw Dean at our table, you put two and two together and came up with three!" she exploded.

"Very nearly," he admitted with a quirking downturn of his mouth.

"What do you mean, 'very nearly'?" she demanded suspiciously.

"Elissa," he said with such quiet intent that her blood ran cold, "when I first saw you and Dean at the same table I was ready to tear him limb from limb and then drag you home and go to work on you!"

She blinked. "What happened? Did you decide to forgo your macho vengeance on him and be satisfied with taking it out on me, instead?" she parried nervously.

"No, fortunately I realized what was going on as I neared the table. It was the way you had neatly engineered the two of them together and the way you were preparing to leave, looking like the satisfied cat that had swallowed the cream. You looked so enormously pleased with yourself I realized you must have intended for Marie and Dean to hit it off.''

Elissa blinked again, this time in astonishment. ''You mean…you mean you aren't really upset? You believe me?''

''I believe you,'' he assured her dryly. ''That doesn't mean I'm not feeling mildly provoked by the whole thing.''

''But if you understood what I was doing…'' she began uncertainly.

''There's something about watching you work your charms that makes a man like me uneasy,'' he confessed ruefully. ''Especially when there's another man involved. I prefer to be around when you're spellcasting. It's safer that way. Which brings me to the one point I want to make this evening,'' he ended on a drawl.

''Which is?'' Elissa began to relax. She was feeling much more comfortable now that she knew Wade believed her. She wouldn't have to fret over his reactions much longer, she told herself encouraging, but until the final showdown Sunday evening perhaps she would watch her step.

''Which is that you're not going to go off on your own after work to the nearest singles bar,'' he concluded in a steady, ironclad tone that brooked no argument.

Foolishly, Elissa tried to argue anyway. ''I wasn't alone. I had Marie with me!''

''That doesn't make one damn bit of difference, and you know it,'' he told her grimly. ''If you're going to go out in the evenings from now on, it will be with me. Two women roaming a singles scene doesn't strike me as any more appropriate than one. Especially when one of those two women is engaged to be married. If I ever catch you wandering off like that again, Elissa, there will be hell to pay. Is that very clear?''

She heard the icy command in his voice and considered it carefully. It occurred to her that she was getting off rather lightly, especially when one took into account the mood Wade must have been in when he first entered the lounge and saw her with Dean. And there were only two more days until the grand moment of revenge. Yes, she could afford to subside meekly.

''Yes, Wade,'' she husked, glancing down at her hands in her lap. She was surprised to find the palms slightly damp.

''That's it.'' Abruptly he smiled. ''You're learning.''

''Learning what?'' she snapped, goaded by his easy acceptance of victory.

''Learning that there are limits to my good-natured patience,'' he explained innocently.

''Good-natured patience!'' she rasped. ''That's the last way I would describe your temperament!'' Her hair swirled lightly about her ears as she whipped her head around to glare across the seat at him.

''I'll admit I don't go to the lengths you do to ensure everyone's pleasant state of mind,'' he acknowledged honestly. ''I would never, for example, go out of my way to ensure that a former girlfriend found herself a new romance before telling her we were finished. I wonder if Dean will ever realize just how much you did for him? Probably not. Why did you do it, Elissa? Is it just instinctive now to make sure everyone is contented? Has it become an automatic part of your charm? Everyone except me, of course,'' he added as an obvious afterthought. ''I seem to be excluded from the list of people whose happiness you so charmingly concern yourself with.''

''You don't seem unduly worried about being left out,'' she declared tartly.

''I'm not. Yet.''

''Meaning you might be someday?'' she persisted sweetly.

''Someday, yes,'' he agreed as he pulled up in front of her apartment building and switched off the engine. He turned in the seat to face her squarely, the gray gaze full of assessing study as he raked her rebellious expression. ''But not just yet. Right now I regard your failure to soothe my poor ego as a hopeful sign.''

''Grasping at straws?'' she asked kindly.

''No, simply analyzing the situation.'' He half smiled, stroking her cheek with one lazy finger. ''Right now it's fine with me to learn I'm an unsettling influence in your life. You need that sort of unsettling. At any rate, it's bound to hold your attention until I can…'' He broke off, and Elissa was startled to see a dark flush creep up his tanned neck. In the limited light of the streetlamp she thought at first she might have been mistaken, but her instincts told her she wasn't.

''Until you can what, Wade?'' she inquired with chilling politeness.

''Until I can terminate the hunt,'' he growled determinedly. ''Come here and kiss me!''

She tipped her head to one side. ''Why should I

kiss you after the way you embarrassed me in that lounge?''

''You should kiss me out of gratitude that I didn't cause a much bigger scene,'' he observed dryly, gray eyes mocking.

''A kiss of gratitude,'' she said reflectively, studying the hard line of his mouth. ''I'm not sure I feel that grateful.''

''Would you like me to impress upon you how close you were walking to the edge tonight?'' he invited softly.

''When are you going to stop threatening me every time you don't get your own way, Mr. Taggert?'' Elissa whispered, supremely aware of the tension and intimacy of the moment.

''When I'm sure you're well and truly trussed in my net,'' he retorted throatily. ''Come, Elissa. Kiss your fiancé, who went so easy on you tonight when he had every right to read you the riot act.''

''And if I don't?'' she hazarded provocatively, aware of the thrilling challenge in him—a challenge that reached to the core of her femininity. ''What happens if I don't throw myself into your arms out of sheer relief and gratitude?''

''Guess,'' he invited succinctly, not moving.

Unconsciously, Elissa nibbled on her lower lip. ''Threats, threats, and more threats,'' she groaned on a mere breath of sound.

''Which you might be able to offset with kisses, kisses, and more kisses,'' he retorted, watching her face in the dim light. He seemed fascinated by the green glow of her eyes.

''A calculated risk,'' she noted, equally fascinated

by the play of shadows on the uncompromising lines of his face.

"Very calculated," he agreed.

Very delicately, not quite certain what was driving her to do it, Elissa touched the tip of her finger to the corner of his mouth, and then she leaned forward to drop the lightest of butterfly kisses on his lips.

The small kiss had a strangely hypnotic affect on her senses. When he didn't move or make any attempt to reach for her, she tried another one. Her fingertips slid along the line of his jaw to rest behind his head, entrenching themselves in the darkness of his hair. Deliberately she pulled his head a fraction closer, her mouth beginning to move more boldly on his. She bared her teeth and gently closed them around his lower lip in the silkiest of daring caresses.

Instantly the world exploded around her as she was pushed heavily back into the rich leather seat. The weight of his chest settled over hers and he seemed to glory in the feel of her softly crushed breasts. The strong, probing fingers of his hand bit into her thigh just as his mouth forced her lips apart.

Wade had one hand behind her neck, holding her head still in the crook of his arm, and the hand on her thigh began moving upward, undoing the buttons of her blouse as it went.

"Please, Wade!" But whether she was going to plead for him not to make love to her on a city street or whether she was going to beg him to continue, Elissa could never be certain. The rest of her words were lost in the warmth of his invading tongue.

And then his hands were invading the small valley between her breasts, claiming the territory there with a possessiveness that left her weak and clinging.

"Elissa, I want you so much." He breathed hotly against her skin as he buried his face in her throat. "Do you have any idea what you do to me? You make me want to take you, to make love to you so completely you'll never, ever forget who owns you!"

She tried to protest and couldn't find the strength. When his lips moved lower until he curled a tongue almost painfully around one vulnerable nipple, she drew in her breath with a desperate impatience. It was hard, so very hard, to think of revenge or anything else when he took her in his arms like this. All she wanted was to give and go on giving until she had taken her fill of him.

"Your body comes to my call so quickly now," he rasped thickly, sliding his hand along the curve of her thigh and up under her wool skirt until she was shivering with the implied promise. "Soon every part of you will answer to me, and you'll see you have to take me into your castle!"

"Wade, oh, Wade." His name was torn from her in short, panting gasps of pleasure and excitement. But even as she was pressing herself more tightly against his hardness, she sensed him begin to pull away.

"Calm yourself, little one," he soothed, beginning to stroke his fingers through her hair in a quieting action that left her at once confused and a little angry. "We can't continue this here. We'll go upstairs to your apartment where I can undress you properly and see you lying naked on the bed, waiting for me!" The gray eyes burned with silver flames as he raked her love-softened face. Without another word, he reached for the door handle, his intent violently clear.

"No, Wade," she managed chokingly, desperately

striving to bring her senses back under control. "No...you can't come up with me. Not tonight!" She hated the hint of panic in her voice, but it seemed to serve the purpose of stopping him cold.

"Why not, Elissa?" he growled tightly. "You want me as much as I want you. There's no way you can hide your reaction!"

"I don't have to explain myself to you!" she stormed, scrambling to rebutton her blouse. "It's a woman's right to call a halt to the lovemaking, and I'm exercising my right!"

Nervously she met his ravaging gaze, uncertain what he would do and knowing she wouldn't be able to stop him if he chose to drag her up to the apartment over her protests. And how long would she protest? she wondered forlornly.

With a small gesture of ruthless power held deliberately in check, Wade tapped the car keys against the leather-covered dash. She could almost see him making up his mind, and the silent tension in the car was frightening.

"All right, Elissa," he finally said in a voice that echoed the small gesture with the keys. "If you're sure this is the way you want it..."

"It is, Wade. Please?" She forced herself to tack on the last word with a suitably beseeching gaze. God! What was happening to her? How could she be behaving like this? The whole dangerous business was threatening to overwhelm her, she realized. Thank heaven it would all come to an end on Sunday. She couldn't take much more of this highly refined torture!

Wade took one last look into her storm-tossed eyes and got out of the car. Without a word more on the subject, he took her politely up to her apartment and left her at the door.

Chapter 10

Saturday evening once more found Elissa waiting with a mix of emotions for the arrival of Wade Taggert. Restlessly she paced the floor, the clinging skirts of her sleekly cut green dress outlining her legs lovingly as she moved. Time was running out, overtaking her in a mad rush that threatened her sense of control. A sense she had always taken for granted before encountering Wade, she reminded herself duly.

Tomorrow night she had to have her revenge neatly packaged and ready to be delivered. She paused in front of the mirror and grimaced wryly at her reflection. It was all happening too fast! She wasn't quite ready...

"But how much more ready do you want to be, friend?" she demanded of her counterpart in the mirror. "There is a safety factor involved here!"

And that safety factor was tied up with how much

longer she could expect Wade to refrain from pushing the physical side of their relationship. Even now she didn't fully understand how she'd managed to hold him at bay. She had been successful only because he hadn't forced the issue, she admitted with a massive amount of self-honesty. There was no understanding it, but since the night she'd tricked him into offering marriage, he had seemed willing to give in to her on this one point.

Of course, the momentous occasion of her marriage proposal had only occurred a few nights ago, she thought morosely, turning away from the mirror with a frown. There was always tonight....

"What the hell's the matter with you, Elissa Sheldon?" she muttered, resuming her pacing. "You should be glad you haven't had to fight that particular battle down to the last ditch. There's a damn good chance you would have lost, and you know it!" Memories of how close she had come to letting him make love to her the previous evening washed over her.

The thoughts brought a flush to her face and a tremor to her full mouth. She clamped her teeth on her lower lip to still the latter. It wasn't fair that the one man in the world who had ever brought her to this stage of excitement and despair and wonder was a man who thought the worst of her. A man who was only marrying her because he assumed that was the price he had to pay to have her. Elissa's fingers closed into fists at her sides. The world had always been fair to her. Why this?

She must think of her revenge, she decided, stopping her pacing as the bell rang. She must keep her mind on dealing with the scene she would be creating

tomorrow evening. The excitement was in her eyes
when she opened the door to Wade.

"I've noticed you've hidden my painting," he
complained an hour later as he seated her gallantly in
the exquisite Continental restaurant with its intimate,
seductive atmosphere. "Is it finished?" he demanded
with a distinct hunger in his eyes as he sat down
across from her.

"It's finished," she allowed, for some reason unable to resist a smile at his expectancy. She reached
for her linen napkin and spread it gracefully in her
lap as the waiter arrived with the white wine Wade
had ordered be brought while he considered the
menus. She decided against telling her escort that she
had finished the painting in a strange rage of emotion
after he had left her on Friday night.

"Where are you keeping it? In your bedroom? I'd
like to think it was in there." He grinned unrepen-
tantly, raising his glass to clink it gently against hers.
"After all, I'm keeping the one I had Hal do for you
in my bedroom."

"What?" She stared at him, floored by this news.
"You've commissioned a picture for me? For our
wedding?" For some reason the information took her
completely aback.

"Poor Elissa." He chuckled, sipping his wine and
watching her over the rim of the glass. "You're so
used to relationships in which you give precisely what
you want to give and take so carefully what you want
in return that the person you're taking from doesn't
even know what he's given. Doesn't it intrigue you a
bit to know you're going to be getting something
from me that you hadn't even guessed existed? Something you hadn't even thought you desired? I phoned

Hal the night after your party, you know, and told him what I wanted. I brought it back with me from California.''

"More witch baiting?" she murmured, the corner of her mouth quirking as she considered his unexpected comment.

"I prefer to think of it as witch tempting," he corrected. "Remember the special toys I told you about that day you came for the picnic? Toys to tempt a witch."

"You also said they might be dangerous, I believe,'' Elissa breathed, knowing the intoxication of bantering with this man and wondering what it would be like when he was gone from her life. When she had *evicted* him from it, she hurriedly rephrased her thoughts.

"I'll be around to make sure you don't get into any trouble you can't handle with them." Wade smiled with undisguised masculine anticipation.

"I've never had much trouble handling toys or anything else before you came along," Elissa couldn't resist putting in spiritedly. If this was to be her last real night with Wade Taggert, why shouldn't she enjoy herself? It had been an interesting interlude in an otherwise comfortable, serene life, she decided.

"But have you had much fun or excitement with your toys?" he pressed, the wolf smile in his eyes now.

"Life's always gone rather smoothly," she countered, taking a sip of her wine. "I don't recall ever wanting for anything."

"It's when you want something that it gets exciting," Wade told her with cool authority.

"Desire is a fleeting thing," she pointed out quietly. "Especially for a man."

"It depends on exactly what is desired. Some things can be taken, used, and forgotten. Other things…" His sentence hovered, unfinished, in the air between them.

"Do you know in advance which things go into the long-lasting category?" She quipped.

"I'm a man, not a boy," he told her softly. "I know which things go where in my life."

She studied him for a moment, feeling the tension and unspoken bonds being woven between them. "What long-lasting desires have you known?" she asked at last, unable to stop the words.

"My work is the main one, I suppose. The one I've taken the most effort to satisfy," he replied unhesitatingly.

"No women?" she dared carefully.

"There have been women," he answered easily, unselfconsciously, and uncaringly. "But none in the long-lasting category. Are you asking which category you'll be in?" He watched the color stain her throat and cheeks.

"You've already told me the answer to that," she said with all the neutrality she could muster.

"I don't believe we've ever set a specific ending date to our relationship," he contradicted. She could hear the deliberate temptation in his words and grimly ignored it. "Would you like to talk about it?" he invited, his gray eyes gleaming with intent.

"No." Elissa didn't hesitate. The last thing she wanted to discuss this evening was the end of their relationship. If he only knew just how soon it was going to come to an end, she reminded herself, trying to feel triumph. The feeling wouldn't come. "I think I'd rather hear about the long-lasting things in your life," she continued. "Tell me about your work, first. Have you always known what you wanted to do?"

"I've always known I wanted to wield power of the sort I've got at CompuDesign," he said without any apology. "Does that make me some kind of animal or renegade?"

"It makes you a wolf, and you know it." She smiled.

He shrugged. "So be it. I need the conflict and the day-to-day assertion of my own abilities."

"Does politics interest you?" Elissa asked curiously.

"Lord, no!" he exclaimed, his mouth twisting wryly. "I couldn't stand the constant compromise and the need to answer to a constituency. Give me the jungle of the boardroom and the marketplace any day!"

"Yes," she agreed abruptly, nodding. "You're far too much the lone wolf to ever fit into the political arena. In this day and age I suppose the business world is the best place for you. You're fortunate in knowing yourself so well." And then she thought of his stark, bleak paintings. "But it isn't all excitement and adventure for you, is it?"

"What brought that up?"

"I was thinking of those paintings you have hanging in your home," she told him, striving for some degree of lightness in her words.

"Ah, yes. The loneliness you think you see in my art selection," he murmured, turning his wineglass to catch the light from the candle on the table. He watched the wine and not her as he spoke.

"Has your taste in art always leaned in the direction of the style you have in your town house?" she persisted, unable to let the subject rest even though he was not encouraging her to talk about it.

"I only became interested in art a few years ago," he said, lifting his eyes back to hers. "But, yes, I think the two in my living room are typical of my taste. My eye for technical skill has improved, but the images are similar to those which attracted me from the first."

Was that the real reason he had decided to take the plunge into marriage? Elissa asked herself with a jolt of stunned dismay. To counteract the loneliness? The thought was an unwelcome one. She wanted to think of Wade Taggert as trying to use her to satisfy one of his temporary desires. It would be so much easier to punish him for what he had done to her if that was the case.

"What about you, Elissa?" he interrupted her agitated thoughts to inquire with what sounded like genuine curiosity. The gray gaze pinned her. "Have your paintings always been of other worlds and the kind of adventure you can't know in this one?"

She produced a little half smile as she thought about the question. No one had ever asked it before. "I don't know what attracts me to that kind of adventure. Heaven knows I should have outgrown it years ago. I thought for a while of trying to write tales like the kind I read, but somehow I discovered painting instead. It lets me create the kinds of scenes that appeal to me. While I'm painting I sort of weave a story in my mind, a story for which the picture represents the main scene in the tale..." Elissa broke off, flushing slightly. "It's hard to explain," she mumbled apologetically.

"Only because you've never tried to do it before, I'll bet." Wade grinned, reaching across the table to fit his large hand over her smaller one. "What about your work?" A shuttered look descended on the silvery pools of his eyes. "How did you get into technical writing?"

She laughed at that. "I fell into it. The same way I fell into an English major in college. I fall into a lot of things in life."

"And always land on your feet?"

"Always!" she shot back with a touch of warning.

"And now you're falling into marriage. With a wolf, at that," he noted slowly.

"It is a little outside my normal activities."

"Not comfortable?" he teased.

"It hasn't been so far! Tell me something, Wade," she drawled deliberately. "What would your reaction have been if our positions had been reversed? If I, as your boss, had told you I wasn't going to give you a promotion you deserved because I wanted to teach you a lesson?"

His face hardened perceptibly, and she knew she'd succeeded in taking him by surprise.

"To tell you the truth, I hadn't considered it from that point of view," he owned gently, the gray eyes alert and wary.

"It gives a person pause, doesn't it?" she observed dryly as the waiter appeared to take their order.

The small consultation which took place over the issue of which fish was fresh and what salad dressing was desired broke the tension of the moment, but it floated back into place the instant the waiter disappeared again.

"I like to think," Wade stated tersely, "that I would have had the good grace to accept the lesson."

"Always assuming you were guilty of having tried to obtain the position by illicit means in the first place!" Elissa smiled brilliantly, sensing a hint of victory.

"Of course," he agreed aloofly.

She leaned forward, the brilliant smile still in place, her blue-green eyes gleaming with derision and laughter. "You know what I think?"

"What?" he asked, clearly sensing danger.

"I think you would have raised hell. Perhaps committed murder. Or at the very least torn CompuDesign apart before storming out the door!" Elissa sat back, grinning triumphantly.

"Regardless of whether I was innocent or guilty?" he hedged.

"Yes!"

"You may be right." He capitulated without even a struggle, and that proved quite disappointing to Elissa, who had been looking for a battle she knew she could win. It was his turn to grin, a slashing smile which held no hint of defeat. "It's fortunate for me you're of a different temperament, isn't it?"

Elissa steered clear of such dangerous subjects for the rest of the meal, chatting willingly about art and Wade's acclimatization to the dampness of a Seattle winter.

"Do you miss California?" she asked at one point during dessert, a luscious cream with a caramelized topping.

"No," he confessed without hesitation. And that

was that. They went on to discuss other matters, and then Wade rose to lead her into the lounge.

"Do you realize we're on the verge of being married and we've never even danced together?" he demanded feelingly as he took her into his arms on the dance floor.

"Perhaps we're, uh, rushing matters," Elissa took the opportunity to suggest even as she floated against him.

"There's no such thing as rushing matters," he informed her gravely, tightening his hold until she was deeply aware of him with all her senses. The spicy hint of aftershave mingled with the clean, earthy smell of his body. The rough texture of his suit jacket was somehow enticing against her cheek. But most seductive of all was the elemental feminine pleasure to be derived from being held by a man strong enough and ruthless enough to protect the woman of his choice. Elissa tried to force the fantasy from her mind but had little luck.

"What do you mean by that?" she asked, sensing his enjoyment in touching her hair with his lips.

"I mean that either a thing is right or it isn't. If it's right, then why not rush it?"

"Do you always see life in such simple terms?" She laughed, lifting her face to meet his eyes.

"It…" He paused, and she heard the laughter deep in his chest. "It *simplifies* things!"

"Spoken like a true lone wolf." She sighed against his shoulder. "Two ways of approaching everything: your way and the wrong way!"

"Perhaps I'll be able to pick up some tips on handling life with more finesse from you," he offered encouragingly in her ear. "Have I told you where we're going on our honeymoon?'' he went on deliberately.

Elissa, who had not thought about anything past Sunday night all day, missed a step and wound up planting the toe of her shoe on top of his instep.

''I take it that's a negative response?'' he remarked imperturbably.

''You know very well you haven't mentioned the issue!''

''I thought we'd take the first few days of next week off and seclude ourselves in Victoria.''

''Go to Canada? In the winter?'' She raised her head again at that.

''I doubt that the weather up in British Columbia is much worse than it is down here, and this is off season for Victoria. I can have you all to myself in front of a cozy fire in a proper old British inn....''

''For someone who comes from California, you appear to know a great deal about Victoria!'' she chided, trying to assimilate the thought of a honeymoon.

''Umm,'' he agreed. ''I made the reservations yesterday. A place Conway in marketing mentioned. Victoria's supposed to be the most British part of Canada. We'll stuff ourselves on tea and scones and crumpets. The inn I've booked is noted for the genuine antiques in the bedrooms and high tea every afternoon. Sound good?''

''Would it matter if I didn't approve?'' she shot back tartly, slanting a glance up at him from beneath her lashes.

He looked hurt. ''I thought you'd like the place.''

''Does it ever occur to you to ask someone else's opinion once in a while?'' she teased, unable to continue protesting once she'd seen the hurt in his eyes. "Lucky I like Victoria in the winter!"

"I thought you would." He smiled and pulled her head down against his shoulder, and Elissa quietly began to panic.

On the drive home much later Elissa settled sleepily back into the leather seat of the Jag and watched the lights of the city through half-shut eyes. She was absorbed in her problems, which seemed to have become greatly magnified during the course of the evening, and didn't notice for a while that the route Wade was pursuing would not lead back to her apartment. She considered the various ramifications of that piece of information and wondered how to bring up the subject subtly.

"Where are we going?" It was difficult to be subtle about such a question.

"Home," he told her easily, sending a quick, amused smile across the seat before returning his attention to his driving.

"Your home. Not mine." She waited, her nerves beginning to tingle with a strange, unwelcome expectancy. The same expectancy that was starting to become very familiar around Wade Taggert. A dangerous, beckoning thing. She remembered unwillingly what he'd said about dangerous and tempting toys for a witch.

"My home," he confirmed unhesitatingly. And then he asked softly, captivatingly, "Afraid?"

"Should I be?"

"No." His voice was still soft. "As of Monday it will be your home, too."

Some of the panic Elissa had experienced earlier returned. She could feel it crawling along her nerves.

But it was having to fight another emotion for space. A weakening, acquiescent urge to forget about Sunday night; to simply go home with Wade tonight and see where it all would lead...

But she knew the answer to that, Elissa tried to tell herself. Agreeing to go home with Wade even for a nightcap was a tacit agreement to staying the night with him. Who was she kidding when she tried to imagine herself only staying for a drink and then leaving? She bit her lip in the darkness of the car and wondered what was the matter with her. Why wasn't she telling Wade she wanted to go back to her own apartment? She could handle the situation adroitly enough there, she thought. Give him a good-night drink and send him on his way, exactly as she had handled Dean Norwood earlier in the week. But Wade wasn't Dean, and Elissa wasn't at all sure she could edge him coolly out the door when the time came. That admission more than anything else seemed to sap her will to argue with him about being driven to his town house.

There was a curious, intimate silence in the car as the Jag sped through the city night. Elissa couldn't bring herself to break it, and Wade showed no interest in doing so, either. Every block which passed was taking her that much deeper into enemy territory. Enemy? Elissa considered that. Surely she had the ability to deal with an enemy on his own terrain. She was no coward, and she had a goal: Sunday night. She lifted her chin and unclenched the fingers in her lap. She could afford to go home with Wade this evening because she could handle the situation. She could handle anyone!

A few minutes later, Wade parked the elegant car

in the drive, opened his door and paused to turn and smile at Elissa, who sat very still as the light came on in the Jag. He said nothing, but the heart-stopping smile and the warmth in his eyes told the whole story. An ancient story of magic and sorcery on the most fundamental level. Elissa swallowed and felt the muscles and bones of her body begin to melt. A second later he was out of the car and striding around to open her door.

"Honey, you're trembling!" he said with immediate concern as he tucked her against him, his arm wrapped around her like a band of steel. But the steel felt protective, not imprisoning, she realized dazedly as he walked her toward the front door. Desperately she tried to rally her scattered forces by reminding them that was the most dangerous mistake of all. She must not delude herself into believing Wade's feeling toward her had changed. She was still only a woman he had decided he wanted. Wanted badly enough to agree to the price he thought she was asking.

"It's cold," she mumbled by way of explaining the trembling.

He pulled her close against the heat of his body, and she could feel his smile above her head. "We'll get you inside and I'll fix you a nice hot toddy. You'll be warm enough soon. I promise!"

The depth of meaning in his last words nearly caused Elissa to stumble. But even if she had, he probably wouldn't have noticed; he was holding her too tightly. She stood pressing her cheek into the roughness of his coat while he fished out his keys and opened the door. He felt so good, she thought wonderingly. What would it have been like if he'd fallen in love with her? If he hadn't believed her capable of the sneaky, conniving behavior of which he'd accused her? It was such a temptation to forget the origins of their relationship and give herself up to the moment. The door opened, and she was pushed gently inside.

For an instant Elissa stood staring at the harsh seascape which had first caught her attention on the day she had come to his house for the picnic. Did lone wolves ever seek mates? The door closed behind her, and she turned to watch as he dropped his keys onto a nearby table and pulled off his suit coat.

"Poor little Elissa," he murmured on a note of affectionate humor as he tossed the coat aside and came forward to cup her face in his hands. "You look confused and cold and about to melt at my feet." The silvery gaze swept her face.

"I could hardly be cold and about to melt at the same time," she said with an attempt at some sophistication and lightness.

"No? It's possible to feel two conflicting emotions at the same time. Why not two conflicting sensations?" Wade's mouth curved into what was probably meant to be a smile of reassurance but which managed to increase Elissa's uncertainty. It showed in the jewel brightness of the gaze she turned up to meet his.

"I'll get you that hot drink," he whispered, bending his head to drop a small kiss on her nose. "Then I'll build a fire and we can talk." His hands dropped from her face, and he turned to walk toward the kitchen. Elissa followed slowly.

"Talk about what?" They had been talking all evening. What was left to discuss at this hour?

"About us. Why don't you find something you like

in my record collection and put it on the stereo while
I get the toddies?''

Grateful for the small task which would keep her
from standing in the kitchen doorway and staring at
him, Elissa wandered over to the stack of albums.
There was a distinct pleasure in discovering that his
collection contained much of the same music she had
in her own. She tried to subdue her reaction. It meant
nothing, she told herself, selecting something rich and
elegant from the eighteenth century.

"Music to ravish the senses," Wade said, walking
into the living room with two steaming mugs a few
moments later. He surveyed her as she sat curled in
the corner of the leather couch. "And a woman who
does the same."

Elissa felt her body react to the expression in his
eyes. Knowing oneself desired was a seductive thing,
she realized dimly as he set the mugs on the coffee
table and walked over to the hearth. She watched,
sipping at the steaming, soothing brew, as he dropped
to one knee and expertly lit the fire. Wade Taggert
seemed expert at everything he did.

"Have you ever," she whispered slowly as he
straightened and moved back to the couch, "gotten
into a situation you couldn't handle?"

He sank heavily down beside her, reaching for his
own mug. For a second he seemed preoccupied with
the toddy, and then his mouth quirked fractionally.

"I've learned one can handle almost anything if
one is persistent enough."

"You mean, reach out and grab the matter by the
throat and hang on until everyone else gives up?"
Elissa felt her own lips shape into a smile.

"Something like that." He grinned, setting his mug

back down on the table and taking hers out of her hands to do the same.

"And would you," she breathed as he pulled her into his arms with an overwhelming, thrilling strength, "be as persistent in a situation where you knew you'd made a mistake? That you'd been wrong or had misjudged completely?"

His mouth hovered a bare inch over hers as he cradled her in his arms across his lap. "Being right or wrong," he grated roughly, "doesn't particularly affect a man's desire." He settled a very tiny little kiss at the extreme edge of her lips. Then he tried another and another....

"I thought we were going to talk," she managed between the enthralling, tempting little kisses. She felt his hand stroke the length of her body in a slow, languid, exploring caress that made her feel warm and wanted.

"We are. But I think we'll do it later. Right now all I can concentrate on is how good you feel in my arms."

Elissa struggled to maintain a hold on her plans for Sunday evening. But it was becoming clear that she had made a serious mistake allowing Wade to bring her home tonight. The tiny kisses being rained on her mouth were rapidly becoming insufficient to satisfy the desire they aroused. She wanted more. More of the tiny kisses, more of Wade's strength.

"You are so soft, so vibrant," he said against the skin of her throat, his voice husky with desire. "I love to feel you come alive when I'm holding you."

Elissa stirred under his hand, his words entering her head but not making the sense they should have made. His voice was like the music in the background; only another element in the seduction. And there were so many elements it was impossible to isolate and pay attention to any particular one!

How was she going to stop him this evening? she wondered, drawing in her breath as his fingers slid down the zipper of her dress. She had to find a way, of course. Everything tomorrow night depended on her not letting tonight get out of control.

His fingers traced delicate, fluttering patterns along her back and shoulders as the bodice of the dress was lowered. She would only let this go on a few minutes longer, Elissa promised herself, lifting her hands to find the black hair behind his ears. Enroute she used her nails gently, provocatively, on the tips of his earlobes and felt him shudder in response. Instantly the tiny butterfly kisses on her mouth began to deepen.

Elissa's fingertips clenched spasmodically as she felt her lips forced gently, inevitably, apart, and her lashes fluttered tightly closed as his tongue pressed the intimacy far into the territory of her mouth. She felt him loosen the clasp of her bra and she shivered, waiting with a sensual expectancy for the touch of his hand on her breast.

But it didn't come. Instead his warm, strong fingers slid between her breasts, down to rest for a moment on the small curve of her stomach and then move around her waist to the sensitive base of her spine. She moaned in the back of her throat and twisted against the crisp whiteness of his shirt.

"Elissa..." he breathed thickly, with growing, devouring urgency. "My sweet. I've waited too long to make you mine..."

Again the words floated into her head, and again she made a halfhearted attempt to comprehend the seriousness of the situation. She must get back to her own apartment, she knew. It was very important. And she would. Shortly.

But first… Her fingers undid the buttons of his shirt, and Elissa heard him groan, a thread of sound from deep inside him that sounded like a strange, masculine cross between laughter and impatient desire as she fumbled with the knot of his tie. But in a moment she had it free, and her nails raked lovingly across his skin, seeking the lines of his ribs and the curling hairs of his chest.

His hand was on her leg now, stroking, massaging, teasing the curve of her calf and the area behind her knee. Gently, insistently, he began to separate her legs, searching for the softness of her inner thigh. The hem of the dress was gliding higher, and soon she would be completely exposed to the hungry, flaming gray depths of his eyes.

And Elissa, as she had known deep in her heart tonight, realized that she wasn't going to demand to be taken back to her apartment. This was where she wanted to be. Always. She sighed with surrender and something more. Something that wanted to give more than her body to Wade. Something that wanted to give her heart and soul…

It was not common sense or belated memory of her unfulfilled revenge which brought Elissa back to reality with a shattering violence. It was an altogether mundane, chance occurrence.

The doorbell rang. And kept on ringing. It rang until Wade finally surfaced sufficiently to realize he had company.

Chapter 11

"**D**amn!" Wade's single, fiercely muttered epithet cut through the remainder of Elissa's fog.

"Someone at the door," she murmured unnecessarily as he helped her to a sitting position and quickly zipped up her dress. She watched him warily, not needing to be told that this was her escape. She would never have been able to make it on her own. With a rush of self-disgust she acknowledged that fact.

"I know," he growled. "I'll get rid of whoever it is and be right back, honey. Stay right where you are," he added, his eyes smiling down at her with heated promise. He put his hand for an instant over her breast in a mark of possession that remained as he got to his feet and stalked to the door.

Elissa twisted around on the couch to watch as he flung open the door with an annoyed, brusque motion.

She would have to be ready to act when he had dismissed the caller, she told herself violently, her hands thrusting through her auburn hair. She wouldn't be able to risk any more of his caresses tonight. That way lay open disaster.

"Terry! What the hell are you doing here?"

Elissa jumped at the astonished note in Wade's voice. She couldn't see who stood on the other side of the door, but she could hear the throaty feminine greeting.

"I came to see you, darling. What else would I be doing here? My plane landed about an hour ago and I finally got a cab…"

Elissa watched, her heart in her throat, as a blond, beautiful, and expensively dressed woman floated gracefully across the threshold. Not just any sort of blond, Elissa thought grimly, her right hand curling unconsciously into a fist. But the stunning, artfully colored-to-imitate-the-sun blond that only California could produce. The woman was tall, model tall. But her figure was more voluptuous than any model's, and she wore her deceptively casual red silk blouse unbuttoned far enough to make sure that much was obvious. Sleek-fitting jeans worn with high heels completed the West Coast look. The gold chains around the slender neck and woven through the belt loops of the jeans were the finishing touch. Elissa decided she hated the woman on sight.

"I tried calling from the airport," the woman went on, handing Wade her fur jacket and lifting her hands to fluff the ends of her shoulder-length wind-blown hair. "But when there was no answer I decided to grab a cab and take a chance on finding you at home by the time I got here."

"We only arrived home a short time ago," Wade drawled meaningfully, his eyes going toward Elissa, who sat tightly coiled on the couch, her clenched hand out of sight behind the leather cushion.

"Oh, you have company!" Terry exclaimed, not sounding the least upset as she swung around to follow Wade's gaze. Something cool and calculating flashed briefly in the vividly made-up blue eyes which clashed with Elissa's, and then the mysterious Terry smiled. She was, perhaps, twenty-two or twenty-three.

"Terry," Wade began firmly, "I'd like you to meet Elissa Sheldon. My fiancée. Elissa, this is Terry Roberts…"

"Fiancée!" Terry turned her head to fling a laughing, disbelieving smile over her shoulder at Wade, who acknowledged it with a repressively lifted eyebrow.

"Fiancée," he repeated flatly, inviting no further comments from his guest.

"Terry Roberts," Elissa mused, striving to find a way of holding her own in this triangle. "Any relation to John R.?"

"Oh, yes," Terry nodded agreeably, moving leisurely over to stand beside the fire, her hands clasped behind her back, her mouth turned upward in sultry challenge. "The boss's daughter."

The daughter of the head of CompuDesign, Elissa thought, absorbing the implications as she forced an automatic smile. Here to see her good friend Wade Taggert, who was being groomed to take over Daddy's position.

"Fascinating. You've come a long way this evening. How fortunate for you Wade was home." Elissa

decided she could drawl her words just as challengingly as Terry Roberts could.

"Isn't it, though," Terry murmured brightly, flicking a glance across the room at Wade, who was moving slowly toward Elissa. If she hadn't known better,
Elissa thought suddenly, she would have interpreted
his action as almost protective, as if he would put
himself between her and Terry. "I would have had to
take a cab back to the airport and find a motel..."
Terry let the words taper off, making it obvious that
she now expected to spend the night at Wade's.

"Where's your luggage, Terry?" Wade's voice had
the edge of the whip in it, and Elissa could sense his
irritation as if it were a physical presence.

"The cabdriver left it on the steps out front," the
blond pouted vaguely, her inquisitive blue eyes going
back to Elissa's cool expression.

"Fine. I'll put it in the Jag," Wade declared forcefully, heading back toward the door.

Terry frowned ever so slightly. "Why put it in the
car?"

"Why do you think?" he shot back before disappearing out the door. "So that you'll have it when I
take you to the motel!"

For an instant after he left silence reigned in the
room, only the crackling of the fire daring to break
it. Terry's blue eyes held a contemptuous gleam that
made Elissa decide this was one young woman she
wasn't going to go out of her way to charm. She
would much prefer to strangle her!

"Fiancée. How interesting." Terry smiled chill-
ingly. "How long have you been engaged to Wade,
Elissa?"

"The engagement party is tomorrow evening."

"A very new arrangement, then?" Terry's smile dropped another couple of degrees.

"Very."

"I must congratulate you. You've worked rather quickly," Terry commended icily. "How long have you known Wade was in line for my father's position?"

"Since almost the first day he took over the Seattle office." Elissa smiled politely.

Terry began to amble around the room in a slinky, knowing fashion, pretending to examine the furniture, the books on the shelves, and other aspects of Wade's home. Elissa watched her as if she were watching a snake.

"Well, I can't fault your choice, Elissa," Terry murmured idly. "Although, personally, I wouldn't want any male who was on the rebound...." She glanced over her shoulder to see how this news settled. Elissa merely stared back at her.

"I turned him down two months ago, you see," Terry announced smoothly.

"Did you?" Elissa felt her old instincts regarding other people awaken. It was so easy to know what others wanted, she thought. So easy to know what they were thinking, how their minds worked. So easy to know when they lied....

Terry nodded, and Elissa could almost hear the plotting going on in the other woman's mind. "We had a fight," she began, pausing in front of one of the stark paintings and frowning at it. "He can be very possessive, you know," she added with a little disparaging gesture of her red-nailed fingers. "I lost my temper, and the next thing I knew he'd accepted this position in Seattle. I thought I'd give him time to miss me and then tell him all was forgiven..."

"What do you think of the painting, Terry?" Elissa whispered carefully, every sense alert.

"This thing?" Terry grimaced, nodding at the seascape. "I told him before he left California he should get rid of it. It doesn't do a thing for the rest of the furniture. I can't understand why he bought it in the first place!"

"Can't you?" Elissa breathed questioningly.

"I suppose he liked the artist personally and wanted to do him a favor or something," Terry said offhandedly. "I don't care. Whatever the reason, it's going to be gone as soon as I move in."

Elissa could have laughed if she weren't so close to tears. Terry didn't even know! Didn't she realize how much Wade was in that painting? What a little blond-brained fool! Whatever category Terry Roberts had occupied in Wade's life, it definitely hadn't been the long-lasting one!

"But you won't be moving in, Terry." Wade's voice came from where he stood lounging in the doorway behind the two women. "Not now, not ever. You've known from the beginning that you're nothing more to me than the daughter of the man for whom I work. And this little business of showing up on my doorstep in the middle of the night wouldn't have impressed John R. in the least." He walked into the room, shutting the door behind him.

Elissa shivered at the grim set of his face as he came forward to confront the sulky-mouthed blond. Didn't Terry have the sense to see she'd annoyed Wade Taggert?

"He knows me too well, Terry," Wade went on

calmly. "He would never buy the scene you're trying to arrange. He'd never believe I'd seduce you."

"Why not?" Terry demanded, a wave of spite clouding her throaty voice as the pout turned into a full-fledged glare. She suddenly appeared very, very young.

"Two reasons," Wade drawled. "One, by the time you get back home tomorrow night the news of my engagement will already have reached him; and two…"

Terry lifted her head challengingly, apparently not seeing anything she couldn't overcome in the first reason.

"And two," Wade repeated devastatingly, "he knows I want his job too damn much to risk messing around with his daughter!"

Elissa winced at the bluntness of his words. She couldn't blame the other woman for looking as if she were on the verge of tears. What female wants to be told a job is more important than she is? But even as the thought went through her mind, she realized Wade had invented reason number two on the spur of the moment. If he'd wanted Terry Roberts, he would have taken her. Wade took whatever he wanted in life. Hadn't he told her that this evening? And if he'd wanted Terry *and* her father's job, he would have gotten both. He'd simply have fought until everyone else surrendered.

But Terry bought reason number two, hook, line, and sinker. It made perfect sense to her, Elissa saw as she watched the little drama. Just as Terry had never realized in the time she'd known Wade that the paintings on his walls held a part of him, so she lacked any real understanding of the man's nature. She didn't know a real wolf when she saw one.

"Let's go, Terry," Wade growled. "In the car. Elissa, you can wait—"

"I'm coming with you," Elissa declared, rising unsteadily but determinedly to her feet. This was her one chance tonight, and she had to take it. There would be no hope at all for her if she sat meekly waiting for Wade to return and claim his bride-to-be. No hope at all for revenge....

"That's not necessary," Wade began, frowning heavily as he met her eyes across the room.

"Oh, but it is," she corrected gamely, essaying a smile. Her blue-green eyes glittered with her determination. "After all, we have a big day ahead of us tomorrow preparing for the party, don't we? I need some sleep, Wade. You can take me home." She started toward the door, ignoring the scowling blond and the rising thunder in Wade's eyes. Head high, she walked to the door and waited with a supreme assurance she was far from feeling for the other two to follow.

"Wade, this is ridiculous," Terry began. "There's no reason I can't stay here tonight—"

"Shut up, Terry."

Elissa could feel Wade's eyes on her as she led the way out into the cold night toward the car. But he said nothing, stuffing both women into the Jaguar with a complete lack of chivalry and sliding into the driver's seat to twist the key viciously in the ignition. He was furious, Elissa thought, and decided to take a few precautions.

"You can let me off first," she informed him coolly, not daring to glance at his stern profile.

"The hell I will," he retorted, slamming the car into gear.

"Please, Wade?" she tried, deliberately injecting into her tone, the soft pleading that she had discovered the night he had threatened to beat her. "I'm exhausted. It's been a frantic week, and I want to be halfway fresh for tomorrow evening. Everyone will be there…"

"Elissa, I want to talk to you," he began firmly. Both of them ignored Terry, who sat in the back seat and took in every word. Elissa could feel her lapping up the budding argument and hated the idea of the other woman's witnessing the scene. But there was no help for it. She had to get safely back to her apartment.

"Wade, we'll have all the time in the world to talk tomorrow after the party." Elissa put out a gentle hand to touch his sleeve, begging for his understanding. "I want to go home."

He was silent a moment, as if turning her words and her pleading over and over in his mind, and then she sensed his hesitation and knew she had won.

"All right, Elissa," he finally agreed, sounding resigned but not satisfied. "I'll take you home."

Elissa could feel Terry's air of excited triumph, but it didn't affect her at all. Wade would take Terry to a motel and leave her there. Elissa was as certain of that as she had ever been about anything in her life. Terry represented no danger and she never would. The danger between Elissa and Wade went deeper and held much more risk than a spoiled, flighty young woman's attempts to snag herself a husband.

Wade let Elissa go at the elevators in the lobby of the apartment building, his eyes reflecting his dissatisfaction with events but also his reluctant agreement to abide by her wishes.

"I have a feeling this is a mistake." He sighed ruefully, pulling her roughly into his arms. "Damn that little bubblehead! If it weren't for her..."

Elissa summoned a small teasing grin. "Are there a lot more like her trailing you around the country-side?"

"No, thank God! I'm going to wire her father in the morning and advise a severe..."

"Beating?" Elissa suggested demurely.

"A severe cutback in her allowance," Wade concluded smoothly. "Money is the surest way of controlling a spoiled little brat like Terry Roberts."

"But not me?" Elissa taunted lightly, grateful that he wasn't going to protest her decision to return to the apartment.

"No, not you," he murmured richly, lowering his head to kiss her quickly, almost harshly. "You require more subtle methods."

She had told Wade she needed sleep, Elissa thought several hours later as she lay awake in her bed and watched shadows on the ceiling. But sleep was a long time coming tonight. With a restless movement Elissa turned on her side, pounding the hapless pillow in an attempt to fluff it. This was the second sleepless night since she'd gotten involved with one Wade Taggert, she reminded herself grimly. But soon the man and all his arrogant, demanding ways would be behind her. Tomorrow night, she vowed for the thousandth time, she would put a fine and mighty end to the war game they had been playing.

Once more she tried to formulate the exact manner

in which she would announce to Wade that she had
no intention of marrying him and that he could take
his ring and his job and go jump in Lake Washington.
And once again it proved incredibly difficult to work
through the scene in her mind. Every time she tried,
memories of his paintings or the way he talked to her
or the way he kissed her kept interfering.

But he didn't love her, she thought furiously. A
man who loved her would never have accused her of
the things Wade Taggert had accused her of. He
would never have believed the worst of her. Damn it,
no one ever believed the worst of her!

But, then, Wade had never claimed to love her, had
he? Only to desire her.

But such desire, she thought, catching her breath in
the darkness. It was outside her experience. Did it
spring from the loneliness, the independence, and the
power she saw in his paintings? Did he really believe
she could assuage it for him?

No, she mustn't think along those lines. She had
her own role to play in the last act of the charade,
and it did not include falling in love with her tormentor.

Falling in love! Elissa could have wept then. And,
like sleepless nights, weeping was alien to her. Life
was much too comfortable and contented to make cry-
ing into her pillow necessary. And she could not,
must not, love a man who thought so little of her! He
had deserved being tricked into making the proposal,
and he was going to deserve having her walk out the
door laughing, the proposal thrown back at him. In
front of all his employees!

Desperately Elissa forced herself to consider that.
It would be the ultimate humiliation if she handed

him her resignation from CompuDesign and the ring in front of the entire staff.

It was an outrageous, horrifying thought, and it made Elissa sit straight up in bed. Would she have the nerve? Could she possibly cause a scene of that magnitude? Upset the entire staff? It was so utterly unlike her to even consider doing such a thing—regardless of the provocation!

But the past week had made Elissa uncomfortably aware of aspects of her nature she hadn't faced before. She had discovered a temper which could plot revenge on an undreamed-of scale. She had discovered a level of passion within herself she hadn't thought any man could arouse. She had been confronted with the notion that she might have been guilty of using her innate ability to charm for her own ends. She had found an element of excitement in life she hadn't ever expected to encounter in the real world. An excitement she had thought reserved for her flights of imagination in her paintings. And, above all, she had met a man who understood all of those things. He understood everything except the fact that she would never in a million years have tried to sleep her way up the ladder of success.

Elissa muttered a low, tense oath that would have done justice to a cowboy's and threw back the covers. She padded across the room and turned the painting which rested against the wall around so that the moonlight fell on it.

She had gone ahead and finished the small canvas because she had never intended to obey Wade's injunction to give it to him for a wedding gift. It didn't matter what she put into the painting, because he would never see the result.

But she would see it, Elissa thought sadly, despairingly. Even if she destroyed it, she would see it in her mind's eye for the rest of her life. Hopelessly she turned the acrylic creation back to the wall, knowing that what it revealed was something she would have to learn to live with. A legacy from the one period of disturbance and discomfort in an otherwise smooth and comfortable life.

But she was committed to her revenge, Elissa told herself grimly, walking over to the window and gazing unseeingly out at the city lights. What option did she have? She couldn't possibly marry a man who didn't love her and who had, from the beginning, thought her capable of a complete lack of scruples.

But what if he genuinely needed her? a small voice asked beguilingly. What if he truly wanted and needed her? Had pursued her because she was important to him even though he thought her capable of such awful things?

Elissa shook her head in self-anger. Who was she kidding? She was seeking an excuse, a reason for marrying a man she should despise. Why this powerful inner pull to reach out and accept what he offered? And how could she do that in good conscience? She had tricked him into offering marriage. She didn't want his ring, knowing it had not been freely given, that he had only upped the ante in order to stay in the game....

Elissa fumbled her way back to bed. It was all so horribly confusing, and time was running out so quickly....

None of the doubts or confusion disappeared in the night. Morning brought only a continuation of the endless debate going on in Elissa's head, a debate she thought might be affecting her very sanity. She spent the day listlessly doing housework in some ill-defined attempt to work out the frustration and fear. But it had little effect. Time ticked inevitably past, and all too soon she had to begin preparing for her grand evening scene.

The least she could do, Elissa decided with defiance and determination, was dress for the event. She pulled the glittering blue-green sheath out of the closet with a vicious gesture that nearly tore it. The action made her realize the state of her nerves, and she took several deep breaths before proceeding to dress.

The severely cut dress, bought a few months ago for a party which Elissa had changed her mind about attending, slithered down over her head, settling with well-cut precision around her slender curves. The long sleeves were close-fitting, and the plain deeply rounded collar set off the line of neck and throat to perfection. The color was an ideal foil for the dark red of her hair and it matched her eyes.

This was a night when she would need all the witchcraft Wade had accused her of having, Elissa decided, reaching into the closet for a pair of evening slippers that were little more than sandals on heels. She dug through her small collection of jewelry for the tiny gold earrings she liked and a discreet gold necklace. The hunt for the proper jewelry made her think of the ring Wade would be giving her tonight, and she grimaced in dismay.

A glance at the clock while she was brushing the shining mass of her hair drove home the information that time had indeed evaporated. It was four o'clock, and she had promised Wade she would be at his house by four-thirty. He had wanted to pick her up, she but had assured him that was a waste.

She didn't want to think about the real reason she needed her own car tonight.

At precisely four-thirty, Elissa stood on the steps of Wade's town house and prepared for the worst evening of her life. It took all her courage just to lift her hand to knock.

Almost as soon as she had done so, the door was pulled open and Wade was drinking in the sight of her. Almost literally drinking it in, Elissa thought dimly. The hunger and thirst in his eyes were living things that reached out to lap at her body and soul, threatening to take them both in one swallow.

"Elissa," he breathed, putting out a hand to encircle her neck and pull her over the threshold into his arms. "I thought you'd never get here!" He pinned her against him and bent to kiss the curve of her shoulder revealed by the round neck of the dress. His lips seemed to burn for a moment, and then he was gazing down into her eyes again.

"It's…it's just four-thirty. I'm on time," she protested tremulously. How was she going to do it? How was she going to exact her revenge? Now? Before the others arrived? Later, when it would be far more humiliating and dramatic? Elissa felt the panic begin to rise.

"How can you say you're on time when you should have been here this morning, waking up in my bed?" he demanded with a rough, uncertain humor that touched her.

"Speaking of which," she tried to say pertly, stepping aside so he could close the door behind her, "did you manage to get your dear acquaintance on a plane bound for California?''

"Beats me.'' Wade grinned, taking her hand and pulling her toward the kitchen, where bottles and quantities of food filled the counters. ''I stuck her in a motel by the airport last night, sent a wire off to John R. telling him where she was, and forgot about it.''

''Roberts won't, uh, believe you might truly have compromised her?'' Elissa asked dryly, staring at all the beautifully prepared trays of food.

''In my wire I made a point of mentioning my engagement,'' Wade admitted, stacking glasses. ''But even without that he would have had the sense to know whether to believe me or his daughter. He loves her, but he's not blind to her faults.''

''Fathers have been known to lose some of their rational view of life when presented with a situation involving a daughter.''

''Or a wife?'' he suggested, pausing in his task to trap her gaze with his own. ''Are you saying men aren't always rational about women in general?''

Elissa swallowed and tried to smile.

''You could be right, you know,'' Wade went on easily, pushing a pile of napkins into her hand. She remembered having done something similar to him when he'd appeared at her party the week before. The memory made her face burn. ''That's why I sent the telegram and mentioned my charming fiancée. Better to be safe than sorry.''

''And you do want his job,'' she shot back banteringly.

''Not badly enough to marry his daughter,'' Wade declared fervently. ''You can put those napkins on the table in the corner. I thought we'd scatter the food trays around the room.''

''Did you do all this?'' she asked in amazement, indicating all the trays.

''Now, what do you think? Do I look like every woman's dream of a man who's good in the kitchen? I ordered everything from caterer's. The stuff arrived a couple of hours ago.'' He chuckled, picking up one of the trays.

''You may not be an old hand in the kitchen, but you seem to know the easiest way to manage a cocktail party,'' Elissa commented, following him obediently around the living room with her piles of napkins.

''I've done a certain amount of entertaining. To an extent, it's almost a necessity in business.'' He shrugged. ''When I have you to act as hostess, however, my reputation as a giver of good parties should skyrocket!''

Elissa felt her palms moisten as five o'clock approached. Perhaps she should simply get it over with now before anyone arrived. She tried to imagine telling Wade just then that she wasn't going through with the marriage and that he could have her damn job, too. A realistic picture failed to materialize in her mind.

By the time the first guests began arriving, Elissa was a nervous wreck. It was all she could do to maintain a semblance of normality, although no one seemed to notice her discomfort as they came through the door. They were all too concerned about being at a party given by the boss, she thought after a moment. His invitation to the staff had, after all, been tantamount to a command. It was no wonder virtually everyone was showing up—and on time! Elissa began to experience a touch of hysteria. No one but Marie knew the reason for the party yet. His announcement was going to be a surprise, Wade had told her.

Some familiar instinct took over as Elissa automatically began chatting with new arrivals, putting them at ease. It gave her a chance to recover her failing nerve as the soothing patter covered the lack of enthusiasm she knew she would be projecting if anyone cared to look beneath the surface.

But no one ever looked that deep except Wade, and he made no mention of Elissa's unease. Perhaps he hadn't notice it. He had his hands full, pouring drinks and playing host. A difficult role for a wolf, Elissa thought, torn between laughter and despair. The man would be much better off with a wife to help him through the difficulties of business socializing.

And all she had to do was keep her mouth shut and she could be that wife. No, Elissa thought again and again. She would not marry a man who thought her so unprincipled!

Then what was she going to do? She would have to act soon. It was going on six o'clock, and Wade would surely make his announcement at any moment while the crowd was at its peak....

Even as the thought came into her head she saw Wade catch her eye from the other side of the room and grin. The look on his face stopped her in her tracks. He was going to do it now. She knew it. God help her, what was she going to do about it? This was the moment. The moment all her plans had been aiming toward. Across the room Marie smiled knowingly.

Heart pounding, Elissa watched Wade cheerfully

call for everyone's attention. He got it immediately, naturally; he was the boss.

"There is an ulterior motive for the party this evening," Wade began as soon as the room had fallen silent. Very carefully Elissa began edging her way toward him. She had never been so torn or terrified in her life. She had to act. She had to!

Her mind whirling, she listened to him explain the reason for the occasion and heard the combined gasp of amazement from the crowd as he told them he was announcing his engagement to Elissa Sheldon.

And then the cries of congratulations and surprise were pouring over her as she was helped along her way to stand beside Wade.

"No wonder she didn't get the promotion!" she heard someone mutter speculatively nearby. "It would have looked pretty bad for Wade to promote her one week and get engaged to her the next. People would have talked..."

"Not about Elissa," another voice chimed in with great certainty.

"No, not about Elissa," the first speaker agreed. "But Wade might have thought they would. After all, he doesn't know her like we do..."

The words were a kind of balm to Elissa's ears, and she wondered if Wade had heard them. She doubted it. Even if he had, he would only have laughed.

She went forward more steadily now, accepting the hand held out to her and letting him pull her close to his side. He was smiling, warmly, intimately, hungrily, down into her eyes, and she was abruptly aware that he had the ring box in his other hand.

"My sweet witch," he whispered under cover of

the laughter and cheers as he slipped the ring on her finger. And then he kissed her lightly, gently.

In that moment the one unwavering fact which stuck out in Elissa's thoughts wasn't that her moment of revenge had arrived. It was that she had tricked him into doing this. Tricked him into marriage when he had only wanted to toy with her for a time. When all he desired was a woman who could appease the loneliness of a wolf. A woman who could put some softness into a life of near-constant battle.

Elissa hesitated and was lost. When she opened her eyes as he lifted his mouth from hers, the first thing she saw was the seascape on the wall behind him, and she finally admitted the truth. She loved him. She loved this man who had turned her comfortable world upside down and seen aspects of her no one else knew existed. She loved a man she had tricked into marriage.

For Elissa the rest of the evening went by in a whirl of incomprehensible sounds, conversations, and laughter. A laughter which she could not share in her heart. This was her engagement party, and she had never been more miserable in her life.

The party lasted much too long. It was supposed to be over by seven, but the last of the guests hung around until eight. Even as she watched them out the door, Elissa realized she would rather they stayed. Anything to postpone the coming confrontation with her fiancé. For sometime during the course of the evening it had become painfully clear to Elissa what needed to be said. She could not humiliate the man she loved by throwing his proposal back in his face in front of his guests, and she could not marry a man she had deceived in making that proposal in the first place.

"I thought," Wade murmured softly, turning to rake her with his hungry glance as he closed the door on the last of his guests, "that I'd never get you to myself! Come here and let me nibble on you for a while!"

Elissa stood perfectly still, her hands clasped in front of her, and forced herself to say the words which must be said.

"Wade, I must talk to you."

He loosened his tie and opened the collar of his shirt, his gaze never leaving her tense face. The blue-green gems of her eyes seemed huge and strangely lit, holding his full attention.

"We'll talk, Elissa," he promised in a slow, thrilling tone that sent shivers through her. "I know there are things which must be clear between us. But not yet. Not until I've made you mine." He started forward slowly. "Can you understand that, honey? Can you understand how it is for a man who must know his woman accepts his claim? Come close, Elissa, and let me hold you. Let me show you what I've been aching to show you since the day I first saw you...."

"You can't put me off tonight, Wade." She smiled sadly. "You must listen to me, and then..."

"Then what, Elissa?" he prompted, halting a few feet away and watching her intently.

"Then you can do as you want."

"Take what I want?"

She drew a gulping breath. "Yes."

"All right, tell me what it is that's put the fear in your eyes tonight, little witch. Yes, I've seen it," he went on heavily. "Did you think you could hide such a thing from me? But I have the cure for it, sweetheart..."

"Wade! Will you stop trying to seduce me and listen to what I have to say?" She almost screamed the words at him, and then she flushed, alarmed at her lack of control. "I tricked you into this, Wade! Don't you realize that? I planned it all along. I wanted you to pay for what you'd done by denying me that promotion because you thought I was sleeping with Martin Randolph!"

She drew a deep breath and plunged on. Once stated, the words wouldn't be halted. "I got lucky, or so I thought, when it turned out you wanted me enough to meet the offer you thought I was getting from Dean Norwood. I lied about that. He never offered to marry me. Do you realize what I'm saying? I tricked you. I had plans for tonight, plans you never knew about. I was going to wait until the moment you put the ring on my finger, and then I was going to take it off and fling at your feet and tell you to go to hell along with the stupid job possibilities you were holding out as a lure!"

Elissa paused for another gulp of air. "It was going to be a grand, thoroughly humiliating scene, you understand. One that would tear a wide strip out of your ego and teach you a lesson about jumping to conclusions. And the whole thing blew up in my face when I realized I loved you."

She turned away to stare into the fire he had built earlier, supremely conscious of his massive presence behind her but unable to meet the glittering look which had sprung alive in his eyes.

"I'll go with you to Victoria, Wade, if that's what you want. But I'll go as your woman, not your wife.

I couldn't bear to have you marry me because that was the only way you thought you could get me,'' she breathed in a hushed voice. There. She had done all she could to repair the damage she had wrought. It was in Wade's hands now. Whatever he decided would be binding. At least she would have the miserable satisfaction of knowing she had been completely honest at last.

''And just who,'' he grated in measured, heart-jolting tones behind her, ''do you think was tricking whom?''

Chapter 12

"You've been outclassed, outmaneuvered, and out-tricked every step of the way, my lovely. Ever since I walked into that damn party of yours and was forced to realize I'd made the biggest mistake of my life!"

Elissa whirled, reacting as much to the raw, rasping pain in his voice as to the words themselves. "Wade! What are you saying?" she gasped, lifting wide, uncomprehending eyes to meet the unfathomable gray depths of his gaze. Her heart had begun to pound with an incredulous hope.

"I think," Wade went on judiciously, jamming his hands into his pockets and facing her, feet slightly spread as if he would brace himself, "that I knew before I arrived at the party that I'd made a hell of a miscalculation. I think I knew it the moment I hit you with my accusation that Friday afternoon when I told you I wasn't giving you the job. But I had been so blinded by sheer, raving jealousy when I'd seen you meet Randolph after work that all I could think of was that you must be seeing him on the sly. I put myself in Randolph's place, you see," Wade went on with a wry twist of his hard mouth. "I knew if I managed to get you to meet me after work there wouldn't be a damned platonic thing about it!"

"Wade!" Elissa's sea-colored eyes began to glow. She took a small step toward him but stopped when he lifted a hand to ward her off.

"No, honey, you'd better hear it all first. You started it!" He seemed to gather himself for his next words. "So, where was I? Oh, yes. Standing in your doorway staring into a room full of people there to celebrate June Randolph's birthday. Exactly as you had claimed. I had been a first-class jealous fool and I'd blown everything. There was nothing for it but to keep going. I couldn't think of anything else to do. I spent the whole time at the party trying to figure a way to recover to another, more flexible position, and I couldn't think of one. If I backed down and admitted I'd made a mistake, you'd laugh in my face and probably never speak to me again."

Wade shook his head, running his fingers through his hair in a gesture of male disgust. "On the other hand, I was learning a lot about you in a hurry I saw those paintings on your wall, saw the books in your bedroom, and, most of all, I saw the satisfaction in your eyes when you thought you'd won. It occurred to me that the best, perhaps the only way to keep you on my hook was to make you think victory wasn't going to be all that easy."

"And everything had always been so easy for me?" Elissa smiled, laughter warming her eyes.

"Something like that," he admitted ruefully, slanting her a quick, wry glance. "I could see the lack of challenge in your life, but I could also see the willingness to take on a challenge in your eyes and in your paintings. I decided to give you a toy to play with long enough to whet your appetite."

"A witch's toy?" she whispered happily.

"Yes."

"Oh, Wade," she breathed joyously. Still neither of them moved. "Why didn't you tell me?"

"I was going to try to explain everything last night. I kept asking if you wanted to talk about our future, if you'll recall, but you kept shying away from it. I wasn't sure what to do, but I decided the most straightforward approach was probably the best under the circumstances...."

"So you were going to bring me back here and make love to me and then confess all?" she demanded, laughter bubbling up inside.

"In that order," he admitted. "When that didn't pan out, I decided to try it again tonight. It was becoming increasingly important to make love to you, lady witch," he growled. "I had tried to avoid it while I was securing you in the net."

"Why?"

"Because I knew that once I had you would realize the full extent of your power over me. I needed to keep you tantalized, curious, off balance, and, perhaps, looking for revenge..."

"You knew? You knew I was plotting terrible things?"

"I knew I'd aroused your temper as well as your interest." He smiled bleakly. "It seemed likely you'd go looking for a bit of your own back if there was a way to get it. But I also knew you were coming to know me better, and I started banking on the fact that you were basically too gentle, too warmhearted, to send me back to my paintings where I belong. You thought I'd made things easy for your plans of revenge when I agreed to marry you, but the truth is, as far as I was concerned, you fell into my palm like a ripe plum!''

"But I tricked you that night you came back from California! I deliberately brought up the subject of Dean Norwood!''

"As I said, I got lucky. All I was aiming for was to get you to stop seeing him. I figured if I made love to you enough to make you realize I was a much more interesting proposition…''

"You never did intend to spend the night in my bed!'' She remembered how he had refused to let her completely undress him.

"I didn't intend to, but I'm not sure I could have avoided it.'' He grinned, starting toward her finally and putting his hands on her shoulders. "But when marriage came into the matter I was suddenly aware of the fact that you had just given me several free moves ahead in our game. All I had to do was keep pushing along the lines you'd already started.''

"Didn't you wonder why I was agreeing to the marriage?'' Elissa whispered, standing quietly under his hands.

"I thought you probably had your own schemes going, but so long as they coincided with mine…'' He left the sentence unfinished.

"You figured you'd just hang on until everyone else gave up?'' she charged, laughing up at him with love.

"Yes!" The single word was ground out with so much grim determination that Elissa believed him.

"What would you have done, Wade Taggert," she demanded boldly, "if I'd gone through with my own plans for this evening? If I'd really hurled the ring back in your face?"

"Beaten you in front of the entire assembled staff of CompuDesign," he retorted unhesitatingly.

Elissa tilted her head to one side and studied the innate arrogance and unshielded iron will in his face and shook her head. "You really mean that, don't you?"

His voice dropped to a new, thick, and almost unsteady pitch as he pulled her closer. "I love you. I couldn't have let you walk out of my life. Not when I was so close to…"

Elissa finished the sentence for him with a tiny, bantering grin. "Not when you were so close to winning?"

"I'm glad you understand me so well. It's going to make life much simpler in some ways," he muttered on a low groan of need. His hands slipped along her shoulders, sliding warmly up her throat to entwine themselves in her chair, and he lowered his head to take her lips.

"Do you really love me?" he asked on a thin thread of steel and anguish.

"Yes." Elissa saw the hunger in his eyes, the wolf's hunger which was more than an appetite. It was a fundamental desire and need and wish and longing. And it was elaborately laced with love. Why hadn't she seen that from the beginning? "I love you, Wade, more than anything else on earth!"

"Or off it?" he charged just before his mouth touched hers.

"Or off it." She heard the deep sigh of pleasure, and then he was kissing her, a soft seal on their love. A binding, chaining, magical kiss that she would never forget. She felt the large hands in her hair tighten and instinctively moved closer to him.

And the doorbell sounded.

"Damn it to hell!" Wade muttered, not lifting his lips from hers. Elissa's eyes flew open, and she was looking directly into rueful gray pools of sheer masculine frustration. She wanted to laugh and knew the humor must be gleaming in her own gaze.

"Probably only a guest who forgot something," she whispered encouragingly.

"It must be that. I couldn't be so unlucky two nights in a row!" He groaned, reluctantly setting her back from him as the bell sounded yet again. An imperious, demanding, commanding summons that made Elissa lift a questioning eyebrow as Wade strode almost angrily to the door.

She saw the incredulous expression on Wade's face before she saw the man standing at the door.

"What the hell are you doing here?" Wade's voice held a new note which Elissa's interested ears picked up at once. The words were blunt enough, but they were tinged with respect.

"Am I too late for the party?" The stranger's voice was deep and gruff, and it suited him very well, Elissa decided as he stepped into the room. A big man, almost as big as Wade, he looked to be in his early sixties, and he also looked, she thought, like an older version of Wade. Not that the two men were similar physically. This man's hair was a rapidly thinning gray and the eyes were blue, not pools of ice and silver. No, the resemblance was more primitive and fundamental than a blood bond. There was the same air of ruthlessness, the same arrogance, the same independence. Another lone wolf. Elissa remembered where she'd seen eyes of that particular shade of blue.

Wade turned toward Elissa, and she could see the surprise still in his face.

"Elissa," he began very carefully, precisely, "may I present John R. Roberts, founder and head of CompuDesign? Our boss."

Elissa smiled straight into the blue eyes so like his daughter's and came forward with welcome and laughing grace. "I have always wondered," she remarked, lips curved dazzlingly, "what the *R* stood for!"

Twenty-four hours later Elissa sat in the middle of a huge four-poster bed which looked as if it had come from a seventeenth-century castle and waited for her husband to emerge from the bath. She fluffed the huge pillows and old-fashioned quilts which surrounded her and leaned back to study the canopy for a moment. She felt like a queen, she decided, her gaze moving on to enjoy the other antique furnishings. This could have easily been a room in a castle on another world for all the resemblance it bore to a modern bedroom. One could almost imagine a dragon standing guard at the gate and a strange moon outside the window. A good room in which to embark on an adventure. The crackle of a fire on the hearth was warming.

Elissa turned toward the sound of the opening bathroom door, her blue-green eyes full of dreams. Wade

stood there, a towel wrapped carelessly around his
lean waist, his dark hair damp from the shower. The
leaping gray gaze raked possessively, lovingly, over
the outline of his wife who had the sheet tucked up
to her chin, and he grinned.

"You look right at home. A witch in her castle.
They still had the sense to worry about witches in the
seventeenth century, you know," he told her.

The firelight gleamed on his powerful, smoothly
muscled body as he came toward her, turning off the
lights behind him. But the flames on the hearth were
no warmer than the ones in the silvery eyes. He
stopped beside the high bed, watchful and clearly
filled with anticipation.

"Did you bring my wedding present?" he demanded softly.

"Yes, Wade." She smiled, reaching for the small
canvas she had propped beside the bed. "Did you
remember mine?"

He said nothing, turning aside for a moment to pull
a square, flat package from the luggage at the foot of
the bed. Silently he handed it to her, accepting his
present from her with an eagerness that touched her
heart.

For a moment they both examined their gifts in the
firelight. When they raised their eyes to meet each
other's gaze, there was little need of speech. The
paintings said it all.

Elissa looked again at the harsh, haunting outlines
of the painting Wade had commissioned for her. The
isolation and aloofness were still inherent qualities in
the work, but there was a new element. There were
figures in this painting. A woman sat high on a rock
overlooking the sea, and her bare arm rested lovingly

on the wolf at her side. She looked totally unafraid of the vicious creature beside her, and her red hair shone in the light of the sun. There was no reason for the woman to fear the beast, Elissa knew. The ruthlessness of the wolf was aimed at the outside world. The woman was well protected.

"I knew when I saw the beginnings of this the night I came to talk about the party arrangements that I couldn't lose in the end," Wade finally whispered deeply, glancing up again from his present. Elissa knew what he saw on the canvas in his hands. A fantasy castle standing on a peak in a scene from another planet. Unfamiliar twin moons threw unearthly light on a landscape full of strange beings and stranger flowers. On the parapet of the castle a woman waited for the black-and-silver wolf who was climbing the tumbling stairs to her side. The wolf looked as potentially lethal as the one in Wade's painting, but he carried a flower in his jaws.

"Well, witch" —Wade smiled with a thrilling, warning timber in his words as he placed the two paintings carefully beside the bed—"your wolf has waited long enough to know all of your magic." He pulled back the covers, letting the towel fall to the floor, and slid into the warm bed, reaching out to pull her close.

Elissa's eyes gleamed with love as she absorbed the unselfconscious male beauty of him. "Don't blame me for having to wait until tonight. *I* didn't have people dropping in at unexpected moments in my apartment!"

"Don't remind me!" He grimaced, his hand running over her modest, old-fashioned nightgown with its demure collar and ruffles and lace. "If it had been anyone besides John R. last night, I would have slammed the door in his face. I couldn't think of an excuse to send him to a motel!''

"I thought it was sweet of him to come all the way up from California to attend your engagement party and act as your best man.''

"Honey, John R. Roberts is not a sweet man, I can guarantee you that much!'' Wade grinned, his fingers toying lovingly with the ribbons at her throat. "He was there because he wanted to know what kind of woman had managed to charm his handpicked heir apparent into marriage. He wanted to see if you were going to be an asset to the firm, nothing more!''

"Do you think I passed inspection?'' She giggled, feeling the ribbons come undone beneath his hands.

"You charmed the socks off him, just like you do everyone else you decide to entrance and enchant, and you know it!''

"Would you still have married me even if John R. hadn't approved?'' she whispered, feeling the heated touch of his fingers on her bare skin above the curve of her breast.

"I would have married you,'' he grated with sudden harsh intensity, his eyes darkening, "if all the dragons in the universe had stood in the way! My career, John R.'s approval, nothing in the world matters to me as much as you, my lady witch. I love you with the kind of love I didn't know existed until I set eyes on you. I would have done anything, fought anyone, played any game, in order to carry off my prize!''

Elissa's breath quickened at the fierceness in him, and she knew he meant every word. Then he lowered his lips to the hollow of her throat, and her lashes fluttered shut with the force of her clamoring emotions.

"I love you, Wade!"

"Not half as much as I love you, lady wife!" His voice was a husky, muffled growl against her skin as his lips followed the ever bolder path of his fingers.

Elissa reached out to first caress and then cling lovingly to the hard leanness of him, exulting in the strength beneath her questing hands. She moaned softly, luxuriously, as he slipped the nightgown off completely and leaned across to drop burning, stinging, entrancing kisses over every inch of her skin from throat to waist.

"Do you know how intoxicating it is," he grated roughly, hungrily, "to own full and exclusive rights to a genuine witch?" He raised himself to settle her more tightly against him, and the plundering, searching fingers of his hand wandered down below her waist, finding her intimate warmth.

Elissa shivered as she felt his nails grate roughly and then soothingly over her thighs, and her legs shifted languidly as her body arched instinctively. She heard his groan of desire and need as she sought the sensitive masculine nipples with her tongue and teeth and felt his rising passion.

His lips burned for a moment at her waist, and then he nipped the vulnerable flesh of her thigh, eliciting a tremor in her that seemed to increase his own passion by great bounds. His lovemaking grew increasingly demanding, inflamed.

"My God!" he breathed, "I don't think I can wait any longer for you, my little love. You pull me into your spells so quickly..."

"Love me, Wade," she gasped, clutching fiercely to him to draw him closer. "I need you so much!"

She felt him shift his weight, lowering himself onto her with urgency and power. Her legs were forced gently apart, making a place for him that he assumed with the authority and arrogance of a conqueror who loves the land he takes.

Elissa felt her body surrendering, enveloping, charming even as Wade claimed his witch with an uncompromising mastery. She gasped at the loving assault, wrapping her arms around his neck and holding him as close as it was possible for a man and a woman to be.

The rhythm and strength of Wade's lovemaking launched them into a glittering galaxy where Elissa viewed at first hand the stars and planets in her paintings. She cried out with the wonder of it and heard his wolfish growl of response. For an indefinable number of light-years they raced and soared through the universe and then, with shattering intensity, found themselves caught in the heart of an exploding sun. Slowly, slowly, they returned to earth, riding the last of the magic spell back into the witch's bedroom in the inn on the tip of Vancouver Island.

For a long time Wade simply held her close against him, his head buried in the pillow beside her as his body recuperated with long, full breaths. Elissa was content to curl into his heat and contemplate the wonder of being married to Wade Taggert. Eventually she felt him stir. The gray eyes opened and met hers.

"In the beginning," he told her finally, smilingly, "I thought I could handle your charms and spells, even when I found myself trapped in them. Now I realize I was only fooling myself. I may have caught you in my net, witch, but I'm in there with you. Promise me you'll never want to escape. I could never let you go!''

Elissa's full lips shaped into a warm, dazzling smile, her eyes full of reassurance and promise for the future. ''You're not really a wolf, you know,'' she teased.

''No?'' One black brow lifted interrogatingly.

''No. You're a sorcerer who uses the shape of a wolf because it suits your personality. But your spells are every bit as powerful as you claim mine are. And I am as thoroughly enmeshed in your magic net as it's possible for a woman to be. I would never leave, Wade. You make the magic and fantasy in my life real,'' she concluded simply.

''And to think,'' he murmured, his hand moving possessively across her bare skin, delighting in the texture of her, ''that there was a time when I didn't believe in witches!''

There was a moment of contented, satisfied silence, and then the gray eyes began to gleam with a warning look Elissa recognized only too well.

''Wade?''

''Just thinking, honey.''

''About what?'' she prompted suspiciously.

''About what you said on the ferry coming over to Victoria. That business about quitting your job and going to work somewhere else because you can't abide working for a tyrant.''

''Oh, that.'' She smiled serenely.

''That. I have some arguments to offer on the other side of the issue,'' he began purposefully, his fingers beginning to trace a more detailed pattern on her skin.

"You just want me to stay at CompuDesign so that you'll have me under your thumb all day long!"

He contrived to look hurt. "It's not that. It's only that I don't like the idea of you using your charms on some poor unsuspecting employer in order to land a fabulous new job."

"You're on a campaign to protect the employers of this world from the likes of me?" she enquired interestedly.

"My civic duty."

"Well, I'll listen to your arguments," she agreed generously. "But I can guarantee they won't change my mind."

"My arguments," he warned deeply, pulling her close, "aren't based on reason."

"No?"

"No," he assured her, lowering his mouth until he was a heartbeat away from her lips. The gleam in his eyes had erupted into flames. "They're based on magic, you see. Much more effective."

"For someone who once didn't believe in witches, you're learning fast." Elissa felt her pulse begin to throb and the excitement begin to build again.

"A wolf is a very practical creature. He uses whatever works. And against a witch the only weapon is magic."

And he proceeded to demonstrate.

* * * * *

AFFAIR OF HONOR

For Edna and Louis—
Edna because she always reads each book
and says nice things, and Louis because he
always says nice things even though he doesn't
read the books. And because I love them both.

Chapter 1

"**D**on't stop now. This is just getting interesting."

The voice out of the darkness was as cool and deadly as the sound of a revolver being cocked. It has precisely the same effect on Brenna Llewellyn. She froze, one leg already swung over the sill of the window. She was trapped.

Fear-induced adrenaline surged into her bloodstream as she stared, wide-eyed, into the thick shadows of the bedroom she had been attempting to enter through the open window.

The price of a little impetuosity, she thought with fleeting hysteria. *My life.* Even as the words floated through her brain she was making the decision to flee. In such a situation there was little to lose. She had apparently surprised a thief or perhaps someone who had been using the deserted Lake Tahoe cabin as a hideout. Someone who would not particularly want any witnesses.

"No, I wouldn't try it if I were you," drawled the dangerous, darkly timbred masculine voice. "It's too late to change your mind."

Brenna's fingers clenched on the windowsill, knowing he was right. She was an easy target outlined against the moonlit sky behind her. By the time she could scramble back outside, the man concealed in the bedroom's shadows would be able to get off a shot. Assuming he was armed, of course, which was a perfectly reasonable assumption given the circumstances. Knuckles whitening under the strain, Brenna sat very still, straddling the window frame. She had to think. Panic would only hasten a disastrous ending.

"Look," she tried in a taut but amazingly quiet tone, "I haven't seen your face yet. There's no way I can identify you. Just let me go back the way I came and I give you my word of honor I won't tell a soul you're here."

"Your word of honor," mused the deep voice. Brenna winced at the amused sarcasm. "An interesting concept for a cat burglar."

There was a subtle flicker in the depths of the shadows, and Brenna caught her breath with sharp fear as her captor moved into a shaft of moonlight. "No, please…!"

It was too late. The silver beams streaming in the window behind her fell across the man who had halted her with his voice. Brenna swallowed tightly, her heart pounding with fear and the effort to control it. He was barefoot and naked above the waist, wearing only a pair of close-fitting black denim jeans. As he moved into view he lowered the weapon in his hands with a frighteningly casual motion that spoke of his utter familiarity with it. It was a bow and arrow.

Brenna, who had been preparing herself for the sight of a gun in his fist, was momentarily stunned by the unexpectedness of the primitive weapon.

"My God," she breathed. What had she stumbled into tonight?

"You might as well come all the way inside," the man ordered in a gentle voice that didn't fool Brenna for an instant. "You can't straddle that particular fence forever."

"Please, this is all a mistake..."

"I'll bet it is," he murmured, coming toward her with a deliberate, gliding movement that covered the distance between them much too quickly. "Life has a nasty way of making sure we pay for our mistakes. Haven't you learned that lesson yet in your profession of cat burglary?"

He reached out, setting aside the curving bow and the wicked-looking arrow without once taking his eyes off his victim. If she was ever going to have a chance, Brenna thought wildly, this was undoubtedly it.

With a frantic rush of tensed muscles, she twisted, trying to throw herself back out the window. But it was too late. A hand that felt like a manacle closed around her wrist and she was abruptly yanked over the sill and into the dark bedroom. Even as she stumbled and barely found her balance the man extended his free hand and flipped on the light switch.

Damn it, she wasn't going to give up without a fight, Brenna decided fiercely as her eyes locked with a pair of unbelievably cool gray ones. Something about the icy silver in that gaze fed the instinctive response of her body as she swung her foot in an arching kick and simultaneously went for his face with her nails. The cool silver told her this man was at home with the prospect of violence.

And in the next tempestuous moments, that gave him a distinct advantage. Before she had time to assimilate what had happened, Brenna found herself flat on her back, lying on a braided rug that had done little to cushion the impact of her fall. She was anchored beneath the unrelenting weight of a lean, masculine body that held her with ease. Shutting her eyes reflexively, Brenna gasped for the breath that had been partially knocked out of her.

"Damn you," she managed to hiss defiantly as he calmly caught her wrists in one of his fists and pinned them over her head. Then he knelt across her hips, a leg on either side of her body, and smoothly, efficiently began to run one hand over her.

Panic of another sort flared to life, and Brenna's body went rigid beneath his touch. "I swear to God if you rape me I'll see you hunted to the ends of the earth," she vowed, fury battling with fear.

"Relax," he growled. "I'm just trying to find out how lady cats are equipping themselves on the job these days."

Brenna stared up at him, confused. Then, through the haze of her terror, she realized that the touch of his hand was brisk and entirely impersonal as it moved across her red cotton knit pullover and jeans. Belatedly it dawned on her that he was searching for concealed weapons.

"I'm...I'm not armed," she managed, having to pause once in the middle of the short sentence in order to moisten her dry lips. "For God's sake, I'm not a burglar!'' Instantly she regretted that confession. If he were a criminal hiding out here in the cabin, perhaps he would be more inclined to treat her leniently if he thought she was also on the wrong side of the law.

"Could have fooled me,'' he announced almost cheerfully, completing his search of her slender form and releasing her wrists. He continued to kneel astride her hips as he straightened and began to eye his captive in more detail. ''Most of the people I've met who make a habit of crawling in through other folks' windows in the middle of the night have what are usually termed larcenous tendencies.''

"Then you must hang out with a slightly different crowd than the one I run around with! I was not crawling through someone else's window,'' she added caustically, finding a heretofore undiscovered sense of nerve. "I was crawling through my own!''

One tawny brow lifted quellingly above one silvery eye. "I'm sure you've heard the old saying that possession is nine-tenths of the law. And as I happen to be in possession of these premises at the moment...'' He let the sentence trail off meaningfully, waiting for her reaction.

"Illegally in possession!'' she reminded him, more of her courage returning as she sensed some of the danger seeping out of the situation. She didn't know why her instincts told her things were looking more hopeful. After all, he was still pinning her to the rug, and the way he'd aimed that arrow at her earlier would probably give her nightmares for months. But there was a sort of calm *professionalism* about the man that made her think she wasn't dealing with an outright lunatic. At least he didn't appear to be the sort who was going to panic and kill her out of hand. That last thought reinforced her budding hope.

Looking down at her, he shook his head once in mock wonderment. "Illegally in possession," he repeated. "Imagine the world having come to the point where thieves in the night use phrases like that."

"Are you denying it?" she charged tightly.

"Oh, yes, I'm denying it. Want to see my lease?"

Brenna's amber eyes went very wide as she absorbed the implications of that casually dropped bombshell. "Your lease!"

"For three months beginning two weeks ago on the first of June," he told her easily, rising lithely to his feet and reaching down to grasp her wrist.

If there is a trauma as severe as facing danger, it is the horror of having thoroughly embarrassed oneself, Brenna reflected. In a very painful silence she allowed him to pull her to her feet.

"I think," she finally began very carefully, "there may have been some mistake."

"As I mentioned earlier," he drawled softly, watching her tense face, "mistakes tend to be paid for, one way or another."

Mutely she stared up at him, yanking her chaotic thoughts back into line with an effort of will. Surely she couldn't have clambered through the wrong window! But all the evidence was beginning to point to that, she realized grimly as she tore her gaze away from the silver-eyed man and hastily scanned the very lived-in looking bedroom.

The rumpled bed in which he had apparently been sleeping was a tumble of white sheets and patchwork quilt. The closet door stood open, revealing a collection of clothing that could only have belonged to a man. On the floor stood a pair of expensive-looking leather boots in an Italian design and a couple of pairs of casual shoes. Papers, books, and some magazines filled a small bookcase in one corner.

Brenna drew a long breath as she jerked her gaze away from the interior of the rustically designed bedroom and back to the man who was claiming possession. He was waiting, mouth smiling faintly at the corners as he watched the expressions flit across her features.

As she met his eyes once more, it struck Brenna that the faint edging of amusement around his hard mouth was enormously reassuring. This was not a man who would smile while still contemplating violence. She had the distinct impression that he could be ruthless and she'd had ample evidence that he could be dangerous when provoked, but he wasn't a nut, in spite of that bow and arrow sitting across the room.

Her nerves began to settle down and she raked an assessing glance over the man in front of her. He was about half a foot taller than she was, which made him nearly six feet. A rough estimate of the lines of experience that bracketed his hard mouth and narrowed gray eyes made Brenna think he was somewhere in his late thirties, perhaps thirty-seven or thirty-eight.

There was a sprinkling of silver at the temples of the tawny brown hair, which confirmed her age estimate. The hair itself was thick, cut a little too short for her taste, and was, at the moment, rather rakishly tousled. Only to be expected, she thought wryly, given the fact that she had clearly just gotten him out of bed.

There was nothing particularly handsome about the

strong contours of his face, but the innate self-reliance and authority stamped there were oddly compelling. The silvery eyes were edged by lashes a shade or two darker than his hair. There was a hawklike quality to the forceful nose and a rough-hewn look to the aggressive chin and the taut line of his high cheekbones.

Against her will, Brenna found herself aware of the expanse of smoothly muscled, bronzed male chest with its covering of curling tawny hairs. The low-riding black denim jeans sheathed a lean, boldly masculine frame that promised strength and grace.

For some reason she remembered how he had looked stepping into the moonlight, the bow and arrow in his strong, thoroughly competent hands. Calm, in command of himself and the situation; a true professional in the ultimate sense of the word. She had no idea what, exactly, he was professional *at*, but it was a cinch he would have been totally out of place at one of the college faculty meetings she was obliged to attend during the academic year.

She knew she was getting the same scrutiny in return and endured it with a sort of wry disdain. The bittersweet-chocolate-colored hair that fell to the middle of her back had come free of the clip at the nape of her neck and hung now in tangled disarray. It framed a face that had been alternately described as interesting and appealing but never beautiful. Wide, faintly slanted eyes of an amber-brown shade reflected intelligence and knew how to laugh when the occasion warranted laughter. A mouth that smiled easily was counterbalanced by the firm angles of her nose and jaw.

The red cotton knit pullover fit sleekly down over her slender body, clinging a little too closely to the small, unconfined breasts. Brenna shifted with a self-consciousness that annoyed her as she recalled the fact that she had dressed for the drive to Tahoe on the assumption that she would not be seeing anyone. Her jeans were snug and faded from numerous washings, and the moccasins on her feet were worn and comfortable.

At the age of twenty-nine, she ought to show more self-confidence in a trying situation, Brenna told herself. After all, she was now a faculty member of the philosophy department at a small but respected college. But she didn't feel particularly self-confident tonight. It had been a trying week in general, and this evening's fiasco was a fitting end to it.

"I'm sorry about this," she began with an attempt at decisiveness. "I appear to have crawled in through the wrong window." She lifted her chin at his mocking speculation. "I have a lease, too," she pointed out coolly. "It's the owner's fault for having booked two of us into the same cabin for the summer!"

"The owners are friends of mine. I don't think they would have made an error of that magnitude. May I see your lease?" He held out a hand promptingly.

"It's in the car," she hedged, frowning.

"Fine. Let's go and get it, shall we?"

"There's no need to be so rude about it!" Brenna gritted as he took hold of her arm and led her out of the bedroom and down the hall to the living room of the cabin.

"I thought I was being remarkably patient," he noted, opening the front door and propelling her firmly out onto the porch.

Brenna had a brief mental image of what the graveled drive was going to do to his bare feet and found herself leading the way to the cream-colored Fiat with alacrity.

He made no complaint, however, following her with a long, pacing stride that was utterly silent and catlike. He seemed oblivious to the rough gravel underfoot. When they reached the car, he leaned casually on the low roofline and waited while she opened the door and scrambled around in the front seat.

"Here it is," Brenna announced with a note of triumph she couldn't quite conceal as she found the folder that contained the papers.

Wordlessly he took them and bent forward slightly to read them in the pale light of the car's interior bulb. "You're Brenna Llewellyn?"

"I can prove that, too!" she retorted tartly.

He smiled at that, straightening. "I'm Ryder Sterne. Your neighbor for the summer, it would seem."

"My neighbor!"

"You tried your breaking and entering techniques on the wrong cabin, I'm afraid. That's yours, the one over there behind mine." He waved a hand toward the woods behind the house Brenna had attempted to enter.

"I don't see…oh." Brenna stared into the darkened grove of pines, barely able to discern a structure in the shadows. "I never even noticed it," she confessed ruefully. "Damn it to hell. What a lousy way to conclude a lousy day," she added half under her breath. With an effort she made herself turn back to face the stranger standing beside her car.

"Do you always make it a practice to go in through windows?" he demanded almost pleasantly, silver eyes reflecting the moonlight.

"Don't be ridiculous," she told him stonily. "I tried the key and it didn't work. That's why I was using the window."

He nodded. "I heard you fiddling with the lock. If you'd waited I would have answered the door and saved us both a great deal of trouble. As it was, when I heard you leave the porch and start around to the back of the house, I was left to assume your intentions were less than honest."

"So you waited for me with a bow and arrow?" Brenna tossed back accusingly.

He shrugged, offering no apology. "It was the only weapon I had conveniently at hand. How did I know who or what was going to come through that window? Come on, let's get your things out of the car. It's two in the morning and I'd like to get some more sleep tonight!"

Alarmed, Brenna put her hand restrainingly on his bare arm, withdrawing it almost at once as she became acutely conscious of the feel of sinewy muscles.

"That's all right, I can manage," she told him imperiously. "I'm very sorry for the mix-up, but you can feel free to go back to bed. I don't need any help tonight."

He glanced down at his bare arm where she had touched him briefly. When he looked up again, it was with the faintest of smiles. "I'll carry your things over to the cabin," he repeated very gently. "But I think I'll put some shoes on first. Hang on, I'll be right back."

Brenna watched him move back toward the house with that effortless, silent stride, her mouth open in astonishment. She was accustomed to men who would have argued, perhaps, or backed off once their offer had been rejected, or, in some instances, men who might have tried to reason with her that she did indeed need some help. She was not accustomed to men who simply made gentle pronouncements and then proceeded to carry them out over her expressed wishes in the matter.

She was learning, she told herself laconically as Ryder returned to the car and reached inside without a word to lift out the luggage. The gentler the tone, the more this man meant business. The memory of how softly he had spoken when he'd ordered her not to try escaping was still fresh.

Besides, she consoled herself as she picked up a small case, it *was* two in the morning. At this hour very little seemed worth arguing about.

"If you'll try that key on this lock, I think you'll find it will work," Ryder instructed kindly, pausing on the front porch of the A-frame cabin Brenna had rented.

She slanted him a quelling glance as she dug out the key for the second time that night. "I'll make a deal with you," she grumbled. "Promise me you won't bring up tonight's little fiasco all summer long and I won't spread the word that you greet guests with a bow and arrow, okay?"

In the pale light she saw his mouth skew upward at the corner. "You drive a hard bargain. I'll have to think about it."

The charmingly rustic interior of the A-frame was revealed as Ryder found the light switch. Brenna glanced around interestedly. As promised, the cabin seemed fully equipped. A flight of stairs led from one side of the fireplace-dominated living room to a loft arrangement that served as the bedroom. The kitchen, dining, and living areas downstairs flowed comfortably together and appeared sufficiently furnished with large, low pieces of solid construction.

"Can you really see the lake from here?" Brenna asked dubiously, peering out into the darkness through the floor-to-peaked-roof windows.

"You'll get a better view in the morning. Too many trees in the way tonight." Ryder set down his load. "Come on. One more trip should do it."

"A man of few words. The strong, silent type, I suppose," Brenna muttered behind him.

"Only at two in the morning," he retorted, not bothering to glance back over his shoulder.

Brenna, who was chewing her lip, was just as glad he hadn't turned around to witness her reddening cheeks. What a dumb remark!

"I think, since we're both wide awake now," her new neighbor announced calmly a few minutes later as he lifted out the last suitcase, "that we both need a nightcap. Come on inside." Still holding the last bag, he started toward his own front door.

Brenna saw her property disappearing in the direction of his cabin and hurried to protest. "Thanks, that's very kind of you under the circumstances, but not necessary. I'm sure I'll sleep very well after all the excitement, and it's getting so late..."

"But I might not sleep well at all. Come in, Brenna Llewellyn," he commanded ever so softly, holding the door politely.

Brenna, not knowing what else to do, walked resentfully inside.

"Have a seat. I'll get a couple of glasses."

She watched, narrow-eyed, as Ryder moved into the kitchen with that gliding way he had, and then she turned around to glance automatically at the books lining a nearby shelf. Force of habit, she thought dryly. Always check out a stranger's bookshelf first. With a creature as enigmatic as Ryder Sterne, a person could use a few clues to his personality!

The array of paperbacks on the top shelf produced an ironic expression in Brenna's amber eyes as she reached up to pluck out a volume. Exactly what she should have expected, she decided, perusing the lurid cover, which portrayed a raffish male firing a wicked-looking gun at a cluster of obviously evil types who, in turn, seemed bent on murdering the hero and the sexy blonde clinging to his left biceps.

It was the sort of sleazy, category stuff usually labeled men's adventure fiction, Brenna told herself disdainfully, unaware of how her mouth had curved downward until Ryder's gentle voice came from across the room.

"That's not the worst of it, I'm afraid," he told her as if he'd just read her mind. "I not only read it; I wrote it."

"What?" Startled, Brenna glanced back at the paperback cover. "It says the author is Justin Murdock."

"A pseudonym." Ryder set down the two glasses of brandy he was carrying, making room for them among a clutter of archery texts on the old brass-bound trunk that served as a coffee table. He sank smoothly into the depths of a couch that displayed a genteel shabbiness suitable for a mountain retreat and held out one of the snifters. "Here you go. Don't worry, it's good. I never let my heroes drink anything but the best."

"I'm impressed," Brenna drawled, accepting the

bell-shaped glass and sipping obediently at the very excellent brandy. Cautiously she sat down across from him in a padded rattan chair.

"Impressed by the brandy or the books?" he asked pointedly.

"Both." Damned if she was going to let him put her on the defensive.

"But it's not exactly your kind of fiction, right?" He smiled.

"Not exactly. But who am I to argue with success? I take it you are rather successful at it?"

"Very."

"I see. Well, congratulations."

"And now that we know my line of work, it's your turn."

Brenna sighed, her lips tightening unconsciously as she met his steady gaze over the rim of the glass. "I'm an assistant professor of philosophy at a small college in the San Francisco Bay area."

He said nothing, but something akin to amusement flickered in the silvery eyes.

"You find my career humorous?" Brenna challenged in a tone as dangerously gentle as any he could have used. Damn it, she'd been through enough this past week concerning her career! She didn't have to hear it mocked on top of everything else!

"Your career seems a little at odds with the memory of that cat burglar who came crawling through my window half an hour ago!"

"There was a time, Mr. Sterne," she returned, lecturing with an acid sweetness, "when the philosopher was also expected to be a person of action!"

"But probably not illegal action. At any rate, you'll have to admit that in the modern era the majority of academic types live in the ivory towers of their institutions of higher learning and seldom emerge to face the real world. Unless you want to count those suitably dramatic moments when they sally forth to face the menace of television cameras in the name of a fashionably radical cause," he added reflectively and then shook his head. "No, I don't think you can count those moments. They hardly constitute reality."

Brenna arched a brow, refusing to be drawn. "It would seem we are on opposite sides of an issue that has been around a long time. I doubt that we can settle the age-old hostility between those who promote the use of reason and those who admire the machismo approach to life. You, clearly, have made a nice living out of romanticizing the excitement of violent action. I, on the other hand, have just spent an entire semester trying to drum the concept of ethics into the heads of fifty freshmen."

Which was surely some sort of joke, when you thought about it, Brenna added silently. Imagine having spent all that time teaching an ethics class only to discover one was the victim of the most unethical behavior...

But Ryder was looking more amused than ever. "So we are opposing forces, hmmm? Haven't I heard something about opposing tensions ultimately producing harmony?"

Brenna blinked in astonishment, pausing in the act of raising her glass. "Heraclitus."

He looked blank. "I beg your pardon?"

"Heraclitus," she repeated slowly. " A sixth-century Greek philosopher who theorized that there was an underlying harmony in nature and that it was the product of opposing forces." In spite of herself a slow smile crept into her golden eyes. "As I recall, he used the bow as an example of tension creating harmony."

"A bow?" Ryder suddenly looked intrigued. "Yes, that makes sense. There is a perfect balance of tension involved in nocking an arrow and drawing the bowstring. I like the notion." He nodded decisively. "I'll have to throw it into the book I'm starting next week."

"Just like that?" Brenna demanded. "Wouldn't you want to study the fine points of the philosophy in a little more depth? Shouldn't you read the theory in more detail?"

"I doubt that would prove worth the effort." He shrugged. "I'd only take what's useful, and it sounds like you just gave me the useful part. The main research I'm doing for the book is in the actual use of the bow and arrow as a commando weapon."

She wanted to lecture him on the reprehensibleness of such slipshod research techniques, but Brenna found herself momentarily sidetracked. "A modern commando weapon? The bow and arrow? Good grief! I thought that was left behind after the invention of gunpowder!"

"The bow and arrow was used as recently as Vietnam," Ryder told her, leaning back against the cushions and sipping his brandy. "On a very limited basis, of course. Despite modern technology there still aren't very many ways of killing people quietly from a distance. The bow makes a very useful weapon in the hands of a man who must move silently in and out of an enemy-occupied zone on, say, a reconnaissance mission."

Brenna stared at him and shuddered in disgust. "I

can see why you wouldn't want to burden your reader with the philosophical implications of a drawn bow-string. You are, after all, selling violence and action, not ethical philosophical theory!''

''And sex.''

She glared at him.

''I'm selling sex, too. It goes nicely with the violence and action,'' he explained politely.

''I'm sure it does.'' She'd had enough. Brenna got to her feet, determined to put a decisive end to a fruitless conversation. ''Thank you very much for the brandy and the help in unpacking my car, Ryder. Now I think it's time I let you get back to bed.'' She was already striding briskly for the door. ''You've been very patient, considering the way I woke you earlier,'' she admitted grudgingly.

''I'll see you back to your cabin.'' He was behind her yet he reached the door before she did. The man moved like fog, Brenna thought in annoyance. Silent, smooth, overtaking you before you knew it.

''That's really not necessary,'' she tried valiantly. ''I can find my way.''

''I'll see you to your door,'' he repeated.

She lifted one shoulder in silent resignation. He was using that gentle tone of voice again. Hardly any point in continuing the argument.

Neither said a word until they reached her front porch, and then something occurred to Brenna. Turning in the act of inserting her key into the lock, she peered up at her escort, studying the reflection of moonlight in his silvery eyes.

''What is it, Brenna?'' he prompted indulgently.

''Did you really think I was a cat burglar when I first came through that window?''

His mouth curved upward but his dark voice was very serious. "The thought definitely went through my mind. I don't normally greet ladies with a bow and arrow. Why are you smiling?"

"No reason," she assured him hastily, stepping over the threshold and swiveling to close the door. "No reason at all. Good night, Ryder."

He nodded once and moved off as softly as the moonlight itself.

Brenna hesitated a moment longer in the doorway, the faint smile he had questioned fading slowly. How could she possibly have explained the curious flicker of amused excitement she had felt at the thought of a man like Ryder actually mistaking her, of all people, for a cat burglar?

She was an academician, a student and teacher of philosophy. Not a woman of dangerous action! Slowly she closed the door and stood gazing unseeingly at the cozy interior of her summer home.

And furthermore, Ryder Sterne had been wrong when he proclaimed that her career provided some protection from the realities of life. Brenna's hands tightened on the doorknob before she made herself release it and walk slowly across the worn, flower-patterned rug in front of the fireplace. There was no protection, no escape from the decision that had been forced upon her this week.

Nor, she thought with a return of disappointment and anger, could she look for help from the one man who should have stood by her. Damon Fielding had made his position clear when he'd stopped by her apartment this morning to "reason" with her.

His advice had been thoroughly practical, thoroughly rational, and thoroughly shocking when one considered that it came from a full professor of philosophy and ethics. He had urged her to accept the situation as it was, not to fight back. Her career, after all, was at stake.

Certainly, he agreed, the action of the department head in publishing Brenna's research and analysis as his own was unethical, but that sort of thing happened all the time in the academic world. She must remember that Paul Humphrey was on the verge of retirement. She must also keep in mind the fact that Damon Fielding was widely thought to be the next in line to assume the mantle of head of the Department of Philosophy. If she would just keep quiet and not make any waves, the aging Dr. Humphrey would soon be out of the picture.

Wasn't it worth ignoring the injustice for the sake of her future career? Besides, Damon had pointed out with a practical logic that probably would have appealed to someone like Ryder, she couldn't hope to win in any open confrontation with Dr. Humphrey. She was only an assistant professor, too far down on the rung of the academic ladder to tackle the respected head of the department.

But all Damon's arguments had succeeded in doing was to put a very large question in Brenna's heretofore career-oriented mind. Did she truly want to continue in a profession that taught such concepts as the pursuit of truth and ethical analysis yet practiced the same kind of pragmatic politics found in the far less self-righteous world inhabited by people like Ryder Sterne?

It was a decision she had to make in the next few weeks.

Chapter 2

She might be at a turning point in her career and therefore in her life, Brenna told herself firmly the next morning, but she must not forget her responsibility to Craig. Her younger brother was also rapidly reaching some inner turning point. She could sense it, even though he did his best to appear content with his college studies. Just one more year, Brenna thought hopefully. One more year and he'll graduate. Then he can take some time to explore the various directions open to him. Just so he gets that degree!

It was going to be a decisive summer in more ways than one.

Brenna showered in the early morning chill of the cabin. Then she slipped into the jeans she had worn last night and dug out a white cotton pirate shirt from one of the suitcases. The full sleeves gathered into French cuffs, and the classic, slit-front collar made for a casually dashing look that appealed to her on that particular morning.

Standing in front of the mirror in her loft bedroom, she brushed her chocolate-colored hair straight back from her forehead and twisted it into a loose configuration at the back of her head. The severe style emphasized the slant of the amber eyes that stared back at her with such seriousness this morning. What was she going to do?

Wandering into the kitchen, she located a copper-bottomed teakettle and set it on the stove. A short rummage in the small sack of groceries she'd brought along produced the packet of tea. Brenna was reaching for one of the pottery mugs in a cupboard near the sink when she glanced out the window and saw Ryder.

The uneasy shock she had experienced at their first meeting returned in diluted form. This morning he presented no overt threat, but there was something about this man that suggested a poised menace to her senses. The peculiar sensation had not disappeared overnight.

He stood at the edge of the clearing near his cabin, aiming a bow and arrow at a target that had been tacked to a tree. The morning sunlight gleamed on the tawny hair and clearly outlined the lean, smoothly coordinated masculine figure. A quiver of arrows was buckled to his hip and a leather arm guard protected his wrist beneath the rolled-up sleeve of the yellow shirt he was wearing with his black denim jeans.

The bold stance and the harshly carved features suggested a man who knew and understood the rough side of life. In fact, Brenna decided wryly as she poured the boiling water into her mug, he looked as if he could have doubled for one of his own fictional heroes. All he lacked was the sexy blonde clinging to his biceps!

She looked up from pouring the tea water in time to see him loose the nocked arrow. It came as no surprise when the shaft thudded forcefully into the center of the target. In a smooth motion Ryder removed another arrow from the quiver, nocked it, and drew the bowstring. It found a place on the target very close to the first.

As if sensing her eyes upon him, Ryder glanced toward the kitchen window before reaching for a third arrow. Through the glass their eyes met, and then without a pause he started toward Brenna's cabin.

Reminding herself of her manners and the way she had behaved the previous night, Brenna met him at the door with a cup of tea.

"Thanks," he murmured, accepting it gratefully as he set down the bow and quiver on her kitchen table.

"Not as good as your brandy, perhaps, but drinkable." She smiled.

"I was wondering if you'd brought some food along for yourself. I was going to ask if you needed to cadge a meal off me this morning." He stood looking down at her, silver-gray eyes roving her scrubbed features.

"We philosophers are not so far removed from the plane of reality as to forget things like food!" She chuckled as he dropped into a straight-backed chair at the table and sipped his tea with appreciation.

"You don't look like a teacher of philosophy this morning," he said in a soft purr of a voice that brought Brenna's senses alert. "But, then, you didn't look like one last night, either."

"Appearances can be deceptive. One of the first rules of good philosophy," she informed him with a determined lightness.

"One of the first rules of any intelligent approach to life," he countered seriously. "Would you like to go out with me tomorrow night?"

Startled by the abrupt question following so quickly on the heels of a totally unrelated subject, Brenna stared at him, her lips slightly parted in surprise.

"To the Gardners'. They own these cabins, remember? They have a place of their own a few miles from here. I'm invited for dinner and I thought you might like to come along. I'm sure they would be pleased to meet you in person."

"Oh, Well, I see. That's very thoughtful of you, but—"

"Good." He nodded once. "We'll leave around six thirty."

"Mr. Sterne…Ryder," she amended quickly, her brow furled in irritation, "I was not accepting the invitation. I was thanking you for it and was about to decline, in fact. I have a great deal to do here and—"

"And you've got all summer to do it." Ryder grinned at her. It was the first time she'd witnessed that particular expression. She'd seen his rather serious smiles a few times, but this was an outright, thoroughly wicked masculine grin. It was captivating. "Besides, you owe me. I'm calling in the tab."

"I owe you! That's ridiculous. What for?"

"For the fright you gave me last night, naturally."

It took a second for Brenna to catch her breath. For some strange reason she wanted to stare and go on staring at the slashing grin. "You didn't look particularly frightened, as I recall!'' she finally managed coolly.

The grin disappeared, changing back into one of the sardonic smiles. ''A man learns to deal with it.''

''Fear?''

''Ummm.'' He took a long swallow of his tea. Then he gave her a straight look. ''And I wasn't the only one handling it fairly well last night.''

''If that's some sort of macho compliment you're handing down condescendingly to the little lady, forget it!'' Brenna wasn't quite sure why she was reacting so fiercely.

''There's nothing condescending about it,'' he told her very quietly. ''Courage is an admirable trait in anyone.'' He held up a hand to ward off her rejoinder. ''Wait, I'll rephrase that. Courage is something *I* admire in anyone, male or female. There, I'm not generalizing, I'm speaking only for myself. Okay?''

''I wasn't going to argue,'' Brenna said slowly. ''I, too, happen to admire courage in others.''

''Ah! A point of agreement, perhaps?'' he teased.

''But I have the distinct impression,'' she continued calmly, ''that the sort of courage you would appreciate is somewhat different from that which I would applaud.''

''You think so?'' he charged almost casually, watching her with interest.

She nodded thoughtfully. ''For you courage would consist of a physical approach to danger. I tried to fight you last night and you find that commendable. From my point of view it was only desperation. I panicked and I reacted instinctively. It wasn't courage as you term it. Real courage is the kind shown by men and women who refuse to back down from the conviction of their ideas simply because the majority doesn't like those ideas. Or because someone in authority doesn't approve of those ideas. A brave man is one like Socrates who allowed himself to be tried and sentenced to death for his philosophic teachings even though he probably could have escaped. He respected the concept of law too much to defy it. Or the English humanist philosopher Sir Thomas More who defied Henry the Eighth by refusing to go along with Parliament trying to make the king head of the Church.''

''More got himself executed, too, I take it?'' Ryder inquired sardonically.

''Yes. He was found guilty of treason.'' In a way Damon had tried to convince her it was almost treason to challenge the head of the philosophy department, she reflected.

''Well, I'm not going to say they weren't men of courage and honor,'' Ryder announced judiciously. ''Although I'm not particularly into martyrdom myself. That still doesn't make your bravery last night any less admirable. You knew you were outmatched from the start but you fought anyway. And went on defying me even after I'd pinned you down. That takes guts, lady.''

''Sounds more like stupidity to me,'' she found herself retorting on a note of sudden laughter. ''If I'd tried talking first, I might have got the whole misunderstanding straightened out before I found myself flat on my back being searched for concealed weapons! A clear instance of where reason should have prevailed.''

''Easy to say in retrospect,'' Ryder noted. ''At the time, though, you were forced to make a choice on a limited amount of evidence. There wasn't really an opportunity to try reason first and violence second. Sometimes choices like that are forced on us and we do the best we can in the circumstances. Besides, we each learned something about the other. Something it might have taken longer to learn otherwise."

Brenna cocked a disbelieving eyebrow. "What in the world did we learn?"

He must have caught the challenging note in her tone because a trace of the dashing grin flashed across his face. "You found out I don't let rash little lady cat burglars climb through my window with impunity and that I don't resort to rape." He ignored the wave of red in her cheeks. "I, on the other hand, learned you don't cower when the chips are down and that you feel good under my hands."

"That I feel good!" Brenna repeated furiously, remembering the way his hands had stroked her body looking for weapons. The red in her cheeks darkened in anger and embarrassment. She had thought his touch almost impersonal at the time. Clearly he remembered the search procedure well! "It's hardly gentlemanly of you to remind me of the way you held me down and went through my pockets! In fact, it wasn't the thing to say at all if you're actually trying to ask me out for a date tomorrow night!"

"I'm counting on your remembering that I don't resort to rape." He smiled blandly. "I proved myself unthreatening last night."

"And that's supposed to be a sufficient reason for me to accept your invitation?" she demanded, knowing she was half charmed and half incensed by his approach to the matter of getting a date.

"Don't you want to meet your landlords?" he asked coaxingly.

"I don't see that it's necessary. I have strictly a business relationship with them."

"They're nice people. And as I said, you owe me."

"You have such a persuasive technique," she muttered dryly, knowing her sense of humor was going to get the better of her. Besides, she could certainly use the diversion of an evening out with a man who was totally different from Damon Fielding or anyone else on the philosophy faculty!

"Did you have anything better to do tomorrow night?"

"Not particularly," she admitted. "Okay, I'll go with you to meet the Gardners if you're sure they won't mind your turning up with a stranger in tow."

He finished his tea and got to his feet, looking satisfied. "They won't. I called Sue Gardner first thing this morning and told her I was bringing you along."

Brenna looked up at him, remaining firmly in her chair. "Why do I have this feeling you don't lack self-confidence? Do you always organize and manipulate things so that they go the way you want them to go?"

"I've picked a way of life that allows me to live on my own terms," he told her quietly, holding her eyes.

A current passed between them, an electric tension that Brenna felt with overpowering awareness. The menace her senses responded to in him was back in full force.

"But I'm not part of your life," she heard herself say very clearly. It seemed important to tell him that. She wanted no misunderstandings on the issue. They were neighbors for the summer, nothing more. They were truly from two different worlds.

"Do you philosophy types routinely go around denying reality and the evidence of your own senses? You entered my life last night when you came through my window. This morning I can reach out and touch you..."

He lifted the hand with which he drew the bowstring and put it under her chin. The silvery eyes looked deeply into hers, trapping her momentarily in their glittering depths. "Oh, yes, Brenna Llewellyn. You're definitely part of my life."

"Only...only for the summer," she whispered hoarsely, wishing desperately that she could find the willpower to move away from him. What was she letting him do to her? Was she crazy?

He shrugged dismissingly. "That's long enough, I imagine."

Brenna saw the sudden intention in his gaze and made a belated movement to escape. But she was much too slow. The hand under her chin reached around to anchor her gently by the nape of the neck. Bracing his left hand on the back of the chair on which she was sitting, Ryder leaned down to kiss her.

Summing up the situation immediately, Brenna held herself passively still. She sensed the curiosity in him, the exploratory approach. She was a woman he would be living next door to for several weeks and he was testing the waters. The logical response for her to make was polite, bland disinterest. A struggle might provoke a man like this who believed in action and force. So Brenna sat unmoving as his mouth came down on hers.

His lips were warm, firm and questioning. She had

been right, she told herself. He was curious about her. She kept her eyes open although his own dark tawny lashes flickered against his cheeks when his mouth made contact. The fingers at the back of her neck moved with a massaging sensuality while his lips explored hers.

Brenna's fingers tightened on the edge of the table as she held herself stiff and unresponsive. There was more in this slow, questioning embrace than mere curiosity, she realized abruptly. There was a hunger lying in wait. It was held in check and it was, at the moment, unthreatening. In spite of her resolve, she found herself wondering what it would take to unleash it.

Ryder didn't pursue the kiss long. He brushed her lips one last time with his own and then lifted his head an inch or two and opened his eyes. There was a cloudy veil concealing the truth in the gray depths of his gaze, but there was a whimsical tilt to his mouth.

"No?" he asked very gently.

"No." Brenna's voice was very assured and she met his eyes in a straight look.

"Is there someone else?" He didn't move, retaining his hold on the nape of her neck.

Brenna drew in her breath. "Someone else; something else. A lot of reasons."

The tilt of his mouth widened into the rakish grin for an instant and the silvery eyes gleamed. "Reasons that vague I can handle," he told her with an amused arrogance.

Perhaps it was time to take a firmer stand. "I'm not here for a summer affair, Ryder."

He straightened. "Why are you here?"

"To work. To sort out some things in my life. To make some decisions."

"More vagueness. Does philosophy teach you to be vague in the face of a direct question?"

"Sometimes," she retorted, deliberately being vague again. But humor lightened her tone now.

"Amazing. No wonder they keep your sort locked up on college campuses. You'd flounder to death if you had to stay very long in the real world!"

"Your prejudice against the academic world is showing."

"Your prejudice against my world has already surfaced," he shot back dryly. "Come outside with me and let's see if we can find a common interest."

"How?" she asked.

"I'll teach you to use the bow. When you use it properly, you can think of it as an application and illustration of the philosophic principle of harmony in the universe." He chuckled, taking her hand and pulling her to her feet.

"While you'll be thinking of it as a lethal weapon for one of your heroes!"

"So? Just because it's your nature to look for something intellectually elevating in the exercise, don't condemn me for looking for something practical."

"I wouldn't dream of condemning you for that!" she scoffed, letting herself be led outdoors into the still-cool mountain morning. She glanced to her left, automatically taking in her surroundings en route to the archery target, and gave a sudden gasp of appreciation.

"Oh, you *can* see the lake from here! The rental

agent was right. Isn't it fantastic? It's huge. Like an inland sea!''

The dazzling blue depths, so deep the lake never froze even in the heart of winter when the region was converted into a skiing wonderland, reflected the bright morning sun.

''It's about twenty-two miles long,'' Ryder told her. ''And about eight miles across at this point. Do you gamble?''

''I beg your pardon?'' she asked in surprise.

''I just wondered if you were interested in gambling, since you've elected to spend your summer on the Nevada side of the lake,'' he explained as they reached the point near the target where he had been standing earlier.

''Oh, I see what you mean. No, I'm not particularly interested. I saw the casinos as I drove through town last night,'' she added. ''I just happened to wind up here because this looked like the most attractive area available from the agent.''

''Fate,'' he suggested dramatically, loosing her hand to unstrap the leather arm guard from around his wrist.

Brenna chuckled. ''I'm afraid there is no empirical evidence to suggest that fate is a genuine factor in the world.''

''Lively conversation like that must limit your dating to other faculty members,'' he murmured, taking hold of her left wrist and attaching the guard. ''So I can assume the 'someone else' is another member of your philosophy department staff?''

''You do a pretty good job of lining up the evidence yourself,'' she commended casually, examining the wrist guard.

"He doesn't love you, you know," Ryder continued, bending down to pick up the quiver of arrows.

Brenna swallowed in a wave of uneasy anger. She should not let herself be drawn into this kind of conversation. "That's your opinion!"

He put the bow in her hand and looked into her eyes.

"That's another deduction from empirical evidence," he corrected.

"What evidence?" she asked huskily.

"He let you come alone to Tahoe for the summer."

"And from that you assume he doesn't love me?" she challenged, amber eyes kindling.

"I'm a man. Given what I know about being a man, that's a reasonable assumption."

"You're very sure of yourself," she taunted, vividly aware of his closeness and the confidence in which he was enveloping her.

"Want to hear another assumption?" he baited softly.

"I doubt it!"

"You don't really love him, either," he concluded inexorably.

"You'd like to believe that so you don't have to feel guilty when you make a pass at me," she tossed back, proud of the coolness in her voice as she studied the weapon in her hand. Why was she standing there, letting him goad her like this? She should drop the bow and walk back to the cabin and lock the door. But that would be admitting that she couldn't deal with him, wouldn't it?

"I won't feel guilty when I make a pass, don't fret." He laughed far back in his throat. "I don't feel even a pang about that kiss, for example."

"Why do you say I don't love him?" She couldn't resist the question, even though she was disgusted with herself for asking.

"Because you are a woman who concerns herself with such things as honor. If you were in love you would not risk conversations like this with another man," he told her simply. "Now," he went on before she could find an answer, "this is called a recurve bow. The way the ends curve and deflect back give a lot more leverage. You're right-handed so you stand with your left side toward the target. We'll start with an open stance..."

He knelt in front of her and guided her sandaled feet into the appropriate positions. Brenna found herself listening submissively for a while as he directed the placement of her hands, talked about the basics of safety, and generally involved her more and more deeply in the first lesson. He was good, she realized. An excellent teacher, in fact. If there was one thing she could admire other than sound scholarship, it was the ability to teach.

"My God! It's hard," she suddenly complained in astonishment when the time came to practice drawing back the bowstring. "I'll never be able to draw it far enough to nock an arrow!"

"Sure you will. This is considered a very light-weight bow. A strong woman like you can handle it."

"What makes you think I'm strong?" she protested, taking a deep breath and attempting once more to draw the bowstring.

"I was the one holding you down on the floor last night, remember?" he said, grinning.

"I thought we agreed you wouldn't bring that up again," she muttered caustically.

"I agreed to think about the bargain you suggested. I haven't made up my mind to accept it yet. There, that's it. I told you that you could do it."

She slackened the tension on the bow so it wouldn't snap and threw him a glare. But she said nothing else as he took her through the basic fundamentals of archery.

"These are aluminum-shafted arrows," he told her as he handed the first one to her. "The best. Which means they're expensive. Lose one in the grass or the pines and you're going to be spending the rest of the day looking for it."

"Is that a threat?"

"That's an added inducement to try to hit the target. Okay, remember that the trick is to combine a relaxation of the muscles in the hand drawing the bowstring at the same moment that you need maximum concentration on aiming. Just relax and release the arrow gently. Hold the release position until the arrow reaches the target."

"Or until it misses the target completely," Brenna sighed as the first one went wide.

"It takes practice. Don't worry about the arrow, I've got it spotted over there near that tree. Try another."

The thrill of having a few actually strike the target was greater than Brenna would have expected. She was elated and not a little exhausted a long time later as she walked with Ryder toward the target to remove the few that had managed to find their way in the right direction.

"Craig would love this," she remarked enthusiastically, inserting the arrows back into the quiver as he handed them to her.

"Craig?" There was a tight curiosity underlying the neutralness of the question. Brenna heard it and smiled to herself.

"My brother. He's going to be starting his senior year at the University of California at Berkeley this fall," she told him.

"You sound proud."

"I am. He's a good kid."

"If he's almost a senior in college, he should be a good *man* by now," Ryder observed, giving her a strange glance.

"He is." She smiled easily. "Sometimes I lapse, I'm afraid. There are a lot of years between us. He's only twenty and I'm twenty-nine. It's hard not to keep thinking of him as a kid brother."

"You sound as if you're pretty close to him."

"After Mom and Dad were killed a few years ago, all we had was each other," Brenna explained quietly as they walked back toward her cabin.

"With that much difference in your ages you must have wound up more or less raising him through his late teens," Ryder said thoughtfully.

"It was a struggle sometimes." She laughed, thinking about those years. "But Craig was a very responsible kid and he always seemed to keep in mind that I was a sibling, not a parent. He didn't deliberately challenge me the way real parents get challenged by teenagers, if you know what I mean."

"I know. Not from personal experience, because I've never had kids, but I've seen it in others," he admitted. "The Gardners, as a matter of fact, had a little trouble with their oldest boy a couple of years ago."

"But he got straightened out?" she asked with idle curiosity.

"Yes."

She looked up, intending to ask another question about the Gardners, but Ryder was already turning the conversation toward lunch.

And somehow lunch turned into an afternoon walk along the lakeshore in front of the cabins as she and Ryder explored a few of the picturesque coves and beaches that dotted the shoreline. The mellow warmth of the day hung on until the sun finally began to set behind the soaring peaks to the west. Then, regardless of her firm intention to the contrary, Brenna found herself sharing a whiskey sour with her neighbor as he broiled steaks over the barbecue on his back patio.

When she went back to her own cabin after dinner, there was an element of peace in the atmosphere between herself and Ryder. He dropped the smallest of brushing kisses against her mouth before seeing her safely inside, but it was a calm, good-night salute. It reminded her a little of the impersonal touch he had used when he'd searched her that first evening.

I was, she reflected uneasily, a little confusing. She had half expected to find herself fighting him off at the door. Given his aggressive nature and his apparent interest in pursuing a summer flirtation, it seemed logical.

So why did she feel a little let down? she demanded briskly of herself as she went about climbing the stairs to her loft bedroom. She should be grateful that he wasn't going to be the pushy type!

The next day she pulled out some of her notes and thought about outlining her fall classes. But that only brought back memories of the decision she had to make that summer. It was difficult, Brenna discovered, planning course work for her students when there was a possibility that she would not even be returning to the college!

Conscious of the stylish casualness of Lake Tahoe in the summer, she selected one of her few dresses with care that evening. After all, she told herself, she wanted the Gardners to have a good impression of their tenant! It was a perfect, summery white eyelet with full sleeves and a skirt that stopped at the knee. The dress was held low at the waist with a narrow sash of bright red, and she paired it with her red sandals, relying on the darkness of her sleekly knotted hair to provide the final touch of contrast.

It wasn't until Ryder knocked at her door that she admitted she might have dressed as much for him as for impressing the Gardners. She found the notion disturbing.

"Good evening," she began with the sort of cheery enthusiasm she imagined appropriate to a friendly date. As she caught sight of him after flinging open the door, her amber eyes widened first in surprise and then in appreciation of the picture he made on her doorstep.

"Don't tell me," she drawled, taking in his attire with a complete head-to-toe glance. "Your heroes not only get to drink the best brandy, they also buy their clothes from Italian designers!"

Not everyone could have worn the crisply tailored linen jacket in the palest of gray-blues, the narrow-legged white linen trousers, or the royal-blue silk shirt with such nonchalance. Ryder carried it off beautifully.

"You only live once," he responded easily. "And it does go with the Ferrari, don't you think?"

"Oh, yes, definitely," she agreed, laughing up at him as they started toward his car, which had been parked at the back of the cabin on the night she'd arrived. The Ferrari was a vivid red that, Brenna realized in amusement, was going to nicely complement her sash and sandals!

"You look very good tonight, lady," Ryder whispered as he assisted her into the cockpit of the beautifully designed automobile. She glanced up as she swung her bare legs inside, and the silver mesh of his eyes seemed to snag her gaze for a moment. She knew what the next question was going to be even before he asked it. "All for me?" He half smiled, taking in the whole of her with a leashed hunger.

"I wanted to impress my landlords," she retorted brightly, determined not to be drawn into such an admission. What was it with this man, anyway? She was beginning to realize she couldn't quite figure him out. A part of her warned that he was capable of reaching out and taking what he wanted, and that restrained hunger in him indicated that he wanted her. Yet other than that exploratory kiss yesterday morning and that quite mild good-night salute last night, there were few indications that she was going to have to fight him off.

The conflicting signals she was receiving both intrigued her and made her wary. She must remember that he wasn't from her world. He operated under a different set of rules than the average college professor or graduate student. It was best to keep a certain distance between them, and he seemed willing to cooperate.

But she wasn't fully aware of just how different Ryder Sterne's world was until she was introduced to Adam and Sue Gardner. A middle-aged couple of charm and affluence, they greeted Brenna with delight.

"Do come in, we're so pleased to meet you!" Sue Gardner exclaimed graciously as she welcomed her guests into the lovely lakeside home. "When Ryder phoned to say he was bringing you, we were so pleased! This is my husband, Adam."

Adam proved to be a handsome man with a wealth of graying hair and a friendly, open smile. His wife was equally attractive. Both had that country-club look of health. Brenna couldn't help wondering how they had met Ryder. She couldn't really imagine him coming from their polished world of business success and prestige. No matter how well he wore his designer clothes, Brenna was certain he hadn't sprung from that kind of background.

Yet there was no doubting the pleasure the Gardners took in greeting her escort nor the obvious, almost maternal affection with which Sue Gardner kissed Ryder on the cheek.

"It's so good to see you, Ryder. I'm glad you were able to take advantage of the cabin again this year." She smiled, leading everyone onto the front deck, which soared outward toward the water.

"It makes a nice change from the apartment in Los Angeles, and you know damn well I can't beat the terms of your lease!" Ryder accepted the salt-rimmed margarita Adam Gardner handed him. "Actually I'm enjoying myself more this year than last. Your taste in tenants for the other cabin is improving," he said with a meaningful glance at Brenna, who occupied herself with demurely tasting the tart tequila drink she had just been handed.

Adam laughed. '' The luck of the draw, I'm afraid. Wish we could take credit, but it was all in the hands of the rental agent.''

''Brenna doesn't believe in fate so she probably doesn't believe in luck, either,'' Ryder murmured.

''Which leaves sheer chance,'' Brenna said firmly, deciding to take charge of the conversation before the two men ran it downhill at her expense. ''Do you come up here every year, Ryder?''

There was a pause and the hesitation startled her. The Gardners seemed surprised at the question, and Ryder looked as if he wanted to head off the answer. But he was given no chance. Sue Gardner threw a very warm, very grateful smile at her guest and then turned to Brenna, who was beginning to feel as if she had accidentally tread on awkward ground.

''The cabin is available to Ryder anytime he wants it, Brenna,'' Sue said calmly. ''We are only too glad when he takes advantage of it.''

''I see.'' Brenna knew her tone sounded a little blank but there wasn't much she could do about it. She simply didn't understand the undercurrents that had begun to flow between the other three on the redwood deck.

''Hasn't Ryder explained about us?'' Adam asked with a glance at the younger man. Then he answered his own question as Ryder's mouth hardened. ''No, I can see he hasn't. We are very deeply in his debt, Brenna.''

She frowned her lack of understanding, switching her questioning gaze to Ryder, who was ignoring all of them now. He sauntered to the railing and stood leaning on it, his eyes on a boat that was roaring across the lake trailing two water skiers. She had the distinct impression that he wanted to get the next few minutes over with in a hurry.

"He saved our son."

Brenna's gaze swung back to Adam's faintly smiling features. "Oh," she blurted out.

Surprisingly it was Ryder who spoke next, his voice distant and remote. "Brenna doesn't approve of this sort of thing. I think that's enough for now, Adam." He kept his gaze on the lake.

"But, Ryder, that's ridiculous! How could I not approve of your saving a boy's life?" She turned back to Adam Gardner. "What happened?"

Adam seemed torn between wanting to answer her and his obligation to respect Ryder's wishes. It was Sue who resolved the matter.

"He led a small group of hand-picked mercenaries in an assault on a prison in South America where Evan was being held on drug charges. The regime in power at the time was not at all sympathetic to U.S. citizens, and we were told we would probably never see our son again once he disappeared inside that prison," Sue Gardner explained quietly. "Ryder got him out and brought him home."

The margarita in Brenna's fingers sloshed precariously as she absorbed the full implications of the story. "Oh, my God!" Her attention went to the silent man at the rail. "You make a living doing things like that?" she breathed.

He swung around and caught her bemused expression. "I make a living writing books," he stated with a trace of challenge. He swirled the margarita in his glass and took a man-sized swallow.

"Books that relate your own exploits?" she persisted, shocked at what had been revealed about him. Somehow she had thought the violent side of him was safely confined to his adventure fiction. Now she knew it existed in real life, too.

"Brenna, he was doing us an incredible favor," Adam Gardner put in deliberately, sensing the tension in her reaction. "He's not exactly a paid mercenary."

And suddenly Ryder was grinning, that wide, slashing, wicked grin that had such a strange effect on Brenna. This time there was a fierce challenge in it as his eyes met hers. "Not exactly," he agreed very distinctly, swallowing the remainder of his margarita. "Not anymore. Now I am a writer of sleazy men's fiction. Period. Let's eat."

Chapter 3

"**I**'ll have to admit you recovered very nicely and maintained your end of the social repartee for the remainder of the evening," Ryder told Brenna much later that night as he helped her back into the front seat of the red Ferrari. "But I imagine you're just about to burst, so why don't you go ahead and get it over with?"

Brenna slanted him an assessing glance as he slid into the seat beside her. She was aware of the challenge in him. It had been radiating from him ever since the full truth about his rather violent past had come out. He was virtually daring her to hold it against him. For some reason, perhaps because of several margaritas and a swing in her mood toward objectivity, she found that amusing and a little touching.

"You think I'm going to chew you out because you saved some kid's neck?"

There was a small hesitation. "He wasn't guilty, you know," Ryder finally said in an even, almost conversational tone. He watched the winding road with care, seemingly totally occupied with his steering. "He got involved with some people who used him. Set out to see the world and escape from his parents' lifestyle and got more than he bargained for. You'd like him now. He's a stockbroker!"

Brenna smiled. "Thank God Craig never decided to defy all authority and see the world!"

"You must have handled him well."

"The only thing that's worrying me is that he's not particularly happy at the university." Brenna sighed. "But I think I've convinced him to finish now that he's come this far."

She sensed Ryder taking a long breath as if to steady himself. "Can I take it that I'm not in for a long lecture on the evils of my rough-and-ready past?"

"It's not my place to lecture you, Ryder."

"Please don't be condescending," he warned very quietly.

Brenna thought about that. Was she being condescending? "How did the Gardners find you when they, uh, needed someone to get their son out of that prison?" she surprised herself by asking.

"I was an officer in the Marines. Served in Southeast Asia and later in…other places. When I left the service to start writing full time, it occasionally became convenient to pick up a little extra money. I kept in touch with some friends I'd made in the service. There's a kind of network out there, Brenna, and when people like the Gardners start looking for help, it can be found. Getting in and out of awkward places is something I happen to be good at,'' he added with a disparaging shrug.

''And perhaps something you like doing?'' Brenna smiled perceptively.

''Not anymore. I'm satisfied with the writing these days,'' he told her in a tone that once again dared her to contradict.

Brenna's smile widened as she drank in the crisp mountain air through her open window. She felt good tonight. It was good to be driving around the lake with a man who was totally different from any she had known. It was as if she were someone else this evening, and she wanted the illusion to continue for a time.

''Does that mean I am out tonight with a successful author of sleazy men's fiction rather than an ex-soldier-of-fortune?'' she teased lightly.

He flickered her a quick, almost uncertain glance. ''Yes.''

''Good. Talk to me of storytelling, Ryder Sterne. Or is it Justin Murdock?'' she corrected, thinking of his pseudonym.

''Would you mind a personal question?''

''Not at all, not at all,'' she assured him happily.

''How many of those margaritas did you have tonight?''

''I'm not drunk,'' she declared, aware that she sounded vaguely defensive about it. But she wasn't, not really. She was just feeling temporarily free and vitally aware of the man beside her. She'd never been aware of Damon in quite this way. Why was that? she wondered silently.

''Then why don't we try our hand at cards tonight, lady?'' Ryder suggested. ''I'll stop at one of the casinos and we can see if your philosophy does you any good when it goes against luck, one on one.''

"That sounds…different. Yes, I think I'd like that.''

Brenna didn't hear the dreaminess in her voice but she felt it in her mind. A wonderful sense of being in another reality. As if she had somehow stepped into a different plane of existence just for this evening.

As for Ryder, she had the impression that some burden had been lifted from him. He sounded happier suddenly; more than willing to forget the discussion of his past and devote himself to the remainder of the evening.

"I feel lucky tonight,'' he told her as he parked the Ferrari in one of the lots of a luxurious, highrise casino-hotel in the south-shore town of Stateline. "Luckier than I have for a long time.'' He helped her gallantly out of the car and took her arm as they walked toward the brilliantly lit casino. "What do you call luck in your world, lady?''

Brenna's lips curved invitingly. "Well, there is something known as the probability theory. Otherwise called chance.''

"Close enough,'' he proclaimed as they stepped through the casino doors.

Before them lay the glitter, the excitement, and the pleasure-bent crowds of a big Nevada casino. The chandeliers, well-dressed croupiers, and scantily clad cocktail waitresses all combined with the tinkling of slot machines and the spin of a wheel of fortune to add to Brenna's glow of unreality. There was an overstated aura of luxury that seemed to swallow one up and form a world of its own. It suited Brenna's unusual mood exactly.

She clung gracefully to Ryder's arm as he led her onto the gambling floor. Even if she had not felt like clinging that night, Brenna wasn't certain she would have been able to free herself. Ryder was ensuring her proximity with a possessive grip that was inordinately pleasing to her senses. Damon never kept her close like this when they went out together. Dr. Fielding didn't believe in archaic masculine emotions such as possessiveness. Normally, Brenna tried to remind herself, she didn't believe in such notions, either. But tonight was different. Perhaps because the man involved was different.

"Do you know how to play any of the card games?" Ryder asked, glancing down at her animated expression with a warm, amused look in his eyes.

"No, I'll watch you for a while. I think the slot machines are going to be more my speed."

"Stand close behind me and we'll see just how much good luck you're capable of bringing me tonight," he drawled, taking a place at one of the green baize-topped tables. The young and attractive woman dealing the cards turned a very brilliant smile on her latest customer.

"I think the croupier is trying to make a pass at you," Brenna warned Ryder in a dramatically low tone.

"Nonsense." Ryder grinned cheerfully. "She's paid to smile like that at everyone. Now keep very quiet while we're playing and put your hand on my shoulder so I'll know you're there."

"You think the hand on the shoulder is necessary?"

"It's how the luck gets channeled from you to me," he explained.

"Oh."

And then it was too late to say anything else. The attractive croupier began to deal the cards and Ryder gave the game his full attention. Brenna dutifully kept her crimson nails resting lightly on the pale blue-gray jacket shoulder and watched in fascination. Ryder played with the professionalism with which he did everything else, she thought fleetingly. Fully alert but serenely in control of himself and, apparently, of his luck. He was winning.

"There you go," he concluded, pocketing his chips at last and turning away from the table. "What did I tell you? Tonight is my lucky night. Come on, lady, let's go find another game to play."

At the wheel of fortune Brenna took a chance herself, putting an entire dollar onto the number she had chosen. When it came back doubled, she lifted happy, glowing eyes to Ryder, who was standing close, his arm around her waist.

"This could be an easier way to make a living than teaching philosophy," she announced.

He laughed. "Is teaching philosophy so hard?"

That question brought back unwelcome reminders of the real world waiting for her at the start of the fall semester. "It isn't the teaching that's so bad, it's…never mind. I want to try the slots!"

He made no attempt to force her back into the unpleasant path the conversation was taking, guiding her instead to the nearest of a bank of quarter slots. There she began to plunk in quarters with an enthusiasm that would have astounded her at another time.

"Somehow it doesn't seem like real money here," she explained apologetically as the machine politely gobbled up quarter after quarter. The apology in her voice was due to the fact that it was Ryder who had financed her go at the slots.

"Go on trying," he instructed, unperturbed. "I keep telling you we can't lose tonight."

With the next quarter he was proved correct. Instead of swallowing it and waiting implacably for the next feeding, the machine began to tinkle with the delightful sound of cascading quarters.

"Ryder, look! We're rich!"

"I'll get a cup to put the loot in," he said, grinning.

Brenna stood trying to estimate her winnings as he disappeared momentarily and then returned with a cardboard cup. Laughing with delight, Brenna scooped the coins into it.

"We'll never be able to carry all this!"

"All we have to do is get it as far as the cashier's stand. They'll turn it into nice lightweight bills," he told her.

"The casino management will probably ask us politely to leave if we keep this up." Brenna chuckled as they moved off down the aisle of slot machines.

"A couple of hundred bucks isn't going to break them. Still, maybe we should take a little time out."

"I thought you were supposed to stick with a hot streak once you had one going," she protested.

"Oh, I intend to pursue the hot streak. On the dance floor."

Brenna thought about that as he guided her toward the lounge that overlooked the gambling floor. A sophisticated trio was playing while more of the scantily clad waitresses moved back and forth among the intimate cocktail tables. She thought about it carefully, trying to analyze the situation. For the first time that evening she asked herself silently what she might be getting into, but when Ryder took her in his arms, the questions faded back beyond the edges of the pleasant dream world she was inhabiting this evening.

He wrapped her close, the possessiveness she had sensed in him all evening seeming to escalate by several quantum leaps. His hand moved down her back to the base of her spine, pressing her audaciously into his warmth. Ryder's breath moved a tiny, loose tendril of hair as he inhaled the scent of her. Without protest, Brenna settled her head on his strong shoulder.

"Enjoying yourself this evening, lady?" he growled very softly.

"Yes," she admitted unhesitatingly. "Very much. And you?"

"I thought things were going to be a bit rough for a while but now everything seems to be going smoothly, doesn't it? Yes, I'm enjoying myself. I'm enjoying *you*. I think I mentioned once before that I like the feel of you under my hands."

An unexpected tremor went through her as he suited action to words and moved his fingers compellingly along her spine. Brenna found herself drinking in the feel of his hard body, the totally male fragrance of his skin, and the indefinable, incredibly complex combination of factors that were attracting her senses. It was a magic night, made even more so because she didn't believe in magic. With a sense of curiosity and desire she moved her nails lightly at the back of his neck, twisting her fingers delicately in the tawny depths of his hair.

His reaction was immediate and electric. His hold on her tightened and his deep voice became very soft indeed. The whisper of silk on a knife blade, Brenna thought, intrigued. What was it about Ryder's voice that she should remember?

"Dangerous," she suddenly said dreamily, her eyes closing.

"What's dangerous?"

"You are when your voice gets very gentle and soft." She smiled without lifting her lashes.

"I'm not the one who's dangerous tonight," he whispered, finding the curve of her ear with the tip of his tongue in a quick, sensuous tasting action. "You're the one who represents a real threat."

"Hah!" She snuggled closer, moving her fingers on the back of his neck this time just inside the line of his collar. "I am a prudent, circumspect, well-behaved faculty member of a very respected college."

"Who goes around climbing through the bedroom windows of unsuspecting males and seducing them on the dance floor," Ryder concluded for her throatily.

"I am not," Brenna stated categorically, "seducing you!"

"That's a matter of opinion."

Brenna opened her eyes and found him watching her face with an intensity that stirred her senses. "Do you feel seduced?" she asked interestedly.

"I feel as though I were being swept out into the middle of Lake Tahoe. It's very deep out in the middle of the lake, lady. A man could be dragged under and never find his way back to the surface," Ryder murmured, his voice vibrating with the purr of a lion.

"I have the feeling you're a very strong swimmer."

"The danger is that I might not want to swim away in time."

"Is this some sort of cryptic warning?" Brenna dared.

"Perhaps."

"A cryptic warning," she repeated wisely. "Then I shall have to be very careful, won't I?"

His shoulder lifted easily in a movement that suggested the matter was out of his hands. "Perhaps. Then again, if it's all a twist of fate, nothing you do will have much effect."

"You forget that I don't believe in fate."

"In which case you're stuck having to take full responsibility for your own actions, aren't you?" he taunted huskily, inclining his head to drop the smallest of suggestive little kisses on the curve of her throat.

"I," she announced bravely, aware of a pleasant warmth creeping through her veins, "am a great believer in personal responsibility."

"So am I," he returned. "Because even when fate and luck are involved, there are always choices to be made. The choice tonight will be yours, lady. Think twice before you select the riskier option, because I will hold you to it."

"Another cryptic warning?" she teased.

"I suppose," he sighed and pulled her closer.

They danced several more numbers and Brenna found herself surrendering to the natural grace of his body. She had the feeling that she wasn't nearly as coordinated, even though no one had ever thought her ungraceful. But he made it easy to slide into the pattern of his rhythm, and once into it, she didn't want to back out.

"It's nearly two," Ryder said at last as they walked off the floor and back to their small table.

"Really?" Brenna stifled a delicate little yawn. "Time for me to be crawling through somebody's window, hmmm?"

"Not unless it's mine. Are you ready to go home?"

"Yes." She took another look at the still-lively casino gambling floor. "Don't these places ever close?"

"No. Come, lady. Let's go home to bed."

She looked up at that as he got to his feet beside her, searching his voice and expression for innuendos and double meanings. But Ryder merely smiled back, taking her arm and leading her through the casino and out into the parking lot.

Safely inside the cockpit of the red Ferrari, Brenna leaned her head back against the leather seat and watched the passing scenery of night-darkened pines and lake with a pleasant, floating feeling. Ryder didn't speak as he drove, but she was aware of a sense of closeness that didn't seem to need words. A man apart. Different, complex, intriguing. But there was a vulnerability in him, she thought fleetingly. A vulnerability he tried to mask with self-confidence and self-reliance. She had seen it briefly this evening after the truth about his past had emerged.

"Did you want me to know, Ryder?" she whispered suddenly.

"Know what?"

"About the way you used to make your living."

He hesitated. "I'm not sure. I told myself it would be better if you didn't find out, but then I found myself taking you to meet the Gardners. A part of me must have guessed the truth would come out there. I guess I must have wanted it out in the open before things went very far between us."

"A question of honor?" she chided gently.

"In a way," he replied evenly.

"Admirable." She nodded, smiling. "But you needn't have worried."

"Because you're not going to hold it against me?" He slid her an enigmatic glance.

"No, because things aren't going to go so far between us that it will matter," she retorted lightly, knowing that her response was a kind of challenge.

But it was a challenge he evidently didn't intend to pick up. Ryder said nothing, concentrating on his driving.

He still said nothing as he parked the Ferrari and walked her to her front porch. Then he turned to her and spoke with gentle urgency.

"Invite me in, lady. For a nightcap."

She met his eyes, aware of her own quickening pulse and the sensuous silver of his gaze. "I…I don't have any brandy."

"Tea will be fine."

For a moment the force of his will seemed to collide with the wavering shield of her ambivalence. It was a contest in which ambivalence stood little or no chance. Fingers trembling ever so slightly with an excitement and a fear she didn't want to name, Brenna handed him her key.

Without a word he inserted it in the lock and pushed open the door.

"I'll build a fire," he said as he closed the door with a decisiveness that made the creeping warmth in Brenna's veins flare a little hotter. She watched him move across the room with that easy, catlike stride and then she turned and went toward the kitchen.

A few minutes later she stood staring unseeingly at the teakettle, waiting for the water to boil and listen-

ing to the sounds of Ryder constructing the fire. What
was she doing? Did she even want to think about it?

An air of inevitability settled on her. It was something that seemed to have been enveloping her for
most of the evening but that she had deliberately
avoided facing. It was easier to take each event as it
occurred even though common sense saw the ultimate
conclusion to the pattern that was forming. Brenna
poured the tea water over the leaves in the ceramic
pot and prepared a tray with cups and saucers.

She found Ryder sprawled on the sofa, staring into
the fire as she emerged from the kitchen with her tray.
He looked up as she came forward, silvery eyes roving over her with a muted hunger that couldn't quite
be hidden. It was a hunger that found an answering
response deep in Brenna, and the cups rattled a little
as she set down the tray on the round wicker table.

"To a night of decadent pleasure," she toasted
with a determined lightness as she poured the tea and
handed him his cup.

"Philosophy professors don't usually spend their
summer evenings cavorting in gambling dens with
writers of sleazy men's fiction?" Ryder queried dryly
as he took the cup.

"I don't. Not usually," she stated calmly, lashes
dropping as she sipped the soothing brew.

"Come now, surely there have been philosophers
who have argued in favor of what is commonly re-
ferred to as the good life?" Ryder seemed willing to
follow her mood. That surprised Brenna a little. But
it fit in with the conflicting signals she had received
before from him. She could be absolutely certain one
moment that he wanted her and in the next he made

it clear that she could set the pace and determine the direction. She didn't quite understand.

"Oh, there have been several who advocated a life of pleasure, but I'm afraid they had the pleasures of intellectual discovery in mind, not the more worldly ones," she lectured flippantly. "Even poor, maligned Epicurus was much more concerned with the pleasure of the pursuit of knowledge than the pleasures of the body. His opponents were the ones who made the word 'epicurean' a byword for a luxurious lifestyle. Epicurus and his circle of followers were really quite restrained. Even so, I suppose he was a little radical compared to some of the others who advocated a very stoic existence," she finished speculatively, glancing into the fire.

"Nevertheless," Ryder persisted softly, "there are philosophical theories that could be used to justify either life in the fast lane or a more cerebral existence?"

"Probably," Brenna agreed with a small smile.

"And a man trying to decide which path to follow is allowed the choice?"

"There's always the doctrine of free will," she acknowledged, amused.

He set down his teacup and removed the one in her hands. "Then I choose to kiss you and the hell with the risks."

Brenna held her breath, her nerves tingling and alive as he swept her into his arms. She made no protest when his mouth came searchingly down on hers. She wasn't certain in that moment that she *could* have made a protest. This was where the evening had been leading, and she knew she wanted to taste a little of what this man had to offer her senses. The urge to do so was overpowering.

The first thing she realized as he wrapped her against him was that the hunger in him was still leashed. She felt that hunger in the hardness of his body, knew it in the warmth of his mouth, but it was under control. A deep feminine instinct made her want to be the woman who could release and satisfy that hunger.

The knowledge shook her and the trembling in her slender frame seemed to seek solace from the rising heat of his passion.

When his lips moved persuasively on hers, Brenna lifted her arms to encircle his neck as she opened her mouth to him. His questing tongue surged inside with a reckless aggression that thrilled her. He explored the warm, wet secrets behind her lips with an arousing, exciting boldness that left her the hungry one.

She sank heavily against him and he accepted the weight of her, letting it carry them both backward until she was lying on top of him. When Brenna tried to catch her breath and her common sense, he tangled her legs in his own and held her head close.

"A little more," he breathed huskily and she obeyed. Of their own volition her tender hands framed the rough, craggy planes of his face as she responded to the kiss. Her mind was whirling with the sensual pleasures that beckoned and seduced. He was altogether different, and she felt compelled to explore whatever it was he offered.

Their tongues met in an intricate dance of primitive courtship as Ryder flattened his palms along her back and began to stroke her in long, rhythmic motions.

Unconsciously Brenna's body arched into him in response, glorying in the lean strength awaiting her.

When she moaned, he drank the sound from her throat as if it were nectar and then he asked for more. Her small, muffled cry came once more, and this time he splayed his fingers across the curve of her hips and forced her gently against his thighs.

With that sensual contact Brenna was made fiercely aware of the thrusting, potent strength of his desire. The dazzling surge of excitement through her body suffused it with a warm flush that seemed to elevate her temperature. He wanted her and heaven help her, she wanted him! Never had it been like this. Never had a man fascinated and intrigued her in quite this way. She wanted to forget about the future and the past and do anything in her power to continue in this delightful plane of unreality.

"Ryder?" His name was a question and a plea on her lips as she lifted her head an inch to meet his eyes.

The tawny lashes rose, revealing the molten silver behind them. He looked deeply into her drugged and dream-filled gaze for a long moment.

"I told you on the dance floor that the choice would be yours tonight, lady," he said with dark velvet in his words. "Just remember that I will hold you to your decision if you choose to take the risk."

"What risk?"

"The risk of inviting me into your bed."

Hearing it spelled out so bluntly sent a tremor through her but she managed not to lower her lashes in spite of the confusion she was experiencing. "What is the risk, Ryder? That you won't stay long in my bed?'' she provoked deliberately, ignoring the pain of that possibility.

His mouth crooked and he lifted his fingers to spear them through the sleek knot of her hair, dislodging the clip. ''No, you little idiot, the risk you're taking is that I will stay there. Don't you understand, Brenna? I won't let you go after I've made you mine. Hell, I might not let you go even if you back away entirely tonight!'' he ended forcefully.

''What are you talking about?'' she whispered.

''I'm talking about commitment, and the fact that you have to ask the question means it's probably much too soon for me to claim you. It means you're probably not thinking in those terms.'' He twisted his hands through her unloosened hair and his mouth continued to smile gently even though his eyes were gleaming and largely unreadable.

''You want a…a commitment from me? That's something of a switch, isn't it?'' she tried to ask mockingly and failed miserably. Her amber gaze was darkening with tension and the unknown aspects of the moment. ''Isn't it usually the woman who—'' She broke off, unable to continue. Her crimson nails dug anxiously into the blue silk shirt.

''I'm not concerned with how it 'usually' is,'' he rasped. ''I'm only concerned with how it is for me and you. I want you, Brenna, but I'm willing to take the time to make it right for both of us. I'm willing to wait for you. I'm warning you that if you give yourself to me tonight, you won't find yourself free of me in the morning. Do you understand now? I won't play the part of a summer novelty for you to explore while you're running around outside your ivory tower.''

"No! I never meant…"

He shook his head. "I know I represent a different world to you, and perhaps under the spell of the evening and your own curiosity you find yourself attracted. If that's all it amounts to, you'd better back away from the flames before you get singed."

"It's not like that at all!" she proclaimed fiercely, the need to reassure him somehow more important than a close look at the truth. "Believe me, Ryder, it's not like that…"

Knowing no other way to counter his accusation, Brenna caught his face once more in her hands and ground her mouth almost savagely down on his. She would not, could not, examine her options in the intellectual way she ought to. Brenna only knew that the night must not end with Ryder Sterne walking out her door.

Ryder's arms tightened around her with rough gentleness as he slowly sat up against the pressure of her slender weight. He never broke the kiss but Brenna found herself cradled across his thighs, her arms wound passionately around his neck.

Then, in a surge of masculine power, Ryder was on his feet with Brenna in his arms. Still holding her mouth in the compelling mastery of his own, he started toward the stairs of the loft.

Chapter 4

One of Brenna's high-heeled red sandals slipped off and fell on a step as Ryder carried her effortlessly up the stairs. She wasn't really aware of the small loss, but the toes of her nylon-clad foot curled in a tiny gesture of gathering sensual tension. Ryder's arms felt strong and secure about her, and she nestled against his chest in languid, delicious abandon.

At the top of the stairs he at last broke the enthralling, lingering kiss to lift his head and search her bemused, heavy-lidded expression.

"Tonight you're a golden-eyed witch," he told her huskily.

"And you?" she countered, touching the corner of his mouth with a fingertip. "What are you tonight?"

"Only a man. But one who wants you very much. Will that be enough for you?"

What was he asking? Brenna wondered distantly.

Whatever the real question, she wanted nothing more than to reassure him.

"It will be enough." Perhaps he was concerned that she would ask too much of him, demand more than he could give. Yet he had been the one who had talked of commitment. She didn't understand but she didn't want to get too involved in an analysis of the situation, either. Not now, not tonight. Tonight was a special place and a special time and she wanted only to exist within those borders. "Ryder, I'm not truly a witch. Only a woman. Will that be enough for you?" she heard herself ask a little anxiously.

"It's all I want," he whispered, his voice as deep and gentle as she had yet heard it.

He carried her to the bed and lowered her carefully to her feet beside it.

"Oh!" The small exclamation came as Brenna stumbled slightly against him and instinctively braced herself with palms splayed across his shoulders.

"What's wrong?" He steadied her at once.

"My shoe." She smiled in soft amusement. "I seem to have arrived with only one."

"Playing at being Cinderella after the ball?" He eased her to a sitting position on the edge of the bed and went down on one knee in front of her.

"Only if you're interested in the Prince Charming role," she tried to say nonchalantly and was very much afraid she failed.

She didn't feel nonchalant tonight. She felt elated, nervous, passionate, and high-strung. She felt a dizzying conglomeration of emotions but she didn't feel at all nonchalant.

"No, I'm not quite right for that role." Deliberately Ryder put his hand on her uncovered knee and slid it silkily down her calf to the foot that still wore a shoe. Slowly he began to unfasten the buckle of the tiny red strap. "I'm much more interested in undressing you than I am in finding you a slipper that fits. Tonight I'd make a lousy Prince Charming." His mouth twisted in a wry self-mockery that touched her heart.

Instinctively Brenna threaded her hands through his hair and moved them slowly down to rest on his shoulders. An unbidden, feminine perception told her that he was asking obliquely for reassurance of her desire for him. How could she refuse? Tonight she wanted to give this man everything he asked.

He looked up at her from under the tawny lashes and she smiled tenderly. "Tonight you're a perfect Prince Charming. Exactly as I always thought Prince Charming would be."

Without a word he lifted his hands to pull her head down to his, and this time she knew from his kiss that the hunger she sensed in him was rapidly coming unbound. Why had he maintained it under such restraint? A man's desire, she had always thought, was a relatively simple thing and certainly not something he bothered to conceal or control when the opportunity to indulge it occurred.

But Ryder was different and the quality of his desire was different. She felt a hunger that was not strictly sexual underlying it and knew a fierce joy at being the one who could unleash it.

When she moaned throatily under the impact of the spiraling kiss, Ryder lowered one hand to trace the distance from her shoulder to the tip of her breast. He drew in his breath sharply when he discovered the taut outline of her nipple and pushed her back against the quilt. He followed, coming down heavily beside her while he continued to move his thumb provocatively against the sensitive peak.

Brenna arched upward, seeking more of his touch, and whispered his name softly into his mouth. His hand went to the bright red sash that held the white dress low on her hip. It loosened magically beneath his touch. Slowly he continued to undress her, finding the fastenings of the eyelet dress while he buried his mouth at the pulsepoint of her throat.

"Oh, Ryder!"

Brenna's head tipped back over his arm in silent supplication and surrender and her eyes shut tightly against the wonder of the moment. Everything was so perfect; he was so perfect.

"You're so exactly right for me," he grated in a velvet-gentle voice as the white dress slipped down to her waist and the curves of her breasts were revealed. Only the filmiest of lace and satin remained and the thrusting tips of her nipples were clearly outlined. "Small and sleek and sensuous."

He found the center clasp of the demicup bra and undid it. When the lacy covering fell aside, he groaned as he began to trail a string of kisses from the base of her throat to the rose-tipped crests.

"My little lady cat burglar," he whispered thickly as he stroked the length of her to her hips. "I wanted to do this the night you crawled through my window!"

"No," she protested even though the excitement was flaming through her at his words. "You didn't want me like this. Not then..."

"You still don't know me that well, do you?"

But he gave her no chance to reply as he curled

his tongue coaxingly around her nipple and traced a circle that made her breath catch in her throat. Her red-gilt nails sank into the shoulders beneath the blue silk shirt as she cried out.

Her response seemed to arouse him still further. In an swift, smooth movement he slid his palms down the curve of her hips, pushing the remainder of her clothing all the way to her ankles and off the bed. In one long, sweeping stroke she was suddenly and completely nude.

Brenna's eyes opened to find him drinking in the sight of her as his fingers went to the buttons of the blue shirt.

"No, let me," she managed, struggling to a sitting position and finding the buttons with fingers that trembled from passionate excitement.

The tawny lashes feathered his cheeks as he let his own hands fall aside. Ryder sat very still as she worked at the fastenings of the blue shirt. But when she slipped her palms beneath the open edges to find the curling hair that covered his bronzed chest, he muttered her name a little violently and caught her wrists.

"Brenna, my golden-eyed witch, you'll drive me crazy if I give you free rein! I want this to last all night!"

"I'm the one who will go crazy if you try to make it last forever," she protested huskily. "I...I *need* you too badly."

She bit off the words, a part of her astounded by them. She had never truly *needed* a man in quite this way. This was different than mere affection tinged with sexual attraction. This was different than the time in graduate school when she had thought she was truly in love. This was different than the way she felt toward Damon. She needed Ryder Sterne and she ached to please him.

"Do you, Brenna?" he growled in his dragon's purr. "Do you really need me?"

"More than anything else in the world," she answered with an honesty that would have surprised her in another context. She lifted her lashes and the gold in her eyes met the silver in his. He groaned in satisfaction and a kind of relief. She knew in that moment that the strange hunger in him was finally and completely unleashed. He made no further protest as she fumbled with the remainder of his clothes.

"You're beautiful," she breathed in wonder as he finally lay naked beside her. With delicate, questing fingertips she traced the shape of him, moving across the contours of his smoothly muscled chest, down to the flat stomach and over the muscular shape of his hip.

Unable to resist, she bent to kiss the center of his chest as her hand clenched a little aggressively into the hard male buttock. Instantly his fingers wrapped themselves in her hair and he pulled her forcibly up to find his mouth.

"We'll make the next time last," he promised thickly against her mouth. "This time I'm not going to be able to play the gentleman!"

"Ryder!" His name was choked from her as, his hands still entwined in the depths of her bittersweet-chocolate hair, he moved, shifting her firmly onto her back. He sprawled heavily across her, his thigh pinning hers as he quenched his thirst at her mouth.

"I'm sorry, sweet lady," he muttered against her lips as he held her face cupped fiercely in his excit-

ingly rough palms. "I meant to play the gallant lover
but I can't. Not this first time with you. All I can
think of now is making you mine completely and absolutely. Do you understand? I can't be sexually sophisticated tonight and impress you with my charm
and gallantry. I want you too badly!"

Brenna couldn't answer. Her own passion was running too high and her senses seemed to swim. Her
nails dug compellingly into his shoulders and she
arched her hips against the pressure of his body. It
was the only response she could manage.

It was enough. With a violently tender exclamation
Ryder slid his palm over her breasts, down the small
contour of her stomach, and found the tangled thicket
below. He forced her legs gently apart with his knee
and let his probing fingers discover the intimate secret
of her.

When she writhed beneath him at the touch, he
whispered her name hoarsely and pressed the hard
strength of his body testingly against her thighs.

"Please. Ryder, please!"

"My God, sweet lady!"

He lifted himself, his shoulders looming briefly
over her in the shadowy light, and then he settled
himself along the length of her, fitting himself between her legs with a gentle aggression that sent shivers through Brenna's nerve endings.

She reached up, clinging to him as if he were all
that mattered in the world, welcoming him completely.

He came to her with a bold power that shocked her
senses. Her nails raked the contour of his back and
his name was a silent cry of desire and passion on
her lips as he held her with a strength she couldn't

have defied even if she had been so inclined. Then he was surging against her body, taking it by storm and sweeping her along into a vortex of swirling color and sensation. Ryder Sterne made love as if he were staking a claim; tuning a fine instrument only to his personal touch; taming a wild creature. The experience overwhelmed and consumed Brenna's senses.

He established a rhythm to which she responded at once. She locked her arms and legs around his driving body, thrilling to the potent, sinewy feel of him. When her nails dug deeper in a convulsive reaction, he nipped passionately at the smooth flesh of her shoulder. The small, tingling pain only served to heighten her awareness to new levels.

Together they spun through their own private universe, so tightly entwined they were as one as they made the sensual journey. When the coiling, flickering tension in Brenna's loins began to flare out of control, she gulped for air and tensed in Ryder's hold.

"Ryder! Ryder, darling!"

He must have heard the amazement and wonder and perhaps even an element of fear in her words as she faced the blazing conclusion of the trip.

"Let yourself go, lady," he rasped. "Give yourself to me!"

As if his words were the last impulse her body needed to send her over the edge, Brenna went abruptly taut beneath him, and then the explosion took her in a series of tiny convulsions that swept her from head to toe.

"Oh, Ryder!"

As if he, in turn, only needed her finish to spark his own, Ryder swept into her body once more, filling her completely and holding her with total possession as he reached the end of his journey.

Long moments later Brenna stirred beneath the heavy male body still covering her own. At the hint of movement Ryder lazily lifted his tousled, tawny head from her breast and looked down at her, the faintest of smiles edging his mouth. The molten silver in his eyes had cooled to be replaced by a warm satisfaction that pleased Brenna. She had fed the hunger in him.

They stared wonderingly at each other in silence for a time, each absorbing the fullness of the moment, and then Ryder ducked his head briefly to drop a tiny kiss on her love-softened mouth.

''I know this is going to sound ridiculous in the light of events, but when I picked you up at your door this evening, I honestly had no intention of winding up in your bed later,'' he confessed.

''Was it fate or free will?'' she teased dreamily, playing with the perspiration-damp hair at the back of his neck.

''I don't know and I don't particularly care. It happened. That's all that matters now.''

She opened her eyes a little wider at the forcefulness of the statement. ''Are you upset about what happened, Ryder?'' Please, no, she thought. She only wanted him to be happy!

''Of course not,'' he drawled, his expression softening at once. ''It was a little too soon and involved some risks because of that, but perhaps there wasn't any other way it could have gone. You're mine now, Brenna. I've waited a long time to find you, lady, and now that I have I won't be letting you go.''

''I'm not going anywhere. Not tonight,'' she

soothed, uncertain of his meaning and unwilling to press for clarification. The night was too precious.

He stroked back the dark hair from her damp forehead and smiled with incredible gentleness. "No, you won't be going anywhere tonight." Then he shook his head once in amused bafflement. "A professor of philosophy. How could I have possibly guessed?"

"Guessed what?" she prompted curiously, enjoying the soothing touch of his fingers across her brow. She wriggled beneath him contentedly.

"That I'd find the woman I wanted and needed, the one who understood about things like honor and the one who was capable of sending me out of my head with desire, on the faculty of some small college of which I had never heard. Hell, Brenna," he added with a wry chuckle deep in his throat. "I finished college in the Marine Corps, and I can assure you there wasn't much attention paid to subjects like ethics and philosophy!"

"A limited education?"

"A practical education," he corrected with a small grin. He lowered his head for another nibbling kiss, drawing back with some reluctance. "Are you happy with the results of your seductive techniques tonight, lady?" he taunted lightly.

"I refuse to answer on the grounds that it might tend to incriminate me," she murmured, drawing inviting little circles on his upper arms.

"Well," he retorted deliberately, "I suppose it doesn't much matter whether or not I manage to drag a confession out of you. It's done. You're mine."

Brenna thought about that, aware of the determination in him and not quite comprehending his full meaning. He was a possessive man, it would seem.

And tonight he possessed her. She didn't want to think any further than that.

"Don't go to sleep on me, witch," he drawled humorously as her lashes lowered to her cheeks. "That first time was to settle the issue. Now that it's settled, I'm going to take the time to make a good impression."

Her mouth curved. "Is that a threat?"

"Just try to stay awake so you can applaud the performance, okay?"

He shaped her head with his fingers and lowered his mouth once more to hers. This time his kiss was slow and lingeringly passionate as he set about stoking the banked fires back to shimmering brightness.

Ryder took his time, as promised, moving over her languid body with finesse and an arousing strength that pushed aside the remnants of earlier passion and set about creating a new experience. She was stroked from breast to thigh, teased with sensitive fingers that knew exactly where to tempt and tantalize. And his kisses, she thought deliriously, his kisses were a sweet ravishment. He poured them without restraint across the roundness of her breasts, dropped them delicately onto the softness of her stomach, and branded them into the exquisitely tender skin of her inner thighs. Brenna had temporarily lost herself in his arms the last time. This time she thought she might never find her way back out.

When he came to her at last, enveloping her in his warmth, she never gave another thought to the prospect of being permanently lost. He flowed into her body and across it and there was no way she could have resisted. This time, when the shimmering conclusion approached, she gave herself up to it without any fear at all, welcoming the flames of surrender in the safety of Ryder's arms.

When it was over he turned her gently on her side, pulled her tightly into the curve of his glisteningly damp body, and ordered her to sleep in the softest of whispers.

"Ryder, I feel like I'm floating."

"So do I. Go to sleep, lady."

"Why?"

"Because that's what I'm going to do and I can't bear the thought of you lying awake staring at the ceiling while I'm snoring blissfully!"

"Oh, dear. Do you snore?" She chuckled.

"It's a little late to worry about it. Tonight you've agreed to take the good with the bad." He yawned, nestling his head against hers.

"Tonight's almost over, Ryder," she pointed out wistfully.

"There's tomorrow to look forward to. Good night, sweet lady."

"Good night, Prince Charming."

He laughed sleepily and then he was asleep. A moment later so was Brenna.

She awoke the next morning in a warm, tousled bed, the down quilt snuggled close to her chin. Her first impression was that something was wrong.

Brenna's eyes opened slowly to find the sunlight filtering brightly through the window cut in the peaked roof. It was late. But that wasn't what was wrong. Her legs stretched idly and she became aware of a faint soreness in the muscles of her thighs.

Not an unpleasant sensation in and of itself, but it brought back memories of the night with alarming speed. Brenna struggled to a sitting position, glancing around her bedroom with a kind of fear. Where was Ryder?

It wasn't his absence that seemed wrong, it was the possibility that he would step out of the bathroom or come up the stairs with breakfast at any minute that sent a wave of panic through her senses.

My God! What had she done last night? She must have been out of her mind! With heartfelt anxiety she tossed back the quilt and stumbled to her feet, chilled in the morning light. Shakily she reached for the fluffy, high-necked, saffron-colored robe lying across the foot of the bed. It was only as she belted it on that she remembered it hadn't been there last night. Ryder had put it out for her. She stood very still for a moment, listening to the quiet sounds of the cabin. Then she began to relax slightly. He wasn't in the house, she was certain now.

A bath, she thought grimly, that was what she needed first. The scent of him seemed to have somehow combined with her own. She made her way to the bathroom and locked the door behind her.

What the hell was the matter with her? Brenna demanded of herself in the mirror. Why was she so nervous this morning? So she had let herself be seduced by a mood and a man unlike any other she had ever known. What was so terrible about that? It wasn't as if she had been unfaithful to Damon. Her relationship with Dr. Fielding hadn't even progressed as far as the bedroom yet and she'd known him, worked with him, for months!

Which didn't make her feel one bit better. Brenna looked away from the anxious expression in her own eyes, turned on the shower, and stepped underneath the spray with alacrity.

No, her relationship with Damon hadn't gotten to the point her association with Ryder Sterne had reached in three days! With a shock of startled realization, Brenna knew that even if she were to know Damon Fielding another ten years, even if she were to go to bed with him every night of that ten years, her relationship with him would never be quite what she'd found with Ryder last night.

The knowledge made her catch her lower lip between her teeth, and another rush of panic seemed to tingle through her bloodstream. Why had she gotten herself into this mess? She closed her eyes at the thought of how Ryder had given her a chance to halt matters before it was too late.

But it had already been too late, even at that point. Somehow the culmination of the evening had been inevitable. Not a pleasant thought for someone who taught the ethics of responsibility and free choice! Brenna's fingers curled into a small fist and she braced her forearm against the tiled wall of the shower. Leaning her forehead against her arm, she let the warm water pound over her while she tried desperately to think.

Over and over again she told herself that nothing all that devastating had happened. She had never been a promiscuous person and she needn't condemn herself for succumbing to the incredible attraction Ryder had held for her last night. There had been very, very few serious romances in her life, she reflected bracingly. Surely a woman her age was allowed the mind-spinning excitement of a night like last night at least once.

She knew, though, that she was, in a sense, chastising herself to no purpose. It wasn't that she felt guilty; it wasn't that she felt as if she'd been disloyal to Damon, who certainly dated other women. There was no point in berating herself for any of the traditional reasons.

The real problem, the one that had to be faced, was that last night had been, in some indefinable way, an act of surrender. She had given herself to Ryder and he had taken possession.

What if he chose to retain that possession now that the night of passion had passed?

With that thought, the full truth surfaced amid the chaos of her thoughts and Brenna straightened away from the shower wall. Facing a truth with intelligence and dispassionate calm was something she was normally very good at.

Unfortunately the kind of truth she was usually compelled to face was of an intellectual nature that made no real impact on her emotions. This was of an altogether different nature and she swallowed unhappily at the implications.

What was Ryder thinking this morning? Where was he? Perhaps he would make everything easy for her by letting the happenings of the night slip away into oblivion. Perhaps he would make no further demands now that morning had come. He, too, had been sharing her separate reality last night. With the advent of day he might have returned, as she had, to the real world.

But then she remembered the curious, restrained hunger in him that she had been so eager to unleash and satisfy. Brenna knew instinctively that it was more than a physical appetite. She had sensed that from the beginning. What had she done by giving it herself to feed upon?

It all came down to an emotion more primitive than she would have imagined could still exist in a civilized, intelligent, reasonably sophisticated human female. She felt claimed.

Unnerved, Brenna turned off the shower and reached clumsily for one of the thick, striped towels. Claimed. Possessed.

What if Ryder chose to exercise his claim?

This was ridiculous, Brenna told herself violently as she furiously towel-dried her dark hair. Utterly ridiculous! What was the matter with her? Number one, he probably wouldn't dare presume too much on the basis of one night, and number two, she was a mature, independent woman who could handle the matter firmly and politely if he did!

Oh, lord! Who was she kidding?

Her scattered thoughts ricocheted around inside her head as she dragged a comb through the wet tendrils of her hair and twisted the dark mass into a long braid that hung down between her shoulders. The severity of the style suited her mood, she thought wretchedly.

Where was Ryder?

Sooner of later she was going to have to deal with the man, she told herself tensely as she pulled on her jeans and found a long-sleeved plaid shirt. She was tucking in the ends of it and groping under the bed for her flat sandals when she heard a knock on the door. Brenna froze.

Blindly she glanced down at the shoe she had retrieved. It wasn't her flat, casual sandal at all. It was the red high-heeled dress shoe Ryder had removed last night. The knock sounded once more, this time with a note of impatience that surprised her.

Why was Ryder knocking in the first place, and in

the second, why should he sound impatient? He was the one who had left her bed this morning. Knowing him, she couldn't understand why he didn't feel quite free to walk back into her cabin at his leisure.

"Brenna! Are you inside?"

With a gasp Brenna got to her feet, still clutching the red sandal. The voice outside her door wasn't Ryder's. It belonged to Damon Fielding!

The next knock jolted her into action. As she started down the stairs she shook her head in annoyance. She had to get a grip on herself.

It should have been harder to open the door to Damon Fielding than it would have been to open it to Ryder. Damon, after all, occupied a much more important role in her life and there was a great deal unsettled between them. He was the man who could assist her in her career, guide her through the intricacies of faculty politics, and lately, she had begun to think, the man whom she might eventually marry. But somehow, when she turned the knob, all Brenna could think of was how grateful she was that she wasn't going to have to face Ryder just yet.

"Damon! What in the world are you doing here?"

She looked up at the dark-haired man of medium height who stood on her doorstep. Professor Damon Fielding had spent a year studying at Oxford sometime in his academic past and it still showed. He wore the tweed jacket with its leather patches on the elbows, the button-down shirt, and the slacks and loafers with aplomb. Nearing forty, Dr. Fielding was aware of his position as next in line to assume the responsibilities of head of the Department of Philosophy when Paul Humphrey retired. He was a good-looking man with stylishly cut hair of the proper length and charmingly blue eyes. He had been divorced from his first wife, a professor of English, for three years. He was, above all else, a highly respected scholar in his area of expertise.

"Good morning, Brenna. Going somewhere exciting?" He smiled down at her and the red sandal she still held in her hand.

"No, no, of course not." Hurriedly Brenna backed away, gesturing him politely inside. "I'm astonished to see you, Damon. Did you drive all this way just to find me?"

"Who else do I know in Lake Tahoe?" He chuckled, stooping to kiss her lightly. "Got a cup of coffee for a man who's had a long trip?"

"Right away. How about breakfast? Did you stop along the way?" Thankful for the excuse, Brenna hurried toward the kitchen.

"No, and I'll admit that sounds like an excellent suggestion." Damon wandered interestedly into the living room, glancing around. "Enjoying the summer, Brenna?"

"It's hardly started," she protested a little weakly, searching the refrigerator for something edible. It would have to be eggs and toast and coffee. "Did you...did you drive up just for the day?"

"No, I was visiting a colleague in Sacramento and decided on the spur of the moment to come on up to Tahoe. I was a little worried about you, darling."

She glanced up to see him watching her, his hands thrust into the pockets of his jacket. Any moment now he would light his pipe and the image would be complete. Her lips tightened as she closed the refrigerator door.

"It's kind of you to be concerned, Damon," she

began formally, "but this is something I'm going to have to think about for a while."

"That's why I'm here, darling," he explained magnanimously, "to help you think. Normally you're one of the most rational, analytical people I know, but on this one subject you can't seem to be realistic."

"Damon, Paul Humphrey is publishing my work under his own name, for God's sake! That's wrong, any way you look at it! Unethical, unprofessional, dishonorable, and unworthy! What the hell do you expect me to do? I may only be a very junior assistant professor but I've got my rights!"

"You also have your future to consider!" he snapped forcefully, clearly annoyed with her inability to be reasonable.

"My future involves teaching things like ethics and the honorable quest for truth! How can I presume to teach such things when I'm personally choosing to ignore them!"

They faced each other across the short space of the kitchen. Where in the world was Ryder? Brenna wondered incongruously. Where had he gone when he'd left her bed this morning? And why was she thinking about him at a time like this? Damon Fielding had come all this way to talk sense into her. She should be thrilled at this sign of his concern!

"Brenna, you're living in the real world, not some perfect construct where everyone behaves according to an ethical code! Be reasonable. Paul Humphrey will be retiring very soon, perhaps even earlier than we thought. His career is over and yours is just beginning. You can't punish him, because it would always be a case of your word against his. He's got a brilliant academic career behind him. You've got virtually nothing yet, except your doctorate and a bottom rung on the faculty ladder. You'll only wind up hurting your own future, perhaps even destroying it, if you accuse him of stealing your work!''

"No wonder you're so good in front of a class full of students, Damon." She tried to smile weakly. "Your logic is impeccable and your delivery is perfect!" She pulled out the frying pan and began to crack eggs into a bowl. "But it's no good. I honestly don't know if I can go back and work for the man in the fall."

"You little idiot," he declared tightly, his temper apparently on edge. With reason, she thought fleetingly. He hadn't even had breakfast yet and here he was trying to deal with a crazy young faculty member. "You'll be back in the fall and you know it! What else can you do? Jobs for philosophy professors are damn scarce! It could take you months, maybe a year to line up another one. And in the end you would have achieved nothing."

"How about my pride and self-respect?" she hazarded dryly, beating the eggs violently.

"What good are they going to do you in a world where there are a lot of Paul Humphreys? And that's the way it will be, Brenna. Our faculty politics are no different than those of any other college or university. If you're going to get ahead, you've got to play the game. That means not embarrassing men like Paul Humphrey or making yourself look like a fool!"

"Good lord, Damon! You make it sound like corporate politics in the business world! All the maneuvering and power struggles and the pains taken to avoid embarrassing the boss or yourself!" She dropped the egg beater and whirled to face him, her hands on her hips.

"That's exactly what it's like! There's a price on success in any sphere, and playing the political game is part of that price," he grated.

"You're telling me you think it's all right to pay the price?" she challenged tersely.

"Yes, damn it! It's the only way one can make a contribution to his or her profession!"

"The ends justify the means? Do you realize what you're saying, Damon? We're talking about theft and dishonorable conduct. Do you realize what you're condoning? What that makes you?"

She didn't know why she pushed him that far. She certainly never intended to do so. Perhaps it was because she was so unnerved and upset with herself this morning. Brenna only knew she hadn't meant to enrage the man she had actually been contemplating marrying!

But she had done exactly that. She saw the red flush sweep into his face, saw the hardening line of his mouth, and the next instant his palm connected with the side of her cheek in an instinctive reaction to the insult in her words and eyes.

Even as she flinched automatically from the blow, Damon was being whirled around by the shoulder. Ryder was in the room.

She had never seen him enter, never heard that silent stride as he crossed to the kitchen. The first intimation of his presence was when he swung a fist that collided with Damon's jaw.

Dr. Damon Fielding toppled to the floor before Brenna's horrified gaze.

Chapter 5

"Damon!"

Rushing to the fallen man's side was an automatic reflex, Brenna realized even as she did so. She would have gone to the aid of whichever man had taken the fall.

"Leave him alone, Brenna, he'll be fine." Ryder's voice was incredibly soft.

But she was already kneeling on the floor beside the other man even as Damon groaned and opened his eyes weakly. She threw a furious, accusing glare up at Ryder, who stood easily, feet slightly braced, his expression utterly unruffled. He had obviously been back to his own cabin, because he was again wearing the black denim jeans he favored and an open-throated white shirt with a tiny stripe in it. His brown and gold hair was lightly raked by the morning breeze and his recent exertion, and when his silver-gray eyes met Brenna's angry glance, she saw the memory of last night hovering just below the surface. For some reason that fueled her own fury and disgust.

"There was no call for this kind of violence, Ryder," she stormed. "Is this how you handle any problem that comes along? With stupid acts of unthinking machismo? This man is a colleague of mine! A respected professor of philosophy! Do you realize what you've done?"

Ryder looked down at her, his eyes momentarily unreadable. "He deserved it. He struck you."

"Well, I deserved that!" she raged. "I said some terrible things to him, insulted him!" And she had, Brenna thought, horrified. She'd unforgivably insulted the man who had cared enough about her future in the academic world to come all this way to talk sense to her. Why had she done such a thing?

"Get away from him, Brenna. Come here." Ryder didn't seem inclined to argue at the moment. His attention went to his victim, who was slowly lifting a hand to touch a tender jaw.

Defiantly Brenna didn't move, turning a worried glance down at Damon. "Damon, Damon, I'm so sorry about all this! I never meant to insult you like that and I certainly never meant to involve you in a fight with Ryder. Are you all right? Here, let me help you…"

"Brenna, I said get away from him. Come over here or I'll come and get you."

This time something in his voice reached her and Brenna tensed. She had heard that soft, gentle tone before—when he was giving a command and when he was making love. In both instances, she had discovered, it was equally dangerous. Uncertainly she got to her feet, her worried eyes still on Damon, who was painfully sitting up. The other man's attention was focused narrowly on Ryder.

"Who's the cowboy, Brenna? Friend of yours, I take it. Is this how you always spend your summers? Shacked up with some stud you wouldn't normally be seen with during the academic year?"

"Oh, Damon, please, you don't understand..." Brenna began plaintively. She heard the enraged humiliation in his words and wanted to soothe it away. It was all her fault.

"That's enough from both of you," Ryder cut in dryly. "In case either of you has failed to notice the fact, I happen to be the one in charge here at the moment and I'm not in the mood to listen to any more accusations, apologies, or uncouth comments. You, Professor, will get to your feet and get out of here. You're not badly hurt and you know it. If, however, you ever lay another hand on Brenna, I will personally take you apart, is that quite clear?"

"Go to hell." But Damon was on his feet and moving resentfully toward the door. When Brenna would have put out a placating hand to touch his sleeve, her face anguished, Ryder stopped her with a single word.

"Brenna!"

Her hand fell away and she watched the other man walk out the door. She knew even as she watched his retreating tweed jacket that it wasn't just a man walking out of her life, but in all likelihood, her entire future at the college where Damon Fielding would someday be head of the Department of Philosophy. She hadn't been ready yet to make such a final decision, and now that decision had been made for her.

Eyes flaming, she whirled on Ryder as Damon slammed the door.

"Do you have any idea of what you've just done? How did you dare? How could you presume to walk in here this morning and ruin my whole life!"

He stared at her for a moment. "Brenna, I walked in here and found a strange male slapping you around. What the hell did you expect me to do?" She had the feeling he wasn't accustomed to explaining his actions to anyone.

"I would have expected a rational, intelligent, civilized man to ask a few questions and find out what was going on before he interfered!"

He arched an eyebrow. "Okay." He shrugged. "So what was going on?"

"Damn you! It's a little late to be asking that now, isn't it?"

"You mean too late now that I've, uh, ruined your whole life?" he queried wryly.

"It's not a joke!"

"You can say that again! Do you have any idea what it's like for a man to walk in on a scene like the one I just witnessed? My God, Brenna, he's lucky I didn't beat him to a pulp!"

"What stopped you?" she gritted scathingly.

"Chalk it up to the fact that I was feeling magnanimous after spending such a delightful evening," he bit out far too gently. Belatedly it began to occur to Brenna that Ryder was furious.

"A delightful evening enjoying the novelty of seducing a college professor?" she hissed tauntingly.

"A delightful evening being seduced by one," he corrected coolly. "I wasn't the one who rushed matters, as I recall. I distinctly remember saying I was prepared to wait.''

"You're saying that last night was my fault?" she blazed, her anger now at such a high level, she had momentarily forgotten Damon.

He considered that. "Yes."

"Why, you ill-bred, ill-mannered, ill-behaved..."

"Stud?" he offered helpfully, a new emotion rousing in the silver eyes to douse some of the controlled fury. Humor?

It was more than Brenna could stand, coming as it did after everything she'd been through in the past twelve hours. She swiveled and grabbed at the nearest object that came to hand, a philosophy text as it happened. Without a pause she sent it sailing toward her tormentor.

The flicker of amusement vanished in Ryder's expression as he stepped aside and let the missile crash into the wall behind him. For an instant after the text had landed harmlessly on the floor, there was utter silence in the room. Brenna stood staring, eyes wide, lips parted in shock at her own violence. And then Ryder started toward her.

Panic overwhelmed her. She wanted to turn and flee but couldn't find the muscle control to do so. The combination of her own guilt, the trauma of the morning's events, and remnants of her anger somehow combined to make it impossible for her to run from him. Since there was no alternative, Brenna stood her ground, hands curled into fists on her hips, chin tilted in a defiance she was far from feeling.

He paced toward her with the gliding, deliberate stride of a hunting cat, and when he reached a point less than a step away he stopped.

"As I've said before, you don't cower when the chips are down, do you?" His words were almost whimsical.

Brenna said nothing; her breath was coming a little too quickly and her pulse was racing, fired by the adrenaline of her emotions.

"Can I take it from your reaction that you don't consider me merely an amusing stud with whom you've decided to shack up this summer?" he persisted dryly.

"You're being insufferable," she managed tightly.

"I know," he admitted on a sigh of regret. "You'll have to forgive me. I've had a trying few minutes."

To her utter astonishment he spun around on one booted heel and started toward the kitchen. "There is a time for action and a time for talk, lady. There is also a time to eat. The action's over and I suggest we proceed to the other two items on the agenda. Ah, good, you've already started," he added calmly as he plucked another egg out of the carton.

Driven by an impulse she didn't quite understand, Brenna narrowed her eyes and said meaningfully, "I was fixing breakfast for Damon."

"Damon's gone," he pointed out blandly.

"Ryder…"

"Sit down, Brenna. We're going to talk."

The underlying steel in the too-gentle voice was enough to convince her to do as he said. He wasn't the only one who'd had a trying few minutes. Mutely she crossed slowly to the round wooden table near the window and sank into the chair, watching as he methodically fixed breakfast.

He took in the sight of her tightly folded hands and stiff shoulders and the silent resentment in her eyes and shook his head once before he went back to cracking eggs. "I'm not going to apologize for what just happened, Brenna. Any man who walked in on a scene like that would have reacted in the same manner."

"Any man who makes it a habit to indulge his physical, violent reactions to a situation, you mean!"

He lifted one shoulder dismissingly. "If you think that was bad, you ought to see what I would have done if I'd walked in and found him kissing you, instead! Besides, if I may take the liberty of saying so, the man was engaging in a little violence himself!"

Brenna squeezed her eyes shut in pained memory and seemed to sag a little in despair. "Oh, Ryder, you should have heard what I said to him!"

"I did hear some of it but I didn't understand it all. What was going on, Brenna?" he prompted quietly as he poured tea.

She looked up at him bleakly. "The man came up here to help me. He's concerned about me, my career. I'm…I'm in the middle of a major decision, you see. Whatever I decide to do will affect my whole future. Poor Damon was only trying to make me see the reasonable side of the situation…" She gave a muffled exclamation and reached for the tea he had poured. "Never mind, it's complicated and I doubt that you'd really be interested—"

"You know damn well I'm interested," he interrupted grimly. "Go on."

Brenna hesitated a moment longer and then gave in. What did it matter if she told him the tale? "You must have heard how it is in the academic world when it comes to the importance of faculty members getting published in their field?''

''Publish or perish?''

''I'm afraid it truly is that bad. If you want to advance and gain tenure, it's an absolute necessity. I have been working for months on a major paper on the subject of computer ethics...''

''Computer ethics!'' Ryder appeared startled for the first time.

Brenna smiled a tiny, wan smile. ''It's a hot new field for philosophy as a whole. Practically speaking, philosophy departments have fallen out of favor on a lot of campuses. Not everyone still sees the study of philosophy as critical to a modern education. The issue of the ethics of computer use and abuse in the modern world is a way for philosophy to get back into the mainstream and help keep itself alive as an intellectual field. It's kind of an *applied* philosophy.'' She paused and looked at him uncertainly.

''Okay, I'll take your word for it,'' he muttered, peering closely at the scrambled eggs in the frying pan.

''At any rate, I've put a lot of work into a paper that assesses the logic and ethics of computers in the light of historical philosophical thinking. Relating what people like Aristotle and Kant and others have written to the modern problem of computer use is fascinating, Ryder. It provides all sorts of new insights, opens up all kinds of questions...'' For a few seconds the enthusiasm she felt for her subject wiped out the dull anxiety in her amber eyes.

Ryder half smiled. ''Again, I'll take your word for it.''

Brenna gave herself a slight mental shake and returned to the main issue. "I had a lot of notes and a rough outline of what I wanted to say in my office. It was no secret that I was preparing the paper in order to submit it to a major journal in the field. One weekend I went into my office on a Sunday, which is something I rarely do. I had intended to put a little extra time in on the project. When I arrived, the whole file of my notes and the outline were gone."

"Stolen?" he demanded, obviously intrigued by the turn of events.

"They were back in my desk drawer on Monday morning," she told him flatly. "I couldn't figure out what in the world was going on. I got paranoid and started taking the file home with me, but by then the damage had already been done. Lord only knows how many Sundays the file had spent out of my desk and on someone else's!"

"Whose?"

"The head of my department, that's who!" Brenna proclaimed with renewed anger. "The eminent Dr. Paul Humphrey, who wanted to mark his last year in the academic world with a paper that would give the impression that he was at the forefront of modern philosophy! I suppose I should be flattered," she added disparagingly. "I didn't know the work I'd done was *that* good!"

"How did you find out?"

"It was announced this past week that a major monograph written by him had been submitted and accepted for publication in an important philosophical journal. Copies of the monograph were passed around so that the faculty could read and admire the work of their department chief. I hadn't finished the first page before I realized I was reading my own research and analysis!''

"So you stood up at the next faculty party and accused your boss of being a thief?" Ryder asked interestedly as he served up the eggs and toast and sat down across from Brenna. "Must have been a sight worth seeing."

"I did not make any open accusations. I was in a quandary so I went to the person I felt closest to on the faculty, the man who will very possibly be the next department head..."

"The man I just kicked out the front door?"

"His name is Damon Fielding. Dr. Damon Fielding," she emphasized through clenched teeth.

"And he immediately took up cudgels on your behalf?" Ryder hazarded coolly, chewing on a slice of whole wheat toast.

Brenna sighed. "He sympathized; said he believed me but there was nothing either of us could do about it. Humphrey is a law unto himself, he said, and I would only get hurt if I tried to challenge the man over an issue like this. He's a well-known established scholar and I'm just a beginner. He tried to impress upon me the fact that if I'm going to succeed in my chosen profession, I've got to learn to play the politics of the situation. He...he made it sound as if we were out in the corporate world with all its nasty in-fighting and games on the way to the top."

"He's probably right," Ryder surprised her by saying readily.

She blinked at him owlishly, not having expected quite that reaction.

"Any situation in which there's a lot of competition for the top rung of a ladder is going to create a climate of that sort. It's true in the military world, the corporate world, and, I'm sure, in the academic world. You can't change that fact of life, lady, all you can do is decide whether or not you're going to play the game. The thing to remember is that the choice is yours.''

"You seem to have given the matter some thought," she said thinly.

"Sure, I've faced the situation before. That's one of the reasons I've done some of the things I've done and one of the reasons I'm writing adventure fiction. I made the choice of living life on my own terms as much as possible. This is the way I do that,'' he concluded simply.

Brenna stared at him in consternation and then asked the question that was uppermost in her mind. "What would you have done if you'd been Damon?'' she breathed.

He gave her a steady glance. "You mean if you'd come to me with proof that the head of the department had stolen your material? Something ill-bred, ill-mannered, and ill-behaved, no doubt. Also something violent. Lady, I would have fought on your behalf and in the process probably gotten us both kicked out of the college,'' Ryder told her bluntly. "All of which is not to say that my way is any better or worse than your friend Damon's. In the end you're the one who has to make the decision.''

"Yes.'' She nodded, acknowledging the inescapable truth. "Although it looks as though I've already made it. Damon won't forgive that little scene this morning. And it was all my fault; I should never have precipitated it by pointing out to him that he was condoning unethical and disreputable behavior by not speaking up on my behalf.''

''That's the comment that made him lose his temper and slap you?''

She nodded. ''I insulted him terribly when you think about it. He was only trying to help me. He came all this way to help me, in fact.''

''Exactly how much does the man mean to you?'' Ryder demanded with sudden intensity. ''I'm getting the impression he's more than merely a colleague.''

''He is…was…'' Brenna lifted a hand vaguely. ''We were quite close. We date regularly and…'' She couldn't quite meet the piercing silver eyes now.

''And you were thinking of a more permanent arrangement?'' Ryder growled.

''I thought we were rather well matched, as a matter of fact. We respect each other, enjoy each other's company, have an enormous amount in common…'' she began belligerently.

''None of which means anything after last night,'' he broke in to say in a very even tone. ''And don't look at me as if you're experiencing total shock. You don't have all that much in common with Damon Fielding or you wouldn't have been so hurt by his failure to champion your cause. If you'd had so much in common, you would have known him well enough to predict exactly how he'd react in the situation you described. On the other hand,'' he added imperturbably, ''you knew me well enough after only three days to be not at all surprised at how I reacted to that little scene this morning!''

''What are you talking about?'' She glowered at him, her stomach tensing with premonition.

''Whatever you had with Fielding is over,'' he explained calmly. "You made that decision last night when you invited me into your bed. I warned you I'd hold you to your choice once you made it. You belong to me now, Brenna Llewellyn."

You belong to me. The words hammered into her mind as she sat staring at the man sitting across the table from her. "No," she whispered desperately. "No, you don't understand..."

"Are you going to try running away?" he asked as if only academically interested in the answer. Ryder reached for another slice of toast.

"If you think we have so much in common that we can predict each other's reactions, you tell me!" she shot back furiously. How dare he sit there so calmly and talk about her *belonging* to him? Maybe in his world people thought in such primitive terms, but certainly not in hers! But she had known ever since she awoke this morning that this was coming. It was the wrongness she'd been aware of since she'd opened her eyes. She had known she'd made a tremendous mistake letting herself be swept away by the mood of the evening. How could she have been so incredibly *stupid?*

He was chewing his toast and contemplating her question. "To tell you the truth I can see you going either way," he finally stated with a nod. "You might run just to see if I really will come after you."

"That would be childish in the extreme!" she snapped, incensed because the question had leaped into her mind the moment he had suggested the fact that she might actually choose to run away. Would he come after her? It was useless to speculate. Brenna Llewellyn didn't resort to such emotional tricks. She had been trained to deal with problems much more intelligently than that!

"Not childish, but perhaps tritely feminine," he corrected judiciously. "To save you the bother, I'll tell you right now that I would, indeed, come after you. And I probably wouldn't be in the best of moods when I found you, either. But if I had to bet on the most likely reaction, my money would be on the side that says you'll stay and battle this out even though the conclusion is a foregone one after last night."

"Hardly!"

One tawny brow arched in cool mockery. "The conclusion *is* foregone, lady, but if it will soothe your frazzled nerves I'll reassure you that I'm still willing to wait. Just as I was willing to wait last night. I won't push you back into bed."

"You're too generous!" Brenna couldn't believe what she was hearing. The morning was shaping up disastrously!

The brackets at the edge of his mouth softened although he didn't quite smile. "It's not a question of generosity, Brenna. It's just that I know you well enough to realize that what happened last night happened a little too soon. I knew it at the time but I did warn you that I'd hold you to your decision. This morning you're feeling panicked and unnerved and I'd just as soon you didn't run away from me, so I'm giving you the time you need to settle everything in your own head to your satisfaction. There are obviously some other major decisions awaiting you in regard to your career. You've clearly got enough on your mind without having to worry about what you'll do if I try to carry you off to bed."

"You're so damn sure of yourself," she whispered incredulously.

"It's not me I'm sure of, it's you. You're a woman of honor—I know you won't be able to turn your back on what happened between us last night. You only need a little time to deal with it. Don't panic, lady, I'm a very patient man when the goal is this important," he concluded kindly.

Brenna swallowed, stricken. "Aren't you reading a great deal into one rather reckless night?"

He did smile this time, memories dancing in his eyes. "It was reckless, wasn't it? All things considered, you're turning out to have quite a streak of recklessness in your makeup. Did you know that about yourself before this summer?"

For some reason tears began to threaten behind Brenna's amber eyes. It was all too much. She didn't know how to cope with everything happening at once like this: the crisis in her career; the crisis with this man. He was right about one thing, she thought wretchedly, she did need time. Brenna got to her feet in a quick, convulsive movement, her hands gripping the edge of the table. "If you'll excuse me," she began very formally, striving to conquer the tears, "I'm going to take a walk. It's been a difficult morning." She turned half blindly and left the cabin.

Half an hour later she sat, knees drawn up and arms resting on top of them, and gazed out over the crystal-blue lake. She had found the small private cove a short distance from the cabin and it was exactly the place she needed. The tears had never actually fallen, to her vast relief. They had been a product of frustration and panic, and she was proud to have resisted the impulse to cry for such reasons. She could handle her life successfully without resorting to tears. Hadn't she always managed to do so?

But she needed to think and so far she hadn't gotten very far with the process. She still felt too on edge, too hemmed in, and a little frightened. The thought of calling her brother occurred briefly and was immediately dismissed. There was nothing he could do and a full explanation of the situation would only anger him. That thought brought a wry twist to her mouth. He wasn't altogether unlike Ryder in his reactions. He'd come out of the corner fighting on her behalf even though this was clearly a case where violence was not very useful. It never was, she reminded herself staunchly.

A faint warning tingle made her glance up sharply to see Ryder emerging on catlike feet from the pines behind her. He was carrying a couple of books and a thermos.

"It's a perfect day to sit and read by the lake with a cup of hot tea, isn't it?" he inquired conversationally, sinking down beside her with a masculine grace that stirred up images of last night in her mind. The silver eyes met hers with a measure of understanding and reassurance.

"Ryder, I don't—"

"I brought you a book," he interrupted quietly, unscrewing the cap of the thermos.

Automatically she glanced down at the two volumes resting on his lap. One was the philosophy text she had thrown at him and the other was one of his own adventure tales, complete with lurid cover.

"Thanks," she told him stiffly, "but I'm not in the mood to study philosophy at the moment."

"I brought the philosophy book for me to read,"

he murmured, handing her a mug of tea. "I brought the other book for you."

Their eyes locked as his meaning registered. "You want me to read one of your stories?"

"I know the stuff isn't exactly your taste in fiction, and I know I'm not the most brilliant of authors, but I would like you to read one of my books. Will you?"

"Why?" she heard herself ask huskily, picking up the paperback in his lap and examining it curiously.

"Because there's something of me in my books and you're an intelligent woman. You'll find it. Maybe in the process you'll learn something about me."

She felt dazed, taken totally off guard. "And you're going to tackle that book of philosophical readings?"

"I'm interested in finding out more about what you do for a living," he answered smilingly, leaning back against the large boulder behind him and opening the textbook.

"There's no point in this exercise," she protested halfheartedly, focusing on the cover of the paperback. "We're totally unlike, Ryder. What are you hoping to accomplish?"

"I've told you, a little mutual understanding. I think it's important since we're going to be living together," he added, already flipping through the introductory pages of the book and studying the table of contents.

"Living together! Are you crazy? Ryder, last night was a mistake, you must see that!"

"Why?" he asked simply, lifting his head to study her earnest face.

"Because you're assuming far too much from what happened!"

The silvery gaze moved over her. "The night you came sneaking through my window I knew I wanted you. Last night you proved you want me."

"That's not sufficient grounds on which to make a decision like living together," she got out huskily. The tension his words generated in her was frightening. A part of her longed to agree with him, to surrender herself to the summer and to him.

"We also happen to need each other, lady," he told her coolly.

"How can you say that? We hardly even know each other," she exploded.

"I can't explain it completely, not yet. I don't have all the right words. But I'm sure of the feeling. Maybe that's why I want you to read my book. Perhaps I'm hoping you'll understand something of what I'm trying to say."

She felt helpless in the face of the quiet plea. She was right, of course, there was no point to the exercise, but she didn't know how to refuse him. Brenna glanced down again at the paperback he had given her.

"What if this doesn't work? What if I'm still of the same opinion after I finish the book as I am now?"

"I don't think you've got any clear-cut opinions right now." He chuckled. "You're much too mixed up at the moment to be thinking with any great clarity."

"Hardly a good time to be studying your character through your stories," she retorted, knowing already that she was going to do as he asked and read the book.

"I'll take my chances."

"Maybe you're the one who will be put off by my character when you get into that long, dry book of philosophy readings!" she challenged, settling back against the same sun-warmed rock he was leaning on. "Have you thought about that? You're likely to realize I'm merely a dull, staid, unapproachable teacher of a subject that never interested you much in the first place."

"Is that how you see yourself?" he asked in amusement.

Her mouth turned downward a little ruefully. "To tell you the truth, I've never thought of myself or my profession as dull and unapproachable, but I'm fully aware that others might see both that way."

"There's not much this book could do to change the image I already have of you, lady." Ryder grinned. "It's just going to give me a little more complete view, that's all."

Brenna hesitated, wanting to ask him exactly how he did see her but not quite having the nerve. Instead she said casually, "Ryder, about last night..."

He leaned forward and stopped her words by the simple expedient of sealing her mouth with a slow kiss. It was a lingering, tasting caress that spoke of remembered ecstasy and satisfaction. It spoke of satiated hunger that could be roused again with very little provocation. Brenna stayed quite still beneath the impact of it, finding it strangely soothing after the chaos of the morning.

"Let's not spoil last night with any more words,

sweet lady,'' he growled, lifting his head with obvious reluctance.

Fingers trembling very faintly, Brenna picked up the paperback novel in her lap.

Chapter 6

It was called *The Quicksilver Venture* and the cover guaranteed it to be another tale of action and intrigue by Justin Murdock. The artwork featured the predictably lusty, well-muscled hero, menaced apparently by an assortment of cobras. The beautiful woman sprawled in terror at his feet was a redhead this time, and while the pose was decidedly sensual, Brenna had the impression that the manner in which she was clinging to the hero's ankle was hampering his attempt to defend them both from the cobras. He was armed only with a thin-bladed knife.

Not quite certain why she had let herself be talked into reading the paperback when, by rights, she should have been trying to sort out the growing confusion of her career and her relationship with Damon Fielding, Brenna turned the page and began to read. Perhaps it was a form of procrastination, she told herself fleetingly. Things were happening in her life, forcing choices upon her that she really didn't want to face. Reading *The Quicksilver Venture* was a way of avoiding the facts. Or was it? she wondered as she began to read.

He was good, I had to admit, but he was probably still new to the business. He didn't make allowances for either the age of the old hotel window or for the fact that agents who have stayed alive as long as I have tend to sleep a little differently than people who have nice, normal, routine jobs. Then, again, perhaps I was still half awake because of the dream about the blonde in Paris. Whatever the reason, I heard the faint creak and I didn't spend any time telling myself it was the normal sort of sound one expected to hear in a venerable English inn. My hand under the pillow closed around the handle of the stiletto.

I didn't move as he slipped silently into the room. Then I sensed my uninvited guest taking that quiet, mind-steadying breath you need when you're aiming a gun at a target shrouded in shadows and you know you'll only get one chance.

The stiletto left my hand in the same instant I dove for the floor on the opposite side of the bed. Sensing disaster, my visitor fired, but the muffled shot went wild because the long, thin blade that had become an extension of my fingers over the years was already burying itself in his throat. Like the silenced automatic, his scream was also muffled.

I picked myself up off the floor and flipped on

the overhead light with a sigh of regret. It was, all in all, a hell of a way to start a vacation.

In spite of herself, Brenna experienced a flicker of wry amusement at the memory of how she had awakened Ryder that first night. Then the amusement faded rather abruptly. Perhaps she'd been rather lucky!

The action-packed tale moved quickly. By the end of the first chapter the hero, one Hunt Cameron, found himself immersed in a dangerous mission to bring a defector known only as Quicksilver out of Eastern Europe. But the relatively straightforward adventure was given a few twists. Cameron was assigned to work with a beautiful new agent, Cassandra Vaughn, who, Brenna presumed, was the redhead on the cover. Cassandra, apparently, was from a modern, technologically sophisticated school of espionage. She was highly skilled in computer-assisted analysis techniques, used the latest in communications gadgets, and was trained to work by the book. Quicksilver was to be her first mission.

Hunt Cameron, on the other hand, had thrown out the book years ago in order to stay alive in the field. He relied on such unscientific things as hunches, well-developed instincts, and a very non-routine way of handling matters. The only tool in which he put any trust was the stiletto he carried always, even to bed. He didn't bother to take the risk of trusting people. Hunt and Cass clashed from the moment they met.

Underlying the conflict between the admittedly chauvinistic professional and the lovely, disdainful beginner was, of course, an undeniable physical attraction. Of course. Brenna found herself reading the love scenes with great attention.

At lunchtime she and Ryder, by quiet agreement, went back to his cabin for a sandwich and more tea. They ate in near silence, and Brenna was conscious of a certain restlessness to finish the story. Ryder eyed her obliquely but made no move to detain her. Within half an hour they were both back at the cove, immersed in their reading.

Out on the shimmering lake the occasional outboard roared past. The sun gleamed on the cold water. It was a peaceful mountain setting and Brenna read the remainder of *The Quicksilver Venture* without interruption. She was aware of Ryder beside her, seemingly engrossed in the book of philosophy readings, but all her attention was on the breakneck pace of the paperback adventure in her hands.

When she finally closed the book on the last page late that afternoon, she had to admit that Justin Murdock had given his readers their money's worth. She wondered how many would realize he'd given them something more, too.

"Finished?" Ryder asked softly, closing his own book.

Brenna nodded, her chin resting on her folded arms, which were, in turn, propped on her drawn-up knees. She stared thoughtfully across at the opposite side of the lake. "You tell a great adventure tale, Ryder, but you've probably been told that any number of times."

"I like hearing it from you," he admitted. She wasn't looking at him but she could feel the faint smile.

There was a short silence and she knew he was waiting for her to go on. "Lots of violence in the story," she mused, knowing she was stepping around the main issue.

"There are certain conventions to be followed in writing that kind of tale," he pointed out dryly. Brenna sensed he was well aware that she was going to have to take her time working up to the important aspects.

"Are the love scenes part of the 'conventions'?" she heard herself ask and immediately could have bitten out her tongue. She sat very stiffly as she awaited his response.

"They aren't love scenes," Ryder murmured. "They're sex scenes. And, yes, they're one of the things the reader expects. I told you once I'm selling sex along with the violence and intrigue."

Her head swung around sharply as she turned to stare at him. "But they *were* love scenes!" she protested.

"Why do you say that?" he asked blandly, but there was a flicker of hungry curiosity deep in the silver gaze as he watched her frowning features.

"Because, aside from wanting each other, Hunt and Cass learn during the course of the story that they need each other. What they have together isn't just sex, Ryder. Good lord! Why am I telling you that? You're the one who wrote the scenes!"

"Go on," he urged. "I'm fascinated to hear the way a professor of philosophy analyzes a sleazy pulp novel. How can you say the sexy parts were love scenes, though? Never once during the whole course of the story does Hunt tell Cass he loves her."

"And she never gets around to telling him that she loves him, either," Brenna finished on a note of complaint. "You could have put that in on the last page,

Ryder. I mean, it was obvious they were deeply in love by the end of the book, anyhow.''

''There was nothing mushy or sloppily sentimental about how they felt toward each other.''

''You think love is sloppy and sentimental?'' she queried, aware of a sense of disappointment.

''My readers would!'' he retorted with great conviction.

Brenna laughed at that and turned back to look at the lake as she contemplated another thought. ''I like the ending,'' she finally said simply. ''I liked the fact that they both realized they wanted something else out of life and had the courage to go looking for it.'' Hunt and Cass had both decided to get out of the hard, dangerous profession they had chosen. At the conclusion of the story they had mutually agreed to quietly resign and find another life for themselves, one they could build together.

''You didn't find Cameron too much of a male chauvinist?'' Ryder taunted gently.

''Well, strictly speaking, he certainly was in many respects,'' Brenna said. ''I mean, he was always stepping in to handle the rough stuff because he didn't trust Cass to be able to do it. No, I take that back. He stepped in to do the bloody work because he didn't *want* her to have to do it. He simply used his lack of trust in her commando training as an excuse. He was trying to protect her from finding out how devastating it can be to kill another human being, wasn't he? And to shield her from danger.''

''Yes.'' Ryder spoke the single word very softly.

''Definitely a male chauvinist. He was also aggressive, cynical, ruthless, and dangerous. But I liked him,'' Brenna whispered, staring very hard now at the opposite shore. "I would have trusted him to the ends of the earth. He was a man of honor and integrity, even if he did make his own rules. Or perhaps he was that way *because* he made them," she added with a sense of wonder. "How much of yourself did you put into Hunt Cameron, Ryder?" she asked very steadily.

"Beats me," he retorted smoothly. "I think I'll leave that for you to decide."

She didn't look at him as she mulled that over. In her trained, analytical brain some unavoidable conclusions were beginning to form. Brenna wasn't at all sure she liked them.

They revolved around the fact that she really had wound up admiring Hunt Cameron and the code he lived by. Like Cass in the story, she found herself attracted to the strength and integrity in the man even though she periodically became thoroughly irritated with his methods and manners. And Brenna was honest enough with herself to realize that her feelings for Ryder were in danger of paralleling those of the heroine in *Quicksilver* for the hero. The knowledge was frightening. It washed over Brenna like a cold wave and automatically she raised the first defense she could find.

"You didn't have to hit Damon this morning!"

As if he could read her mind, he followed the non sequitur immediately. "You belong to me now, Brenna. There's no way on earth I could let another man get away with striking you. He's lucky I didn't kill him."

Brenna absorbed the impact of the quiet, forceful statement, knowing the truth behind it. Ryder lived by his own code. He felt she had given herself to him last night and he would protect what was his. But, as

with Cass in *The Quicksilver Venture,* Brenna felt a
need to protest his autocratic assumptions. Ryder was
not the right man for her! She needed and wanted
someone like Damon Fielding...

But she knew even as she repeated the words to
herself that the reason she had hurled accusations at
Fielding that morning was precisely because he had
fallen far short of her ideal. She had wanted him to
defend and protect her in an uncompromising manner.

It wasn't that she wouldn't or couldn't take a stand
on her own behalf. Brenna knew she was fully capable of defending herself. But an undeniable part of
her had wanted the man she was contemplating marrying to prove himself totally on her side when the
going got rough. She had wanted to know that she
was the most important thing in his life and that he
would not make compromises when it came to pro-
tecting her.

All of which was totally unfair, she reasoned deliberately. Damon had tried to protect her in his own
way. He had logically advised her to think of her
career and her future first, rather than the injustice of
the moment. His method was the right approach.

But Ryder would have gone to war for her.

And gotten them both kicked out of the college,
Brenna reminded herself ruefully.

On the other hand, something in her knew the line
had to be drawn somewhere. Logical compromise was
all well and good, but each individual had to decide
just how far he or she would go before saying that
the limit had been reached. In that moment of self-
understanding and analysis, Brenna acknowledged
that Damon would go a great deal further than she

would when it came to compromising for the sake of a career. How much further?

Before she could explore that question, though, another matter had to be dealt with. Talk about drawing the line somewhere! She was most definitely going to have to do exactly that with Ryder Sterne. Every instinct warned that the attraction she felt for this man was dangerous in the extreme. She realized now, after having read *The Quicksilver Venture,* that his appeal was all the more hazardous because it wasn't simply physical. A very elemental part of her sought the straightforward, utterly unyielding, fiercely independent strength in him. But it was all wrong to find those qualities in this man! She dared not let herself admit that she could give herself completely to a man who was not of the intellectual and academically sophisticated world in which she lived. She had worked so hard gaining entrance to that particular world! It was a kind of heresy to even contemplate the notion that she could fall in love with someone who did not share it with her.

Fall in love! No! Brenna's chin lifted and her amber eyes flared gold as she turned her head to fix Ryder with a condemning stare.

"I do not belong to you, Ryder. Not in any sense of the word. We…we only went to bed together last night, we didn't pledge our love, for heaven's sake!"

He put down the thick philosophy text and leaned forward to capture her face between his palms. The silver in his eyes was a banked flame. Brenna sensed impatience and an equal determination to control that impatience radiating through the lean, hard body.

"I, like my readers, am not interested in sloppy, sentimental words such as 'love.' Please don't use them to cloud the issue. We want each other, Brenna, and we need each other!''

''How can you say that?'' she pleaded. ''We don't *need* each other! Not in any meaningful way!'' But she heard the lie in her own words and was desperately afraid he would see it. A part of her *did* need him; needed his honor and passionate way of living by his own code.

He studied her face searchingly. ''Lady, I have spent the day reading the works of the men and women you admire. Shall I tell you what I've learned?'' Ryder didn't wait for the answer. ''You are a member of a profession that is not afraid to ask questions. The most incredible questions! The questions your predecessors have asked were so fundamental that they literally opened up the areas of human knowledge. They are the questions that are the foundation of science and mathematics and ethics and communications and logic. My God, woman! If you are going to follow in the footsteps of such people, surely you must find the courage to ask a few personal questions of yourself!''

''Such as?'' she challenged tightly, her pulse racing as she met the will and the power in him.

''Such as what you want out of life! Such as what you want out of a relationship. Such as what you need from a man and what you're capable of giving in return.'' His voice deepened, becoming as deceptively soft and gentle as silk. ''Such as why you made the decision to invite me into your bed last night.''

''I didn't! I...'' Brenna closed her eyes against the accusation she sensed in him. ''All right, so I did. That's all there was to it, Ryder. I don't know what it is you want from me!''

"You," he told her gently. "All of you. And I want exclusive rights. If I ever find your precious Dr. Fielding touching you again I'll take him apart. I mean it, Brenna. I warned you last night that when you gave yourself to me it would be completely."

"You can't blame me for not understanding how…how completely you meant!" she argued, aware even in frustration and anger how much her body longed to call off the battle. It would be so blissful to simply go into his arms and forget the past and the future. But the need to resist his challenge was just as strong. Brenna knew better than to succumb to the repressed streak of recklessness in her own nature. She could not trust that side of herself; she was sure it would lead to disaster.

"Don't pretend you misunderstood me," he admonished with a wry quirk to his lips, his features softening. "I just finished the chapter on the philosophy of linguistic analysis! Even if I hadn't read it, I would still, as a writer, have a great respect for the power of language, lady. And I know my words last night were very direct and to the point."

"This isn't a joke, Ryder," she protested, sensing the flash of humor in him. "You're trying to push me into a full-scale affair and I won't be driven like that!"

He shook his head once in denial. "I'm not pushing, Brenna. I keep telling you I'm willing to wait."

"You say that and then turn around and make all sorts of demands!"

"You gave me the right to place those demands," he said evenly.

"No!"

"What are you going to do? If you choose to run,

I think you know by now that I'll come after you. If
you stay here and work things out, I'll give you some
time in which to come to terms with yourself and the
situation. Take your choice.''

Anger surged to life in Brenna. In part it was directed against herself for even being tempted by this
man, but she aimed it at him, nonetheless. With a
swift movement she pulled herself free of his hands
and leaped to her feet, the tension in her stiffening
every line of her body.

"How dare you presume to give me such choices,
Ryder Sterne! No one, especially no man, has that
right! I'll do as I damn well please and I sure as hell
don't intend to let myself get boxed into a corner by
you. Your conceit and arrogance are amazing! Do you
really think I'll let myself be used by you for an affair
this summer? Someone to provide a little light relief
after a hard day's writing?"

At her words his jaw tightened and his silver eyes
became narrow and assessing. Brenna knew she was
running a risk but she couldn't seem to stop. She was
feeling trapped both by the events of the morning and
by the bonds Ryder was attempting to place on her.
Her instincts were telling her to fight while there was
still some chance of freeing herself. But when Ryder
got almost lazily to his feet to stand in front of her,
another instinct jerked into awareness. This one instructed her to be prepared to run.

"You know damn good and well that I'm not looking for a 'little light relief,' as you put it," he stated
coolly. "If I were, I wouldn't have told you that I
was willing to wait politely for another invitation to
your bed. Use your head, lady, and stop looking for
flimsy excuses to attack me."

"What sort of excuse should I look for?" she tossed back flippantly. "Something tells me you'll label all my excuses flimsy!"

"Oh, you've got some good grounds for being afraid of me at this point," he drawled dangerously. "I represent a threat to your whole way of life."

"The only threat in my life right now is the one to my career!"

"You're wrong, Brenna. That's the easy one to handle. I'm another kind of threat altogether and you're going to find me a lot tougher to deal with."

"You're beginning to sound like the character in your novel," she spat furiously. Her temper was raging and she didn't seem to be able to bring it under control. Too much had happened to her today, and somehow Ryder seemed the focus of all the problems she faced.

"Maybe you've got it all backward. Perhaps he's the one who sounds like me," Ryder taunted softly.

"Well, I'm not the sexy, beautiful redhead in *The Quicksilver Venture!* I don't intend to let myself be swept off my feet by a tough-talking macho type who thinks that because he wants a woman she should immediately surrender herself, body and soul!"

The only response to that was a casually raised eyebrow. It had the horrifying effect of bringing a warm flush into Brenna's face. She already *had* surrendered herself once. How could she deny it? Brenna drew herself very straight, her head lifted proudly.

"I can see there's not much point in continuing this discussion. If you'll excuse me, I'm going back to the cabin. It's been one hell of an interesting day, I assure you!"

Whirling in the sand, Brenna started for the safety

of the pines and her own cabin. She refused to give
in to the inclination to run. Not for the world would
she allow him to think she was afraid of him! At
twenty-nine she was not about to admit to fear of any
man. Disgust, disdain, and irritation, perhaps, but not
fear!

"Brenna."

Her name was the quiet, snaking coil of a whip. It
spun through the air behind her, reaching out and circling to bind her as it settled about her body with
almost tangible force. Brenna wanted to run from it
but she knew she couldn't. Slowly she halted and
turned to face the man who had managed to make the
single word a command.

For a long, tense moment they stood staring across
the distance between them, each one assessing the
other. Brenna felt the palms of her hands grow damp
with the force of the conflicting emotions coursing
through her.

"Don't give me orders, Ryder."

"I haven't issued any orders. I only called your
name," he said quietly.

But it had been an order and they both knew it;
one she couldn't deny because it demanded that she
have the courage to stand and deal with the threat and
the challenge in him.

Without a word he started toward her slowly.
"Don't be afraid of me," he growled deeply. "Don't
be afraid of yourself."

She watched him come closer and wished she could
run. But she couldn't, and there was no point thinking
about it. "Ryder, I won't let you seduce me," she
whispered.

"No," he agreed, halting a pace away.

She tried again. "I'm...I'm sorry about what happened last night, about the way you interpreted it."

"I'm not."

"Please, don't tease me!"

"No," he agreed again.

"Are you angry?"

"A little provoked," he temporized dryly.

Brenna lifted a hand, feeling helpless. "What are you going to do?"

"Keep pressing my claim until you acknowledge it," he told her calmly.

"Is that a threat?"

"No threats. I won't be back in your bed until you invite me."

Surely that was safe enough, Brenna told herself. She could trust this man. With that thought came another, more impulsive one. She felt compelled to tell him that last night had meant something to her even though she didn't want to be bound by the commitment he was invoking. It was an incredibly difficult thing to say, Brenna discovered.

"Ryder, about last night..."

"Let the subject of last night rest," he said tersely.

"Why?" she demanded in sudden annoyance. "Because we can't agree on what it meant?"

"You know what it meant. You just don't want to admit it. Not yet."

"But you think I will in time?" she challenged.

"We'd better let that subject rest, too." He held out his hand. "Would you like to come over to my place for a sundown drink, dinner, and a little philosophical conversation?" He smiled in whimsical invitation.

She hesitated suspiciously, knowing she was longing to accept the offered hand. The longing and the wariness in her were creating an unbearable tension, she realized. Her fingers quivered slightly as she slowly accepted his hand in a small surrender.

"All right, Ryder. Thank you." There was a sense of relief in the way his fingers closed warmly around hers. She took a steadying breath and then declared, unable to resist, "I still say you should never have struck Damon. Violence is never the answer!"

A slow grin sliced across his tanned features, a knife blade of a grin. "I disagree. It can be satisfyingly decisive at times! You must occasionally crave for something decisive in your life after dealing with all those endless questions of philosophy."

He started back toward the cabins with her in tow, ignoring her withering glance. "What are you going to do about your job situation?" he asked after a moment.

"I don't know. I honestly don't know. Damon is very influential. He's sure to be next in line for the position of head of the department. After the way I insulted him this morning, I can probably assume I've burned my bridges at the college." Brenna caught her lower lip between her teeth as she considered that. What a mess. The worst of it was that she couldn't determine how she felt about it.

"My decking him probably didn't aid your cause any," Ryder muttered laconically. "Will he fire you or get you fired?"

"I don't think he could do that but…" She let the sentence trail off.

"But he could make life difficult for you on the faculty, right?"

It was the truth. "Yes."

There was a small pause while Ryder appeared to be searching for the words he wanted. "The important thing is that you don't really love him, Brenna," he finally announced forcefully.

"You think love is a sloppy, sentimental emotion, remember? Since you don't have much respect for it yourself, you're hardly in a position to tell me whether or not I'm in love!"

"Take my word for it," he retorted sardonically. "You're not in love with Damon Fielding. You would never have gone to bed with me last night if you loved him!"

Brenna shook her head, abandoning what was sure to be a fruitless argument. Ryder was too certain of himself and of her. As for herself, Brenna couldn't seem to view her feelings toward Damon with any objectivity today. Ryder had occupied her thoughts from the moment she'd awakened in the empty bed, and it was Ryder who had set the pace for the strange day.

It was easier during this time of uncertainty about her future to simply put the whole subject out of her mind and let Ryder continue to guide the evening. It was, she admitted privately, an unusual way for her to behave. Brenna Llewellyn couldn't even remember the last time in her life when she had allowed someone else to direct the course of events. She had known where she was going, been aware of her responsibilities, and felt the obligations of her duty to her career and her brother for so long that any other way of responding seemed abnormal.

But definitely easier for the time being, Brenna reflected a few hours later as she sat curled deep in the corner of the sofa in front of Ryder's fireplace. Much easier. She had spent the day sidestepping her problems, and the technique had some definite attractions. She smiled a little ruefully to herself as she sipped the excellent brandy and gazed into the flames.

The conversation all evening had been about philosophy and the characters in Ryder's books. Brenna had been drawn comfortably into the folds of the conversation, giving herself up to the safety of it with pleasure and undeniable relief. There had been no more talk of her career or of the claim Ryder was making, and over the past few hours she had finally relaxed.

At the opposite end of the sofa Ryder raised his brandy snifter in a small, intimate salute.

"To another perfect evening."

Brenna's lips curved as she turned her head to look at him. Her state of relaxation gave her the courage to tease now about a matter she would not have dared to bait him with a few hours earlier. "Perfect? Even though you'll be sleeping in your own bed tonight?"

As soon as she spoke the words Brenna regretted the impulse to tease. It was the first time the conversation had come back to sex all evening and she wished she hadn't been the one to bring it up now.

"My own bed," Ryder repeated thoughtfully. "There's nothing wrong with my bed. At least there are no stairs to climb." He hesitated long enough to catch her full attention. "Will I be sleeping alone in my bed, Brenna?"

Her head came up with a challenging movement. The room seemed suddenly very warm to Brenna. Keep it light, she told herself firmly. Keep it light.

"Don't worry, Ryder. You're safe enough tonight. I won't be seducing you."

"I've always had a certain reckless streak," he informed her gently. "Some forms of safety just don't appeal. I think you share the same brand of recklessness, Brenna Llewellyn." Very deliberately he sat up and placed his snifter on the brass-bound trunk in front of the sofa.

Brenna saw the waiting trap in the silver eyes and felt her pulse quicken. In fear or desire?

"You said you would wait," she reminded him, her voice a thread of sound.

"For an invitation," he agreed with a nod, making no move.

"There isn't going to be an invitation." But her fingers were trembling and she had to set down her snifter.

"No?" He put out a hand and traced a tiny design along the line of her throat. The erotic little caress made her catch her breath. The gold in Brenna's eyes was suddenly very warm. "Can you bring yourself to deny either of us tonight what we found last night?"

"Have you been seducing me with the philosophy and the brandy all night?" she tried to ask flippantly.

"No, you've been seducing me again," he whispered throatily. "Talking to you is a seduction in itself, lady. Don't you know that?"

With an effort of will Brenna got to her feet. "I think I'd better go, Ryder," she murmured. "Good night. Thank you for dinner." Wrenching her gaze away from his, she tried to snap the bonds settling around her. But every step toward the door was like a step through quicksand.

He was behind her, soft and silent and all leashed masculine power, when she put her hand on the doorknob.

"I have to go, Ryder." She stared down at her fingers as they tightened fiercely around the knob.

"I'm not stopping you."

"Damn it!" She looked up furiously. "You're not helping, either!"

"That would be asking too much, lady," he drawled very gently. "Far too much."

She wrenched open the door and came to a halt on the threshold, glaring out into the dark shadows. What did she want tonight? Surely she could not take the risk of letting this man make love to her again. Where was her common sense? Where was the rational, logical side of her nature when she needed it?

"Ryder, I can't stay tonight," she began tightly, whirling to face him. "But about last night. I want you to know...oh!"

When she swung around on the threshold, he was right behind her. She hadn't heard the step that brought him so close, but when she turned he was there and his arms came around her as she collided with the hard, compelling planes of his chest. Wordlessly she stood in the circle of his embrace, eyes very wide and questioning as she looked up into his taut features. She saw the hungry longing in him and couldn't move.

"Last night," he said very gently, "was perfect. Tonight will be perfect, too."

He swung her off her feet and into his arms. Turning, he kicked the door closed behind them and carried Brenna back toward the warmth of the fire.

Chapter 7

Ryder lowered himself to the sofa with Brenna across his thighs. For a long moment he simply cradled her close. She nestled her head against his shoulder, aware of his lips hovering near her hair. He wanted her. She could feel the power of the hunger in him and knew the surge of desire in herself. It was easy, far too easy, to simply suspend all thought and give herself up to the night and the man who held her.

"Well, lady?" he prodded with carefully controlled urgency. "Do I get my invitation?"

"I thought you were inviting yourself." She lifted her lashes and raised a fingertip to toy with the curl of tawny hair on his neck.

"You'll have to say the words. I don't want there to be any question in your mind."

"About who is seducing whom?" she mocked softly.

"Exactly."

She felt the tension within and sought for a way out. "Ryder, I don't want the responsibility tonight. All day long I have been avoiding decisions about the important things in my life, and I don't want to make any decisions tonight. Do you understand?"

"I understand," he surprised her by saying. "You want me to make this particular decision. You want me to assume the responsibility for both of us."

She flinched. "That makes me very weak, doesn't it?"

"It makes you very vulnerable." He smiled crookedly, threading a hand through the dark chocolate of her hair and loosening the strands. "Are you sure you're ready to trust me to make the right choice? You must know I'm already convinced we belong together tonight."

"Don't talk to me about it," she cried softly. "I don't want to think about all the rational implications!"

"All right, sweet lady," he crooned, feathering her ear with his tongue. "Just remember in the morning that you turned all the responsibility over to me tonight."

Brenna didn't say anything; she couldn't. She relaxed against him with a small sigh of desire as the caress on her ear became damp and warm and teasing. Yes, it was much easier this way. She luxuriated in the sensation of being safe and warm and wanted.

Abandoning herself to the enthralling illusion being spun around her, Brenna moved her palm lovingly down Ryder's cheek to his throat. There she found

the first of the buttons on his shirt and set about un-
fastening them. His breath fanned her ear and his
hand slid up from her waist to seek out the shape of
her breast.

"Ryder," she said on a long sigh as his thumb and
forefinger coaxed forth the tight bud of her nipple
beneath the fabric of her shirt. "Oh, Ryder..."

"You feel so right, so good in my hands," he whispered huskily as he undid the buttons of her shirt and
moved his hand inside to cup the breast he had been
teasing. "Thank you, sweet lady, for turning the decisions over to me tonight. You won't regret it."

Brenna, who didn't understand exactly what he was
talking about, ignored the words and moved her lips
tenderly to his throat as he traced patterns of desire
across her breasts. She stirred as the delicious sensual
tension began to build inside her and gloried in the
evidence of his own rising passion.

When her fingers fluttered lightly down his chest,
twining and untwining in the crisp, curling hair, he
groaned urgently at the touch. The sound, uttered
deep in his throat, emboldened her. She let her delicate fingertips wander lower until they settled lightly
on the blatant male hardness covered by the fabric of
his jeans.

"You see what you do to me?" he complained
ruefully. "It's not easy for a man to be subtle when
he wants a woman as badly as I want you!"

Brenna thrilled to the confession, experiencing a
feminine power that was reflected in her amber eyes.
Ryder saw it at once and laughed a little as he gathered her closer. "Witch," he growled. "Just remember you've turned all the authority over to me this
evening!"

She smiled invitingly and lifted her mouth for his kiss. He obliged at once, his tongue surging hungrily between her lips. Slowly he lowered her down onto the cushions of the sofa, pressing her deep with his weight until she was thoroughly trapped. Her arms encircled his neck as he pushed aside her shirt and crushed her breasts against his chest.

Ryder built the fires in her with an insistent, persuasive rhythm that made it seem the most natural thing in the world for Brenna to surrender. She arched her hips upward into his as he lifted himself momentarily to slip off her shirt and his own.

Instead of coming back down on top of her at once, he boldly put his palm flat against the feminine mound still hidden by her jeans. His eyes met her heavy-lidded gaze as he waited for a moment, feeling her warmth. The touch was possessive to an incredible degree and the look in his eyes challenged her to acknowledge that possession.

"Tell me you want me, lady," he commanded with utmost gentleness.

"I want you, Ryder." The words were forced out from between dry lips and she automatically put the tip of her tongue to those lips after she had spoken.

"You take away my breath, lady."

Slowly he undressed her under the flickering warmth of the firelight, and when she lay naked and bathed in gold before his gaze, he stood up long enough to tug off the black jeans he wore. Then he knelt beside the couch and ran his fingers from her throat to her ankles as she lay open to his touch.

Brenna's heated eyes wandered hungrily over the hard, sleek shape of him as he knelt beside her in the firelight. His tawny hair caught the flames, and the muscled contours of his shoulders drew her fingers. When she turned toward him convulsively, Ryder's hand on her thigh moved up along the delicate inside skin and probed the dark mystery between her legs.

"Oh!" The bold touch brought a gasping cry to her lips and she squeezed her lashes closed in response. Ryder leaned closer to kiss the tips of her aching breasts and she clutched at him, a tremor singing through her.

"Come here, sweet lady. I want to feel you all over me," he groaned and pulled her down on top of him as he lay back against the rug. Brenna sprawled across him in a tangle of silky skin and unbound hair.

Feeling marvelously pagan and excitingly wild, she began to do as he bid, scattering tiny, nipping kisses across his shoulders and down the hardness of his thighs. She reveled in his response, taking a primitive delight in seeing how far she could excite him before he lost his control. It was a game she had never played before and the danger implicit in it only acted as a lure.

He caught her head, his fingers winding tightly in her hair, and held her still for a moment so that he could drink from her lips. Then he released her once more and let her continue showering the tasting, impulse-driven kisses across his body.

When she rose briefly on her knees beside him, bending low to find the flat, masculine nipples with her mouth, he lifted his hand to trace the line of her spine down to the sensitive base. When she arched instinctively at the caress, he trailed his fingers further, sliding them erotically down her buttocks to the dampening warmth below.

"Oh, my God, Ryder," Brenna breathed, collapsing against him in an agony of passionate need. Her kisses became a little desperate as she reached out for him.

"Come and take me, sweet lady. Come and take me."

Catching her hips, he guided her astride him, fitting her body to his with urgency. Brenna gasped at the uncompromising invasion of the throbbing heart of her passion. His fingers clenched deeply into her buttocks as he held her tightly and began to thrust upward with a surging power. She buried her lips in the curve of his shoulder and gave herself up to the wonder of the moment.

The sensual pace quickened and intensified until Brenna was moaning helplessly over and over again. Her nails raked unconsciously along the strong shoulders beneath her, and when she gave in to the impulse to sink her teeth lightly into his flesh, Ryder grunted.

Then, quite abruptly, she was on her back, the intimate connection of their bodies never broken in the process. With a muttered exclamation of need, Ryder surged against her, wrapping her to him until she felt utterly consumed. It became impossible to tell where the heat of her desire stopped and the heat of Ryder's body began.

As the passion flared higher between them Brenna could only cling and cling and go on clinging to the one rock-hard reality in her private universe. Ryder seemed to lose himself in her even as he demanded everything from her, and when the shattering culmination took them both, their husky cries of satisfaction mingled together.

In the aftermath of their sensual battle Brenna lay curled into Ryder's body, his hair-roughened thigh trapping her smooth one, his palm moving lazily along the curve of her hip. When he spoke, his mouth was close to her tangled hair.

"You're so incredibly responsive," he murmured wonderingly. "You seem to go up in flames in my arms. It's enough to make me want to keep you under lock and key. I couldn't bear to have another man so much as touch you now that you're mine, lady. I've never felt so...so..."

"Possessive?" Brenna supplied with a smile as she pulled back a little to look at him. "Chauvinistic? Demanding? Irrationally jealous?"

"You take the words right out of my mouth," he drawled on a note of dangerous humor as he dropped a kiss on the tip of her nose. "Take heed, lady, I shall be a very possessive, chauvinistic, demanding, and jealous lover."

"Your basic technique must be pretty good in spite of all those drawbacks," she retorted saucily, adding in a little rush as his silver eyes narrowed, "Because I've certainly never known what it feels like to go up in flames before."

"Brenna!"

He pulled her close, stroking the smooth contour of her back down to her waist. It was a moment of great tenderness, not passion, and Brenna found it captivating. She nestled against him, delighting in him. Together they lay watching the flickering flames on the hearth die.

A long time later Ryder got to his feet and led Brenna down the hall to his bedroom

"I should have just kept you here that first night when you climbed through my window," he said as he tucked her in beside him and found the tip of her breast with his fingers. "Much simpler."

But the next morning Brenna awoke with the feeling that things weren't going to be simple at all. She lay for a moment beside Ryder thinking of all the realities she had postponed facing the day before and wondered where to start. Slowly she turned her head to look at him, taking a subtle pleasure in the harshly carved planes of his face and the sprawled grace of his body.

He had seduced her yesterday, she thought wonderingly. But it was a seduction she would never be able to hold against him, for in his arms she had found a depth of feeling she wouldn't have guessed existed. With all her heart she was glad she had given him the invitation he had wanted last night.

But now morning had arrived and with it a return to the problems that needed solutions.

The tawny lashes shifted on the high ridge of his cheek as Ryder came awake and opened his eyes to meet her gaze. Without a word he put out a hand and dragged her face lazily down to his for a lingering kiss.

"Lady, you look very good here in my bed."

Dear God, Brenna thought as everything began to click into place at the sight of his contented, indulgent grin. I'm falling in love with the man. And it's all wrong. He's not the right one at all. He can't be!

"You wouldn't look so bad, yourself, if you could wipe that expression of smug, male satisfaction off your face," she tried to say lightly as she pulled free of him to sit up on the edge of the bed.

"Can you blame me for appearing a little relieved this morning now that I know I won't have to beg for invitations to your bed in the future?'' He reached behind him and adjusted the pillows so that he could sit up against them. The silver eyes watched her with possessive pleasure as Brenna, clutching the sheet to her throat, turned to look at him.

Why did it have to be this man? Why couldn't it have been someone like Damon? Someone from her own world? Ryder Sterne was so different from everything she had known all her life...

"A gentleman always waits for an invitation, Ryder,'' she told him deliberately.

"Not after the lady has turned over the responsibility to him,'' he corrected with a knowing chuckle. "Last night you did exactly that, Brenna Llewellyn.''

"For one night!''

"Forever.''

She blinked, taken aback by the conviction in his tone. Try to keep it light, Brenna. She repeated the instructions over and over to herself. You must keep things light. There must be ways of handling this kind of an affair. Heaven help her! She needed time to think. She had to sort out the alarming mixture of her emotions for this man. Perhaps once she was free of the devastating intimacy of his bedroom, she would be able to think properly.

"Aren't you presuming a great deal on the basis of what happened last night?'' she tried to say repressively.

"And the night before,'' he added helpfully. "Don't forget what happened the night before, either. Yes, I guess you could say I'm presuming.'' He reached out and snagged her wrist, yanking her down on top of him in a soft tumble. A silver devil laughed at her from the depths of his eyes, but there was tender possession in the touch of his hands as he smoothed her nakedness. "I'm presuming that I'm going to be the only man in your life, sweet lady. I'm presuming that you have given yourself to me and I'm presuming that you can't take back the rights you handed over last night when you turned over the responsibility for what happened to me."

"That's a hell of a lot of presumption!" she pointed out carefully as he cradled her forcefully in the crook of his arm.

"What are you going to do about it?" he provoked, refusing to appear the least concerned by her mood. "Allow me to point out that I'm bigger than you are."

He was only teasing her, Brenna told herself firmly, taking a short rein on her temper. She might be nervous and on edge because of the implications of the last two nights, but there was no need to lose her self-control just because he was in a playful mood. The intelligent way of handling this was to respond in kind. She must be cool and at ease with the situation until she could escape to think it over properly.

"Size is not always an asset," she noted demurely. "It didn't do the dinosaurs much good."

"A poor analogy. The dinosaurs didn't combine brain with brawn the way I do," he declared immodestly. He swept back the sheet, sliding his legs over the edge of the bed and getting to his feet. He stood grinning down at her, his hands on his lean hips for a moment. "Guess which of us is going to win in a one-on-one confrontation. All your fine philosophy isn't going to do you a bit of good in a situation like this!"

Before she could divine his intention, Ryder was

reaching down to scoop her up and toss her lightly over his broad shoulder.

"Ryder! What the devil do you think you're doing? Put me down!" But she was laughing in spite of herself. The mood of boyish bravado and playfulness in him was difficult to withstand this morning. And she was falling in love with the man.

"I'm going to teach you how to scrub my back," he announced, spinning around to stride toward the bathroom. "I've always wanted my own personal back scrubber."

"A private fantasy of yours?" she demanded caustically. Deliberately she dug her nails into his side.

"Ouch!" he yelped and promptly retaliated by slapping her vulnerable, bare rear. "Damn right it's a private fantasy. Very private." He walked into the bath and turned on the shower, stepping into the stall itself with Brenna still draped over his shoulder.

"This is ridiculous," she groaned.

"Start scrubbing."

It was an hour before Brenna was finally able to free herself of the exuberant mood Ryder was indulging, and then it was only because she demanded an opportunity to go back to her cabin to put on some fresh clothes.

"If you'll settle down and promise to stop picking me up and bouncing me around as if I were a toy, I might even make you some breakfast," she volunteered before she could stop herself. The thought of making his breakfast was strangely pleasing. And he certainly had fed her enough lately.

"It's a deal," he agreed, sending her on her way with an affectionate pat on her derriere. With a last, wary glance over her shoulder, Brenna escaped.

But being alone for a while with her own thoughts did not prove to be the steadying, rational time Brenna had assumed it would be. She padded barefoot around her kitchen making pancakes from scratch and heating syrup and tried to think through the crisis in her life.

It wasn't fair that everything traumatic should be happening to her at once: her career at a crucial point; her love life dominated by someone who was not at all as she had secretly imagined the man of her dreams would be. It was just too much!

What was she going to do? She added the butter-milk to the pancake batter and told herself that as far as her career was concerned, she had to decide on a logical course of action that would also satisfy her own inner sense of honor and integrity. In some ways that crisis was going to be the easier one to deal with. But what did one do about falling in love with a man like Ryder Sterne? A man who, in his own words, found love a sloppy and sentimental emotion. A summer affair? She bit her lip in a rush of pain. It was difficult to think in such terms when one hovered on the brink of love...

She threw a chunk of butter on to the heating griddle as a knock came on the front door. It struck her as funny that Ryder should still be politely knocking after what they had shared during the past two days and she was smiling when she opened the door.

"Craig!"

Brenna took one startled look at the dark-haired young man on her doorstep and then hurled herself delightedly into his arms. "Craig Llewellyn, did you come all the way up here to see me or are you here to mooch a few free days at Tahoe!" Laughing, she hugged her brother and stepped back. "You're just in time for breakfast. Come on in."

"Thanks, you know I'm always available for a free meal. How's it going up here, Brenna? Having a good summer?" Craig stepped into the room, his arm draped around his sister's shoulders. He had inherited the deep brown hair of all the Llewellyns and the gold in his amber eyes matched Brenna's, but she had always privately thought him rather handsome into the bargain. The natural bias of a sister, she decided warmly, glancing up at him. His body had a young man's lean ranginess, which reflected his interest in outdoor pursuits. The planes of his face were maturing into strong features. She already knew he didn't lack for female companionship although he'd never gotten overly serious about anyone since the night of his high school prom when he'd come home convinced he was in love. The emotion, however, had faded within a week, Brenna remembered. She had been enormously thankful at the time.

"Is everything okay back in Berkeley? I thought you were taking some summer classes this year?"

"Everything's fine," Craig said slowly, taking a seat at the table while she puttered around the kitchen.

Brenna looked up at the careful steadiness in his words. "I'm glad to see you, Craig, but how is it you're here during the week? I would have thought you wouldn't have any free time until the weekend. I know how intensive summer classes usually are."

He seemed to take a long breath. "Brenna, I came up here to talk to you about...about next year."

She froze, straightening from the drawer where she had been looking for an extra setting of stainless. "Next year?"

"Brenna, I'm not going back to school in the fall."

All the other crises in Brenna's life were quickly pushed to a back burner. "Oh, Craig, no! You're not going to drop out! Not now when you're so close to finishing. You can't!"

The breakfast preparations forgotten, she came across the room in a daze to stand at the opposite side of the table. Her face was a mask of anxiety and protest. Two pairs of amber eyes stared at each other in pain and determination.

"Brenna, please try to understand. I've had enough of school. I want...I want to go out and see a little of the world. I have an opportunity to get a job on a freighter next month."

"A freighter!"

The young man's mouth tightened at the disbelief in her voice, but he kept his own tone level and desperately reasonable. "It's a unique opportunity and it's something I want to do very badly. It feels right for me, Brenna, do you know what I mean? This past year at the university hasn't had the feeling of being right. I've just been marking time..."

"Well, can't you mark another year of it? Craig, your education is so important, you must see that! You can't abandon it all now!" Her fingers curled into the wood as she clutched the chair in front of her. "It's only another year."

"And then I'll have a degree for which I have no use. Brenna, I'm a history major, for God's sake. Do you realize what that means? The only thing I can do with that is go on to graduate school and that's the last thing I want!"

"It makes a hell of a lot more sense than shipping

out on some damn freighter! Craig, that's like a kid talking of running off to join the circus! It's crazy!''

"It's what I want," he repeated quietly. Craig's hand was coiled as tightly as Brenna's. She read the determination in him and wanted to cry with frustration. To have come so far and then give it all up now. It was wrong. Very wrong. She had to convince him.

"Please, Craig," she tried, keeping her voice under control with a tremendous effort. "There's only one more year to go. After that you can decide if you really want to leave the academic life altogether. But at least you'll have that degree to fall back on if you ever change your mind."

"I can always go back to school to finish if that's what I want to do…"

For the second morning in a row Brenna was so wrapped up in the tension generated by an early visitor that she failed to hear the front door of the cabin open. The first either she or Craig knew of Ryder's presence was the sound of his dangerously laconic voice behind her brother.

"This is getting to be a habit, isn't it? Finding strange men sitting down to have breakfast with you in the mornings is not one of my favorite ways to start a day."

"Ryder!" Brenna looked up quickly, her eyes suddenly anxious for reasons other than the immediate crisis with Craig. "Wait, this is…"

But Craig was already getting to his feet to face the newcomer. He was apparently unruffled by the challenge in the older man's words. There was a physical tension in him that Brenna read at once as preparation for battle, but when he spoke, Craig's voice was calm and clear.

"I'm Craig Llewellyn." He waited as Ryder assessed him with a cool silver glance. "Brenna is my sister."

"Yes, with those eyes and that hair, you'd have to be related, wouldn't you?" The moment of strain dissolved as Ryder stuck out his hand, his grin inviting Craig to forgive the brief male challenge that had threatened for a few seconds. "I'm Ryder Sterne."

Craig accepted the proffered hand and accompanied the handshake with a searching, curious smile. "You obviously feel you have some right to be concerned with other men at Brenna's breakfast table?"

"Craig Llewellyn!" Brenna gasped, horrified.

"Every right in the world," Ryder was saying easily, sinking lithely into one of the chairs and smiling with brilliant casualness at an infuriated Brenna. "She belongs to me, you see."

"Don't listen to him, Craig," Brenna instructed tightly as her brother reacted with only a mildly inquiring eyebrow. "He's been in this...this *teasing* mood all morning."

"All morning?" Craig glanced speculatively from Ryder to his sister, the question-behind-the-question there for all to hear.

Brenna, for the first time in her life, felt as if the tables had been somehow turned between her brother and herself. Suddenly it was her little brother who was questioning her actions. She knew the flush in her cheeks was not going to go unnoticed by either man at the breakfast table. Hurriedly Brenna got to her feet.

"Would either of you care for a cup of tea?" she demanded frostily.

"She's still a little shy about the situation," Ryder explained to Craig.

"Understandable." Craig nodded, still eyeing his table mate. "The kind of men Brenna usually dates don't generally go around claiming she belongs to them. They tend to talk a slightly different line."

"I asked if either of you wanted any tea!"

"That will be fine, Brenna," Ryder agreed soothingly. "I'm sure Craig will have some, too." As she turned to put on the teakettle he asked Craig interestedly, "What kind of line do they usually talk?"

"You have to understand that there haven't been all that many men in her life," Craig answered reflectively.

"During the years I was in high school, she had her hands full making a home for me and getting her career started. It didn't leave her much time for a social life. Lately the one or two men she's introduced me to have been the kind who talked about career-oriented partnerships and having intellectual interests in common. They tended to worry a great deal about personal freedom in a relationship and not being stifled by such outmoded concepts as possessiveness. The kind of guys who would probably be involved in affairs with their graduate students six months after marrying Brenna."

"Craig!" White-faced, Brenna whirled to confront her brother. "You've said enough. Please shut up!"

"I'm sorry, Brenna," he apologized at once, sensing her genuine anger and embarrassment. "You're already upset. I shouldn't have teased you like that," he sighed ruefully.

"Why are you already upset?" Ryder demanded

an she began to pour pancake batter with an unsteady hand.

"It's a private matter between Craig and myself,"
she told him stiffly.

"If you're this upset about it, you'd better tell me
what's going on," he returned coolly. She could feel
his narrowed, searching gaze on her taut profile but
she refused to look at him.

"I don't wish to talk about it," she stated flatly.

Ryder pinned Craig matter-of-factly. "Are you in
trouble?"

Craig straightened a little warily at the chilled softness in the older man's voice. "No," he said quickly.
"No, I'm not in trouble. I'm…I'm dropping out of
school. That's what I came to tell Brenna."

"And that's why she's upset? What are you going
to do, Craig?"

Brenna set down the pitcher of pancake batter and
stared in frozen silence as the two men faced each
other. She had obviously been cut out of the conversation completely. Or perhaps she'd cut herself out
when she'd refused to discuss the matter with Ryder.

Craig hesitated and then plunged earnestly into the
reasons behind his decision. In a few minutes he had
summed it up, and when he sat back in his chair,
Brenna had the impression he was awaiting Ryder's
opinion as if it really mattered.

Ryder was silent for a while. He folded his elbows
on the table and fixed a considering glance on Craig's
expectant features. "You're absolutely certain this is
what you want to do?"

"Absolutely certain," Craig vowed feelingly. He
didn't look at Brenna, who stood taut and silent by
the stove.

"What's the name of the freighter line?"

Craig told him and Ryder nodded thoughtfully. "I've heard of it. They've been around a while. Do you know anything about working on a freighter?"

"Not much," Craig admitted. "They said I'd be trained."

Ryder's mouth tilted upward sardonically. "I'm sure you will be. It's hard work, Craig."

"I know."

"Have you ever been to sea at all?"

"No, not really."

"Well," Ryder suddenly announced calmly, "I'm sure you'll find it very interesting. Remember you can always jump ship if the going gets too rough. It's not like signing on with the military."

Craig's relief at Ryder's apparent approval was blatantly obvious. "I'll keep that in mind. Have you ever done anything like it yourself?"

Ryder paused and then said quietly, "I've done a little traveling the hard way. Seeing how the rest of the world functions is a very educational experience. Probably be worth five or ten years in graduate school!"

"That's enough! Both of you!" Brenna's fury boiled over as they shifted their glances to her tense face. "Craig, this is absolute nonsense and you know it. Ryder, you have no right to encourage him like that! This is a family matter between Craig and myself and I demand that you stay out of it!"

"Lady, you know anything that concerns you, concerns me. This is a decision Craig has to make for himself. He's a man in addition to being your little brother. He has to make up his own mind about what he wants to do with his life."

"You don't understand!" she wailed, feeling at her wits' end. "He's only got one more year of school! He's come this far, why can't he finish? Ryder, what if something happens? What if he gets into trouble like the Gardners' son did?"

Ryder looked at her. "If he gets into trouble I'll go and get him out of it," he stated with gentle simplicity.

Brenna stared at him helplessly for an instant longer as a wave of panic and defeat rolled over her. Then, without a word, she turned and walked out of the cabin, leaving the pancakes to burn on the griddle.

Chapter 8

No one pursued Brenna to try to soothe her or "talk sense into her," and for that she was inordinately grateful. She needed time to think and to adjust. Her sense of responsibility toward her younger brother had existed for so many years, she realized, that it had become almost maternal in nature.

Her mouth twisted ruefully even as the tears stung her eyes. She stood, hands jammed into the front pockets of her jeans, and stared out at the calm surface of the lake. She had walked far enough to be out of sight of the cabins.

Craig was a man now, she told herself. A young man who lacked experience, it was true, but still a man. Ryder had been right to correct her when she had termed her brother a "kid" a few days ago. Even mothers had to let go when the time came, Brenna reminded herself. It was still more important that she, who was not his mother, step out of the responsibility role. After all, she wanted herself and Craig to be friends. It would be unhealthy and stupid to try to persist in the dominant older sister mode.

Funny, she'd never thought of herself as domineering, but when she'd heard herself yelling at her younger brother that he had to stay in college, there was no denying the fact that she had assumed too much responsibility, for too long.

Not that Craig was going to allow her to control his life, apparently, she added wryly. He had come up to Lake Tahoe to break the news to her, not to ask her advice in the matter.

She thought of the tale of the Gardners' son, the one Ryder had been hired to rescue from a foreign prison, and shuddered. Working on a freighter, Craig was bound to encounter the rougher side of life. What if he wound up in real trouble? Her imagination worked overtime supplying possibilities.

Brenna put a halt to that line of thought with a firm mental decision. Craig was not Evan Gardner. He was not a mixed-up kid engaging in an act of rebellion. He was simply ready to start living his own life. And if he got in trouble Ryder would go and get him and bring him home.

Ryder. He had promised her that much and she could trust him. Brenna turned from the shore and started back toward the cabins.

The two men had apparently finished breakfast on their own, Brenna realized as she walked back into her cabin. The dishes had been piled in the sink and the griddle turned off. She was warming it back up again in preparation for her own meal when she glanced out the window and saw Ryder and Craig in front of the archery target.

For a few minutes she simply watched, ignoring the sizzling griddle as Ryder demonstrated shooting techniques to the younger man. Craig appeared fascinated and picked up the basics quickly. Even as she stared at the two men, Brenna slowly acknowledged that Craig and Ryder had a lot in common. There was a self-reliant masculine assurance and determination in both of them that would always set its own standards. They were the kind of men who lived by their own codes and for whom honor and integrity would always be crucial. The kind of men a woman could trust to the ends of the earth even when she became thoroughly annoyed or outraged by the host of macho characteristics that went along with their honor and integrity. Brenna turned away from the window and sat down to eat her pancakes.

It was Craig who came back to the cabin an hour or so later, alone. He looked concerned but very determined. Brenna glanced up from the essay on the dualism of mind and matter that she was attempting to read and smiled. The expression was a bit misty, perhaps even wistful, but it was a genuine smile and Craig relaxed visibly. His mouth lifted in response, and for a moment brother and sister stared at each other in understanding. Then Craig came forward and slipped into the chair across from Brenna.

"It's going to be okay, Brenna, Ryder's going to look after you for me," he said gently.

Brenna, who hadn't been thinking along those lines at all, blinked in astonishment. "What on earth are you talking about, Craig?"

He shrugged, sensing her sudden wariness. "Ryder

and I had a long talk and he let me know how things stand between the two of you. He's going to take care of you. I won't have to worry about your marrying some turkey like that Fielding character.''

Some of the wistful, sisterly gentleness faded from Brenna's startled eyes. ''Craig, I don't know exactly what Ryder told you about our relationship, but I can assure you it is only temporary at best. Furthermore, it's not important at the moment. You're the one who is embarking on a new adventure and I...I want you to know that if this is what you really want to do, I'm behind you a hundred percent.''

He leaned forward and hugged her affectionately. ''Thanks, Brenna. I know what it must have taken for you to come to that conclusion. I know how important the academic world has been to you, and it was only natural you'd feel more comfortable putting me in that world, too. But it's not for me.''

''I think I've sensed that for the past couple of years. The problem has been that it was the only world I knew, the only one I could guide you toward,'' she sighed.

''A man has to find out for himself where he belongs,'' Craig announced very solemnly. ''It's time I went out and started looking.''

They spent the rest of the day together, talking quietly, sharing the closeness of being a brother and sister who had been alone together in the world for a long time. Ryder discreetly disappeared into his own cabin and didn't reappear until Craig went over to invite him for dinner.

Brenna glanced up from the stuffed mushrooms she was removing from the oven and met his calm, in-

quiring gaze as he walked in the door behind Craig.
Wordlessly he was asking her if she had accepted her
brother's decision.

The answer to that one, she found, was easy.
"Hello, Ryder. Have a seat. Craig has picked up a
few interesting skills this past year. He mixes a terrific
margarita. If he got that much out of Berkeley, there's
no telling what he'll pick up on a freighter in the
South Seas!" She laughed, sliding the hot pan of
mushrooms quickly onto the top of the stove.

"A margarita sounds great, Craig." Ryder settled
into one of the chairs in front of the hearth as Brenna
carried in the plate of stuffed mushrooms. Craig
headed for the kitchen with a grin and Brenna was
left to face the second question in Ryder's eyes alone.
The answer to that one, however, was not so easy. He
must have known that Craig had told his sister of
Ryder's decision to "take care of her." The silver
gaze was asking her point-blank if she had accepted
that decision, too.

"You have, I understand, been attempting to re
assure my brother that I'll be all right in his absence,"
she began dryly, taking the bull by the horns as she
sat down across from him.

"He was worried about you," Ryder said simply,
reaching for one of the hors d'oeuvres. If he sensed
the challenge in her words, he chose to ignore it. He
bit into the mushroom. "These are great. Do you realize this is the first meal you've finally gotten around
to preparing for me?"

"Ryder, Craig seems to have a slight misconcep-
tion about our relationship," Brenna pursued firmly.

"No, he doesn't." Ryder was glancing past her
shoulder to where Craig was coming toward them

with a pitcher of margaritas and three salt-rimmed glasses. He grinned appreciatively at the younger man. "I'm glad to see there are still benefits to be derived from a university education."

After that there really was no opportunity to confront Ryder again. Craig was leaving to return to Berkeley in the morning, and Brenna was suddenly anxious not to cause a scene. Somehow it had become very important that the three of them enjoy this evening together. The other crises in her life could wait.

She let Craig and Ryder do most of the talking that evening, listening quietly as they discussed Craig's new venture and Ryder told a few anecdotes about some of his own travels. Ryder did not, Brenna noticed, bring up any incidents such as the assault on the prison that had freed the Gardners' son. For that she was grateful. Craig's future promised to be adventuresome enough without actively encouraging him into any more dangerous directions.

It wasn't until Ryder finally rose to walk back to his own cabin that Brenna finally acknowledged the evening had aroused a new kind of wistfulness in her. The talk had been of adventure and travel and personal discovery. It left her with a strange feeling of restlessness.

Ryder kissed her good night before he left, making no effort to conceal the extent of their relationship in front of Craig. She was the one who pulled back in confusion and embarrassment. But Craig only smiled, appearing satisfied with the situation as he chose to interpret it.

In spite of all her fine resolutions and understanding, there were tears in Brenna's eyes the next morning as she stood with Ryder's arm around her waist, waving goodbye to Craig, who was backing his car out of the drive.

"It's not as if he's going off to war," Ryder teased sardonically as Craig's car disappeared from sight. "And you'll be seeing him again before he ships out on the freighter, anyway."

"I know." Brenna dashed the dampness away from her eyes with a fierce brush of her hand. She stepped out of the circle of Ryder's arm.

"He'll be all right, Brenna. He's not an immature boy, he's a man."

"I know." Brenna started back toward her cabin, not looking at Ryder. The strange restlessness was eating at her. Her emotions seemed to be confusingly scrambled this morning. The traumatic events of the past week were taking their toll. She was aware that Ryder was pacing along beside her, frowning.

"Are you angry at me for sanctioning his decision to go?" he finally demanded softly.

Brenna said nothing. She wasn't sure how she felt just then. She couldn't define her emotions toward Ryder at that moment.

"He would have gone anyway, you know. There was no one who could have stopped him." She sensed Ryder's laconic smile. "He's got his sister's will and determination, I'm afraid."

Brenna bit her lip and still said nothing. She was filled now with a tension that threatened to force an outlet for itself. It angered her because she could not deal with the emotion until she understood it, and it seemed totally incomprehensible.

"Are you upset because I told Craig not to worry about you? That I would take care of you?"

Brenna shrugged, unable to speak. She needed time to herself, she thought. Time to come to terms with this strange, uncoiling tension. She started to push open the door to her cabin and behind her Ryder finally lost his patience.

"Damn it, Brenna! Talk to me! Don't just walk away from this!"

"What the hell do you think you're doing?" she gasped furiously as he clamped a large hand on her shoulder and whirled her around to face him.

"I'm trying to figure out what's gotten into you. I thought you'd come to grips with Craig's decision to leave!" He clamped the other hand on her shoulder and held her in front of him with a grip of iron. The brackets at the edges of his mouth were tight with impatience and the silver eyes were narrowed with it.

"I have come to grips with it!" she flung back, the tension in her crashing toward the surface. "No, I'm not upset with you for sanctioning his decision, either. What else could I have expected from you? You're two of a kind, you and Craig. It was perfectly natural that you'd understand him immediately!"

"Then you must be angry about the way I told him not to worry about you!" He punctuated his words by giving her a small shake.

"Maybe," she hissed, trying unsuccessfully to free herself from his hold. "Maybe I am a little upset about the way you handled that! You certainly didn't have any right to imply the sort of relationship you did!"

"The hell I didn't," he ground out far too gently. "Brenna, you're my woman now and I'll take care of you. It's as simple as that."

"Nothing is as simple as that!" she blazed, the gold of her eyes flaming as she faced him.

"Is that issue the real problem this morning?" He searched her face coolly. "You want a knockdown, drag-out fight over the matter of my claim on you?"

"No, damn it! I don't want a battle over it. That would be admitting your 'claim' exists in the first place!"

"It does."

"It can't exist unless I accept it!" she stormed. "But believe it or not, that's not the reason I'm upset this morning!"

"So tell me the reason," he ordered softly, implacably.

"It's none of your business!"

"Don't be ridiculous," he drawled quietly. "Of course it's my business. Everything about you is my business. Talk, woman. What's driving you this morning? Why are you tense and nervous and spoiling for a fight?"

"You don't think I've had enough cause for an emotional outburst of some magnitude?" she snapped furiously. "It's been a rough summer so far and my vacation's hardly begun!"

"You've had cause, but you were handling things fairly well. What happened this morning?"

"I don't know," she almost wailed. "It's too hard to explain and I really don't want to talk about it. Not with anyone!"

"You're going to talk about it with me."

"This may be a little tough for you to comprehend, Ryder Sterne, but you do not have the right to dictate to me like that!"

"Brenna, so help me, if you don't stop raving and

tell me what the hell is wrong, I'm going to lose my temper,'' he stated flatly.

''Is that supposed to throw me into abject terror?''

''It might,'' he murmured. It struck her that the louder she got the quieter he was getting. It was alarming.

''That's a poor threat, Ryder. We all know you don't lose your temper. You're cool and calm and *professional* under fire, remember?''

''You really are looking for some method of venting your frustration, aren't you? You're even trying to provoke me so you'll have some reason to lash back. That's a dangerous game, lady. Much safer just to talk out the situation, believe me.''

''I thought you favored the use of violence as a means of settling problems!''

''Only under certain circumstances,'' he drawled. ''I don't think this is one of those circumstances. Yet. Now talk, Brenna.''

''I can't even explain it to myself, let alone someone else,'' she whispered tersely. ''Let me go, Ryder. I need to think.''

There was a pause but he didn't release her. For a few seconds he stared down into her simmering gaze and then he asked very coolly. ''Are you by any chance jealous?''

''Jealous! *Jealous!*'' she ripped out, stunned. ''Of what, for God's sake! Are you hiding a model from one of your book covers somewhere nearby? Don't be absurd, Ryder! Of course I'm not jealous.''

''Not of another woman. Of Craig.''

The simple explanation hit home with an impact that took Brenna's breath. Her eyes went very wide with anguished denial and her body went rigid in his grasp. ''Of Craig!'' she repeated in a whisper.

''Of the fact that he's stepping out of the academic world and going off to indulge his natural streak of recklessness and taste for adventure. Do you see him having the courage to make the move and wish you had that courage, too?''

''No! No, that's not it at all! It can't be!''

''Why not? It makes sense to me, lady. There's no denying the intellectual side of your nature. Indeed, you've honed that aspect of yourself very nicely, given it every opportunity to express itself. But there's another side of you, isn't there, Brenna? A side you've always treated with disdain and kept repressed because you're afraid it will conflict with the lifestyle you admire most, the academic world.''

Helplessly she looked up at him. It was the truth. She knew it and she didn't want to face it. Fear was the emotion that roiled within her now.

''That's why you're wary of me and my claim on you, isn't it?'' he pursued steadily as he worked the implications through in his mind. ''Giving yourself to me is a risk because I represent another kind of life, something far different from the one you've been trained to admire. Well, it's true, I'm not part of your college faculty world and I never will be, but you've already taken the risk, sweet lady. It's too late to change your mind. Find the courage to face our relationship the same way you found the courage to face Craig's decision and the way you'll find the courage to handle the crisis in your career!''

''Ryder, you don't know what you're saying!''

''Yes, I do. It's not a crisis in your career or with your brother's future that you're really facing this summer. You're having to make a very fundamental decision about what you want out of life.''

''I know what I want out of life!''

''Yes,'' he surprised her by agreeing, ''I think you do know what you want. The question is, are you going to have the guts to acknowledge that fact? How long will it take you to accept that for you there must be something more in life than the climb up the academic ladder and relationships with men like Damon Fielding who don't know what it means to want and need a woman the way I want and need you? Craig found the courage to strike out on his own and go after what he wants in life. How about you, Brenna? Will you find the same courage or will you scurry back to your ivory tower and force me to come drag you out of it?''

Appalled, Brenna tried to reason with herself. She must not let him do this to her! She was a rational, intelligent human being who knew how to think her way through any situation. She would not let this man drive her to violence. But she was trembling with a combination of outrage and fear as she bit out, ''If I decide to scurry home to my ivory tower, as you so graphically put it, I assure you there's no way on earth you'll be able to drag me back out! I make my own decisions in life and I will not let you control or manipulate me. Just because you've shared a bed with me on two occasions, don't get the idea you have any rights over me! How many times do I have to tell you that?''

''How many times do I have to take you to bed before you stop denying my rights?'' he countered roughly.

It was too much. The events of the preceding days

took their toll with a vengeance. And Ryder became the unlucky focus of all the chaotic emotions surging through her in that moment.

Brenna slapped him. Her hand moved in a wide, swinging arc that he probably could have avoided but didn't. Instead he just stood there and let her fingers create a bright-red brand on the side of his face.

The silence that followed seemed to extend even to the surrounding woods. In utter quiet Brenna stood staring at the man she had just struck, her mind numb with shock at her own behavior. Ryder didn't move.

"The thing about violence," he finally cautioned in a very gentle voice, "is that you have to be prepared for the possibility that it will escalate."

She swallowed. "Is that a way of saying you're going to get even?"

"Do you think I would really hit you?" He appeared almost curious.

Brenna closed her eyes in shame and self-disgust. "No. I deserve it but you won't do it." She took a couple of slow breaths, bringing herself back under control. When she opened her eyes, Ryder was already several feet away, walking back toward his cabin. She could only stand and watch as he moved off with that fog-silent step. He didn't look back.

It wasn't long after she'd served herself a lonely dinner in front of the fire and was focusing on the prospect of going to bed without even being able to say good-night to Ryder that Brenna finally realized it was up to her to end the impasse. She was the one who had created it.

Ryder hadn't emerged from his cabin since he'd walked away after she'd lost her self-control. She could only presume that he'd spent the afternoon and evening beginning work on his book. He was probably the type who could do just that, she told herself unhappily. He was so damn self-controlled, he could probably put the incident with her out of his mind in disgust and go to work. She, on the other hand, couldn't get past page one of the quarterly issue of the philosophy journal in her lap.

Lifting her eyes from the open journal to the flames on the hearth, Brenna tried to rationalize her way out of what she knew, deep down, had to be done. Ryder had no real rights over her, she reminded herself, regardless of how he'd chosen to interpret her willingness to let him make love to her. It would probably be best to let the rift between them stand. It would serve to break off a relationship in which she was swiftly becoming far too involved. Only this morning she had found herself toying with the idea of falling in love with the man.

No, it would be simpler to use the current unpleasantness as a way of easing herself out of a highly precarious situation. It was frightening to think how close she had been to admitting she was in love with a man who was all wrong for her.

All wrong. It was crazy, ludicrous, and adolescent to allow one's emotions to rule one's head that far! Ryder was *different,* far different from any other man she had ever met. It stood to reason that there would be a certain attraction about him, didn't it? But that didn't mean a genuine, solid relationship could be built on that attraction. Sound relationships weren't built on the basis of a man declaring himself in possession of a woman because she had been foolish enough to surrender herself to him!

But even as she lectured herself, Brenna knew there

was more to it than that. Unwillingly she recalled the hero of *The Quicksilver Venture,* a man hardened in the ways of the shadowy world in which he moved but still a man who lived by a code of honor and integrity; a man who could, in a strange way, be trusted. Not unlike Ryder.

No, Brenna told herself firmly, she had no business getting involved with a man like Ryder Sterne. The Damon Fieldings of this world were the kind of men she should be cultivating. Damon understood her lifestyle, her ambitions, and her career. He held modern views on the subject of a relationship, and just because Craig hadn't cared for the man, that didn't mean Damon was wrong for her. Heaven knew Craig was a lot more likely to view the world the way Ryder viewed it! They were two of a kind in many ways.

But Brenna Llewellyn was her own woman who had to make her own path and her own choices. It was all very well for Craig to choose a more adventuresome path in this world, but she, Brenna, had already chosen hers and it did not lead in the same direction. It did not lead toward men like Ryder Sterne.

None of which, she realized grimly, changed the fundamental question before her now. She owed Ryder an apology. Even if the wiser course of action might be to let the situation stand, there was still a matter of simple honor and simple manners involved.

She not only owed him an apology for the slap, she also owed him her thanks for the quiet way he had helped both her and Craig through the difficult time yesterday. His calm, reasonable attitude had been a source of reassurance for her, and clearly he'd had the same effect on her brother, who had been worrying about Brenna's reaction to his announcement.

Yes, she owed Ryder for that and for the slap. Her pride demanded that she take some step toward satisfying its demands. With a soft sigh Brenna got to her feet and located the rust-colored suede jacket she'd brought with her. It was going to be quite chilly outside this late at night.

As she stepped outside her door Brenna saw at once that there was no light on in the cabin across the clearing. Had Ryder gone to bed early? She glanced down at her watch. It was later than she had realized. Perhaps this whole thing should wait until morning.

But something drove her forward. This wasn't going to keep until morning. It had to be done as soon as possible. Too much time had already passed. As she walked across the clearing Brenna reminded herself over and over that going to Ryder like this involved nothing more than an apology and her personal thanks for what he had done for her and Craig. It most definitely did not involve any admission on her part that she was accepting the claim he had placed on her!

She bit her lip as she neared the cabin and realized that even the porch light was off. He must have gone to bed. Well, he would just have to get out of bed to hear what she had to say, she decided determinedly. Having made up her mind, Brenna knew she wasn't going to abandon the project now. With a firm step she began to circle around to the front door of the cabin. Then, quite suddenly, she realized she was about to pass by the open bedroom window. The window she had attempted to crawl through that first night.

Irresistibly Brenna was drawn to a halt beside the window. Ryder would be in there. All she had to do was rap on the panes and he would hear her. There would be darkness to cover her as she made her apology. She wouldn't have to stand in the full glare of the porch light and do it. The idea became incredibly appealing.

She moved a little closer to the open window and lifted a hand to tap on the glass. Nothing could be seen inside the shadow-filled room. Cautiously she scratched at the panes.

"Ryder?" she called very softly.

There was no answer; no sound from within. Brenna tapped gently once more. "Ryder, it's me, Brenna. I have to talk to you. Just for a minute." Why the devil was she whispering?

When there was still no answer, she gnawed reflectively on her lower lip and thought seriously about returning to her own cabin. In the morning she could come back and do this in broad daylight.

That thought was enough to urge her into one more effort. With every fiber of her being, Brenna wanted to get the matter out of the way tonight. Deliberately she pushed the window open wider and leaned inside the room. She still couldn't see much except the vague outline of the end of the bed. In the poor light she couldn't even tell if he was *in* the bed. Brenna frowned and threw a leg over the sill.

"Ryder? Are you awake?"

She was sitting astride the windowsill now, peering into the gloom. Perhaps he was in the bathroom brushing his teeth. Maybe he hadn't gone to bed yet after all.

"I'm awake."

The soft growl didn't come from the bed, it emanated from directly behind her shoulder, from the darkness inside the room at the edge of the window. Brenna gasped and instinctively tried to slip her leg off the sill so that she could stand safely outside the window. He put a stop to that by putting out a hand and clamping it strongly across her thigh. Automatically Brenna went very still as he moved into the pale starlight coming in through the window. When she found his face in the darkness, she drew in her breath a little shakily. He looked very dangerous there in the shadows. He was wearing only a pair of Jockey shorts, and the lean, sinewy lines of his body seemed quite pagan. The expression in his silvery eyes was totally unreadable but the hand on her thigh was easily comprehended. He wasn't going to let her slip back outside the window.

"Good lord!" she breathed. "You frightened me. I thought you'd be in bed. When you didn't answer my tap on the window, I decided you must not be in the room."

"I heard you crunching around outside on the gravel. I wasn't quite sure what to think about having you attempt to crawl through my window, though, so I thought I'd give it a few minutes to see how far you intended to go. Now you're here shall I draw my own conclusions?" The fingers on her thigh tightened but she still couldn't make out the emotion behind his silver gaze.

Brenna decided to plunge into her explanation without delay. That was the reason she had come to his cabin, wasn't it? "Ryder, I'm here for—for several reasons."

He waited, one brow arching slightly.

"First of all, I owe you an apology for what happened this morning after Craig left…" She forced herself to go on in a steady voice. "I lost my self-control. There was absolutely no excuse for that and I can only say I'm sorry. Violence is never an answer!"

"But it can, as I pointed out earlier, give one a feeling of satisfaction," he returned dryly.

"Well, it didn't," she muttered icily. "I'm ashamed of myself and it only served to make me feel like a fool. My only excuse is that I was on edge at the time."

"Yes." There was a pause, and when she didn't say anything else, he questioned carefully, "And your other reasons for climbing through my window tonight?"

Brenna stifled a groan. He wasn't going to make this easy. "I wanted to thank you for helping Craig and me. You somehow managed to reassure both of us and keep things calm. I think the situation would have been a great deal more unpleasant if you hadn't been there. It— it helped when you said that if Craig ever got himself into real trouble you'd go and get him out, and I know Craig felt better when you told him you'd look after me. Oh, I can't explain it exactly, Ryder. It was just that your presence made things easier for my brother and for me."

"I see. Anything else?"

Brenna hesitated. She hadn't meant to tell him the rest. There was no need to confess everything, especially this last matter about which she still wasn't very certain herself. But a rush of self-honesty, aided by the comforting blanket of darkness, brought the words to the surface. "You—you may have been right about my being a little envious of my brother," she mumbled.

"Because he made the break you didn't make years ago?" His tone was gently implacable. There was no sympathy in it at all.

"Perhaps a part of me wonders what would have happened if I hadn't chosen the path I did. But that's natural, isn't it? Everyone must think along those lines from time to time. I did choose the academic world, however, and it's been satisfying. It's my life now and I'm content with it. I'm not like you or Craig."

"Not even a little bit like us?"

"No," she stated very firmly. "No, and even if I were, it's too late. I made my choice a long time ago."

"It's never too late, Brenna," he told her softly. "There are no rules that say we have to stay committed to any single job or career. The only rules we have to follow in life are the ones we make for ourselves."

"I'm happy in my world, damn it," she suddenly flared. "I'm good at what I do and it's satisfying. I may wonder occasionally about the other side of life, the kind of life you have explored, but that doesn't mean I want to explore it for myself. I'm a teacher of philosophy and that's enough for me. I don't entertain any secret admiration for the more adventuresome life. Hell, I probably wouldn't even approve of many of the things you've done, much less admire them! I do admire my own world, or at least a great deal of it,'' she added, thinking of the aspect of it she had been exposed to lately when Paul Humphrey had stolen her work. But there were honorable and dishonorable people in every profession, weren't there?

''Okay,'' Ryder said soothingly, ''so you're happy in your ivory tower. That's your decision.''

''Thanks!''

''But that still leaves one more issue, Brenna.''

She looked at him with sudden wariness. ''What issue?''

''The matter of our relationship. I have a claim on you, lady, and you can't rationalize or argue or philosophize your way out of that. I'm waiting for you to accept it intellectually just as you've accepted it with your body.''

''No!'' She made a startled movement, and his hand on her thigh clenched with gentle warning. ''Ryder, you and I are from two different worlds.''

''That's got nothing to do with it.''

''But it does! I need someone from the academic world. Someone who understands my career and my way of thinking. What you and I have together is a very temporary thing. You need someone who's more—more exciting and venturesome.''

''We want and need each other, lady,'' he interrupted quietly. ''How much longer until you realize that?''

''What about love?'' she flung back, aware that she was inserting a totally irrational argument into what should have stayed a very rational discussion.

''What about love?'' he countered. ''I'm talking about fundamentals, not vague, indefinable concepts like love. You're an intelligent woman: face the facts of the situation. You want me, even if you are a little afraid of me at this point.''

"I am not afraid of you!'' she bit out furiously.

"Yes, I think you are. You're afraid of what I'm going to bring into your cozy, well-organized life, aren't you, Brenna? With me around you might find yourself tempted to give in to the more adventure-some side of your nature. In fact, the mere act of coming to me takes you very far afield, doesn't it? I keep warning you what giving yourself to me really means, and you keep trying to pretend you can slip in and out of my bed without accepting the commit-ment it involves. You're frightened of that commit-ment because it's got nothing to do with your neat little academic world. You're frightened of *me* be-cause I'm not a man from your world. But you've got the courage to handle those fears, Brenna.''

"I came here tonight to apologize," Brenna hissed angrily, "not to become involved in this kind of crazy argument! Good night, Ryder.'' She waited defiantly for him to release his grip on her leg. Not for the world would she admit that she was trembling with an irrational wish that he would simply yank her into the room and into his bed. It made everything so much simpler when she didn't have to make the choice.

"Good night, Brenna. Your apology is accepted.'' Ryder took his hand away from her thigh. He didn't move as she scrambled back out of the window and fled toward her cabin. But he called her name once softly in the darkness and she halted, poised warily in the starlight. "Brenna.''

"Yes, Ryder?''

"You could have kept him here, you know.''

"Craig?" She frowned uncertainly, not understanding.

"All you had to do was tell him about your own messy situation at the college. If you'd told him how bad things are and told him you needed his support, he would have stuck around until everything was resolved."

"That wouldn't have been a fair tactic to use," she protested instantly. "It would have been a kind of emotional blackmail."

"I know." She sensed his smile even though she couldn't quite discern it. "And you're a woman of honor, aren't you? You prefer to fight fair, even when you know you're going to lose. Good night, lady. Sleep well."

Chapter 9

It was Ryder who found the note in the mailbox shared by the two cabins. He walked into Brenna's kitchen the next morning just as she was about to poach an egg for herself. He didn't bother to knock.

"It's addressed to you," he announced, tossing the envelope down on the table and lowering himself casually into one of the chairs. "Tea ready yet?"

Brenna refrained from dropping the egg into the swirling hot water and frowned. She had spent a sleepless night alternating between anger and cool determination. Ryder looked as if he'd had a thoroughly restful night. She wanted to say something firm about the way he had walked in without bothering to knock, but she couldn't think of anything that wouldn't sound childish or petulant.

"It's ready. Help yourself." Wiping her hands on

a towel, she went over to the table and picked up the small letter. It was from Diana Bergen.

"Friend of yours?" Ryder asked easily, pouring his tea.

"She's a member of the philosophy department. A colleague. Yes, she's a friend." Brenna tore open the envelope and quickly scanned the contents. "So," she whispered when she'd finished. "That's the way it's going to end."

"The way what's going to end?" Ryder persisted patiently, his gaze going to the letter.

Brenna looked up. "She says Dr. Humphrey is announcing his retirement unexpectedly early. There's going to be a party for him tomorrow night and she suggests I come back for it. Good politics." Her mouth turned downward derisively at that last comment. "Says she would have phoned to give me more advance notice but found out I didn't have a telephone here this summer." Brenna glanced back down at the letter. "She also says Damon will undoubtedly be taking over Humphrey's position."

Ryder sipped cautiously at the hot tea. "The fall term should prove interesting for you," he observed dryly. "Are you really going to go back and work for the man you insulted so openly a few days ago?"

Brenna tapped her fingers restlessly on the table. "I'll worry about Damon later. I might be able to apologize for what happened and make him understand," she said quietly. "It's Humphrey I'm thinking about now. If I don't go to this party for him tomorrow evening I may never see him again. If I'm ever going to do or say anything to his face about what he's done to me, tomorrow night is the time."

Ryder ignored the last part of her statement alto-

gether. "What the hell do you mean you'll worry
about Fielding later? I thought you said he could
make life very uncomfortable for you this fall."

"He can." She shrugged. "But I don't think he
will. He *likes* me, Ryder. He'll understand how upset
I was just as I understood why he was trying to talk
me into not making a scene with Humphrey. He was
only trying to make me see the political side of the
question." She brushed the remainder of that issue
aside. "The important thing right now is whether or
not I'm going to confront Humphrey."

"Can he still jeopardize your career?"

"I doubt it. Not from retirement. I could still come
out of a scene looking extremely foolish, though. Damon's right in that regard. I'm just a very junior member of the faculty making some crazy charges against
a renowned senior member of the department. But I
can't let this pass! My God! I worked months on that
ethics paper. Some of those conclusions took me
weeks of study and analysis. To see them published
by a man I held in such high regard is unbearable. I
have to say *something* to him, even if I do come off
looking foolish and vicious." Brenna got to her feet
with determination. "I'm going to that party. I'll
drive back this afternoon and have plenty of time to
prepare for tomorrow night." The moment of decision had really arrived and she knew what had to be
done. She had to confront Paul Humphrey regardless
of what he might do to her future in the academic
world. It was a relief to have the decision made.

"What about Fielding?" Ryder asked very softly.

She turned to glance at him as she prepared to finish making breakfast. "It was wrong of me to expect
Damon to help me fight my battles. I shouldn't have

tried to enlist his aid, and I had no right to insult him when he tried to make me see his side of the matter. I'll apologize to him tomorrow night. He'll understand why I acted as I did. I'll explain to him about you, too.''

"That should be interesting."

Brenna felt herself flush furiously and her mouth tightened. "There's no need for him to know all the details!''

"He's already guessed most of the pertinent ones, as I recall. He thinks I'm the stud you're amusing yourself with this summer, remember?''

"Don't say things like that!'' she whispered tautly, shocked.

"You heard him. Is that how you see me, Brenna?''

"Ryder, don't be ridiculous. You're just trying to provoke me." She looked at him pleadingly, the bowl of eggs in her hand. "Ryder, about last night, I hope you understood what I was trying to say."

"You have the most annoying tendency to try to explain 'last nights.''' Ryder's crooked smile expressed a tenderness that took Brenna by surprise. She stood quite still, staring at him as he got up from the table and came across the floor to cup her face in his hands. "But it's the future I'm concerned about. I won't try to tell you that you shouldn't go back for this party. If you feel you have to confront Humphrey, that's your business. It's a matter of pride and honor. I understand that. But I have to know whether or not you're planning on coming back here to Tahoe afterward.''

Brenna went still, her inner turmoil clear in the

amber of her eyes. "Ryder, I don't know if I should. Perhaps this is as good a time to end things as any."

"You won't be ending matters if you stay down in the Bay area," he warned gently. "You'll just make it necessary for me to come after you. I'm asking for your word that you'll come back here instead of going into hiding. I think you've got the courage to return, lady. What do you think?" His thumbs moved sensually along the line of her throat, and the silver in his gaze was a net she couldn't avoid.

"Oh, Ryder," she whispered helplessly.

"Your word you'll come back?" he coaxed softly.

What could she say? How could she resist, even though she knew she should? This man might be all wrong for her, but he held a power over her that no other man had ever wielded.

"Ryder, it would be better if—"

He didn't let her finish. Still holding her face cupped in his rough yet gentle hands, he brought his mouth down to take hers in a sweet, lingering kiss that flooded her with weakness and reminded her all too keenly of how close she was to falling in love with Ryder Sterne.

His tongue moved knowingly along the inside of her lips as he deepened the kiss. When she moaned softly and unconsciously crowded a little closer to his hard frame, he lifted his head to look down into her eyes. "Promise you'll come back to Tahoe. You owe me that much at least, lady."

She didn't owe him anything, Brenna told herself wildly even as she heard her own voice say "Yes."

He pulled her close against his chest. "It's always nice to know one is dealing with a woman who will honor her word."

* * *

Brenna was on her way by lunchtime. She was tense, both from the strain of what she was going to do when she met Paul Humphrey face-to-face and from the look in Ryder's eyes as he watched her leave. He stood in the drive, feet slightly braced and hands shoved idly into his back pockets. The breeze ruffled his tawny hair and the sun seemed to glance along the planes of his set features. He understood why she had to go, Brenna knew. But he would hold her to her word about returning.

What had she done by rashly giving her promise on that score? she asked herself time and again on the long drive back to the San Francisco Bay area. It would have been so much more rational to simply not have returned. Going back to Tahoe would be dangerous. There was no way around that.

No, she had to stop thinking about such matters. Her main concern now must be deciding what she would say to the esteemed Dr. Humphrey. Brenna entertained no illusions about gaining any real justice out of the mess. But it had become important to let the man know she was well aware of what he had done and what she thought of him for doing it. She was the only one who could stand up for her own rights. It had been wrong to hope that Damon would stand beside her. Some things a person had to do for herself. If there was ever a philosophical bit of truth, that was it!

The apartment she had left for the summer seemed almost unwilling to welcome her back so soon. It was closed up and too neat, just as she had left it. There was also no food in the place.

Hours later, tired by the drive and her own nervous tension, Brenna crawled between the cold sheets, turned on her electric blanket, and fell asleep. And dreamed of a man with silver-gray eyes.

She chose her clothes with care the following evening, the kind of clothes that a woman would wear when she knew she would be standing alone. She wasn't about to fade into the room on this particular occasion. The suit was classic white, spare and cleanly designed with a rakish shape to the upstanding collar that framed her throat. Underneath she wore a chrome-yellow silk blouse. The contrast with her dark hair and the yellow-heeled white leather pumps made an impact that would not go unnoticed. Standing in front of her bedroom mirror, she twisted her hair into a sleek, severe knot and added a yellow and turquoise bracelet to one wrist. The amber in her eyes seemed almost gold as she stared critically back at herself. Would anyone else notice the tension and, yes, the fear in those eyes?

Deliberately choosing to arrive late at the on-campus faculty club, Brenna walked through the quiet grounds with a firm stride that belied her inner nervousness. The college was operating some special summer programs this year, but even with those in progress there wasn't nearly the usual bustle of students and faculty as there was during the academic year.

The understated elegance of the faculty club was the result of a bequest from a generous alumnus. The room had been designed to resemble the gracious library of an English manor house and, as was appropriate, sherry would be the beverage served. Brenna wasn't surprised to see the delicate little tea sandwiches that accompanied it. The staff of the campus cafeteria somehow always managed to produce fairly interesting tidbits for these occasions.

The subdued hum of conversation was as appropriate as the little sandwiches and the sherry. The room was full of faculty members from all of the college's various department, including the library. Brenna stood silently in the doorway for a moment absorbing the scene. Dr. Paul Humphrey was, naturally, the focus of attention of the most important of the evening's guests. The provost and his wife, the head of the library, and several other notables stood grouped around the retiring faculty member. At Humphrey's right hand stood Damon Fielding.

"Brenna! You made it! I'm so glad you got my note."

Diana Bergen came quickly toward her, her attractive features cheerfully drawn into a smile of welcome. She was a couple of years older than Brenna and had recently been promoted to associate professor in the philosophy department.

"Thanks for thinking of me when you heard the news, Diana." Brenna accepted the delicate glass of sherry and took a sip. She was going to need it.

"I really thought it would be a good idea for you to show up." Diana nodded, glancing over her shoulder at the group surrounding Paul Humphrey. "I know Humphrey is a little pompous and no one's going to be overly sad to see him leave, but it's important to be seen at functions like this. A good opportunity to show the provost you have a proper respect for senior members of the faculty community," she added with a knowing little chuckle.

A few weeks ago Brenna wouldn't have thought twice about the little customs, niceties, and command

performances demanded of a junior faculty member.
A certain amount of socializing was important in any
job, and she would be the last to belittle the civilizing
factor of good manners. But there was no denying
that her view was jaundiced this evening. A glance
around the room seemed to show nothing but people
playing the subtle political game of climbing the academic ladder. Would any of these people even want
to know about what had happened to her? Would they
care that she had been Humphrey's victim, or would
they just as soon never hear about it? She guessed the
latter. Once they knew about it, they would have to
take sides, and the only sensible side to take was
Humphrey's. Humphrey, of course, would deny the
whole incident.

She didn't have the right to involve anyone else,
anyway, Brenna reminded herself as she circulated
quietly through the crowd. This was between herself
and Paul Humphrey. She glanced again at his aristocratic profile as he held court in the center of the
elegant Oriental carpet. He was a tall man, his thick
mane of snow-white hair lending him a patrician air.
Somehow she was going to have to manage to get
him off by himself.

As she watched him through coolly narrowed eyes,
sipping at her sherry, Damon Fielding glanced across
the room and saw her. She saw the surprise and dismay in his eyes, and then he was moving toward her.

"Brenna!" He sounded wary. "I'm glad you decided to come tonight. It's about time you realized
the facts of academic life. As you can see, Humphrey
is virtually out the door. You won't have to work for
him in the fall. No point in making a scene now, is
there? It was an unpleasant incident but not one worth

ruining your image with the rest of the faculty and the provost. I guarantee things will be different when I take over Humphrey's position!''

''Is it settled then? You'll be appointed head?'' she queried.

''It's definite. In fact, Humphrey decided to bow out early just so that I could take over a little sooner than planned.'' There was no hiding the satisfaction in him and he proved it with his next words. ''I also want you to know I'm not holding a grudge about what happened in Tahoe, Brenna. I realize you were under a great deal of strain at the time.''

''Thank you, Damon,'' Brenna said slowly, surprised at the magnanimousness of the statement. It gave her the opening to make her own apology and she seized it quickly. ''I was so shocked when my neighbor struck you. He overreacted, of course, but you must see how it happened,'' she added earnestly. ''He saw us arguing and he had no way of knowing at the time who you were.''

Damon's mouth twisted ruefully and his handsome face seemed to soften with genuine understanding. ''I should never have slapped you. That was really all he had a chance to see, and he reacted to it without stopping to ask questions first, didn't he?''

''Something like that, I'm afraid. I'm—I'm sorry I provoked you, Damon. I had no right to say the things I did. No right at all.''

''Brenna, who was he?'' Damon demanded with an underlying urgency.

''My neighbor.'' Her eyes flickered briefly across the room to track Humphrey's movements.

''Someone important to you?'' Damon persisted.

"I was angry at the time and implied a few things I had no right to imply."

"He's my neighbor for the summer, Damon. A friend." How could she possibly begin to explain Ryder Sterne's role in her life when she hadn't figured it out herself?

"I see. Did you tell him about us?" Damon sounded almost cautious now. "Did you explain why we were arguing that morning? Who I am?"

"I told him who you are," Brenna admitted slowly.

"Good," he murmured, apparently relieved. "Then he knows what the situation between you and me is."

Brenna looked at him, thinking how she had intended to try to explain Ryder to Damon. She knew now that would be a pointless effort because she didn't have all the right words to attempt such an explanation. In any event there really wasn't time. She was here on another mission altogether this evening, one Damon seemed to have all too quickly misconstrued. Brenna took a deep breath.

"Damon, I came here tonight because I'm going to confront Humphrey."

His expression of satisfaction faded into one that, if she hadn't known better, Brenna might have taken for fear.

"You can't! What would be the point? For God's sake, he's literally out the door! What good can it do you to confront him tonight? Let it be, Brenna, just let it be, will you? You'll only be doing yourself an incredible amount of damage!"

"I just want him to know I'm aware of what he did to me, Damon," she said steadily. "Don't worry, I won't ask you to get involved or take sides. I should never have done that in the first place. This is strictly between Humphrey and myself.'' She smiled a little grimly. ''If it makes you feel any better, rest assured I'm not even going to cause a major scene. That's not my way. I'm not going to stand here and yell at him at the top of my lungs. That would be a—a form of violence, wouldn't it? I'm really not a very violent person. I'm going to take him quietly aside and confront him with what he did. I just want him to know that I know and I want him to be aware of what I think of him. That's all the revenge I'm seeking, Damon, believe me.''

''He could still hurt your career, Brenna.''

''From out of retirement?''

''Going into retirement doesn't mean he'll be giving up all his associations and his friendships, damn it! He could still put a word or two in certain ears and influence certain people against you!'' he argued urgently.

''I'll have to take the risk, Damon. I want to be sure he knows what I think about him for lowering the honor of his profession to this extent.''

''Honor!'' Damon exploded vengefully. ''What the hell does honor have to do with a career? Brenna, compromises have to be made in every line of work. Let this matter go and your own career can only benefit. It will be worth it to your future to be rational about this!''

She looked at him levelly. ''You mean because I won't be running the risk of Humphrey trying to damage my career?''

''I mean,'' he declared with emphasis, ''that if you'll let things ride, I will personally make it worth

your while.'' He returned her astonished expression
with one of cool defiance.

"What on earth…? Damon, what are you saying?"

"I'm going to be the new department head,
Brenna.''

"Yes, I understand that, but…"

"And as such I will be in a position to, shall we
say, *compensate* you for what the outgoing department head did to you." He waited, watching her narrowly, the way Brenna imagined a high-powered
chief of a large corporation might watch a junior manager to whom he had just offered something akin to
a bribe.

"Compensate me," she echoed flatly.

"As head of the philosophy department I will have
a lot of influence over matters such as promotion and
tenure and even publication. You'll find it will be
worth your while not to take any step tonight that will
jeopardize your career.''

"Damon, are you trying to bribe me?" she whispered in mingled astonishment and dismay. She
couldn't quite believe what she was hearing.

"I can't seem to talk sense into you," he bit out
angrily. "And I care too much about you to let you
ruin your future. If bribing you to keep silent is what
it takes to make you act reasonably this evening, then
that's what I'm doing, yes!''

"Oh, Damon," she murmured with a sad little
shake of her head. "You just don't understand, and I
honestly don't know how to explain any further." But
Ryder understood, Brenna thought fleetingly. Ryder
comprehended matters of personal justice and honor
and ethics even though he'd never made a formal
study of them. How could Damon, who *had* made a

formal study of them, be so blind? "I appreciate your intentions but I can't let the matter drop. I feel I have to say something to Humphrey. I wonder how many times he's published other people's work as his own?"

"You're going to go through with this act of stupidity even though nothing you say or do will change the situation? Brenna, listen to me!"

But it was too late for further remonstrations on Damon's part. Even as he opened his mouth to continue the argument, a well-modulated masculine voice was breaking in on his words. "Ah, there you are, Fielding. Wondered where you'd gone. Should have guessed when I saw our charming Miss Llewellyn in the crowd, though! So glad to see you again, Brenna, my dear." Paul Humphrey inclined his head with an Old World grace. "Very thoughtful of you to come back for this little farewell the faculty arranged for me. I understood you were spending the summer in Tahoe?"

So charming, so aristocratic and courtly. So esteemed in his profession. Brenna found herself at a loss to understand how this man could look her in the eye and try to charm her as if nothing had happened. She was aware of a thrill of apprehension. Even when you knew you were right, it wasn't always easy to face this kind of scene, she thought. Brenna met the benign gaze with determination.

"I wouldn't have missed this for the world, Dr. Humphrey." Her adrenaline switched into high gear. She would never have a better opportunity. There was only Damon to witness the confrontation, and that didn't really matter since he knew the facts. If he chose to hang around while she faced Paul Humphrey with her accusations, that was his business, but Brenna wondered why he didn't decide to drift off and leave her to her fate. "You see, there was something I wanted to discuss with you before you retired."

Paul Humphrey smiled charmingly. "You needn't worry about my disappearing entirely, my dear. I fully intend to take advantage of all the privileges belonging to retired faculty members. I expect you'll see me around—I understand I'm even going to be allowed to maintain an office in the north wing of the library. Just an old war horse, I'm afraid. I wouldn't be able to stay totally out of harness. But I am going to take a vacation before I adjust to my new role in life. A trip to Greece that my wife and I have been promising ourselves for years," he confided jovially.

"Dr. Humphrey, I really must speak to you," Brenna began formally, her stomach twisting into a knot of tension. This was ridiculous. She must stand up for her rights. She must let this man know what she thought of him. She owed it to herself and to the honor of her profession.

"Of course, my dear." He winked broadly. "But I'll bet I can guess what it is you want to discuss!"

Brenna parted her lips to begin the quiet accusation, but before she could get the first words out of her mouth she became aware of two things almost simultaneously.

The first was the utterly beseeching expression on Damon Fielding's face. He was silently pleading with her not to continue. Does he really care that much about my future career? she wondered, taken aback.

The second factor that impinged on her consciousness at that crucial juncture was a faint sensation of heightened awareness. It was the kind of sensation that made you turn your head in a crowd and look around to see who was watching you.

For a split second Brenna succumbed to the primitive pull and slid a quick, uneasy glance toward the door. She turned her head just in time to see Ryder enter the room.

For an instant she couldn't move, quite stunned by his presence. What was Ryder doing there? In the next moment she realized that there could be only one explanation. He hadn't trusted her to return to Tahoe.

The knowledge of that mistrust bit deep. It was suddenly more important than anything else this evening, including her confrontation with Paul Humphrey. *Ryder hadn't trusted her to keep her word!*

Across the room, Ryder's glance collided with hers. He barely nodded at the polite but curious hostess who was pushing a delicate sherry glass into his hand. His silver eyes never left Brenna's as he started toward her.

It was like watching a jungle cat glide across the room. Ryder had dressed for the occasion, but apparently without any concern for the style of masculine dress favored in the pompous atmosphere of a faculty club. He certainly wasn't wearing anything like the British tweeds or the quiet, conservative suits that predominated in the room. The fawn-colored sportcoat was cut with Continental flair, not British conservatism, and it was shaped out of the supplest of suedes. The slacks were a darker brown, lean-fitting and expensive. The tie was a bold splash of gold and brown and it was worn over a brown silk shirt. With his tawny hair, he resembled a lion to Brenna's stricken gaze.

"I beg your pardon, my dear," Paul Humphrey prompted politely in a bid to regain her attention.

She forced herself to turn back to the task at hand, fiercely aware of the fact that Ryder was almost upon her. She could only tackle one thing at a time, she reminded herself. Ryder's mistrust would have to be dealt with later.

"Brenna, please!" Damon's tight voice broke into her concentration.

"About the paper you're publishing on the subject of computer ethics, Dr. Humphrey," she began challengingly, feeling as if everything were happening at once and knowing she had to regain control of herself and the situation.

"Ah, yes," Humphrey nodded imperturbably. "I'm not at all surprised you're interested in it. I hope you'll be able to get something useful out of it for your own project. I understand you're working on a related issue?" One white brow arched in polite inquiry.

Brenna nearly choked on her last sip of sherry. "Get something useful out of it!"

"Brenna, listen to me!"

Damon again. With a flash of insight triggered by the knowledge of Ryder's presence behind her, Brenna realized she was strangely glad that Damon Fielding had chosen not to stand beside her in this matter. For if he had, she would need to feel somewhat obligated to him, and the last thing she wanted now was a feeling of obligation toward Damon. She wanted to be free, totally free, to go to Ryder. The impact of that knowledge was almost overwhelming.

"Yes, indeed," Dr. Humphrey was continuing expansively. "But quite frankly, if it's clarification or amplification you need, I suggest you talk to Dr. Fielding, here.''

Brenna looked up at him blankly. Ryder was right at her shoulder now, not speaking or touching her but indisputably *there*. She could feel the power of his presence but she focused her attention completely on Paul Humphrey.

''Dr. Fielding and I held several discussion on the topic before I wrote the paper. He made some extraordinarily insightful comments and suggestions. So many, in fact, that, although he insists he doesn't want any credit, I'm going to see to it that his name goes on that paper as well as my own. No, no, Fielding, don't bother to argue. I believe in giving credit where credit is due, and you know full well I would never have written that paper without your urging and your helpful contributions. It was truly a joint effort, and I'm going to see to it that you receive proper acknowledgment. Some of those conclusions were brilliant, positively brilliant!''

Brenna swung her wide-eyed gaze to Damon. Behind her Ryder sipped sherry, his cool, watchful, prepared attitude registering itself on Brenna's consciousness.

''You contributed *significantly* to Dr. Humphrey's paper?'' she breathed. ''Exactly what contributions did you make, Dr. Fielding? By any chance were the sections on Humanist ethics and twentieth-century logic your work?''

Before a grim and desperate-looking Damon could reply, Dr. Humphrey was again interrupting expansively. ''Oh, yes, Dr. Fielding made a number of points in that area. He also brought in the rather unusual sections on Aristotelian thinking, didn't you, Damon?''

Brenna's fingers gripped the little sherry glass until her knuckles whitened. All of those interpretations and analyses had been hers. All of them!

"And the comments on Kant?" she pursued relentlessly.

"Brenna, I can explain…"

"If you two will excuse me," Humphrey murmured, "I think I'll let you get on with this discussion. I do have an obligation to circulate this evening." He chuckled. "Have to let everyone show how much they'll miss me!" He patted Damon paternally on the shoulder and moved off with a curious glance and nod at Ryder.

He wasn't the only one flicking a glance at the silent Ryder. Damon's expression of grim desperation was tightening. Brenna stared at him.

"Damon, how could you?" she whispered fiercely. "You stole my work. You knew those notes were in my desk drawer. It must have been easy for you. And I spent so much time telling you about my project. It must have been simple for you to outline the best portions and feed them to Dr. Humphrey as your own 'contributions.' But why? I don't understand *why.*"

"Brenna, I can explain," Damon began, his eyes still moving nervously from her to Ryder and back. "But this is between you and me. What's *he* doing here? Get rid of him!"

For the first time Ryder spoke, not moving from his position at Brenna's shoulder. His voice was very gentle and, therefore very, very menacing.

"I don't believe in letting my woman handle the

bloody work on her own, even though she's got the guts to do it.''

"The bloody work!" Damon looked quite dazed.

"She thinks I'm something of a chauvinist, but that's the way it is." Ryder shrugged, downing a swallow of the rich sherry. His cool glance moved meaningfully over Brenna's taut features as she looked up at him and met his eyes directly for the first time since he had entered the room. "Well?" he said blandly. "Is he the one?" He indicated Damon with a casual thumb.

"Apparently so," she got out tightly.

"Brenna, it was a matter of establishing myself firmly enough in Humphrey's mind that he would make an effort to handpick his own successor. Whoever he names will get the nod for department head! Don't you see? In that position I can help both of us!"

"What do you want done with him, lady?" There was a subtle anticipation in Ryder's words that Damon reacted to immediately. He stepped back a pace even though the other man hadn't moved.

"Brenna, this is ridiculous. I can see you're not prepared to listen to reason," Damon sputtered furiously.

"Forget it, Ryder," Brenna murmured icily. "I only came here tonight to tell the guilty party what I thought of his actions. That's already been accomplished, hasn't it, Damon? You surely know what I think of you. Your climb up the academic ladder should be interesting. What will you think of yourself when you get to the top, I wonder?"

Before her colleague could reply, Brenna swung around on a yellow-heeled shoe and put her hand lightly on Ryder's arm. "I'm ready to go now," she told him, lifting her chin proudly. "I've done what I came to do."

"You're satisfied?" he asked, searching her face intently.

"Yes, I'm satisfied. Please get me out of here."

"My pleasure."

Chapter 10

Ryder led her toward the door with an arrogant disregard for the discreetly curious glances they were receiving. Brenna found herself aware of the expressions of her friends and colleagues but in that moment found them fading into unimportance compared with the absolutely critical matter she had to discuss with Ryder. Now that it was behind her, even the scene with Damon was no longer the most vital issue in her world. As soon as the door closed behind them, she glared up at his profile.

"Why did you follow me? I told you I'd come back to Tahoe!"

"I know what you told me, lady," he drawled softly.

"But you didn't believe me, is that it? You thought I'd run? Ryder, I gave you my word!" She came to a decisive halt on the sidewalk and he obediently stopped too, somehow contriving to maneuver her into the light of the streetlamp.

"I know you gave me your word. That's not why I decided to show up tonight," he stated evenly.

"Then why are you here?" she rasped huskily.

"For the reason I gave Fielding, naturally. What else?" He took her arm again and started her along the sidewalk.

"The reason you gave Damon! Oh!" Brenna's lashes closed briefly in sudden comprehension. Then she opened them to slant him a sidelong glance. "You drove all the way down here from Tahoe just to be around in case there was any, uh, 'bloody' work that needed doing?" She found herself remembering how the hero in *The Quicksilver Venture* always stepped in to handle the dirty business so that Cass didn't have to face the danger alone. It had been a manifestation of Hunt Cameron's chauvinism. It had also been a manifestation of his caring.

"Even though you aren't violence-prone"—Ryder broke off to touch the side of his face absently in memory—"or at least not generally prone toward it, I still didn't want you tackling the guy who stole your material by yourself. It's not that I didn't think you could handle it, I just didn't want you doing it alone. I have the right to look after you now, Brenna," he concluded flatly. "I have the right to stand by you when you're facing something serious."

"The right!" Brenna dragged them both to another forcible halt, narrowing her eyes ferociously as she peered up at him. "The *right!* Ryder Sterne, you're a chauvinistic, arrogant male who has presumed far too much, assumed too many rights, made too many claims since we first met, but—'' She had to stop to catch her breath.

''But?'' he repeated, his hands moving slowly up and down her arms. He seemed concerned by her outburst, but utterly determined.

''But at least a woman always knows exactly where she stand with you,'' Brenna admitted frankly. ''And she always knows where you yourself will stand: beside her when she needs you. Thank you for coming tonight, Ryder.'' Impulsively she stood on tiptoe, bracing herself with her hands on his shoulders, and brushed her lips lightly against his firm mouth.

Then she swept on toward the parking lot without giving him a chance to react. He paced silently beside her to where she had parked her car, not speaking until he had opened her door for her.

''I'll wait for you in Tahoe,'' he told her calmly, handing back the keys he had taken long enough to unlock the door. ''Drive carefully tomorrow.''

Brenna paused in the act of slipping into the front seat, confused. ''You're going back? Tonight?''

''Yes. I only came down in case there were fireworks. That's the truth, lady.'' He smiled warmly into her anxious eyes.

''Not because you didn't trust me to return?''

''I trust you to keep your word.''

She caught her breath at the look in his eyes. ''It's a long drive back,'' she whispered tentatively.

''I'll be all right.''

''You could stay here,'' she pointed out in a little rush.

He shook his head. ''I want you to know I trust you. Drive carefully, lady. I'll be waiting for you tomorrow. Go back to your apartment tonight and get some sleep. You've had a rough evening.'' He shut her car door and stepped back, waiting until she reluctantly started the engine before he walked over to the Ferrari and climbed inside. They went their separate ways as they drove out of the campus parking lot.

She could follow him back tonight, Brenna told herself, watching the Ferrari disappear in the rearview mirror. Why hadn't he encouraged her to do exactly that? Because he knew she needed some time by herself in which to think? He was a very perceptive man. She *did* need time to think. A lot of the problems she'd been struggling with had resolved themselves this evening: her future in the academic world, her knowledge of what she wanted out of life, and her acceptance of her relationship with Ryder. Yes, she needed time to think, not to come to conclusions but to adjust to the conclusions that had made themselves plain tonight. It was like studying philosophy, she thought as she drove back to her apartment. You could go over and over a complex bit of logic without understanding it, and then all at once everything fell into place.

For her that falling into place had occurred when she'd looked across the room and seen Ryder walking toward her, asserting his right to be at her side.

He might find the concept of love sloppy and sentimental, Brenna decided the next morning as she repacked the small overnight bag she'd brought with her and locked the apartment again for the summer, but Ryder knew all there was to know about the fundamentals behind the word. More than Damon Fielding would ever know, she added silently to herself as she began the long drive back to Lake Tahoe.

She might disagree with Ryder's way of doing things from time to time, but her respect for him would never be lowered. He was a man who understood the basics of what she had been trying so hard to teach this past semester in Ethics 205. And he'd arrived at that understanding on his own. She wasn't sure where the commitment she was making to him would lead, but she knew for certain that she would be able to trust his commitment to her completely.

The drive back to Tahoe seemed to take forever, but she was on the winding lakeside drive by morning and turning into the lane that led to the cabins shortly thereafter. It was only a summer place but she felt as if she were coming home.

She couldn't explain the wave of shyness that momentarily assailed her as she braked the car to a halt in front of the cabin and saw Ryder coming toward her from behind the house. He set the bow and quiver of arrows he had been using aside on the porch as he came forward. Brenna just looked at him for a long moment, drinking in the sight of him and feeling the sureness of her decision welling up inside her.

When that sureness threatened to block the breath in her throat, she threw open the car door and began to run.

"Ryder, oh my darling, I'm sorry I took so long!" She hurled herself into his waiting arms and he locked them closed around her, swinging her effortlessly around in a circle before letting her find her feet.

"I knew you'd come back," he growled gently, and then he was pinning her close for a slow, savoring kiss that branded and claimed and promised. Time hung suspended for the length of that kiss and Brenna gave herself up to it with willing surrender, for she knew she was staking her own feminine claim. This man was hers.

When he finally lifted his head reluctantly to smile searchingly down into her glowing face, Ryder seemed shaken by the wonder of what her kiss must have told him and by the evident love in her eyes. "Does this mean you're not merely coming back because you've agreed to give our relationship a chance? Have you made your decision, Brenna? Will you be accepting my claim completely?"

She laughed up at him wickedly. "Ryder, you have a way of expressing yourself that badly needs refining for the modern age of equality. I'm here for the sloppy, sentimental reason that I love you. I know," she went on hurriedly, stopping his mouth with her palm when he would have spoken, "you don't think much of the word, but I find it perfect to describe my feelings for you. And someday I'm going to convince you that it's the perfect way to describe your feelings for me," she concluded tenderly.

He kissed the fingers that covered his lips and she lowered them, her cheeks warming at the expression on his face. "I never said I thought the word 'love' was sloppy and sentimental," he whispered. "I said my readers would probably find it so. I avoided using it with you because I figured one had to trap a rational little professor with logic and appeals to her sense of integrity and honor. There's no logic to love."

"But there is honor and integrity," she said.

"Yes." He slid his hands into her hair, pulling free the combs that had anchored it back behind her ears. "Brenna, I love you. I knew I wanted you from the first. It didn't take me long to realize the feeling went much deeper than that. I need you in a way I can't

fully explain. You're like the other half of myself.
I'm more than willing to label that feeling 'love.'"

"So am I, Ryder. So am I."

He drew her close to his chest, smoothing the
length of her hair and sliding his hands up and down
her back with a heavy urgency, as if he still couldn't
believe she had accepted him completely.

"We're on the Nevada side of the lake, lady," he
murmured.

"So?" She smiled into his shirt, luxuriating in the
wonder of being held by him.

"So we can get married this afternoon without any
waiting."

She lifted her head. "Is that what you want, Ryder?"

"It's what I want. I have a very primitive need to
tie you to me with all the bonds I can find."

She shook her head, her amber eyes smiling at him.
"What am I going to do with you? No sense of what
a modern relationship entails at all!"

"Stop making fun of my Neanderthal approach and
tell me you'll marry me," he ordered roughly, using
his hand to pull her head back down onto his shoulder.

"I'll marry you," she agreed obediently.

"If only for the opportunity of straightening out
my male chauvinism?"

"I never could resist a challenge."

She felt a tremor of laughter go through him and
he kissed the curve of her shoulder. Brenna lifted her
arms to wrap them around his neck. "Oh, Ryder, I
love you so. I kept telling myself you were all wrong
for me but I guess that was because I was afraid of
realizing how very *right* you really were."

"In spite of my past? I know I don't have the kind of background you probably expected to find in the man you married…"

"It's not your past I'm interested in." She smiled. "Only your present and your future."

He sighed, a kind of relief evident in the sound. "And your future, Brenna? Do you know what you want now?"

"I know, I want you. As for the rest, I'm open to suggestion," she admitted. "For as long as I can remember I've kept myself on the straight and narrow path of academia. It's a good path and someday I may go back to it. But right now I think I'd like a change. At least for the next few months. I wonder if you would be interested in seeing a little of the world with me? There are some things I've missed during the past few years. Things I'd like to catch up on."

"As a matter of fact," he said gently, "I was thinking of taking a couple of research trips after I finish this current book."

"I should warn you that, unlike Craig, I like my adventure with a few luxuries."

"Oh, it will be first class, all the way." He grinned. "It's the only way I'm interested in traveling now myself!"

"And when we get back I will rethink my career plans. I'm not really sure what I want to do, and it's rather nice thinking that I have the freedom to change everything if I wish. I've never given myself that freedom before."

"Well, since your future is still a little unsettled," Ryder drawled, "would you be interested in hearing some plans for the immediate present?"

"I feel quite open to suggestions."

"Fine. Then this is what we're going to do. First, I will bundle you into the car and whisk you off to the nearest wedding chapel. Then we shall have a light lunch of champagne and caviar and then I shall carry you off to the bedroom where we can celebrate our future in style."

"I love it when you're being masterful," she said, grinning, eyes sparkling.

Three hours later Ryder poured the last of the champagne and saluted his new bride. "To the lady cat burglar who came crawling through my window at two in the morning." He downed the champagne with relish.

"I think you must be running short of toasts to resort to that one," Brenna observed, the gold of her new wedding band catching the afternoon sunlight as she obediently sipped from her glass.

"That's a very important one," he protested, rising to his feet and setting down the glass with a deliberate air. "After all, that was the night I began to realize I was fated to marry a most adventuresome lady. And I was right, wasn't I? Just look how you seduced me the night we went gambling!"

"I didn't seduce you!"

"Our first married argument? How charming."

"Ryder? Where are you going?" She watched him disappear into the hall.

"To get a blanket. We're going down to that little cove on the lake where you read *The Quicksilver Venture*."

"We are? I thought you were going to carry me off to the bedroom."

"I've changed my mind. A captured lady cat burglar needs something a little more exciting on her wedding day.''

Brenna laughed softly. ''So we're going fishing, instead?''

''Not quite.''

He led her down to the private cove and spread the blanket out with aplomb. Brenna watched him lovingly, enjoying the grace in his body and the sureness of his movements. But when he straightened and turned to look at her, she wasn't prepared for the sudden hesitancy in his silver eyes.

''Ryder?'' she whispered, not understanding.

''Brenna, I love you, and now that you're mine, now that you've finally accepted my claim, I find I'm suffering an attack of groom's jitters. See?'' He held out his hand and there was, indeed, a faint trembling.

Brenna stared at his hand and then her gaze flew to his shimmering eyes. ''Are you jittery because you think you may have made a mistake in marrying me?'' The words almost stuck in her throat.

''No! Damn it, don't say such things. That's not it at all!'' He closed the distance between them in one gliding stride and hauled her into his arms. ''My God, woman, how can you even say that? I'm shaking like a leaf because nothing has ever been as important to me as you are. I want to be the perfect husband, the perfect lover. I want you to love me for the rest of our lives. When you want something that much, you get a little shaky!''

''Maybe that's why I'm trembling, too,'' she confessed, collapsing against him in the relief of knowing she wasn't the only one who was suffering from bridal jitters. ''I want to be the perfect wife for you.''

"Lady, lady," he crooned gently, his hands moving on her back, sliding down to her waist.

She lifted her mouth to his and he took her lips with an urgent longing that spoke of want and need and love. They held each other until the case of nerves had subsided. It was a silent time of tenderness and passion that somehow set the seal on the wedding vows they had taken earlier that day.

When Brenna felt the heat rising in Ryder's body, she crowded closer to him and her nails slipped delicately down his back.

"I love you, Ryder."

"My sweet Brenna, I love you so much!" He sank down onto the blanket, pulling her to him in a rush of emotion that could not be halted now that it had begun. With hands that trembled now from passion rather than nerves, he undressed her, fumbling occasionally and cursing a little at his own unaccustomed clumsiness.

The muffled words made Brenna laugh tenderly and she captured his hands to still them for a moment when he would have unzipped her jeans. "Wait, you're getting ahead of me!"

He raised his head from where he had buried his lips in her throat and looked down at her questioningly.

"It's only fair to let me fumble a little, too," she whispered, releasing his hands and putting her fingers to the buttons of his shirt.

"I suppose we'll get slicker at this as we gain experience," he murmured ruefully.

"I suppose."

"On the other hand I may never get used to the idea of really having you all to myself!" With that he went back to sliding off the jeans and pushing aside the edges of her shirt.

When they both lay naked at last, Ryder slipped his hands roughly, passionately along the length of rounded thigh and up to the softness of her breasts. The possessiveness in him was a tangible force.

"Oh, Ryder, my love!" Her voice was a soft moan of wonder and love that he responded to with a flaring desire. She thrilled to the touch of his tongue curling around each nipple, coaxing it tautly awake. His leg moved over hers, forcing her thighs gently apart so that the hand he was trailing across the satin of her stomach could begin teasing the tangled thicket between her legs.

She shifted languidly beneath his exploring, probing touch, her body caught up in the sweet passion being generated between them. Eyes closed tightly in mounting ecstasy, she trailed her fingertips across the crisp hair of his chest, blindly seeking the flat, male nipples. When he groaned she moved, sinking her teeth lightly around the area she had just been caressing.

"Lady witch," he breathed and slipped his hand through the thicket to the dampening heart of her desire. "You open for me like a flower. A hot, luscious passion flower."

"Ryder!" His name was a husky cry on her lips as he boldly stroked the petals of the flower. He leaned close to drink the sound of her moan from the other blossom that was her mouth.

Brenna felt entranced, enthralled, and overwhelmed with the hard strength of him, and she ran her hands again and again across the contours of his back and the muscled power of his thighs. When she trailed them lingeringly, daringly to the point where the tapering chest hair became enmeshed with the provocative curls below his waist, he moved against her. Deliberately he pressed his hardness against her.

"Touch me, lady!" he half commanded, half pleaded. "I love the feel of your soft hands."

But when she willingly did as he asked, his body seemed to surge against her fingers, seeking far more than the caress of her hand. He lifted himself and came down along the length of her body, using his ankles to open her legs farther for his advance. She was ready for him.

"I want you," he grated. And then he was thrusting himself forward against her softness, losing himself in her body even as he mastered it.

Brenna gasped at the delicious impact of him, knowing it would always be thus between them, a kind of mastery and a kind of surrender that blended so that it would be impossible in the ultimate moment to know where the boundaries were or which of them was responsible for which emotion.

He seemed to relinquish all control, giving himself completely even as he took. Brenna clung tightly, her nails raking his back in the heat of her aching need. When he slid one hand down to her buttocks to lift her even more tightly against him, she cried out with husky fierceness and clutched him with a sweet savagery that seemed to call to his most elemental maleness.

His body surged hungrily into hers again and again, sweeping her with him into a taut, whirling vortex from which there was only one exit point.

Brenna let herself go as he flashed with her toward that ending. It was an incredibly exhilarating sensation to know that she could abandon herself to Ryder's embrace, emotionally, physically, even intellectually. They belonged to each other.

The tight, spiraling ecstasy within her snapped with unexpected fury and she heard herself calling his name as if it were a talisman.

"Ryder!"

"Yes, sweet lady, *yes!*"

Her body went into a shivering delight, and the tiny convulsions seemed to be more than his own hardness could resist. In an instant he was sinking his fingers deep into the skin of her shoulders, arching himself against her with a near-voiceless shout of triumph and satisfaction. Brenna held him to her with all the passion and love in her heart.

Slowly, lingeringly, they surfaced, still wrapped tightly together. In a tangle of perspiration-dampened arms and legs they let themselves float back to the real world and the privacy of the cove. Lovingly Brenna pressed her lips to his throat, inhaling the scent of their lovemaking as it combined with the mountain breeze. Ryder's fingers moved with tender idleness along her arm and she felt him smile into her hair.

"My wife," he murmured in tones of gentle wonder. "My God, I waited a long time for you to walk into my life!"

"You've been looking for a wife for a long time?" she teased.

"No. Didn't even realize I wanted one until you came sneaking through my window that night. But once I realized that, I knew I'd been waiting for quite a while."

"I was not sneaking!"

"Scared the daylights out of me," he protested.

"Ah, well, it probably served you right," she decided. "I don't think you've had much opportunity to experience being scared."

"Oh, I've been scared a lot since that night," he vowed gently. "Scared Damon Fielding might lure you back, scared you wouldn't be able to tolerate my past, scared you'd try to run from me after I'd made you mine."

"You overwhelm me," she breathed. "I had no idea. But I've been a little scared myself."

"You've had a hell of a lot to deal with these past few days, haven't you? The crisis in your career, Craig's announcement that he wasn't going back to the university..."

"And you. Above all else there was you to deal with, Ryder Sterne," she concluded, rising on one elbow to gaze down at him. "You were the most complicated thing of all to deal with and you must know that."

"Because I wasn't what you'd always admired and wanted in a man?"

"No, because you were exactly what I'd always admired and wanted in a man but you didn't come packaged quite the way I had expected you to be packaged. No tweed jacket, no year at Oxford, no Ph.D., no academic credits."

"Wait a minute," he broke in, grinning. "I *have* been published!"

"You've got a point there. Of course, it wasn't quite the sort of publishing I had expected my future husband to be doing," she agreed thoughtfully.

"The pay is good," he pointed out hopefully.

She giggled. "And, damn it, the writing is good, too!"

"You liked the story?" He slid her a speculative glance.

"I loved the story. Except for the violent parts. The love scenes were terrific."

"Sex scenes," he corrected. "I don't write love scenes."

"Anybody as good as you are at doing love scenes for real can't help but write them beautifully!" she proclaimed grandly.

He groaned and pulled her down, trapping her head close by locking his hand around the back of her neck. His other hand traced the outline of her breast lovingly, finding the nipple and coaxing it forth. Ryder's mouth found hers in a kiss of recent satisfaction that combined with a promise of future need. Gently his tongue pried apart her willing lips and he tasted deeply for a long moment of the warmth behind them. With slow reluctance he released her mouth.

"So you want to do a little adventuring before you decide whether or not to go back to the academic world, hmmm?"

"Being with you will be an adventure in itself," she said, smiling, knowing it was the truth.

"You won't mind being married to a macho writer of sleazy men's fiction?" The silver eyes were gleaming with laughter but Brenna chose to take the question seriously.

"I don't mind being married to a man who lives by a code of honor, a man who will always stand beside me when the going gets rough, a man who knows how to love even if he'd never allow the word into one of his sleazy novels!"

"Is that how you see me?" he asked wonderingly.

"Yes," she admitted simply. "You know more about honor and ethics than any of my colleagues seem to know. The advantages of being a self-taught man, I guess."

"Some of that learning came at a high price, Brenna," he warned.

"The price, whatever it was, has been paid. It's over. We are concerned only with our future," she declared, leaning close for an instant to brush his lips with her own.

He smiled at her silver eyes full of love. "Speaking of the future reminds me that I have a piece of sleazy men's fiction to write in the next few weeks. I'd best get started on it right away so that we can have the rest of the summer to go adventuring. Come here." He caught her tenderly and brought her down into a sensuous sprawl on his chest. "I want to practice my love scenes."

"I thought you only wrote sex scenes!"

"I think they're definitely going to be love scenes from now on!" He captured her mouth once more with his own and she realized he had spoken the truth.

Ryder Sterne did love scenes perfectly.

* * * * *

The legend continues!

New York Times **bestselling author**

DIANA PALMER

MEN
of the
WEST

**A Collector's Edition containing
three classic Long, Tall Texans novels.**

Relive the spellbinding magic of Harden, Evan and
Donavan when the spirited women who love these
irresistible cowboys lasso their elusive hearts.

Look for MEN OF THE WEST in March 2004.

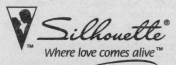

Silhouette®

Where love comes alive™

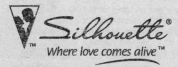

Just in time for Mother's Day
come four favorite stories
in one gift-sized volume...

small wonders

National bestselling authors

Candace Camp

Dallas Schulze

Ann Major

Raye Morgan

Celebrate the joys
and challenges of
motherhood with
this warmhearted
anthology that all
women will love—
whether they're
moms or not!

*Coming to a bookstore
near you in April 2004.*

Silhouette®

Where love comes alive™

JAYNE ANN KRENTZ

83598	THE PRIVATE EYE	___ $6.99 U.S.	___ $8.50 CAN.
83496	LEGACY	___ $6.99 U.S.	___ $8.50 CAN.
83542	WITCHCRAFT	___ $6.99 U.S.	___ $8.50 CAN.

(limited quantities available)

TOTAL AMOUNT	$_____
POSTAGE & HANDLING	$_____
($1.00 for 1 book, 50¢ for each additional)	
APPLICABLE TAXES*	$_____
<u>TOTAL PAYABLE</u>	$_____

(Check or money order—please do not send cash)

To order, complete this form and send it, along with a check or money order for the total above, payable to Harlequin Books, to:
In the U.S.: 3010 Walden Avenue, P.O. Box 9077, Buffalo, NY 14269-9077;
In Canada: P.O. Box 636, Fort Erie, Ontario L2A 5X3.

Name:_____
Address:_____ City:_____
State/Prov.:_____ Zip/Postal Code:_____
Account Number (If Applicable):_____
075 CSAS

*New York residents remit applicable sales taxes.
    Canadian residents remit applicable GST and provincial taxes.